THIS AUTHOR AND BOOK WERE

ADOPTED THROUGH THE

GENEROSITY

OF

## THERESA FRONCEK

THANK YOU

5R

Praise for
BEVERLY LEWIS

"No one does Amish-based inspirationals better than Lewis."
—*Booklist*

"Author Beverly Lewis has come up with a new magic formula for producing best-selling romance novels: humility, plainness and no sex. Lewis' G-rated books, set among the Old Order Amish in Lancaster County, Pennsylvania, have sold more than 12 million copies, as bodice rippers make room for 'bonnet books,' chaste romances that chronicle the lives and loves of America's Amish."
—*Time* magazine

"Much of the credit [for the growth of Amish fiction] goes to Beverly Lewis, a Colorado author who gave birth to the genre in 1997 with *The Shunning*, loosely based on her grandmother's experience of leaving her Old Order Mennonite upbringing to marry a Bible college student. The book has sold more than 1 million copies."
—Eric Gorski, Associated Press

"As in her other novels, Lewis creates a vividly imagined sensory world. . . . And her well-drawn characters speak with authentic voices as they struggle to cope with grief and questions about their traditions and relationship with God."
—*Library Journal*
(about *The Parting*)

"Lewis' readers can't get enough of her tales about Amish life, and this latest installment won't disappoint."
—*Publishers Weekly*
(about *The Forbidden*)

# BEVERLY LEWIS

## the THORN

BETHANYHOUSE

MINNEAPOLIS, MINNESOTA

*The Thorn*
Copyright © 2010
Beverly M. Lewis

Cover design by Dan Thornberg, Design Source Creative Services
Art direction by Paul Higdon

Scripture quotations are from the King James Version of the Bible.

Published by Bethany House Publishers
11400 Hampshire Avenue South
Bloomington, Minnesota 55438

Bethany House Publishers is a division of
Baker Publishing Group, Grand Rapids, Michigan.

Printed in the United States of America

**Library of Congress Cataloging-in-Publication Data**

Lewis, Beverly.
    The thorn / Beverly Lewis.
        p.   cm. — (The rose trilogy ; 1)
    ISBN 978-0-7642-0814-0 (alk. paper) — ISBN 978-0-7642-0574-3 (pbk. ) — ISBN 978-0-7642-0815-7 (large-print pbk.)   1. Amish—Fiction.   2. Sisters—Fiction.   3. Pennsylvania Dutch Country (Pa.)—Fiction.   I. Title.
    PS3562.E9383T48      2010
    813'.54—dc22

                                                                                2010014545

In keeping with biblical principles of creation stewardship, Baker Publishing Group advocates the responsible use of our natural resources. As a member of the Green Press Initiative, our company uses recycled paper when possible. The text paper of this book is comprised of 30% post-consumer waste.

green
press
INITIATIVE

To
*my darling cousins*
*Bonnie, Marcia, Susie, and Marie,*
*sisters four.*

And
*in loving memory of dear Caroline.*
*1923–2010*

# By Beverly Lewis

THE ROSE TRILOGY
*The Thorn*

SEASONS OF GRACE
*The Secret* • *The Missing* • *The Telling*

ABRAM'S DAUGHTERS
*The Covenant* • *The Betrayal* • *The Sacrifice*
*The Prodigal* • *The Revelation*

THE HERITAGE OF LANCASTER COUNTY
*The Shunning* • *The Confession* • *The Reckoning*

ANNIE'S PEOPLE
*The Preacher's Daughter* • *The Englisher* • *The Brethren*

THE COURTSHIP OF NELLIE FISHER
*The Parting* • *The Forbidden* • *The Longing*

*The Postcard* • *The Crossroad*

*The Redemption of Sarah Cain*
*October Song* • *Sanctuary* (with David Lewis) • *The Sunroom*

*The Beverly Lewis Amish Heritage Cookbook*

*www.beverlylewis.com*

BEVERLY LEWIS, born in the heart of Pennsylvania Dutch country, is the *New York Times* bestselling author of more than eighty books. Her stories have been published in ten languages worldwide. A keen interest in her mother's Plain heritage has inspired Beverly to write many Amish-related novels, beginning with *The Shunning,* which has sold more than one million copies. *The Brethren* was honored with a 2007 Christy Award.

Beverly lives with her husband, David, in Colorado.

# PROLOGUE

*September 1985*

At times I wonder what might've happened if I'd gone with *Mamm* that damp, hazy morning eleven years ago. She was so tired—she'd said it herself—preparing for market day. Such a bleak expression dulled her sweet face as she trudged out to the waiting horse and the enclosed gray carriage filled with gourds and squash and other garden vegetables.

A shudder rippled through me as I watched her step into the buggy, carrying the rectangular money tin for making change at market. Was I somehow sensing what was just ahead?

She set the tin box on the front seat next to her and picked up the reins as I stood on the back steps. Then she gave a faint wave and our eyes locked momentarily. In that burning second, I felt the urge to run out to the buggy and stop her, or at least offer to join her, as though my presence alone might keep Providence from having its way.

But before I could do so, Mamm clicked her tongue for Upsy-Daisy to move ahead, and the young mare trotted off by way of Salem Road, where our farm adjoins the bishop's own. Then over one road and down . . . down the precarious Bridle Path Lane that rims the rocky ravine, our shortcut to the main roads leading to Quarryville.

Even now, as a young woman of twenty, I think back to that miserable hour and tremble, wishing I'd heeded the alarm clanging in my brain. Yet there I stood, watching silently in the mist and the fog.

How could I have known Mamm would be found sometime later, lying along the road and unable to walk, the family buggy turned upside down in the rugged ravine below?

~

Around that time, our neighbor, the bishop, brought home a foster child from Philadelphia. I'll never forget the day I met Nick Franco. He was just ten and scrawny as a stick . . . his wavy hair as black as a raven. My mother had taken my sister and me next door to welcome him, a basketful of food tucked under her arm.

There, in the far corner of the big kitchen, Nick had sat all slumped over, as if someone had dropped a feed bag on his slight shoulders. He was dressed like any of the Amish schoolboys round here—the thin black suspenders and baggy pants out of place with his short English haircut. When he glanced up from his perch on a wooden stool, I caught the lost look in his dark, sad eyes and realized he must've been taken away from everything he'd known. Nick never so much as uttered a word when the bishop's wife introduced him as *our new son.* Neither did he speak to a single soul the rest of that week, the bishop later told *Dat.*

Right away, I felt sorry for Nick Franco—an outsider come

to live with our man of God. I learned later that his father had abandoned him when Nick was a toddler and that his mother was seriously ill, too sick to care for him. No other family members were willing or able to take him in, so he wound up in a foster program. Like it or not, the People hoped that he might become Amish.

Nick was sullen and quiet during those early months. Honestly, it irked me no end how aloof he could be. I occasionally got brave enough to attempt conversation, but he would turn away as if he hadn't heard me. Or didn't care to. Even so, I heeded my inner urge to treat him kindly, the way I'd want to be . . . if I had to walk in his shoes.

And I kept trying to talk to him. About the time Nick turned eleven—a year after his arrival—his expression became a bit softer. Sometimes when he looked my way, there was even an inkling of a smile. But the misery lurking in his eyes never completely faded.

It was then he started working for my father on Saturdays and weekdays, after school. I'd wander out to the barn, if my sister was looking after Mamm, to watch him haul manure with Dat and my older brother Mose.

Quickly, I learned not to call *hullo* when I entered the barn, because there was just no getting a response from the bishop's second son. For the longest time, I actually assumed Nick Franco was partly deaf.

Eventually I tried talking to the horses, loud enough for Nick to hear. *"You're growin' a thicker coat, ain't ya, Upsy-Daisy?"* I might say, stroking the mare while glancing at Nick out of the corner of my eye. *"Winter'll be here before we know it, ain't?"*

Nick would sometimes snicker or cough. Now and again he might even mutter something back, like *"Ain't even fall yet,"* and then quickly return to his apathetic whistling.

For the longest time this strange sort of game continued between us. Then one day he began to say a few words directly to me. I felt ever so proud—in a good way, of course. *Jah,* somehow we'd managed to become friends. And considering his sullen nature and the way he normally kept to himself—even during school recess—I daresay I was his *only* friend.

One afternoon, he surprised me by asking if I'd go riding horses with him, "*just for fun.*" He was still quite standoffish, so I was taken aback at this invitation. And I resisted.

Nick persisted the next day, and the next, just as I had all those months trying to draw him out in conversation. At last I agreed. So he took one of the bishop's spirited colts, and I chose our feisty George, and we rode along the narrow treed section of Salem Road, west of our house, down past the Amish schoolhouse and Farmdale Road.

Oh, what a wonderful-*gut* time it was! I'd never felt so carefree in all of my young life, the wind on my face, my hair falling out of its formal bun. Much to Nick's and my own amusement . . . but hopefully not to the Lord's dismay!

It was a turning point in our friendship. And, little by little, I began to feel more comfortable with the shy city boy who rarely spoke as he listened to me chatter on about whatever popped into my head.

~

Last month after Preaching service, Mamm eyed Nick while we sat out on the lawn waiting for the common meal. "I hope ya know that boy's trouble," she said softly from her wheelchair.

"Dat's had him workin' for us all these years," I replied too quickly.

Mamm waved her hand absently. "Workin' and socializin' are altogether different." She let out a long sigh, her eyes growing stern. "Just mark my words: Nick ain't our kind."

I considered that, surprised she was so pointed. "Bishop made him one of us by takin' him in, jah?"

"Plain clothes don't make ya Amish and never will. And just

look at that ponytail he's got." Mamm clucked her tongue. "I honestly pity the girl who ends up married to him."

I nodded my head wholeheartedly. The way he was wearing his hair so long in back made anyone look twice, especially since the rest of him looked downright Amish.

"Hen's blunder oughta be a lesson to any girl," Mamm added.

Always, *always*, my parents set up my only sister as an example to encourage my ongoing compliance. *"Look what Hen went and did,"* they'd say, *"getting herself hitched to Brandon Orringer"*—her *Englischer* husband.

"Don't worry, Mamm. I'd never marry someone who's not *really* Amish."

My mother gave me a fleeting glance, then turned to greet her many sisters and oodles of Kauffman and Blank cousins as they stopped to chat. The steady flow of womenfolk continued, all of them ever so fond of Mamm.

And as they came, I caught their unmistakably sympathetic gaze—since I was stuck there and not off with the other youth. And I couldn't help thinking how very different Mamm's life might now be—and mine, too—if I'd simply gone with my mother to market that long-ago autumn day.

*Roses have thorns, and silver fountains mud;*

*Clouds and eclipses stain both moon and sun,*

*And loathsome canker lives in sweetest bud.*

—SHAKESPEARE, from Sonnet 35

The fear of the Lord is the beginning of knowledge:

but fools despise wisdom and instruction.

—PROVERBS 1:7 KJV

# CHAPTER 1

The history of Rose Kauffman's ancestors was well known in southern Lancaster County. They had fled Switzerland with other persecuted Amish families, eager to embrace the freedom to worship as they pleased, and to settle on valuable land offered by the heirs of William Penn.

Generations of Amish Kauffmans, Hartzlers, and Zooks thrived there in the fertile Big Valley area of central Pennsylvania, hauling limestone in the 1820s, then tilling the soil and planting corn and other vegetables. They raised hogs and chickens and milked dairy cattle, too.

That is, until one of Rose's uppity great-uncles, Yost Kauffman, began to argue with the Big Valley bishop, declaring the Good Lord wanted him to grow a full beard *and* mustache. The Anabaptist forefathers had always forbidden their men to grow hair on the upper lip, a sober reminder of their European persecutors. When stubborn Yost refused to shave off the offensive fuzz, he was ousted and moved his family away to the floodplain southeast of Quarryville, near Bart in Lancaster County. His old clapboard homestead on Shady Road still stood but a half mile from Rose's own father's land.

Rose's father, Solomon, never heard what became of the errant uncle's whiskers. But Yost's gumption meant Solomon and his family were settled in a fine old three-story redbrick farmhouse set back on the westernmost stretch of rambling Salem Road. There, Solomon lived and worked as a crop farmer and a wagonmaker.

Idyllic Salem Road ran west to east, between Bartville and Farmdale Roads, connecting the two oft-traveled thoroughfares, and a short distance from the ill-fated Bridle Path Lane. Quiet Salem Road was populated by farmhouses and outbuildings, including chicken coops, granaries, hogpens, and woodsheds.

During the summer months, Rose Ann's flower beds on both sides of the house boasted profuse colors, as well as a sea of white daisies. There were rows of golden mums, a well-tended rose garden, and Rose's own flourishing grape arbor. Small birds and butterflies fluttered nearby all summer and into the early autumn.

Years before, when Rose and her older sister, Hannah—nicknamed Hen—were younger, they frolicked outdoors on nippy autumn Saturdays, raking leaves into deep piles. Occasionally, if she was strong enough, their mother sat near the front window doing her hand sewing, cloaked in sunlight. On such mornings, Emma Kauffman undoubtedly observed her daughters making quick work of the raking and believed they were as sedate and obedient as any well-mannered Amish girls.

Sometimes, though, when they thought no one was watching, the sisters made a running start and fairly flew into the brittle heap, leaping and scattering leaves with cheerful abandon before stopping again to rake up the strewn foliage.

But those carefree days were long past. Hen's shocking union to an outsider at age twenty-one had made it painfully clear that at least one Kauffman daughter was anything but proper.

~

Rose Ann pressed her embroidery needle into the pretty white pillow slip and pulled the light green floss through the stamped ivy design. She knotted the thread on the underside and removed the small hoop.

With a great sigh, she cast an impatient gaze out the window and watched the fast-moving clouds against the gray-blue sky. Her eyes drifted to the treetops and the tall white martin birdhouse, then to the rolling front lawn. A horse and buggy passed by, and she wished *she* might be heading somewhere this morning. *Anywhere at all*, she thought desperately.

Mamm moaned softly, and a pang of guilt tugged at Rose's heart. She dipped the point of her needle into the pillowcase and set it on the small table nearby, then helped her feeble mother out of the wheelchair and onto the daybed. There, she'd made a cozy nest for Mamm's daytime naps in the spare room just off the sitting room. Later, when twilight fell, Dat would lift her mother into his strong arms and carry her to their bedroom on the first floor, as he did every night.

"Still feelin' chilly, Mamm?" Rose asked.

Her mother nodded.

Rose raised the quilt and gingerly slid Mamm's frail, useless legs beneath the handmade coverlet, as careful as she could be. "That should warm you up right quick."

"*Besser* now," said Mamm. "*Denki*, Rosie."

Rose gave a smile and went to sit on the old cane chair near the foot of the daybed. Because Mamm was in near-constant pain, Rose felt ever so tenderhearted toward her.

Mamm turned her head to face the window, the sunshine spilling over the small bed and onto her brown hair. "Be sure 'n' leave the shades up all the way," she told Rose, "and the door ajar, too." Ever since her injury, Mamm craved the light.

Rose never forgot to do her mother's bidding. She doubted

she ever would, intent as she was on being the best caregiver her mother could have—at least now that Hen was gone.

Honestly, as much as Rose loved her mother, she didn't know how she'd managed these last six months without the daily assistance of her maternal grandmother, Sylvia Blank. In the years since the accident, dear *Mammi* had faithfully helped to bear the burden of Mamm's care, but a sudden stroke had left *Dawdi* Jeremiah incapacitated and dependent on his wife's help, as well as anxious for her company. Here lately, though, Dawdi was able to get out and about on his own again and was nearly his old self, which meant Mammi could once more tend to her daughter most mornings. During those times when Mammi Sylvia came over from their adjoining *Dawdi Haus* or when Mamm took long afternoon naps, Rose could scarcely wait to be in the fresh air, free of the confines of the house. Carrying fresh feed and water for the field mules and the driving horses—Upsy-Daisy, George, and Alfalfa—was one of her few joys.

Her outdoor adventures with Nick were another pleasant reprieve. Sometimes they'd ride horses after nightfall, and other times they'd sneak off to go fishing or exploring in the high meadow, once chores were done. When they were younger, they used to make little floating boats of leaves in the bishop's pond, with sticks for the masts . . . and caught tadpoles, and made tiny mud huts, too.

Then, as now, Rose spent time talking Nick's ear off, and occasionally about the day Mamm became paralyzed. It had long been rumored that their inexperienced driving horse had been spooked by a runaway stallion on the precarious road, though this was no more than hearsay, since the day of the accident had been wiped clean from Mamm's memory.

What they *did* know was that their family buggy had flipped over and rolled partway into the rocky chasm. Mamm had been thrown free when the carriage snapped loose from Upsy-Daisy's hitch. The People called it a "mystery of God" that she and the horse had survived at all.

Nick listened attentively as Rose wondered aloud what had, in fact, happened that frightful day. Neighbor Jeb Ulrich had later told Dat of an English boy who'd appeared at his door, asking for help after the accident. But Dat had always questioned the validity of senile Jeb's farfetched account—especially since there were no English boys around the area that they knew of.

Rose shared with Nick how she'd gone with Hen to the narrow dirt road the very next day. They'd knocked on Jeb's door to no avail and scoured the area, looking for Mamm's money tin with its thirty dollars worth of change. They and their seven older brothers speculated about the cause of the accident for weeks. Yet neither the tin box nor the reason for the accident could ever be found.

For months afterward, Mamm came in and out of herself. Bless her heart, for all she'd been through, their mother looked just as pretty and sweet, if not more so, than before the fateful mishap itself. Her will was as strong as ever, but despite the good care she'd received at the Lancaster hospital, she simply did not get any stronger, and her legs remained as useless as twigs.

There were times Rose would find her singing to herself, sitting in the wheelchair Dat and his father had made for her, darning socks near the black cookstove in the kitchen. Mamm wanted to help out—"do my part," she'd say with a pensive, pained look in her golden-brown eyes. Rose was determined to make her life as happy and comfortable as possible.

Presently, Rose Ann reached for the book she was reading. Opening to the next chapter, she read aloud for a while, glancing at Mamm every so often. Oh, the lovely romance described on these pages!

After a time, she set the book down, daydreaming . . . the story alive in her heart. She couldn't help wondering if she'd ever be so loved and cherished as the girl in the book. Would she someday know the joys of marriage and having children, as she'd dreamed of even as a young girl . . . before Mamm's mishap?

It seemed less likely now with Mamm so frail and growing feebler as the months passed. *And Silas Good no longer pursuing me.* Rose thought sadly of the handsome, likeable fellow, though she was resigned to God's will. If being a *Maidel* and caring for Mamm was her destiny, then so be it.

She stared at her mother, resting peacefully. Rose folded her hands against her black work apron, trying yet again to imagine what it must be like, unable to move her legs to walk or run or move about at will.

*Or to ride horseback . . .*

Quickly, she dismissed her own secret goings-on, knowing her mother would not approve. Mamm would be quick to point out the perils of spending hours with the bishop's wild son on a Sunday night. *Instead of going to Singings to pair up with real Amish boys.*

Rose opened her book yet again, anxious to lose herself in the fictional world as she waited for her mother to drop off. Devouring stories—especially those with surprising twists and turns—was her favorite escape from her semi-isolation.

Later, standing in the doorway till she was certain Mamm was asleep, she whispered, "Rest well." Then, quietly, Rose walked to the coatroom off the kitchen and pulled on Hen's old sweater before hurrying outside.

# CHAPTER 2

The sweet scent of hay drew Rose into the humid stable, where she spotted Nick, disheveled as usual, shoveling out the manure pit. The tall young man's long, dark hair blended in with his black shirt. It was hard to believe that Nick had persuaded Barbara Petersheim, the bishop's wife, to sew him so many dismal-colored shirts. The black, gray, and brown shirts were clearly Nick's favorites, which amused Rose, since the men in their church district wore shirts made of blue and green fabric, as well as white for Preaching services.

Not even the bishop could get him to conform to their ways. Not in Nick's preference for long hair, nor his five-o'clock shadow . . . and definitely not in the bishop's hope for his foster son's living a peace-loving life. No, Nick could bloody a fellow's nose as quick as he could drop his straw hat. Did he think fist fighting was an acceptable sport here? Was it something he'd learned in the city?

*"I learn the hard way,"* Nick had once told her haughtily. And Rose knew it for truth. He'd insisted on using a makeshift fishing pole from a willow branch, even though he could see how many

fish *she* caught by simply using her brother's conventional fishing pole. But he would stubbornly shrug and cast his line into the water. The same was true when it came to cutting hay with Dat or hanging tobacco to dry for a neighbor. Nick refused to imitate what her older brothers—or his foster brother, Christian—did routinely . . . and correctly.

Rose justified his disruptive behavior, considering his difficult childhood—something Nick never talked about. It wasn't surprising to her that he seemed so angry. Angry at everyone, really.

*Everyone but me.*

At twenty-one, Nick had passed the age many young people joined church, yet he still showed no sign of wanting to do so. Didn't he understand that being selected by the bishop to be raised Amish meant the Lord God himself had chosen him? Out of all the lost, worldly souls.

*"But by the grace of God I am what I am."* Rose thought of the verse from 1 Corinthians that she and Silas Good had discussed months ago, when she'd last gone riding with him. *"Sure seems like Nick would look on being chosen as a mighty gut thing,"* she'd suggested to her former beau, and he had agreed. Silas had felt as strongly as she did about the privilege it was for Nick to have the bishop as his father. *"What most fellas wouldn't give for that,"* Silas had remarked as she rode beside him in his black courting buggy.

Now, while she distributed the feed, Rose felt a twinge at the memory of blond, blue-eyed Silas. She had no idea where things stood with him, since her expanded caretaking duties had kept her from attending Singings for quite a while. And, too, the few Sunday evenings she could've gone, she'd chosen to ride horses with her friend Nick instead. The thought of sitting still and singing the same songs put her on edge—hoping a nice fellow would smile and catch her eye for a ride home and all—when she could be out on a galloping horse, breathing in the nighttime fragrances.

It was her nighttime romps through the countryside with Nick that made her life most cheerful. They'd kept their outdoor jaunts secret—between just the two of them. Even now no one was aware of their companionship, apart from the work they did together in the barn. It was best, they'd long agreed, to avoid needlessly raised eyebrows.

She turned now to look at Nick. He smiled back and fixed his eyes on her head, where he'd once snipped off a strand of her strawberry hair when he was sure no one was looking. They had been pruning the grapevines near the road, after harvesting a bumper crop. He'd pressed the curl into his pocket, declaring it the *"most striking red-blond"* he'd ever seen. Rose had worried the clipped spot would show till it grew out again. But not a soul ever noticed.

Nick's scruffiness had amused her from his first day here. And sometimes she caught herself double-checking her own *schtruwwlich* hair, reaching up to push a loose strand over her ear, hoping she didn't look as unkempt as Nick. *Goodness!*

There were times the womenfolk shook their heads, though not unkindly, when they saw her at canning bees or quilting frolics. They took one look at her and must've understood that her mother couldn't rein in her youngest daughter like most able-bodied mothers did. Still, they liked her even as they winced at the stray hairs at her neck. Rose was known, after all, as a dutiful and loyal daughter. Unlike her sister Hen.

*Plitsch-platsch*—slapdash—Hen liked to describe her, but with a loving expression to soften the truth. There was no arguing it—Rose *did* have a penchant for letting things go. She couldn't deny her aversion to tightly twisting her hair on each side to pull it into a tidy bun. After all, she figured no one really noticed her hair beneath the boyish blue paisley kerchief she preferred to wear around the house—nor under her best *Kapp* on Preaching Sundays, either.

But Hen's opinion didn't count for much anymore. Not since she had joined ranks with the "high people," as Nick called them. For the life of her, Rose had never understood why the rough-and-tumble boy from Philadelphia could just blurt out whatever was on his mind one day and clam up the next.

Today, Rose moved along the horse trough. She walked right up to Nick. "I've been wonderin'," she said. "Are all English big-headed, do ya think?"

Nick smirked and returned to his shoveling. "*I'm* English, jah?"

"Ain't what I meant." She shook her head. "Remember what you said about my sister?"

"What about her?"

"That she joined up with the high folk when she married."

"Well, she got herself hitched to an Englischer, didn't she?" His black eyes pierced her own.

"That didn't make her uppity, though."

"Says who?"

"Honestly, I'm tellin' ya, Hen's not stuck on herself like some fancy folk." She stroked Upsy-Daisy's mane. "I'd be more apt to worry over her loss of faith."

"Why's that?"

"She rarely talks of the Lord anymore," Rose said.

"Does she read the Good Book?"

"Not to judge, but I doubt it. And her husband won't let her attend worship services, either, let alone come to our Preaching Sundays."

Nick huffed. "And *that* bothers her?"

"Can't say for sure. But it wonders me sometimes . . . and makes me ever so sad."

Nick ran his hand over his stubbly chin. "So you're worried about her soul, then."

"I pray for her, if that's what ya mean." Rose turned and headed back to the feed bin with her empty bucket. Fact was, Hen had shown her true colors back when she first met Brandon Orringer near the old sawmill on Mt. Pleasant Road. But English as she was

now, Hen wasn't a know-it-all, as the high people were thought
to be.

Rose sighed, rehearsing those hush-hush things Hen had
confided to her years before. Nick would not be hearing any of
that from *her* lips, nor what Rose thought about Hen's impulsive
marriage—and her lack of interest in joining church. Surely he
could see how Hen's stubbornness had broken her parents' hearts.
Rose herself saw the pain clearly in both Dat's and Mamm's eyes
each and every day.

~

Mammi Sylvia was testing the roast for tenderness later that
afternoon, with Mamm sitting primly in her wheelchair near the
woodstove, when Hen's blue car pulled into the lane. Rose heard the
motor before she saw Hen get out of the sedan and open the back
door for blond, curly-haired Mattie Sue. Typically, months passed
and they wouldn't see hide nor hair of Hen, and even less of Mattie
Sue. The elusive Brandon had never once stopped to visit.

*Glory be!* Rose took off running out the back door, straight
to Hen. "Oh, sister, you're here again . . . three times in two
weeks!"

Hen's pretty hazel eyes blinked rapidly. "We came for supper,
if that's all right." She gave Rose a hug and then glanced down at
a smiling Mattie Sue.

"Well, you're just in time. Mammi's cookin' a delicious meal."
Rose fell into step with Hen while four-year-old Mattie Sue hurried
away to the barn to play with the kittens.

Hen paused on the sidewalk, her eyes following Mattie. "How's
Mamm doing?"

"About the same . . . she does complain of bein' chilly lately.
And I'm afraid she's come down with a cold."

"It's getting to be that time of year again."

"Truth be told, I don't think it's just the change of seasons. Mamm's getting weaker."

"That's why I came to check on her."

"Since when are *you* a nurse?" She bristled at Hen's insinuation, as if Rose weren't up to the daily task.

Hen tweaked her elbow. "You silly goose. Don't take things so seriously."

The tightness in her stomach would not give. "I'm doin' just fine looking after Mamm," Rose said softly, motioning for them to go inside.

*Lately I've scarcely done anything else!*

～

After supper, Rose slipped out to the screened-in porch, surprised to hear the bishop's son, Christian, and Nick talking loudly near the side of Dat's barn. Nick's head was down, his posture slouched, as it often was when Christian cornered him.

"Well, you're not listening . . . *Daed* insists you attend the family meetin' tonight," Christian was saying.

Nick looked away, shoving his hands deep into his pockets.

"You'd better be there." Christian leaned forward, his straw hat square on his chestnut-colored hair. He waited for a response, shook his head, and turned to leave. Then he stopped in his tracks. "If you'd just loosen up your tongue, things would go a lot better round here, brother."

Nick raised his head. "I pull my weight, and you know it."

"Anyone can muck out a barn."

Nick's expression soured.

"If ya can't appreciate what Daed's done for ya," Christian barked, "you're downright *dumm*!"

Nick walked to the barn door and gave it a shove to the side.

Christian hollered after him in *Deitsch*, his face red, his eyes blazing. "*Undankbaar*, that's what you are!" Christian stormed off across the pasture to the bishop's house. "Ungrateful!"

The word hung like a broken tree branch after a squall. Rose planted her bare feet on the wooden planks of her father's porch, wondering what had gotten Christian so riled up again.

What she wouldn't give to see Christian offer the hand of acceptance to his English foster brother. Her *own* brothers, especially Mose and Joshua, were the best of friends. They shared each other's farm tools and whatnot, as did Dat and *his* brothers. All of them seemed to be unified in working the land and caring for the animals. But never once had she heard Christian speak a kind word to poor Nick.

What she had heard were Dat's worrisome comments to her oldest brother, Joshua, who came frequently to assist with welding hitches for buggies and wagons and other heavier jobs that had to do with the conveyances Dat made. *"Something must be done to get Nick's attention, to sway him toward the church . . . and mighty soon,"* her father had said.

This had surprised her. Wasn't swaying Nick up to the Lord? After all, God loved Nick more than even his own mother did. "More than anyone," Rose whispered.

Recently, after a Preaching service, she'd spotted Nick walking past the chicken coop, dressed in his black trousers and coat like the other fellows. In that moment, it struck her that although he looked the same as the others outwardly, he did not resemble any of them on the inside. Then and there, she'd wondered if he would ever join the ranks of the People.

Rose wandered down the back steps and across the yard to the barn. From the day Nick had come to live next door, he had been at odds with their community. Especially with Christian.

A year younger, Christian had always enjoyed a solid relationship with his bishop father, having been the only son for nine years—until Nick arrived on the scene. With his dimpled chin and sparkling green eyes, Christian was exceptionally good-looking. Rose had once had a short-lived crush on the tall, muscular boy, till it became obvious that he took much pleasure in picking on Nick.

Hearing Dat come into the barn now, Rose headed straight to the stall to check on the bedding straw for their two new foals. She heard her father's work boots on the cement. "Can ya come early tomorrow to help me lift some boards?" Dat asked Nick. "The old bench wagon's nearly shot after all these years." Her father told him that the bishop thought it was time to replace it. "Your Daed wants it finished up in a few more days."

"Sure," Nick said, pausing. "I'll help ya."

"All right, then. We'll get started just after dawn." Dat glanced over at Rose before he slipped out the barn door.

Rose sat down in the fresh straw, still thinking about Christian's rash remarks. Why had the bishop called a family meeting? She was curious, even though it wasn't any of her business.

"S'pose you heard what Christian said earlier," Nick said, coming her way.

She nodded, wondering if she ought to say what she was thinking—that it might be best not to pay any mind to what his brother said.

"Christian? *Puh!* They should've named him Cain," Nick added. Then he said more softly, "Or Aaron, after his father."

Rose looked at him. "Bishop Aaron's *your* father, too."

Nick wiped his brow with the back of his hand. He stood there, looking dejected, his mouth in a thin, straight line. "Verna and the twins and their husbands and kids are all comin' over tonight," he muttered.

"What for?"

"Same as last week, prob'ly." He stopped abruptly, his ruddy face streaked with a line of dirt on one cheek. "They think it's time for me to join church."

Just then, Hen opened the barn door. Sunlight poured in like a brilliant waterfall. "We're heading for home now, Rosie."

Before saying good-bye to her sister, Rose turned to Nick. "I'll come over and see the bishop's grandchildren later on."

Nick gave a slight wave. "Bring a jar to catch lightning bugs."

She smiled at him, then watched her sister get into the car, wave, and back away, down to the road. And all the while she realized how sad she still felt, for having missed out on seeing Hen as a bride on her wedding day. *How could she have denied me that?* Rose thought. *How, when we were such close sisters?*

# CHAPTER 3

*S*olomon Kauffman finished power-sanding the smooth planks of pine to create the bottom and sides for the new bench wagon. He was mighty glad his bishop allowed compressed air to run his woodworking tools. He ran his callused hand down the fragrant lengths, relishing the light flouring of sawdust on them.

The door to the shop opened, and Bishop Aaron stepped in. "Got a minute, Sol?"

"Sure do." *Anything for the bishop.* He wiped his hands on his coarse work apron. "What can I do for ya?"

The bishop's eyes were sunken, like he hadn't slept much last night. "Havin' more troubles with Nick." He stroked the length of his brown beard. " 'Tween you and me, I found some empty beer bottles back behind the barn."

Solomon held his breath, then said, "Again?"

"Nick's either in with a bad crowd, or he's doin' the drinking on his own."

"Have ya talked to him again 'bout church baptism?"

"Barbara and I have said all we can." The bishop removed his straw hat and stood there looking mighty helpless. "Don't know what more to do." He drew a long, labored sigh. "Unless the Lord gets ahold of him—or one of the district girls catches his eye—I'm afraid we'll lose Nick to the world altogether."

Solomon was sorry to hear it. And he was worried, too, because he knew Rose Ann had befriended the sometimes surly young man. "Is there anything I can do?" he asked.

"Doubt it, really."

Sol knew, as with his own daughter Hen, once the world grips a person, they rarely come back. *An enemy of God . . .*

"Well, it's obviously too late this year, but by a year from now, I'd sure like to see him make the kneeling vow," the bishop said. "I'll keep workin' toward that end."

For that to happen, Nick would have to start attending baptismal instruction classes with the bishop next summer. "*Ach,* growin' up in your house . . . surely Nick's overheard plenty of the teaching for the baptismal candidates. If ya don't mind my suggesting it, what if you made an exception and did some one-on-one training with him right away?"

The bishop eyed Sol. "That could work, I s'pose." He nodded his head. "Might get him committed to the idea, anyhow."

"You don't think he'd just up and run off, do ya?"

Bishop frowned and glanced back at the door. "Hard to say with that one. He's all filled up with a contentious spirit."

Something inside Solomon gripped him. "He won't influence Christian against the church, will he?"

"It's difficult to know what Nick's capable of." The bishop went on to tell about the family meeting they'd had last week. "We've got another tonight. Verna's husband, Levi, is trying to take Nick under his wing, but that's proving to be mighty hard when the boy's keener on the world than God."

Solomon's sons—all of them—had followed the Lord in holy baptism early on, settling down with their sweethearts right away.

Hen, though, had caused enough chaos to make up for all of her compliant and upstanding brothers put together. "I'll keep you in prayer." Sol's throat constricted with the memories of his rebellious daughter.

"Denki, Solomon . . . mighty kind of you."

"The Lord knows what it'll take. You can trust in that." It felt odd counseling the man of God this way, but it was all Solomon knew to say.

He thought back to Rose Ann's own baptismal instruction and was happy she had decided to forgo a typical *Rumschpringe* to join church at age fifteen. That way, when the time came, she could only date Amish fellows, and her promise to God would keep Rose safely in the fold. He'd encouraged his youngest to become a member mighty young . . . *for dear Emma's sake.* Emma had been afraid she might pass on before she could witness Rose's baptism. And everything, after all, hinged on his wife's frail health. Just everything.

The bishop sighed, his expression dreary. "The ministerial brethren are all doin' whatever they can, trying to keep Nick in the church."

"I'm sure you've warned him 'bout touching or tasting the unclean things of the world, jah?" said Sol.

"Oh goodness, have we ever, and you can see what good that's done. Poor Barbara . . . sometimes I believe all this is goin' to break her health," the bishop admitted. "I'd hate to see that."

Thinking again of Hen, Sol offered, "Well, our wayward daughter's startin' to show interest in us once again . . . if that's any encouragement."

The bishop nodded and looked away, as if struggling to maintain his composure. "We're nowhere near that with Nick, I daresay."

"Does he show you and Barbara any respect?"

"Most of the time—'least outwardly."

Sol felt for the man. "Don't give up on him."

"No intention of that. My very calling in the community depends on getting Nick settled down."

Sol understood the bishop could soon be under serious scrutiny from the other ministers if he didn't get Nick into the church, and soon. Having a rebellious son—even a foster one—called his qualifications for bishop into question, even though he'd drawn the divine lot for the office as a younger preacher than most, some fifteen years ago.

"*Da Herr sei mit du*—the Lord be with you," Solomon said as the bishop headed for the door.

"And with you," Aaron replied.

Solomon watched silently as his neighbor—and good friend—left.

~

Rose waved at the bishop, who was trudging across the field toward his house as she went to check the mailbox. While strolling down the driveway, she heard two buggies already turning into the bishop's long lane. Oh, she could hardly wait to go over and enjoy the merriment, as well as the scary stories the children liked to tell.

The sun was falling behind the eastern hills as she walked back toward the house with the mail. She noticed a letter addressed to her, but the handwriting was unfamiliar. Once inside, she placed the rest of the mail on the kitchen table next to Mamm, who was having dessert with her mother, as well as some peppermint tea to ease her congestion.

Without saying a word to either of them, Rose dashed upstairs to the stillness of her room and sat on the bed. She opened the letter and glanced at the bottom of the page. There was Silas Good's name.

*Dear Rose Ann,*

*It's been months since I've seen you at Singings or other youth gatherings. Your grandfather seems to be getting better here lately,*

*coming again to Preaching and all. My family and I pray for him—
and your mother, too—each day.*

*I know it's been a long while since we've talked. But would you
consider meeting me this Saturday at dusk, up Salem Road—remember
the spot near the thicket of oak trees?*

*If it's possible, let me know. Otherwise, if you're not there by
about eight o'clock, I'll just assume you're not coming. But I hope
you will. I'd sure like to see you again, Rose Ann.*

*Your friend,*
*Silas Good*

Rose was amazed—and elated, considering this strange turn
of events. Hadn't she hoped, even prayed that Silas still cared
for her?

Recalling his warm glances before and after Preaching the past
year, her heart beat faster. "He hasn't forgotten me after all," she
whispered, clasping the letter to her.

She spun around and smiled into her dresser mirror, still holding the letter. To think he'd written to her when so many pretty
girls might've caught his eye by now. Oh, she hoped Mamm's cold
would be better enough by then that she might be free to meet
him. She didn't dare to just slip away. It was one thing to go on a
spur-of-the-moment ride with Nick and quite another to plan an
evening out with a potential beau like Silas. And she didn't want
to let Silas down.

Placing the letter in her hankie drawer, she turned to look
out the window and saw the bishop's grandchildren playing on
the front lawn next door. Over several decades, the soaring maple
trees—silver, black, and sugar—and well-established pin oaks and
sycamores had steadily suffused the Petersheims' front and side
lawns, creating a shadowy world beneath. She hurried down the
stairs and saw Mamm nicely settled yet with Mammi Sylvia, the
two of them nibbling sugar cookies. A new pot of coffee—Mammi

Sylvia's weakness—had been put on to boil. No doubt she'd added a few eggshells to take out the bitterness as she liked to do.

Rose slipped out the back door, carrying an empty jar. She headed across the grazing land that bordered the bishop's property. Right away she saw several of the school-age boys bunched up near one ancient tree out back, while the younger boys whittled near the woodshed. The girls played more quietly, staying close to the screened-in porch. Some of them had their little cloth dolls and handmade blankets.

She enjoyed the mingled sound of their play. And as she strolled along, dusk began to fall. Just that quick, the children were drawn to each other, like a flock of birds toward the sky. When they saw her, they shouted, "Come on, Rose!" encouraging her to chase and catch fireflies with them, their laughter clear and true.

After a time, they began to settle onto the back steps to take turns telling stories, each one trying to outdo the other with far-fetched or frightening tales. This evening was no exception. Most every story included some superstition about the dark, rocky ravine that ran below Bridle Path Lane over yonder . . . of disappearances and mysterious sounds in the night. So many superstitions had sprung up after Mamm's near-fatal accident. Despite all of that, Rose shivered with delight at the telling.

She heard the crack of a twig and glimpsed Nick's shadow near the side of the house—she knew what he was fixing to do.

Nick reached the farthest end of the porch, pausing there, still as a tree trunk. Then he jumped out and shouted, "Boo!"

The children's terrified yet merry screams rose straight to the sky. Nick clapped his hands, his laughter ringing across the paddock as he swung one child, then another, around and around. He'd pulled pranks like this before, and the children were always gleefully surprised.

He stayed around, squatting on the top step and listening as the stories took a more ominous turn. The story being told now was of a recent flood that had washed out and destroyed the historic Jackson's Sawmill Covered Bridge not far from there. "Weeks afterward, live frogs and dead fish were found in Gilbert Browning's house, right there near Octoraro Creek," the tallest boy said.

Rose stifled a laugh. While it was common knowledge that last year's flood had washed the old bridge off its moorings and flooded several houses, too, she couldn't envision how this child knew anything about the interior of Gilbert Browning's abode. The eccentric man rarely let in any outsiders except Lucy Petersheim, who'd quit working there several weeks ago. That was how Rose came to be hired in her place, to cook a variety of meals for the week, as well as clean the kitchen and wash up a small mountain of dishes. Since he was a widower, there was surprisingly little to keep tidy. As meagerly furnished as the main floor was, Mr. Browning's house could've easily passed for Amish.

She was thankful to her father, as well as to the bishop, for agreeing to let her work for Mr. Browning on a trial basis. She had no idea why Lucy had stopped working so suddenly, unless she was planning to marry come fall.

Rose's mind drifted back to the voice of the young storyteller. "It's awful dark in the holler." He went on to describe the very location where Mamm's buggy had flipped over, adding, "There's a hobgoblin who lives deep in the ravine by the crick. If you ain't careful, he'll grab ya!"

Now the children were squirming with fright. Rose had never been one to fret at such tales or grimace at the thought of the sun going down. Truth be known, she relished the nighttime hours— enjoyed stepping out of the house after dusk to sit on the back porch before family worship. She liked to simply breathe in the savory freshness, especially during the autumn months. The resonance of a thousand crickets in the vast underbrush along the horse fence . . . nothing quite compared.

Hen, on the other hand, was petrified of the dark. In fact, at supper tonight, Hen lamented the shorter days now that it was late September. Rose, however, secretly thrilled to the longer evenings. For one thing, Mamm went to bed earlier in the fall, giving Rose more time to read her library books. And ride with Nick.

And back when she was going to Singings in the fall of last year, Silas Good would arrive at dusk—pulling up Salem Road a ways and parking his open buggy beneath the turning trees to wait for her. It had been nearly one full year since he'd first taken her home in his new courting buggy . . . last September twenty-eighth. But in that year they'd only gone together a handful of times.

It had been Hen who'd urged Rose to attend Sunday Singings again. *Love can't find you if you're hiding at home*, her sister had said last week. Yet Rose had been almost reluctant to go again—until Silas's letter had come today.

Starlight slanted in the sky as Rose sat there listening to the last of the stories. Looking at the top of Nick's head as he leaned in toward one of the children, she wondered how it might be if Silas asked to court her. How would it change her life?

*A dream come true*, she decided, cherishing the delicious warmth brought by this new excitement as she said her good-byes to the little ones and to Nick, then headed toward home.

But as Rose walked through the white moonlit pasture, the vision of Nick attentively sitting with the children lingered.

# CHAPTER 4

*B*ack home now, Hen opened the front door to the modern two-story house she and her husband had purchased four years ago. She remembered the first time she'd spotted the For Sale sign standing like a beacon in the front yard. Her heart had skipped a beat as she pulled the car off the road to jot down the real estate agent's phone number.

She still caught herself hesitating slightly before entering by way of the front door, even after living this long in the wonderful house. Everything was different from her growing-up years, when the entrance to her father's farmhouse was through the back door.

*I should be used to it by now. . . .*

As they went inside together, Hen leaned down to kiss Mattie's forehead, lifting her daughter's thick blond hair over her shoulders, beneath the little black candlesnuffer bonnet Hen had gotten for her just today at a quaint general store on the back roads. Other than her daughter's bangs, not once had she actually cut Mattie's long hair, only trimming the dead ends every few months.

Brandon's negative reaction to Mattie Sue's long locks had caused conflict between them. That, and the fact she'd pulled Mattie's hair back into a thick knot a couple times recently. She'd occasionally pinned up her own hair, as well, though not in the traditional Amish bun.

Going into the living room, she saw Brandon sitting in the breakfast nook across the house, his gaze focused on notebook pages spread out all over the table. Mattie Sue removed the bonnet and dashed to her daddy, throwing her arms around his neck. Brandon kissed Mattie on the cheek, making over her as he always did when they returned home from shopping or running errands.

Mattie leaned on his arm for a moment, gazing up at him. "Look what Mommy bought me." She held up the black outer bonnet. "See, Daddy—it's just like Aunt Rosie's."

"I see that." Brandon raised his eyebrows at Hen.

Hen cringed inwardly. "It's almost bedtime, Mattie."

Mattie Sue looked back at her, then turned again to Brandon. "Do you like it, Daddy? It's for dress-up—make-believe."

"Why don't you get ready for your bath," Hen suggested quickly.

Brandon groaned, then frowned as Mattie scampered back to her and she patted Mattie's head. "I'll come in and draw the water soon," she said.

"Okay, Mommy." Her little girl's bright eyes held hers momentarily before she darted down the hallway to her room, swinging the bonnet behind her as she went.

Hen stiffened as she walked toward the kitchen to pack Brandon's lunch for tomorrow. She opened the refrigerator and found the lunch meat and the mouthwatering dill pickles she'd put up last summer. She felt her husband's eyes on her.

"So . . . you've been out." He sounded tense.

She nodded, not wanting to tell him about their relaxing time this evening, enjoying her grandmother's wonderful dinner and all the pleasant chatter around the table. True, her father had seemed a bit quizzical about their making yet another unannounced visit, but her mother had appeared content just having Hen eating with them once again. She didn't say a word, either, about going through piles of Mom's piecework with Rose Ann, choosing enough squares to make a quilted wall hanging for Mattie Sue's bedroom. And she certainly would not mention Mattie's delight at getting more than a peek inside the Amish general store.

Brandon looked up suddenly. "No need to make my lunch, by the way. I have a noon appointment tomorrow."

"All right," she said quietly. She forced a smile, wishing she could return to the lovely time at her parents' house. If Hen tried hard enough, she could actually picture Brandon sitting next to her at the table back home—but years ago, when she'd finally gotten the nerve to introduce him as her boyfriend. Well, by then Brandon had been her fiancé.

*So much water under the bridge,* she thought as she returned the lunch meat to the refrigerator. She opened the lid on the dill pickles and halved a long spear down the middle. For as long as she could remember, she'd loved eating dill pickles just plain.

*Plain,* she thought, *like I used to be.*

"Anything else I can get for you?" she asked Brandon, holding the sliced pickle in midair.

"No, thanks."

"Okay, then . . . as you wish."

He sighed loudly. "*That's* an interesting concept."

She hoped he wasn't picking a fight.

"What *do* I wish for, Hen?" He shook his head and looked away. "Do you even know anymore?"

She noticed how spotless the kitchen was. "Nice of you to redd up," she said, attempting to change the subject.

"Must you always talk that pig Latin?"

"What?"

"You know what I'm talking about."

"It's Deitsch," she insisted.

"You aren't Amish anymore."

She shrugged absently, already weary of the undertow between them. "Anyway, thanks for straightening up after supper."

"I actually didn't—I went out" was his taut reply. "Remember, my wife didn't bother to cook tonight."

*First time in months.*

"There were plenty of leftovers," she replied gently. "You could've heated up something."

He rose from his chair and stood there, scratching his head. "Look, Hen, I don't get it. I really don't."

She was slow to speak. "What do you mean?"

"You're never here anymore." He stared at her, no pain in his eyes. It was more of an accusation.

"Never? I'm almost always home."

"Before these past few weeks, sure. But now?" He ran both hands through his crop of hair. "And what's with the Amish bonnet for Mattie?"

"It's just the one worn outdoors, not the sacred Kapp."

"Hen, c'mon . . . what exactly is sacred about any of that backward nonsense?"

She opened her mouth to speak but didn't. They were getting nowhere. And she needed more time to let her thoughts simmer deep in her heart, where she would know how to answer him eventually.

"Really, hon," he said. "You left that life behind, remember?" Looking tired, Brandon wandered to the refrigerator, pulled out a can of soda, and popped open the lid. He took a long swig before giving her a sideways glance. "So . . . where *have* you been all day? Is something bothering you?" Surprisingly, his tone was softer.

"I'm fine," she muttered. Truth was, the only time she felt

this crazy pressure in her chest was when Brandon fired questions at her.

"So you're not going to say."

She ignored him and put the pickles back in the fridge, relieved when he returned to the breakfast nook—deep into the abyss of his work, which was rarely finished. Always, more time was required to finish this project or start the next. She was surprised he'd even noticed her absence.

*At least he's home with his work and not at the office all hours.* Her friend Diane Perlis's husband was hardly even home. Behind his back, Diane referred to him as a workaholic. Thankfully, Brandon's unfinished tasks could be taken up after hours in the comfort of home, so Mattie Sue could see her daddy. See him but not interact much with him, especially not during the week.

Hen heard the patter of feet in the hallway. "Ready for my bath, Mommy."

Moving away from her modern kitchen, Hen didn't look over her shoulder at the confident land developer she'd hopelessly fallen for at age twenty-one. What a charmer he'd been! She had never known what being swept off your feet could possibly mean until she met Brandon. And she'd savored every minute of it.

*Where did we go wrong?*

She scooted her daughter along the hallway, toward the main bathroom. "Let's get you into the tub, munchkin." She was getting better at putting on a playful tone . . . becoming more accustomed to shielding Mattie Sue from the truth. It was in her blood to keep grown-up issues behind closed doors, to force her voice into submission and be as sweet as Brandon had always said she was. *Until now.*

She closed the door to the attractive bathroom, complete with a corner shower and a separate soaking tub, and let a sigh escape.

"Can you pour in lots and lots of bubbles?" Mattie asked.

Hen nodded and leaned down for the pink plastic bottle

beneath the sink, her smile still plastered on her face. No need to spoil Mattie's bath time.

"Does Auntie Rose put bubbles in her bath, too?" Mattie Sue's wide blue eyes blinked up at Hen.

"What'd you say, honey?"

"Auntie Rose . . . does she like bubbles, too?"

The phone rang loudly. "Just a minute, sweetie." Hen opened the door and looked back at her unclothed daughter, who was cautiously pointing her little pink foot into the water. "Don't let it get too high, all right?"

Mattie nodded her head slowly, transfixed by the mound of billowy bubbles.

"I'll be right back," she said. Brandon despised the phone ringing when he was working. Rushing to the receiver, she answered, "Hello, Orringers."

"May I speak to Brandon?" came a stiff-sounding male voice.

"Who's calling, please?" She knew better than to bother her husband at this hour for a phone solicitor. She had to know for sure who was on the line. "Is he expecting your call?"

"He is, in fact. I'm returning *his*."

"Just a moment." Hen hurried to the breakfast nook and covered the receiver with her hand. "A man . . . for you."

*You sure it's not a solicitor?* he mouthed silently, and she assured him the caller had some business with him.

Brandon reached to take the phone from her. Moving away from the room, she heard his opening response and realized the caller was someone connected to his brother's law firm in Lancaster.

*Some legal hassle*, she guessed.

Hen made her way to their bedroom, distantly aware of the sound of running water. Suddenly fatigued, she sat on the neatly made bed and leaned her face into her hands. She stared at the carpeted floor and relived the first time she'd met Brandon—his irresistible eyes and winning smile. Her memories pulled her back to the past.

That February had brought with it a biting cold. Winter had hung like an icy curtain around her father's barren farmland as Hen hitched up the driving horse and headed to visit her dearest friend, Arie Miller. Arie was heartsick over her beau's sudden interest in another girl, and Hen wanted to cheer her up.

Several hours after Hen's arrival at the Millers' house, a steady snow began to fall, coming in large flakes. In a short time, the storm turned to blinding swirls and a harsh wind roared down over the dark hills near the Millers' stone farmhouse. By the time Hen was ready to start out for home—down the gently curving road leading through the old covered bridge, near Jackson's Sawmill—the snow had become an old-fashioned blizzard. The two buggies that passed her on the road were mere dots of gray in the vicious current of white.

After some time of merely walking the horse, Hen could no longer see well enough to keep going. She reined the animal off the road, disoriented in the whirl of white and wind. She feared she might become stranded in the dangerous storm—might even freeze to death. *O Lord, guide me safely home,* she prayed.

Minutes later, Brandon Orringer had arrived in his red car and pulled onto the drifting shoulder. An immediate answer to her prayer! He got out and trudged against the wind and snow, right up to her carriage, asking if he could help. He'd saved her that day by guiding her slowly through the blizzard as she trotted the horse close behind his blinking car lights. And, months afterward, she believed he'd rescued her from the tiresome, ordinance-laden life she'd dreaded, as well.

A godsend, Hen had thought at the time. Even though there had been plenty of nice Amish fellows interested in her during those years, none of them was half as intriguing as Brandon—and none of them had come along to save her from a terrifying storm.

*"Be careful what you wish for,"* Brandon had once told her soon after they'd met. Despite that, Hen had cherished their unlikely relationship and attempted to keep pace with his lightning-speed ways.

When Hen considered it now, the short length of their engagement—a mere seven weeks—actually stunned her. Yet no one could've steered her away from Brandon if they'd tried. Not even her own mother, who was completely in the dark about her plans to marry a worldly boy . . . at least until it was too late. Hen's eyes had been fixed on the goal of wedlock outside the church, as far away as she could get. And she'd let Brandon know it, too, in every way that mattered to him.

With a shudder, she threaded her fingers through her shoulder-length hair, remembering all the years she'd worn her hair in the Amish bun. She raised her head to stare at her wedding photograph on the dresser. Posing for the camera was another rule she'd broken during the very year her younger sister—and near shadow—had obediently made her vow to God and to the church.

*Being happy was all I cared about.* She remembered the delirious days and weeks of first love—fully believing she was cut out to be an Englisher. She'd told Rose this privately in their bedroom. Rose, poor thing, hadn't known what to make of Hen's rash insistence, especially with their mother ailing so. Mamm was as helpless as the rag dolls Rose sewed for their many young nieces.

Hen had never forgotten the look of astonishment she'd received when she told dear Rose she wouldn't be joining church with her that September after all.

"I let my sister down," Hen whispered now. Looking at herself in the dresser mirror, she arched her back to better see her face and hair . . . the worldly makeup, too. "I let everyone down. . . ."

Mattie Sue called to her, and she hurried into the hallway. She'd lost track of time. Pushing open the bathroom door, she found her daughter's little head peeking up from the bath, encircled in sparkling bubbles.

"Honey—what on earth . . ."

"I'm having fun," Mattie said, a small bubble clinging to her long eyelashes. "Sorry, Mommy. I turned off the water soon as I remembered, honest I did."

*Honest I did . . .*

Mattie's expressions reminded her of the way she'd talked as a little girl. "It's all right—this time." She knelt beside the tub and reached her arms deep into the water, up past her elbows, letting the warmth and the suds soothe her as she washed Mattie's back.

"I go see Karen tomorrow," Mattie said, eyes wide. "My bestest friend."

"We need to get you to bed. You want to be wide-awake in the morning, don't you?" Nearly every other Tuesday for the past year, Mattie had spent most of the day with Hen's friend Diane and daughter, Karen, who was the same age as Mattie Sue. Two Fridays a month, Hen returned the favor and took Karen to give Diane a break, as well.

"Karen wants a hair bun like Auntie Rose's and Grandma Emma's."

*Auntie . . . Grandma.* Brandon had insisted Mattie call her Plain relatives by the English names.

"Did you tell Karen about your Amish relatives?"

Mattie nodded her head rambunctiously. "She doesn't know what a Kapp looks like up close," she said in her sweet little voice. "I tried to draw one, but it was too sloppy."

Mattie's remark reminded Hen of the verbal battles she'd had with Brandon over what was appropriate for Mattie Sue. Now that their daughter was older and more aware of what was going on around her, they'd had numerous arguments over worldly VHS tapes and, especially, MTV. Her husband definitely enjoyed his cable TV. Hen felt the pressure build whenever she thought of her precious girl growing up in such a sophisticated environment. *I never once considered this when Brandon and I were dating—never cared about it.*

The thought amazed her now. She certainly loved her husband, but she'd never thought there would be such a tug-of-war over their child's upbringing.

"Can I show Karen how to make a cradle like Uncle Josh made for me?" Mattie's words broke through her musing.

"Out of wood?"

"No, cardboard." Mattie frowned, the sides of her mouth turned down, dismayed by Hen's distraction.

"Oh jah."

"Mommy?" Mattie giggled. "What'd you just say?"

She looked at her daughter, still immersed in the sudsy water. "Did you mix up your other language again?"

Smiling, Hen picked up the washcloth and lathered it with soap to wash Mattie's face. "When you do something the same way for many years, it's hard to stop," she explained.

Mattie glanced at the door. "Is Daddy upset about my new bonnet?"

The question startled Hen. So the strained atmosphere between her and Brandon *was* affecting their daughter. But she absolutely refused to talk about Brandon in a negative way. "Daddy's just busy with his work, honey."

"His face looks sad sometimes." Mattie returned to playing in the bubbles.

Hen inhaled deeply. If Brandon was angry, she had been the one to trigger it. She probably shouldn't have gotten the black bonnet for Mattie Sue, but she could scarcely resist it. Knowing her husband, he'd be sure to bring it up again to her when they were alone.

"*It's your fault we fight so much,*" he had said recently. Earlier tonight he'd said as much again with his eyes. Hen hadn't anticipated how motherhood would change her priorities so profoundly.

She shook herself and pulled her arms out of the water. "Five more minutes, honey."

"Aw, can't I stay in longer?"

Mattie would beg and plead all night if Hen allowed it. Her daughter was not as submissive as she and Rose had been as children . . . or their many brothers. There had been no back talking to "those who have the rule over you" without serious consequences. She'd heard the account of two of her brothers giving Dat some lip and quickly regretting it—rubbing their backsides through their work trousers—after a sound whipping behind the barn.

"You can stay in the tub longer another time," she told Mattie, getting up to reach for a towel.

"Daddy lets me—"

"Mattie Sue, not tonight."

Tears welled up in Mattie's big eyes. "Why not, Mommy?"

"Because I said so." *Words Mamm used with Rose and me . . .* Quickly, she added, "It's bedtime now."

"But, Mommy . . ."

"No more whining. I'll come back and dry you off soon." Hen opened the door and stepped outside. There was no question in her mind: Her permissive husband had encouraged this sort of behavior in Mattie, as well as exposed her to all kinds of ungodly "entertainment" right here in their own home. Where would it end?

She leaned her head against the wall, aware of Brandon's voice across the house. Something was "preposterous," he said. Then, finishing up his phone call, he concluded, "We'll talk more tomorrow."

*Always the negotiator,* she thought, going to Mattie's room for some clean pajamas. She remembered the Rainbow Brite nightshirt that got away, so to speak . . . the one Mattie had pleaded for at the mall with real tears. This was Hen's worry about planning playtime get-togethers with the Perlises' daughter—Mattie Sue was constantly being immersed into the worldly way of thinking. Even though she was just a little girl, Karen was obsessed with Barbie dolls, dressing them in outfits complete with skimpy underwear that made Hen cringe. Why wasn't little Karen more interested in Glo Worm or Strawberry Shortcake dolls instead?

It wasn't that Hen didn't enjoy Diane or having coffee in the Perlises' beautiful home. She also delighted in Mattie's gleeful excitement at seeing her little friend at the door. Even Brandon agreed it was a wonderful arrangement. *Anything to keep our daughter away from her Plain cousins*, she thought. Her husband was adamant that a conservative lifestyle wasn't for them.

But Brandon couldn't possibly know what Hen planned to do tomorrow during her free time. The mere thought of it gave her goose bumps, even though she felt a bit hesitant, considering what was at stake.

She hurried back to Mattie Sue with the soft pink pajamas in hand, wondering what her father might think of her plan . . . if he knew.

# CHAPTER 5

Rose kept to herself Tuesday afternoon, contemplating Silas's invitation as she carried buckets of fresh feed for the animals. With Mamm's cold worse today, she didn't see how she could accept it just yet, much as she wanted to. Perhaps things would look more promising in a day or two.

When her barn chores were done, she headed out to roam the pasture alongside one of her favorite horses, Alfalfa, enjoying the sunshine and the fresh smells of autumn in the air. She noticed the bishop and his son, Christian, and several of the bishop's sons-in-law digging potatoes within spitting distance of her father's pastureland.

*Tomorrow I'll make scalloped potatoes for Mr. Browning—his favorite,* she thought, anxious to see how the cuttings she'd made from some of her purple and pink African violets were faring. She was eager to bring some cheer to the dreary kitchen where the man spent most of his time. Although his wife had died several years ago, Rose was sure he was still in mourning. At times he even seemed to talk to his deceased wife while he sat in his usual spot, smack-dab in the doorway between the kitchen and front room.

If she were an Englischer, she'd definitely spruce up that kitchen of his. Give the walls a nice, soft coat of yellow paint, for one thing. Since starting to work there three weeks ago, Rose had pondered multiple ways to open up the gloomy abode with additional light. "Like Hen's wonderful-*gut* kitchen," she caught herself saying. Oh, she could only dream of ever having such a fine place to cook and bake!

Laughing at herself, Rose herded two of the horses into the barn for grooming. By currying at least two each afternoon, she could squeeze it in between her other chores, especially if Nick helped, too. But so far today, he was busy checking the hanging harnesses for any weak points, as Dat had directed. One of their neighbors, another farmer, had broken down on the road early that morning for just that reason, Dat had reported.

Rose was especially careful with the oldest horse as she moved the rubber curry brush from the neck down to the rear, working most gently on the back and shoulders. She had to watch where she stood when brushing this one, not wanting to get kicked, which had happened to several of her brothers. Clumsy Mose was especially a target for this horse's kicking.

Thinking suddenly of Christian, she was reminded of his rude treatment of Nick. He'd never seemed so unkind to anyone else, including his nieces and nephews. She was still captivated by last night's stories, especially the one about the floodwaters—and frogs and fish—seeping into Gilbert Browning's house. She'd even had trouble concentrating on her library book last night as she recalled the bishop's grandson's peculiar tale.

*Was it just made up?*

Tomorrow she hoped to ask Mr. Browning about the flood to see what he remembered. That is, if he managed to stay awake long enough. Most of the time when she was there, Gilbert sat stiffly in his chair, puffing on his pipe till he fell into a sleepy stupor—twice he hadn't even known when she'd finished up for the day. Since he left her day's pay in bills sticking out of a ledger on the little table in the corner of the kitchen, there was no need to awaken him to say good-bye. Still, she wondered what made him so tired. Was he depressed, perhaps because of his grief?

Nick sneezed loudly across the barn, where he was sweeping with an old push broom.

"Blessings on ya," she said.

Nick scratched his dark head beneath the rim of his straw hat. "Ya know, I never once heard that . . . not before comin' here." He moved toward her.

"Well, lots of folk say it."

He was silent for a moment, then added, "I sure never heard my dad say anything like that." He looked at her. "Don't think I ever heard him pray, neither."

His comment stopped her short. He talked only occasionally about his parents. Rose was wary, not wanting to mention something offhand when he looked so serious. "Pardon my askin', but did your folks ever have a say about where you lived . . . when ya came here?"

He reached for a dandy brush and began to groom a horse. "I doubt it. My dad was long gone by then—left my mom and me when I was little. Might be why Mom drank so much."

She'd assumed his birth parents had no Plain family roots. But she knew little about the private agency that had placed Nick with the bishop and had supervised him only minimally till Nick turned eighteen. The way she'd heard it, the bishop had gone clear over to Philly to handpick a boy who was considered most needy.

She wondered sometimes if Nick still thought of himself as an outsider amongst the People. He so rarely shared anything personal. At least not verbally. His eyes, well . . . it was downright uncanny how he expressed his thoughts with a brooding gaze. As for her, there were plenty of occasions when she'd talked *his* ear off. Moments when she considered him a right good friend, or nearly like a cousin. Then, other times, he acted like the worst ever brother, ignoring her completely—or tormenting the daylights out of her.

"Do you ever hear from your mother?"

He drew a quick breath. "Before I left, she said she'd come get me one day . . . when she got herself sober." Tugging on his gray shirt sleeve, he looked down at his scuffed-up work boots. "Still waitin' for that."

"Ach, Nick. Surely she'll come." *If she promised.*

He brought up the family meeting last night, at the bishop's. "I was there only a short time before I was asked to leave. Kinda like the meetin' last week," he said more softly.

Rose listened, feeling sorry for him.

"As for my *real* dad, I doubt he even cares where I am." Nick's voice sounded empty. "From what Bishop tells me."

Rose curled her toes inside her old black boots. *How awful sad!*

"Will you continue to stay on with the bishop's family, then?" she asked.

He fingered the dandy brush in his hand. "Hard to know what to do, really." He raised his head and looked her square in the face.

"Don't forget, they're your family, too." She sighed and glanced in the direction of the farmhouse, remembering what Christian had blurted out to him yesterday. "Actually, if ya think about it, *all* the People are." She hoped and prayed Nick might sometime accept the bishop as his father.

"Time I make my own way," he said flatly. "My own choices, too." Nick blew out his breath and looked away just that quick, like he'd told her too much.

"Well, Christian's a church member, though he still works at home—and sometimes over here, too," she pointed out.

"He'll be getting his own place soon enough. Wait and see."

"Get himself hitched, ya mean?"

"I doubt he's found his girl yet." Nick paused, then handed her the stiff-bristled dandy brush to flick the dirt out of the horse's thick hair. "Here," he said, "you'll be needin' this next."

She stooped to put the rubber curry brush on the floor, away from the feeding trough. It was a mystery to her and everyone why Nick had stayed on at the bishop's after his eighteenth birthday. And since he hadn't yet become a church member, she wondered if he was thinking of returning to the English world from whence he'd come. There had been talk amongst some of the older folk that he was a bad seed. And there was Mamm's worry that his Plainness had been for the bishop's benefit all these years. Still, Nick hadn't caused any *real* trouble, as far as Rose knew.

She brushed the horse more vigorously now. If Christian hoped to keep working for his bishop father till he married, could Nick do the same? If so, he ought to start attending the Sunday Singings again, instead of riding horses with her. She'd only seen him once with a girl at the youth gatherings in the few times he'd gone.

*I'm more sociable than he is, even being stuck at home with Mamm these months!*

She considered Nick's willingness to share openly with her today. It made her sad to think his father had been so disinterested as to run off like that. Nick's solemn eyes and downturned mouth revealed that he'd never recovered.

Nick waved as he headed off to another part of the stable area, and she offered a smile.

"Goodness, I need to hurry 'n' finish up," she whispered, suddenly remembering her mother, who would be awakening from her long afternoon nap about now.

There were times when she tucked Mamm in for a nap and slipped out to tend to the animals that she almost forgot her mother's plight . . . and how it affected all of them.

Being the main caretaker had been more difficult than Rose

anticipated, and she'd chafed against the fear that she might miss out on getting married. The fact that Silas Good had bided his time gave her more than a single ray of hope.

～

Solomon and the bishop were in the woodworking shop, leaning over the workbench, talking about ordering a small load of horse manure for their vegetable gardens. The bishop suggested they go up to White Oak Road themselves and help to load it.

"How'd last night's family meeting go?" Sol asked.

Bishop Aaron shook his head. "Not so *gut*."

As familiar with Nick as he was, Sol didn't think one iota less of the bishop for voicing this.

"The whole situation really wore on me yesterday. So much so that I crept into Nick's room last night . . . stood there in the dark at the foot of his bed," Aaron said. "A terrible temptation came over me—one I'd never experienced before."

"Oh?"

"It was all I could do to keep from going over there, while he lay sound asleep, and cutting that scandalous ponytail off his head!"

Sol was downright startled. Bishop Aaron had always seemed to be a tolerant father. "How'd ya keep from doin' it?" he asked.

"Gritted my teeth, that's what . . . and turned away from the pull of righteous indignation." The bishop's face was stern.

"What would cuttin' off Nick's long hair accomplish?"

The bishop nodded slowly and tugged on his suspenders. "That's just what I asked myself in bed later. What *gut* would it do?"

Sol thought on that. "You've always treated Nick as your own."

Bishop looked at him askance. "Well, how else would I treat a boy who's been with us all these years?" Then, with a thoughtful sigh, he added, "Who the Lord handpicked to come here . . . and who I'd always hoped to adopt."

Solomon felt sorry he'd uttered a word.

Scuffing his feet on the woodshop floor, Aaron admitted it wasn't easy to live with such a defiant boy.

Pulling his pencil from behind his ear, Sol asked, "You ever ask Nick to cut his hair, in accordance with the *Ordnung*?"

"Oh, more times than I can count."

"Well, what's he say?"

"Nothin' . . . just shrugs and keeps on working."

"What if Barbara asked him?"

Aaron frowned. "I'm tryin' to keep the stress off her. But my daughters have teased and tormented Nick something awful over his 'Samson locks.' "

Sol shook his head. "I guess I'm with you, then—I would've wanted to cut his ponytail off, too."

The man of God let out a restrained chuckle, and they both returned to figuring up how much manure they'd need, planning to divide the expense of having it hauled in on a manure spreader to make quick work of the chore once it arrived.

# CHAPTER 6

An hour before supper, Hen surprised Rose with yet another visit. As she walked with Nick across the barnyard, Rose's legs felt sluggish from sweeping and redding up the barn.

"See ya tomorrow," she told Nick, who'd spotted Hen's car.

He nodded abruptly and scooted off toward the grazing land without saying more.

Immediately Rose looked for Mattie Sue, but this time Hen was alone. It was actually startling to see her sister here again. *Shouldn't she be at home cooking?*

But then Rose remembered "mother's day out," or so Hen called the days Mattie spent with her little English friend. "Hullo, sister," she called, lifting the barnyard gate and going toward the backyard. She waited for Hen to make her way to the sidewalk.

"You look all in, Rose."

She gave a little laugh. "Almost said the same 'bout you." She motioned to the screened-in porch. "Can ya sit awhile?"

Hen dropped her purse on the wood floor and sat down with a sigh. "Might do me some good."

Rose pulled a wooden chair over next to Hen's.

"How's Mom?" asked Hen.

"Still restin', hoping to knock this cold. Mammi Sylvia has an ear out for her."

"I hope she's feeling better soon." Hen picked at her floral print skirt, like the ones the Mennonite girls up at the Bart general store sewed for themselves. "Maybe you won't know what I mean if I say this, but do you ever wish you could relive your life?" Hen leaned back against the chair. "Do you ever have regrets?"

"What sort of regrets?"

"Do you wish you could go back and make different choices?"

Rose was surprised, but she considered the question for a moment, and thought of Mamm . . . and the day of the accident. "Jah, I guess I do, sometimes." *No, all the time.* She caught Hen's eye. "What about you? Do you ever regret marrying Brandon?"

"Well, no . . . we wouldn't have Mattie Sue if I hadn't."

Rose noticed a glint in Hen's eye. Something was amiss. "Are you all right, Hen?"

Her sister wore a sudden frown. "No need to tell Mom any of this. Promise?"

"Any of what?"

"Just what I said."

Rose couldn't understand why she was being asked to promise, but because she knew Hen very well, she suspected her sister must be struggling with something. *Hopefully it's not about her and Brandon!* The thought made her awful sad.

"I'm planning to make an Amish dress for Mattie Sue," Hen said quietly.

"Why?"

"And I've been teaching her a few words in Deitsch, too." Hen glanced over her shoulder tentatively. "It's time for Mattie Sue to know more about her Plain heritage."

Rose did not understand this new talk whatsoever. She had observed through the years of her sister's marriage that Brandon was determined to keep Amish ways out of their home and life. And besides, the People were always saying that once a person left, the world swallowed them up. Yet if that was so, why was Hen coming back to visit so often?

Hen grimaced faintly. "Oh, Rosie, my daughter's missing out on so many of the old traditions."

Rose Ann hardly knew what to say. *Wasn't that the reason for marrying an Englischer?*

"I just can't figure out how to mix the Plain ways with the modern. It's so hard." Her sister's voice cracked.

Rose lightly touched Hen's wrist. *But you didn't want anything to do with our ways. . . .*

They sat there silently looking at the barn, where the bishop and his son, Christian—and Dat, too—were going in and out of the sliding wooden door. A heavy feeling pervaded the atmosphere, and Rose hoped Hen wasn't going to get herself into hot water with her husband.

After a moment, Hen leaned forward and clasped her knees through her long skirt, linking her fingers. "If I tell you something, will you keep it mum?" She looked at Rose.

"Two promises in two minutes?"

"I'm simply *asking* you to keep everything we've just talked about private. That's all."

Rose tried to absorb the seriousness in Hen's eyes.

"I need to tell you this, sister to sister," Hen said. "Do I have your word?"

It was easy to say she'd be silent about something and quite another to remember what she'd promised. With a sister like Hen,

Rose had often had to keep track of what was a secret and what wasn't. "Of course you do," she said at last.

Hen's face beamed, like she was ever so relieved. "I did something today I've wanted to do for quite a while."

Rose braced herself.

"I filled out a job application."

"You did what?"

Her sister nodded happily. "I'm holding my breath I'll get the job."

Rose groaned. She felt she knew where this was going.

"And I'll be expected to put my hair in a bun when I work."

"You want to work at an *Amish* store?"

"Rachel's Fabrics."

*What does it mean?* Rose's heart was torn.

Hen continued. "Rachel wants me to look Plain, which shouldn't be too hard, right? After all, I am."

"Will you start talking Deitsch again, too?" Rose gave a nervous laugh, not sure she wanted to know all that Hen was up to.

"I feel desperate, Rosie. I really miss the old life . . . and my family." Her sister smiled sadly and looked down. "You have no idea."

"Oh, Hen."

The silence hung in the air. So her worldly sister had finally woken up and realized she'd made a terrible mistake.

"I'm hopin' you might be able to help with Mattie Sue . . . if I get the job, I mean."

Rose didn't see how she could take on more responsibility, but she loved her sister's little girl and felt sorry she'd had no choice in being raised English. "Just remember I'm busy in the afternoons, and Wednesday mornings, too."

"I know Mom and Dad need you to help around here—and

you're working at Mr. Browning's. Certainly I don't expect you to adjust your work schedule to baby-sit Mattie Sue."

"I'll do what I can." *That is if Brandon lets you take the job.*

Hen waved her hand casually. "Or . . . maybe one of our sisters-in-law might be a better choice."

Rose immediately thought of Josh's wife. "Kate's home all day with her three girls. Maybe between Kate and me, something can work out."

Hen paused and glanced toward the pastureland. "I'm determined to pull this off, Rose."

*You always do what you set your mind to. . . .*

The sound of songbirds was thick in a nearby tree, and Rose tilted her head to watch them, feeling a bit awkward. Hen had come here to bare her soul.

They sat quietly and observed their father talking with the bishop and Christian near the entrance to his woodshop. Nick had returned—Rose hadn't noticed when—and glanced their way. Hen looked at Rose, seemingly nervous. "Is Nick eavesdropping on us?"

Rose almost made an excuse for him, but she kept still. Maybe he *was* eavesdropping.

Hen kept her voice to a near whisper. "You mustn't think poorly of me, Rosie. Please don't."

Rose looked at her sister. "Ach, my mind's just a-spinnin'—I can't help it."

The distinctive sound of a horse's hooves on the road was the perfect background to Hen's peculiar news. What Hen had told her about wanting to work at the Amish fabric store was the very last thing Rose had expected to hear from the sister who'd shunned her own people and upbringing to marry the English boy she loved.

"You and I both know what Brandon will say when you tell him," Rose ventured.

"Well, I'll have to sometime." Hen fussed with her plain-looking skirt, flicking off imaginary bits of lint.

"Your husband despises your Amish roots," Rose whispered, a lump in her throat. "You know that as well as anyone."

# CHAPTER 7

Wednesday morning Rose didn't have to wait around for her gray-haired grandmother to arrive from the larger of the two Dawdi Hauses next door. Mammi Sylvia came right over and began making blueberry muffins and scrambled egg and cheese sandwiches. Mamm smiled broadly, since she loved this kind of breakfast.

Mammi Sylvia took Mamm's smooth hands in hers, like Mamm was just a child, and leaned down to kiss her forehead. At times the way she treated Mamm made Rose wonder if she thought Mamm had regressed in her mind.

"You feeling up to hot cocoa with your breakfast, Emma?" Mammi asked.

Mamm's eyes lit up. "With some whipped cream?"

Rose had to smile. "And a cherry on top of that, jah?"

Mamm turned and nodded her head. "Sweets on sweet, I always say."

"Which reminds me, we should be havin' more snitz pie."

Mammi Sylvia went to the pantry and opened the door, peering inside. "Looks to me like you're nearly out of sugar."

"You need me to get some?" Rose offered.

"No, no." Mammi waved her hand. "I've got extra next door."

Having her mother's parents living on the other side of the wall from the main house was as handy as all get-out.

She eyed the wicker basket next to Mamm's wheelchair and thought of the market baskets and other items, including the tin money box, lost to the ravine the day the buggy tipped over and rolled. Sometimes, when Rose thought of it, she had to keep from marching down there in broad daylight to scour the craggy creek area. Surely Mamm's old tin was still sitting deep in there somewhere.

After a delicious, filling breakfast, Rose took the family buggy to Mr. Browning's, at her father's urging. She was hesitant to inconvenience Dat in any way. Mamm, of course, could ride with her mother anywhere she needed to go, if necessary, although it was doubtful Mamm would be going anywhere today. Rose knew Mamm was still hoping to attend Friday's birthday get-together for Mamm's older sister Malinda. All of them—Mammi Sylvia, Rose, and Mamm—were going up to Bart for some birthday cake and ice cream, and Dutch Blitz, a lively card game they liked to play. And a mystery meal was also planned. Rose loved a good mystery—craved them nearly as much as the wholesome romance novels she liked to read.

When she arrived at Gilbert Browning's farmhouse, Rose tied Alfalfa to the hitching post still there from a former Amish home-owner. Any of their other horses might have balked at being tied to the post for long. But she knew she could go about her work and return to find Alfalfa contentedly nibbling on the grassy row near the lane.

The landscape seemed to pour over her as Rose took in the enormous cornfields in several directions. The little woodshed to the side of the house had been piled with newly split logs just since she began working there.

She studied the house with its three prominent dormer windows facing the road, wondering when the exterior had last been painted white. The fact that electricity had been installed at some point made the clapboard house, with its peeling front porch, more comfortable for Mr. Browning, who had to be in his late fifties if he was a day.

She nuzzled the horse and gave her a sugar cube. If Rose found she was needed longer, she would free her from the buggy, but that always took extra time. Last week, she'd cleaned the kitchen so thoroughly she knew she would be primarily cooking today. She hoped Mr. Browning or his neighbor had purchased everything on the grocery list she'd jotted down last time.

One thing for sure, the man had a fondness for meals with chicken as the main ingredient. He'd insisted she make him fried or baked chicken, chicken salad, and chicken casseroles with noodles or rice. He was a man of peculiar habits, having explained that his late wife liked to cook lots of chicken dishes for him. So, for now, chicken it was.

Rose made her way up the front steps, noting the sagging front porch railing. She wished someone would sand, prime, and paint the whole porch, because a good sprucing up was definitely needed.

She knocked on the door, noticing Donna Becker, Gilbert Browning's neighbor, across the yard, shaking throw rugs. Donna gave Rose a jovial wave.

"Come over before you leave today, all right?" the dark-haired woman called. For a moment Rose considered the Englischer, whom she guessed was in her midthirties. Certainly the woman was older than Hen.

Rose agreed, smiling and waving back. "Might be ten o'clock or later till I'm finished here."

"By then you'll be ready for some warm cookies," Donna said as her fluffy white Old English sheepdog, Farley, came out onto the back porch.

"I'll look forward to it. Denki!" Rose turned back to the house just as Mr. Browning called from inside. She said, "Good mornin' to ya," as she pushed the door open.

Usually, he came to the door when she knocked or rang the bell, but today he was quick to say he'd had a bad night and was tired. "I'll try to make it snappy, then," she told him, setting about to wash the many dishes.

"I don't mean it's necessary for you to hurry." He tapped his black pipe on the arm of his oak chair. "Take your time."

She again recalled the bishop's grandson's tale and wondered where in this house the frogs and dead fishes had been discovered after the flood. A quick glance at Mr. Browning, and she doubted he felt up to talking about such things just now. She could only imagine where the critters had shown up. *If they had.*

She looked in the refrigerator and was pleased to find the items she'd requested. The fridge had been organized and cleaned, which surprised her, as she hadn't done a thing to it last time she was there. The butter was located in its designated spot behind the small compartment in the door, and so were the fresh eggs, all lined up in a neat row. The spills she'd noted last time had been wiped clean, as well. Had the man taken time to straighten up?

When she'd gathered the thawed chicken breasts, butter, and milk onto the kitchen counter, she glanced toward the pantry. "Do ya like brown rice or white better?" she asked, not turning to look at him.

"Doesn't matter, Miss Rose. Whatever you want to cook."

*Well, how about some pork chops or a nice juicy steak?* She smiled at herself, knowing she'd never talk up to him that way.

70

A quick trip to the pantry, and Rose found both brown and white rice on the shelves, along with several kinds of nuts, boxed cereals, and oatmeal. "Have you ever eaten homemade granola bars?" she asked, making small talk as she emerged. "I have a delicious recipe."

"What's in it?" he asked.

"Well, let's see—oats, Rice Krispies, marshmallows, and nuts, too. Oh, and sunflower seeds and coconut."

"Any peanut butter?" He suddenly looked chipper.

She smiled over her shoulder. "Yes, peanut butter and some honey, too."

"Sounds tasty."

"All right, then. I'll make up a nice batch for ya. You can nibble on them all week." First, though, she set to work making a large chicken casserole with brown rice to make it more filling to eat for several days. Next she mixed up the ingredients for the no-bake granola bars before readying his weekly dish of scalloped potatoes.

Once the side dish was in the oven, she cleaned the counters and the double sink. Then she swept and washed the kitchen floor, as well as the hallway that led to the first-floor bathroom.

After she had also scrubbed the bathroom, she returned to the kitchen to wash her hands. Looking over at Mr. Browning, she offered to dust and sweep in the small sitting room adjacent to the kitchen. It was the room behind the doorway where he always sat, like a guard. "Wouldn't you like more of the house cleaned today?" she asked, holding the broom and dustpan. "I'd be happy to."

"No, no . . . and besides, the sitting room rarely gets used." He gave an uncomfortable chuckle.

Rose wasn't one to argue with a man, yet it was apparent the dust stood thick on the lamp table not but a few feet from Mr. Browning's chair. "Looks like the tables could use a good dusting, at least."

He stared back at her. "There's plenty to keep you busy in the kitchen," he said, a gruff edge to his words.

Backing away, she didn't understand why he expected her to clean only the kitchen and one small bath. "What about your bedding and linens? Don't you want them washed?" At home, every Monday morning without fail, she and her grandmother stripped the beds to wash up all the sheets and towels, and every stitch of clothing from the week, then hung them out to dry on the clothesline. She had no idea when Mr. Browning had last done his laundry.

"I do my own washing," he replied, a hint of pain in his eyes.

She guessed he must be telling the truth, since he smelled fresh enough. Even so, she suspected the upstairs had to be languishing, not getting a thorough cleaning. "Just want to help out," she said, going back to sit at the kitchen table to write the next week's grocery list.

"Well, if you want to do something more, you can bake me a chocolate cake," he suggested, his tone more friendly. "Would you mind?"

"I know the best German chocolate cake recipe."

"I should've asked when you first came in." He seemed embarrassed.

"That's all right." She brightened and went to the pantry again, closing the narrow door after her in order to get to the shelving behind it, where the flour and sugar were kept.

She was startled by a rustling sound overhead as she reached for the flour. Looking up, she eyed the ceiling. "Hmm," she whispered, "maybe Mr. Browning has mice instead of frogs."

She carried the dry ingredients to the counter and set them down. Reaching for a clean measuring cup from the cupboard directly above her head, she couldn't remember having seen a single mousetrap anywhere along the kitchen floorboards. Didn't Mr. Browning know it was important to have several set in a drafty old farmhouse? Especially one situated on the very edge of a cornfield.

Glimpsing the man, she saw that his rounded chin had come to rest on his chest, and for a fleeting moment she pictured how his face might appear with a full beard like her father's.

She couldn't very well ask him about mousetraps at the moment. Sighing, she wrote on the grocery list for next week: *3 mousetraps.* He could read it when he woke up.

Quickly, Rose mixed together the ingredients for the cake, wondering if today was the lonely man's birthday. Or, if not that, then a "*special memory day,*" as Hen's best friend, Arie Miller, now Zook, used to say, back before she and Hen parted ways.

Whatever the cake represented to him, she hoped Mr. Browning wouldn't have to celebrate alone. For the life of her, she wished he'd wake up before she left the house in another hour or so, since now she had to stay to bake and frost the cake.

Once she'd put the cake in the oven, she set the timer and made the frosting. Then she wandered to the window and pinched off the dead heads on the African violets she'd brought over, and tested the soil for dampness.

She walked down the hallway on the south side of the sitting room that led to the back door and looked out past the woodshed, wondering if she'd have time to stop in and see Donna today, after all.

Standing in the doorway, she noticed the latch was locked. She took in the sweep of the large backyard, where a single rope swing hung from a gnarled old tree. Why had Mr. Browning chosen to rent such a large house? Was he accustomed to this much space in Illinois, when his wife was still living?

The rich chocolate aroma began to fill the house, beckoning Rose to return to the kitchen. She pulled out a chair and sat at the table, leaning her elbows there. Looking around, she was aware of not a single picture of Mrs. Browning anywhere—not even in the sitting room, which, truth be told, she'd peered into twice since working there. It wasn't that she was looking for anything in particular, but she had noticed the lack of photographs, especially of such a well-loved deceased spouse. The English folk she knew—her sister, Hen, included—had oodles of framed photographs sitting on tables and desks, and mounted on walls, too.

There *was* an interesting framed jigsaw puzzle on Gilbert Browning's wall, however. A majestic snowcapped mountain named Longs Peak near Denver, Colorado—a "fourteener" Gilbert and his late wife had climbed once. *"We loved a good physical challenge, the wife and I,"* he'd said proudly on Rose's first day of work. *"Wasn't the only mountain over fourteen thousand feet we conquered together. But it was our very first."*

He'd explained that, all in all, they'd hiked fifteen mountains in the "fourteener" category before his fortieth birthday. *"We were young then,"* he'd said. *"We called ourselves 'weekend warriors.' We would have hiked a mountain every weekend, if the Good Lord had allowed it."*

She'd gotten the distinct feeling that something had altered their passion for hiking mountains around the time Gilbert Browning had turned forty, though he hadn't said just what.

Later, after the cake had cooled enough to frost it, Rose bid Mr. Browning good-bye and let herself out, feeling rather sad the man would be alone with his memories for yet another week.

# CHAPTER 8

The sun was high overhead when Rose hurried down the steps and made her way across the side yard to the waiting horse. The mail carrier was coming up the road, stopping at the house two doors away.

Going to Alfalfa, she gently tapped her fingers on the mare's muzzle, caressing her. "I'll get you some water over yonder," she whispered, leaning closer again. She'd seen a well on the side of Donna Becker's house and assumed the friendly woman wouldn't mind if Rose gave her horse a drink.

She was looking forward to seeing Donna again, as she'd been invited before to her charming home, which was as snug and well kept as Gilbert's was drafty and untidy. She'd learned recently that Donna was a distant cousin of Arie Miller Zook through marriage. What a small world! The first time Rose had taken tea with Donna, Rose had been surprised to learn of the connection to Hen's former close friend. *Hen's best friend,* thought Rose as she watered Alfalfa and gave her a sugar cube.

Later, when they were having cookies with some raspberry tea with honey, near the kitchen window, Donna again brought up the relationship she shared with Arie, Rachel Glick's cousin. "Rachel has a job opening at her little fabric shop. She's been interviewing potential employees all week."

"Oh?" Right away, Rose thought of Hen. She hoped Donna might fill in the blanks, since Hen hadn't given her much to go on other than that she'd applied for the job.

"Can you keep a secret?" Donna said, eyes twinkling.

"I'm ever so *gut* at that." Rose smiled.

"Well, my cousin told me she's very excited about your sister, Hen. What a cute nickname!"

Rose nodded her head, explaining how her older sister had gone from Hannah to Hen as a youngster. "It's remarkable that any of us keep our given names, especially if we have younger siblings, ya know," she said, then sipped her tea.

Donna laughed. "Whatever her name, Hen made a very good impression on Rachel and the other clerk."

"I can certainly vouch for Hen's ability as a seamstress. And she knows what fabrics and colors Amish find acceptable."

Donna smiled. "Sounds like a good fit."

Rose laughed at the pun. She was curious how Donna's family had come to have an Amish cousin, but before she could ask, here came Farley, barking for a treat. Donna rose quickly and went to the counter, taking a treat from a cookie jar. "This one's spoiled . . . and not just a little."

"Hen really wants a puppy." Rose didn't know why she brought it up.

"I'll bet it's for her daughter, right?" Donna said. "Every child longs for a pet."

"I wouldn't be surprised." Rose thought Donna must know more about her sister than she was letting on. She steered the conversation to the reclusive neighbor. "How's Mr. Browning's health, do ya know?"

"Mental or otherwise?" Donna glanced out the window toward the older house. "I don't know what to do to help him. He sits and broods most of the time, at least when I've gone over with a pie or cookies. He must miss his wife, but it can't be good for him to hole up in that house."

Rose nodded her agreement.

"My husband invited him to go small-game hunting, but Gilbert declined."

"Maybe he's not a hunter," Rose suggested.

Donna reached for her tea. "Maybe not."

"Well, I baked a cake for him today . . . at his request." She paused, looking across the yard at Mr. Browning's house. "Might today be his birthday?"

"Who would possibly know? He has no friends that Roy and I've ever seen. He hardly says a word to us."

"Too bad, ain't?" Rose felt sad. "No close family, prob'ly."

"Not that I know of," Donna said. "Makes you count your blessings for a close-knit family . . . and good friends, too."

They continued sipping their tea, and then suddenly Donna put down her cup. "Come to think of it, there's an Amish fellow wandering about over there now and then."

This surprised Rose. "Doin' odd jobs, maybe?"

Donna nodded. "Mowing and raking and other light chores."

"Nice to know he has that sort of help." Rose looked at the stove clock and wiped her mouth with the dainty cloth napkin. "Well, thank you for the delicious tea," she said. "It was nice of you to invite me over." She went to look out at Alfalfa. "Goodness, you might not have to mow your side yard anytime soon!"

Donna clapped her hands and laughed when she got up to see. "You'll have to stop by with that horse more often."

Rose had to laugh, too. "Well, thanks again!"

On the way to the horse and buggy, she realized she'd forgotten to collect her pay from Mr. Browning and decided to run over to his house. Inside, the man's favorite chair was vacant, but her money was lying on the kitchen table. Not knowing if she ought to take it without letting him know, she went into the sitting room and stood at the bottom of the stairs.

Looking up, she opened her mouth to call to him, but heard his footsteps overhead, then water running. Rose couldn't help noticing again how badly the room needed dusting and, for a fleeting moment, she thought of cleaning it up right quick, while she had the chance.

Instead, she headed back to the kitchen to write a quick note, stating she'd returned for her day's pay. *I'll come again next Wednesday morning. I hope you enjoy the chocolate cake. If it's your birthday, have a real happy one!—Rose Ann K.*

With that, she left the house and picked up her long skirt as she ran back to Alfalfa and the waiting carriage.

≈

"I see you've been playing dress-up again."

Hen wished Brandon would keep his voice down. She moved to close their bedroom door.

"I don't want my wife looking Amish. Not ever." Brandon stared at her. "You're stunning with makeup, so what's with the washed-out look today?"

She held her breath, suddenly feeling faint. Did he truly dislike the person she was—the girl he'd met and married?

"Where are those cute sweaters I bought you?" He motioned toward the closet. "And the hundreds of dollars of sexy jeans?"

*Too tight fitting,* she thought. Aloud she said, "The sweaters seem so, well—"

"Revealing?" he said with a sneer.

She'd felt comfortable wearing them for only a couple of years after they were married. "I really can't wear those anymore."

"Can't . . . or won't?" He eyed her.

"Honestly, Brandon . . ." She couldn't finish. Truth was, she felt sinful parading around in those clothes. Maybe it was being a mother. Or maybe her upbringing had taken root at long last.

*Train up a child in the way that is right. . . .*

"So, are you comfortable in those long skirts you wear all the time?" he asked, shaking his head in disgust.

She couldn't refute it. "Yes, I am."

"C'mon, Hen. This is ridiculous." He moved swiftly toward the door, opened it, and headed into the hallway.

She felt discouraged, and after showering, she dressed for bed. Hen lay quietly under the covers, feeling the soft sheet beneath her fingers and reached slowly, inching across the king-size bed, missing the warmth of her husband. Much later, in her sleepy haze, she stretched farther, hoping he'd returned as she rolled closer to his side.

Not finding him in bed, she raised herself slightly to look at the clock on Brandon's lamp table—2:25 A.M.

Glancing again at the clock, she placed her hand on his pillow to see if it was warm. Perhaps he'd merely gone to the bathroom and would return soon. But his pillow was cool to the touch, and Hen wondered if it was possible he hadn't come to bed at all. She groaned softly, realizing he must have chosen to stay up working. *Or to stay away from me.*

When she finally fell back to sleep, Hen dreamed she was a little Amish girl again, playing with a favorite barn kitty. But in the end it was her daughter's wide eyes looking back at her, her wispy blond hair parted down the middle. She wore a pretty white prayer cap atop her head and held the old Kauffman family Bible in her small hands.

Hen heard Brandon's reprimand in the background of her dream. *"You left that life—for me."*

~

When Hen awakened to daylight streaming across the dresser and the wall beyond, she looked again for her husband's long frame but saw only his pillow and the smooth covers where he had not slept.

She felt apprehensive; there was a horrid kink in her neck as she pushed the blankets back and pulled herself out of bed. Fumbling for her slippers, she reached for her blue bathrobe at the foot of the bed and hurried to splash cold water on her face. When she reached for the hand towel and dabbed it against her cheeks, she looked into the wide mirror and wondered how to explain to Brandon what she was feeling. No, it was more than a feeling—she was experiencing something, a gnawing at her very soul.

Hen replaced the crimson-colored towel and stumbled across the floor to the small scale out of sheer habit. She hadn't gained a single pound since having Mattie Sue.

She wandered down the hall and out to the living area and kitchen, hoping she wouldn't find Brandon asleep at the breakfast table, his arms cushioning his head. She sighed as she looked for his usual spot for posting a note to her. Nothing.

She glanced in the living room, where the rumpled afghan on the sofa indicated he'd slept there, though she saw no sign of him now.

*He's gone to work early*, she told herself before looking in on Mattie.

Lining the hall on both sides were favorite photographs from her life with Brandon. Farther down the hall, baby Mattie Sue's sweet little face appeared in several lovely frames, and then the three of them together, the picture-perfect family. As much as Brandon had seemed to love their beautiful baby, he'd once told her he wanted only one . . . and no more than two. Hen, of course, had been eager to start a family. She'd even hoped she might be pregnant again recently but was sadly disappointed.

Staring at the picture of the three of them last spring, near their backyard forsythia bush, she wondered if some men, more than others, possessed a natural way with little ones. Her father came to mind. He had always been loving and warm, not as austere and rigid as some Amish fathers she'd known, including a couple of her own married brothers.

She remembered the first time Brandon had seen newborn Mattie Sue. He'd kissed her tiny peach of a cheek, tears sparkling in the corner of his eyes. *"She's beautiful, honey. Our baby looks just like you."* He'd kissed Hen, too, his tears wet on her cheek.

She smiled, the sweet memory lingering as she stepped into Mattie's colorful, cozy room. Soft pink and yellow floral designs adorned two of the walls, while the others were painted the palest shade of yellow Hen could find. Mattie was still sleeping, but a sunbeam peeked under one window blind and was spilling over her favorite dolls. *Like a blessing*, thought Hen, smiling sleepily as she sat on the edge of the small bed.

There were days, not so long ago, when she and Brandon had crept happily into this very room and stood holding hands, watching their darling girl in her slumber. Hen breathed slowly, recalling the times she'd asked to take Mattie to visit her Amish grandparents, only to have Brandon recoil as if he'd been slapped. *"What for?"* he'd asked when they were out of their daughter's earshot. *"Aren't you finished with that life, Hen?"*

He'd had every right to think that, given the joy she had exhibited on their wedding day . . . minus any Plain relatives. Hen had lived to regret not having her parents or Rose there to witness their marriage vows. What had possessed her to shut them out, breaking their hearts? Months later, Rose had traveled by horse and buggy to try and find Hen's new residence and gotten tearfully lost in the process. *"Didn't you want Dat's and Mamm's approval?"* her sister had asked, astonished. But to Hen none of that had mattered then.

Now she reached down to pick up Mattie's favorite stuffed animal—a soft brown puppy with a white spot around one eye.

*Foofie*. She placed the beloved toy on the bed near Mattie so her daughter could see it when she awakened.

Hen rose and shuffled back to the living room, still contemplating Brandon's night on the sofa. She picked up the afghan—the large, comfy throw made by her own mother, of all people—and folded it neatly.

*If Brandon's this upset now, how will he feel if I get the job at the Amish shop?*

# CHAPTER 9

The phone rang just as Brandon stepped into the house for supper that night. Hen reached for it as Brandon set down his briefcase to pick up Mattie Sue. "Hello," she answered, then was mortified to realize that Rachel Glick was on the line. *Such bad timing!*

Glancing toward the hall, Hen crept back to the master bedroom, listening as the fabric store owner chattered away, eager to know when she could start working. "I . . . uh, I'll have to let you know," she said quietly, wishing now she'd mentioned something to Brandon sooner.

"Well, I'll be needin' someone by this comin' Monday," Rachel said in her Dutchy-sounding voice.

Almost more than anything, Hen wanted to say she could be counted on to be there bright and early. "Can I call you back tomorrow?"

Rachel paused, undoubtedly confused at Hen's uncertainty. "All right, then," she said. "I'll wait to hear from ya."

Hen thanked Rachel for her patience, not daring to reveal that her husband could very well nix the whole thing.

All during supper Hen fidgeted, thinking ahead to the conversation she needed to have with Brandon. She wondered, too, why the subject of last night hadn't been addressed. *Why didn't he sleep with me?* Fortunately, Mattie Sue was especially amusing at the table, which captured Brandon's attention and gave Hen a bit of slack.

She and Mattie were clearing the table when Mattie asked again if she could have a real puppy. Hen, too, was fond of dogs and had thought of bringing up the idea to Brandon at some point. But tonight was definitely not the best time to discuss buying a puppy, even if she knew where to get the pick of the litter. "We'll talk about this later, honey."

Mattie Sue was not to be put off.

"Karen's daddy is getting *her* one." Mattie's lower lip protruded. "*Her* mommy thinks she's old enough."

"I didn't say you aren't, honey."

Her daughter batted her big blue eyes. "Can't we get one, Mommy . . . please?"

The whining and pleading were uncalled for. She and Rose had never carried on like this as youngsters. And if they had, well, her father—or Mamm, before her accident—would've nipped it right in the bud. More and more, the way Hen viewed her own childhood was evolving . . . as was the childhood she now wished for Mattie Sue.

"Sweetie, go get your coloring book, please."

"I want to talk about the puppy," Mattie insisted. "And my crayons are all broken." She began to sob.

Hen refused to let her daughter get the best of her. She looked around for Brandon, thinking he might entertain her while Hen loaded the dishwasher and cleaned up the kitchen. "Where's Daddy?" she asked, hoping Mattie might take the hint and go looking.

"Downstairs working." It sounded like *wahking*.

Hen wasn't sure when Brandon had slipped away, but with one quick look toward the stairs, she noticed the lights on in the family room. "Maybe Daddy will color with you," she suggested, although she guessed it was unlikely.

Mattie Sue plopped down on the kitchen floor and rubbed her fists into her eyes. "I really want a puppy. You'd get me one if you loved me. . . ." she whimpered.

Hen folded the dishcloth and placed it on the counter. *I won't tolerate this behavior*, she thought, heading for the bedroom. Quietly, she closed the door and sat on her side of the bed. "Mattie doesn't know how to obey," she whispered. Brandon's and her permissiveness had produced a self-indulgent child with little respect for parents. Sure, Mattie was still very young, but when Hen looked at her daughter, she saw so little of herself. *Hardly a speck of Christian rearing . . . because of Brandon's worldly influence. And mine.*

After a few minutes, Hen returned to the kitchen with new resolve, only to find that Mattie had taken her broken crayons and coloring book and gone downstairs after all.

~

After Mattie was comfortably tucked in for the night, Hen approached Brandon. Quietly, she sat at the breakfast table across from him, where he was having a piece of leftover pie. "Honey, can we talk?" she said when he looked up.

He put his fork down and folded his hands beneath his chin. "What's on your mind?" His light brown hair was mussed from raking his fingers through it. The soft blue of his eyes was faded, washed out from a hectic day.

The joy of having found the ideal job welled up in her, and Hen momentarily hoped he might be as happy as she was for herself. "I've been offered a job," she told him. "A really terrific one, Brandon."

A deep frown appeared on his face. "A job? You know you don't have to work."

She nodded. "But I *need* to."

A long silence ensued, and then he shook his head. "Are you bored at home?"

"Oh, Brandon . . . no. I love taking care of Mattie Sue." And she did. "It's just that—"

"You're restless?"

She looked down at the woven tan place mat, working up the nerve to share her inner thoughts. It was much more than a restless feeling. "I guess so. And to be honest with you, I feel like a fake," she said in a near whisper. "I want to reconnect with my roots."

He cleared his throat. "Your *roots*? What sort of job are we talking here?"

"Rachel's Fabrics—there's an opening for a clerk. She wants me to start this Monday."

"Hen," Brandon said, shaking his head, "that's an Amish store, right?"

"I really want to work there."

"That's not possible."

"I can see why you'd think that, but—"

"No, it's completely unnecessary."

"What about how I feel?" she asked. "Don't you care how I feel?"

Brandon leaned forward on the table, his eyes steely blue and bright. "I really don't want you to get sucked back into that life, Hen. Remember how you felt before we were married? You were so done with being Plain—at least you convinced me you were."

She remembered all too well. But she wouldn't admit to having made a mistake in leaving, because marrying him was a big reason for that. And she did not believe their relationship was a mistake. "I married you because I love you, not to escape my Plain life, if that's what you're thinking."

He shook his head. "You felt trapped, Hen . . . afraid you would be expected to help care for your mother. Afraid you wouldn't have your own life."

She suppressed the urge to cry. How dare he pull this out of a hat—the vulnerable thoughts she'd shared with her new husband a few weeks after they'd wed. "I didn't mean that I *only* married to get away from my family and my heritage, Brandon. You know better than that."

"Well, I can see where this is heading," he said more softly. "And I don't want to lose you to a life you despised."

Feeling all spent, she tried again. "The job's only part-time—a few mornings or afternoons a week." Their eyes locked. "Please, Brandon, can't I do this?"

"You mean until you get this out of your system?"

She couldn't answer; she felt so torn. She wanted to be completely honest, to share her concern about Mattie Sue's missing out on the simple gifts, the characteristics of obedience and kindness, generosity and tranquility . . . all the lovely things the Amish taught their children. But it was impossible for him to understand. Besides, it was unwise to bring her assessment of Mattie's needs into the equation tonight.

"Look, honey . . . you and I both know you're impulsive by nature. You run with what you want. You decided to go out with me on the spur of the moment—never blinked twice. You've lived your whole life like that."

"That's unfair."

He shook his head slowly, still looking at her. "But it's true."

"Maybe before Mattie Sue was born . . . but I'm not that way now." Hen fought the lump in her throat.

His mouth twitched, and Brandon pushed away from the table. "It's getting late."

"Yes." She sighed, feeling desperately sad.

They looked at each other, the tension between them so strong it was palpable. Brandon was beyond peeved, and Hen felt helpless and terribly frustrated.

She rose and began picking up the house, straightening magazines and tossing out snippets of paper. She stacked up the mail scattered around the coffee table and watered her plants. Then she washed her hands to make tomorrow's lunch for her husband. Once that was accomplished, she looked in on Mattie Sue, who was sound asleep. *Blissfully so.*

Heading back to the master bedroom, Hen found Brandon already sprawled out on the bed, asleep. She reached for her robe on the back of the bathroom door, careful not to bump the oval mirror nearby. Staring at the small crack on its surface, she had never forgotten the disoriented bird that had caused it, flying into the bedroom a few hours before she walked down the bridal aisle. As terrible as having a black cat walk across your path.

*Please, God, let me have a glimpse of the life I left behind. Don't let Brandon stand in my way. . . .*

# CHAPTER 10

*E*ven before the rooster crowed the next morning, Rose Ann flung off her bed quilt and went to find her writing paper and a nice pen. Padding over to the windows, she raised the shades and looked out to the south, where the pastureland sat like a large blanket between the bishop's property and her father's.

The day might bring rain; the pending dawn could not disguise the clouds. But Rose's spirits were bright—Mamm had announced last evening at supper that she felt well enough to attend Malinda's party today . . . which meant Rose should be free tomorrow evening to do as she wished.

Going to sit on the chair nearby, she reached for her current library book and used it as a little writing desk. She clicked the pen and began to write a reply to Silas Good.

*Dear Silas,*

*It was nice to receive your letter this week. I'll plan to meet you at the appointed spot tomorrow night. Hopefully this note will find its way to you in time.*

*Denki* for praying for my grandfather. He is indeed much improved, and we are all very grateful the Lord has restored him to us. *Mamm*, however, is very frail. She has suffered greatly this past year. Your prayers for her mean a lot to my family and to me.

Until we meet again.

Your friend,
Rose Ann Kauffman

Should she have closed the letter differently, perhaps with a *Most sincerely* or *Always?* Just to be on the safe side, Rose chose to follow Silas's lead in this.

～

Rose had always liked Aunt Malinda Blank's house, set back as it was on the sheltered side of Shady Road. Her aunt lived in her own Dawdi Haus, surrounded by trees and low-growing bushes—a small brick house so well hidden from the road some folk would get partway into the drive before they realized they had the wrong address, especially since her mailbox had no numbers on it.

*En aldi Maed*—an old maid—Malinda was reasonably proud of her single status. It was commonly known that she'd felt love wasn't just sacred for those who married. As a youth, she had lost her own dear beau to a barn fire, and she said the memory of their affection was enough to carry her through the rest of her life.

Since parties for a grown woman were rare, Rose guessed this must be a landmark birthday for her mother's sister. Yet Rose, polite as she was, did not ask her mother or grandmother Aunt Malinda's age as she guided the horse to the fence post. She supposed her aunt had reached the half-century mark.

Several buggies were already parked along the side yard as Rose tied the horse to the post. Malinda came out the back door, smiling and chattering, and invited them inside as if she'd known they were coming, even though this was intended to be a surprise party. She held open her ample arms to Rose and planted a kiss on her cheek, as she often did—seeking Rose out whenever there was a gathering. Mamm had shared privately that Malinda had felt a special connection with Rose since her infancy, when Malinda had come to the house to help out for a few days after the birth.

By the time all the birthday well-wishers had arrived at Malinda's, there were more than a dozen relatives and friends gathered in the front room. They sat in a wide circle on the wooden chairs brought in from the kitchen and some folding chairs from the main house, where Malinda's nephew and family lived. The birthday girl looked as vivacious and bright-eyed as always in her green dress and black apron. Her brownish-blond hair was graying only slightly at the temples and toward the front of her middle part.

The deacon's daughter-in-law, Nancy Mae Esh, slipped in next to Rose. "Would ya have time next week to watch my Abe for a morning?"

"Why sure, bring him over anytime," Rose said of Nancy's autistic son. "Happy to help out."

"Denki," Nancy Mae said. "Abe and his twin brother, Sam, surely need a break from each other." It would not be the first time Rose watched the deacon's special grandson. She enjoyed having him around.

In a short while, Rose went to help the other young women set up for a card game of Dutch Blitz. Out back, one of the large dogs barked and came right up to the back screen door, where it whined till Malinda poked her head out the door. "We've got company, Laddie . . . now go on with ya!" She shooed him off, then came back to start passing around small sheets of paper and pencils.

Malinda's niece by marriage—fair-haired Lydia Zook—took

over from there. "We can't eat our mystery meal till everyone guesses what these words stand for," Lydia said from across the room.

Rose had played this guessing game before and enjoyed seeing who worked extra hard to be creative enough to fool the luncheon guests. She scanned the list of descriptive words, smiling at some of the more obvious clues—she suspected some might not be food items at all. *Fence posts, Grandma's dandruff, honeymooning, rabbit snack, flour power, brown eyes, scratch, jiggle berries, rodent's glee, cow pies, red wheelbarrow wheels, and udder delight.*

Right away, she knew that Grandma's dandruff had to be table salt, and udder delight? She hoped that was ice cream and couldn't imagine anything else.

In a bit, Lydia announced it was time for everyone to put their papers and pencils under their seats to play Dutch Blitz, Rose's favorite game. The fast-moving game meant you could not blink an eye—not if you wanted to win. As there were plenty of decks of cards to go around, they divided into groups of three or four, and Mamm and Mammi appeared delighted to end up together, though each was wise to the other's tricks.

They were in the process of scooting their chairs into smaller groups when Lucy Petersheim arrived late, rushing into the front room. Catching Rose's eye, she asked if she could sit with her, and Rose agreed. "I hear you're doin' some cooking and cleanin' for Gilbert Browning," Lucy said while the cards were being counted into piles of forty for each player.

"I've only worked for him three times so far, since I'm goin' just once a week."

Lucy lowered her voice. "Not to be unkind, but do ya think he's a little strange?"

"He seems normal enough . . . quite sluggish, though. But I'd have to say he's harmless." Rose didn't mention hearing the mouse above the pantry. Lots of farmhouses had a running battle with rodents.

"Did he forbid ya to go upstairs?"

"Wasn't quite as blunt as that."

" 'Under no circumstances,' he told me."

Rose said that he *was* a little jumpy when she'd suggested dusting the sitting room or stripping his bedsheets.

"Oh jah, I know just what ya mean." Lucy nodded her blond head. "Honestly, he gave me the heebie-jeebies."

"Is that why you quit?" Rose studied her.

She leaned near Rose to whisper, "I daresay that old house is truly haunted."

"You mean it?" A shiver ran up Rose's back.

"Mighty creepy, 'tis."

Not one to get caught up in too much gossip, Rose was glad it was time to start the game.

Any thought of Mr. Browning was soon swept from Rose's mind as she became caught up in the rhythm of play. It turned out Lucy was one fierce player—she shouted "Blitz!" quite loudly, ending the game at their table. Mammi Sylvia called out the same within seconds at the table next to theirs.

Putting down her cards, Rose waited for the final tally from Lucy, thinking how much fun it would've been to have Hen here, too. She felt worried for her sister and wondered if Hen had any idea what havoc she might cause with her husband.

But then, Rose did not want to entertain such thoughts, afraid pondering them too hard might just make them come true.

Rose stared out the nearby window at the turning leaves of the trees along the road. The colors seemed more vibrant against the gray sky. Suddenly, out of nowhere, a young fellow dressed all in black came riding bareback across the vacant field. *Is that Nick?*

She must've made a sound, because Lucy turned to her and, seeing Rose staring outside, moved her head to look just as quickly. But Lucy had missed the black horse and its matching rider . . . so very swiftly they had passed.

"You all right?" Lucy asked Rose, who had returned to counting her cards.

"Jah—'twas nothing," Rose reassured her, yet spotting Nick or someone just as tall riding a driving horse in broad daylight made her ill at ease. The ministerial brethren weren't keen on driving horses being used for recreational purposes. If it had been Nick, might he know she was here and be sending her a message? Did he want her to go riding with him tonight, maybe?

Soon it was determined that both Lucy and Mammi Sylvia were indeed winners, and the other tables continued to play while these two tables shuffled cards and prepared to play again. Meanwhile, Rose dismissed her suspicions as ridiculous.

Even so, when the card games commenced again, Rose could not keep her mind on the game. Her thoughts turned toward a book she'd read years ago, when she was just a girl. She'd forgotten the title, but the childish story was about a pony named Misty who was content to graze the pastureland by day, but who broke through the fence each night to gallop wildly across the windswept moors.

*If the rider was Nick, why'd he ride past so boldly?* she wondered again. *Is he so brash, he doesn't care if he's caught?*

Her questions went around in her head during the mystery meal: lettuce, carrots, biscuits, sliced tomatoes, cheese, chicken, strawberry Jell-O, brownies, and ice cream. Of course, the one who got the most items correct earned an extra brownie!

Even so, the jumble of thoughts did not let up even as Rose turned the carriage toward home, oblivious to Mamm's and Mammi's chatter, or to the rain now making down. She fretted over the possibility Nick had been on that horse. Might he have been seen by someone who would tell the bishop?

And what about Lucy's jitters over the Browning house? *Haunted, she called it!*

Rose wondered what Silas Good might say about either subject.

He seemed like a level-headed sort of fellow, and she yearned to get to know him better. She wished she hadn't been so slow to accept his invitation for tomorrow evening. Hopefully she hadn't given him the wrong idea. She was eager to see him again—and to join the other youth in their festivities, as well—but she felt so disconnected from all that had gone on these months. What would it be like to go back now? Could Silas help Rose make sense of her life and her future? Truly she wished for far more than what she woke up to each morning. *Ever so much more!*

~

That afternoon, Rose Ann saw Nick over near the goat pen. She waited until she was certain no one was around to approach him, then took the letter from her pocket and held it at her side. "Any chance you might have an errand to run yet today over near the Goods' farm?"

Nick shrugged. "Maybe . . . why?"

"Here." She pushed the folded envelope into his hand. "Would ya mind putting this in their mailbox?"

"What for?"

"It's a letter, silly. If I send it by regular post, it won't reach the recipient in time."

Nick unfolded the envelope and read the address. "To Silas?" He paused. "Awfully forward, ain't?" He frowned as he studied her.

"He wrote me *first*."

"Well, why?"

"None of your business. Just make sure you get it over there before suppertime, jah?" Rose said, ready to return to her outdoor chores.

Nick shrugged. "I'll see 'bout that."

She groaned, then gave him a good look. "You're just pullin' my leg, ain't? You'll take it over, won't ya?"

"Say 'perty please with marshmallows and cream,' " Nick said, scowling. But there was a twinkle in his black eyes.

"I'll say nothin' of the kind!"

He chuckled. "Well, then, you'll just have to *hope* I can be trusted."

It was her turn to shrug her shoulders and smirk back. Rose knew Nick well enough to be assured that he'd do her bidding. He always did.

# CHAPTER 11

By Saturday, Nick's demeanor had turned as gray as the tattered work coat he liked to wear. Rose greeted him cheerfully all the same before she set to work freshening the bedding straw for the new foals, not bothering to attempt conversation. Back and forth, sunshine and shadows, this was Nick's pattern. On such days, she'd learned to just let him be.

She fed and watered the half-dozen goats Dat had taken to raising recently. Her father spent most of his afternoons in the shop, where he built all kinds of wagons—market wagons, bench wagons, pony carts, and the like. The bulk of his work was commissioned by neighbors in the church district. For those who were strapped for money, he might either charge a small fee or, occasionally, none at all. His generous nature was well known far and wide. Dat believed the Lord would supply his family's need if he was openhearted to those who were less fortunate.

Rose wished her father's manner might yet influence Nick. This day, however, Nick worked in close proximity to her without ever making eye contact. Rose's own spirits were high as she worked and talked gently to the beautiful new foals, stroking their silky manes . . . her hopes and dreams set on seeing Silas Good again.

*Tonight!*

~

Once the sun had slipped below the western hills, Rose managed to leave the house unnoticed. Wearing her best blue dress and white apron, both nicely pressed, she draped a long black woolen shawl over her arm and headed down the lane, toward the main road. She'd taken her hair down to brush it thoroughly before pinning it up again, wanting to look extra nice for Silas, who would also be wearing his for-good clothes for their Saturday-night date.

*He'll probably get nominated for deacon or preacher by the time he's thirty,* she thought, turning onto Salem Road, her arm brushing against her skirt. *Even Dat would say Silas is cut out to draw the divine lot someday.*

In a few minutes, she should see his pretty chestnut mare and open black buggy. And Silas himself, blond, tall, and handsome as any fellow she'd ever known, standing on the shoulder near the carriage, waiting just for her.

She willed her heart to slow its beat. Fondly, she recalled her first ride home from a Sunday Singing with Silas, just last year. He'd seen her home a few times after that, but she'd been so haphazard about attending the youth activities this year, she was still a little surprised he hadn't found himself a steady girl by now. *Am I to be that girl?*

A horse and buggy passed by just then. The carriage was filled with children, some perched on their parents' laps, others loaded into the back. Rose wondered what it would be like to be blessed with so many children. As a young girl, Rose had played with baby dolls until she was altogether certain Mamm would think her too old to do so. Oftentimes Rose would wait till the gas lamps were all blown out before secretly retrieving her dolls from her dresser

98

drawer. Quietly, she tucked them into her bed, whispering to them after her silent bedtime prayers.

But Rose hadn't been able to hide her fondness for dolls—or young children—from her only sister. So when Mattie Sue was born, it broke Rose's heart to think she wouldn't see her new niece very often. She'd never forgotten how it felt to hold darling Mattie hours after her birth—Rose had gone with Dat and Mamm that once to the hospital. The touch of a baby's grip on her finger was unforgettable.

Oh, that she might someday be a good and kindhearted mother to her own little ones! Next to being married, this was her dearest hope. Perhaps belonging to a large family accounted for her desire for many babies. She wondered whether Hen and Brandon would have more children, or if Mattie would remain an only child, like Nick had once been. Rose could not imagine being so alone . . . nor would she ever wish it on anyone.

The sight of Silas at that moment caught her almost off guard. The blond bangs that peeked from beneath his straw hat shimmered like gold in the moonlight, and he beamed an enthusiastic smile as he moved toward her, taking her hand as he helped her into the carriage. "Rose Ann," he said, like a special pronouncement. There was something exceptionally nice about the way he said her name.

When they were settled together in the seat, Silas lifted the reins and clicked his tongue. The horse pulled them slowly forward without the slightest jolt, reminding Rose that Silas was a masterful carriage driver, among other things. He could easily handle a team of eight field mules, too. Although Silas had never spoken with her about the details, she knew from the grapevine that he was set to take over his father's farm. And she thought he would be a good and honest farmer, as well as a wonderful husband and father.

"I received your letter yesterday," he said. "But I didn't see a postmark."

"Hand delivered," she replied quickly.

"It was awful nice." He smiled, tall next to her in the buggy seat. "Denki, Rose."

She smiled back, careful not to sit too close, so as not to bump him while he held the reins. She wanted to be as ladylike as Silas's own sisters.

Being proper with a young man while courting—not like the tomboy Rose had been in her younger years—wasn't something Mamm had ever discussed with her. Despite the years of being apart from her sister, she'd gleaned what she could from Hen, who had been attended to by several nice Amish boys before Brandon came along. These days Mamm was more interested in reading the Good Book or having it read to her than she was in the mysteries between a beau and his girl. The pain Mamm endured doubtless occupied the majority of her thoughts, and though she tried, Mamm could not hide from Rose the grimace or sudden catch in her breath as she reacted to it without complaint.

*If only more could be done for her . . .*

Rose breathed in the cool night air, thankful Silas had invited her. "Thanks for mentionin' my mother in your letter," she said into the stillness.

"My sister-in-law Naomi says she heard your mother can't tolerate any type of pain medicine."

"That's true . . . sadly. It unsettles her stomach." She wondered how much she should say. "Poor Mamm just grits her teeth when the worst comes."

Silas shook his head slowly. "Must be terrible for her. And you, too."

She wondered if he had responded in that way because of mere sympathy. Or . . . was he thinking about their future as a couple, and Rose's concern for her mother's care, perhaps? Oh, she could only hope!

On the other hand, she didn't want to be foolish and jump to conclusions. There *was* the real possibility he was simply making polite conversation. After all, Silas was the most well-mannered fellow she'd ever known, with an upbringing that was an example to many. Silas's grandfather, Reuben Good, had become so well integrated into his adopted Plain community that most folks soon forgot he was ever an Englischer. His many children, including Silas's father, Reuben Jr., were devoted to the Lord God and *Das alt Gebrauch*—the Old Ways. Other than Silas's family, Rose knew of no other Goods who were Amish in all of Lancaster County. There were some who were Plain, but none were Old Order.

They traveled for another stretch of road before Silas asked, "How would ya like to spend part of the evening at Jonathan and Naomi's place?"

"Sounds nice."

His married brother and sister-in-law had invited them for a game of Ping-Pong and homemade ice cream one other time. Rose had so enjoyed that visit, especially because they had the dearest twin boys ever. She had helped Naomi by dressing one of the twins—she wasn't sure whether it was Leroy or Davy—in his homemade sleeper. To think the boys had just turned three last month, and like some twins, they talked in their own made-up language. Rose had gotten a chuckle out of seeing the two of them conspiring together at the common meal following Preaching service. No one, not even their mother, could understand them.

"I wonder if the twins will still be up," Rose said quietly.

"Wouldn't be surprised." Silas smiled down at her. "Naomi knows how fond you are of them."

*Does she also think I'm fond of Silas?*

Rose blushed and she leaned against the buggy seat, enjoying the sway of the carriage as Silas's horse pulled them forward at a nice clip. The sound of the horse's hooves on the pavement created a relaxing rhythm, and she delighted in this pleasant reprieve from her responsibilities.

Several of her older brothers thought Rose was a mite too sheltered, spending as much time at home as she did. And, too, they thought she had taken the vow to consecrate her life to God and the church too young. Yet Rose had been sure of her choice—she'd done it for Mamm, wanting to bring some peace to her mother's poor, troubled heart back then.

There *were* times now when she wondered if she had done the right thing. But Nick had once told her it was a good thing she joined at fifteen, lest she run herself too wild during her "running-around years" and fly right out of the church. Like Hen.

*Puh, there's no chance of that happening!* After all, a vow was a vow.

Glancing at Silas, Rose felt so happy to be here with this wonderful-good fellow. While other couples took advantage of the longer evenings to ride up and down the back roads, late into the night, Silas was one to thoughtfully plan their evening together, limiting their time alone in the buggy to the drives to and from their destination. If Mamm ever inquired about this, Rose could say that her beau—if she could consider him such—was indeed honorable. Surely this was a concern for nearly every mother in the church district.

"Do ya like peppermint in your ice cream?" Silas asked as they neared Jonathan's farmhouse.

"Oh jah," Rose said. "And I like making it almost as much as eating it." She hoped they might take turns turning the crank on the ice cream maker.

The barn and other outbuildings came into view, and Silas reached for her hand as they entered his brother's lane. The feel of his leather glove against her own bare hand made her feel safe somehow.

"What's your favorite flavor?" she asked.

"Definitely chocolate."

There was no yard light at Jonathan Good's house as there was next farm over at the Mennonite neighbors', and Rose was grateful for the large flashlight Silas held to light their way. She stepped down from the buggy into his strong arms, but they were around her for only a second.

"Wouldn't be surprised if Naomi's made your favorite treat," he said as they walked across the yard.

"Brownies?" She smiled back at him, and he reached for her hand again. Her heart sped up. The thrill of his big, warm hand around hers surprised her no end. Just then, she realized he'd removed his gloves, and she pressed her lips closed to keep from smiling too broadly.

"We'll have us a *gut* time tonight," Silas said as they approached the back walkway leading to the porch.

*Jah, because we're together,* Rose thought merrily.

# CHAPTER 12

Brandon rattled the newspaper as he read while Hen hung up her jacket in the entryway closet. She and Mattie Sue were late getting home again, and Hen glanced at Brandon, hoping she could somehow make it up to him. She had stayed longer at Diane's than she'd planned, talking girl talk when she had stopped to pick up Mattie Sue from Karen's birthday party. "I'm going to put my dolly to bed," Mattie Sue said, running off to her room.

Hen nodded absently, realizing she had a challenge on her hands, the way Brandon was snapping the paper around. He was obviously upset and would eventually ask when she was thinking about making supper. Things could rapidly deteriorate from there.

"Sorry, hon, the day just got away from me." She hurried to the kitchen and took some leftover turkey out of the refrigerator. Then she turned on the radio on the counter, scanning for something other than news.

She recalled how delighted Rachel Glick had sounded when

Hen called her yesterday morning, as promised. Against Brandon's wishes, she'd accepted the job.

Her husband closed the newspaper and folded it. "There's an interesting article here about attention deficit disorder in adults."

"Really?"

He carried the paper into the kitchen and placed it on the bar. "I'd like you to read it."

"Sure." Hen kept busy, hoping he wouldn't decide to camp out right there. She didn't enjoy having people watch her make meals, not even her husband.

"I've been thinking," he said more softly. "This job you're dying to take . . ."

She looked up, heart in her throat, and searched his eyes. "You don't mind, then . . . if I start working?"

"Actually, I was thinking that if you're so eager to bring in some extra money, why not find a stay-at-home job? I've circled several options in the paper." He locked eyes with her.

"I guess you didn't hear me the other night."

Brandon turned to look out the window. "Hen . . . honey, is this some sort of crisis you're having?"

Tears stung her eyes. "I know, I know . . . I don't *need* to work, at least according to our budget." She paused and leaned down to get a pan out of the cupboard. "But I'd really like to take the job at the store. I want to do this."

"So much for submission," he shot back.

"Oh, now, that's not fair. You know I was never the most obedient Amish girl." She sighed, trying to think what she could say that might make sense to him. "But I do miss my Plain life, Brandon. Or parts of it."

He dug his hands into his pockets and jingled his coins.

"I love you . . . this isn't anything about us, really." She hesitated. "Working at the Amish store really might be the answer for me." It was the best compromise she could think of.

But a craving for the peace of her former life wasn't the only impetus behind wanting to work at Rachel Glick's shop. Hen felt strongly that Mattie Sue needed more than a mere glimpse of the tranquility of Plain living she got during their infrequent visits to her parents' home.

Brandon picked up the paper again. "Hen, take a look. There are lots of terrific jobs listed here."

She held her breath, then said, "I told you what I'd like to do."

"And I'm not in favor of it." He gave her a sidewise glance. "You left the Amish for a reason."

She placed the lid gently on the pan and set the burner to medium. Turning to face him, she said as sweetly yet as firmly as she knew how, "Don't you care how I feel, Brandon?"

He chuckled. "How *you* feel?" He moved around the counter, coming to her, arms outstretched. "I married a girl who wanted my life. *Mine*, Hen. How could you have forgotten?"

She hadn't, but the memory of how easily she had cast aside all she had ever known pained her now. Every enticing aspect of the modern life she'd desired—a comfortable house, a beautiful car, pretty clothes—had come with her marriage to Brandon.

"I won't let you return to the very thing you despised." He slipped his arms around her waist and drew her near. "We'll have another baby—wouldn't you like that?" He leaned down, head tilted, his breath on her ear. "Wouldn't you?"

Hen didn't know if he was being tender or baiting her. "I'd love more children—you know that." She let him kiss her cheek. "But right now, I really want to work at Rachel's Fabrics."

Brandon pulled back, holding her at arm's length. "I've always liked your spunk," he said. "But tonight you're impossible!"

She cringed.

"I want you to let this job go, Hen." With that, he gradually released her and then left the kitchen for the downstairs family room.

Clenching her teeth, she stood next to the sink, her heart pounding in her ears. There were days—and nights, too—when she thought of nothing else but her former life. All the good aspects of it, and everything Mattie Sue was missing. Yet she also wanted to be a loving wife to Brandon. So she had seen the part-time job as something of an answer to her dilemma. *Why can't it work?*

Her husband had just forbidden her to take the job, and there was no getting him to surrender. Hen was stuck—either she obeyed him or she followed her heart . . . and defied him.

Her breath caught in her throat as she rushed after Brandon, coming to a stop at the top of the stairs.

Mattie Sue's sweet voice rose from the family room. "Daddy, will you play a game with me?"

Hen sighed, refusing to create a scene. Besides, she was drained emotionally. Her throat ached with tears that threatened to come.

She made her way down the stairs as Brandon switched on the TV and sank into his favorite chair. Horror rose in her at the sight of Madonna prancing seductively on the screen in a revealing wedding gown of sorts, singing "Like a Virgin." *Oh, dear Lord, no!* It was all Hen could do not to speak her mind as she had in the past. She wanted to go over there and turn off the wickedness pouring into their house. *Into our daughter's mind.*

What she wouldn't give to unplug the "one-eyed monster," as Bishop Aaron Petersheim had sometimes referred to a television.

Clenching her jaw, Hen waited for the seemingly endless music video to finish. She looked at precious Mattie Sue, who was carrying her game to the sofa. Then, seeing Madonna on the screen, Mattie Sue dropped her game and broke out in song as she picked up Karen Perlis's Barbie doll from the sofa. Hen had never seen the matching Madonna bridal gown before, yet there it was on the shapely doll, and now, to her dismay, Mattie Sue began moving the doll around to the sensual rhythm of the song, keeping time with the worldly woman . . . to Brandon's seeming amusement.

She bit her lip, deciding once more it was best not to speak her mind. Not now. Turning, Hen hurried back up to the kitchen, tears prickling behind her eyes. She thought of the psalm: *I will set no wicked thing before mine eyes.* She went to the cupboard and reached for three dinner plates with trembling hands and carried them to the breakfast nook.

*"It's no big deal,"* her husband had insisted days before when they'd argued about MTV yet again. *"Mattie doesn't know what she's singing, anyway—does she, Hen?"*

"How can he abide this in our daughter?" she whispered now. *"How?"*

When she set down the third plate on her own cloth place mat, something snapped in her—everything converging in her at once. She'd experienced this sudden flash of rancorous emotion before, the night her father forbade her to marry Brandon. The bitter feelings had propelled her right out of the house, after the gas lamps were extinguished and her parents and Rose Ann had gone to bed. Hen had run straight to the phone shanty, dashing barefoot all the way, and phoned for Brandon to come and get her.

Looking down now at the dinner plates, she knew that if she followed her impulse this minute, she might not finish making supper tonight. She might also regret switching off the burner and heading like a hornet to Mattie's room. But at the moment, Hen didn't care about the consequences. She went to her daughter's closet and pulled down the little suitcase and started stuffing in her pajamas and a set of clean clothes. She felt an urgent need to save her little girl from MTV and all the other distressing things Brandon allowed into their home.

*He doesn't know the first thing about holy living—or child rearing!*

∼

When Rose arrived home from her date close to eleven o'clock, she was shocked to see Hen's car parked near the woodshed. A strand of dread ran through her as Silas walked her to the back door.

*Why's Hen here at this hour?*

"Did ya have a nice time?" Silas paused near the step, his eyes crinkling as he looked at her.

"Ever so nice."

His face burst into the dearest smile. "You're very sweet, Rose."

She put her head down, the blood rushing to her cheeks. "Denki," she said quietly, hoping she was doing right by acknowledging his compliment.

Was he leading up to the courtship question? She certainly didn't think this was leading to his popping *the* question—not as proper as he was about everything else. Surely he would approach that like any other Amish young man, by shining his flashlight on her window and asking her to be his wife in the privacy of the house.

When she raised her head, he was still smiling. Then, tapping his straw hat rather comically, he said, "*Gut Nacht*, Rose Ann . . . till next Sunday Singing. I hope you'll be there."

*A whole week away.* Though she felt quite *ferhoodled*, she thoroughly enjoyed this newfound giddiness. Silas waved fondly and she watched him hurry down the lane to the road, where he'd left the horse and buggy. Oh, to think Silas Good liked her . . . and very much, too!

*Maybe he's ready to get serious and settle down!* she thought, not wanting to move from the spot.

Silas had just turned twenty-one, after all. Like her, he'd joined church several years earlier, so he didn't have to wait to be baptized to move ahead with marriage. She suddenly felt peculiar about rushing ahead in her thinking.

Turning toward the house, Rose's gaze fell on Hen's car again.

When she let herself into the house and tiptoed upstairs to her bedroom, she could not believe her eyes—Hen and little Mattie Sue were sound asleep in her bed. "Goodness' sakes," she whispered, baffled. "They're stayin' all night?"

Then, lest she awaken them, she carefully opened her drawer to find her nightgown and noticed the pile of quilting squares there on the dresser, the ones for the wall hanging Hen wanted to make for Mattie's room. Wondering why Hen had brought them, Rose carried her nightclothes downstairs to the room where her mother rested by day.

*Hen and Mattie Sue . . . here?*

It didn't take long for her to surmise the possible cause as she lay on Mamm's daybed, covered by three layers of homemade quilts. Most likely Brandon had rejected the idea of his wife's working in the Amish community. But what could've possessed him to ask Hen—and Mattie Sue—to leave?

Rolling over, she didn't care to contemplate Hen's plight anymore. It blemished her wonderful-good evening with Silas. Oh, she wanted to hold this date near to her heart . . . cherish their night under the white full moon, with the invisible nocturnal creatures humming their lovely song all around them.

*Glory be*, Rose thought, not one bit sleepy. *O Lord, do I dare trust my heart?*

# CHAPTER 13

Hen awakened early to the medley of frogs and birds. How long had it been since she'd really listened to the sounds of morning? Lying next to Mattie Sue, she looked affectionately at her little girl, all curled up in a soft bundle there in Rose's bed. The happy memories of growing up in this house came rushing back—of learning to cook with her mother and Mammi Sylvia, of helping to whitewash the fences with Rose, and of gathering eggs with her best friend, Arie, whenever she'd spent the night.

*"Idle hands are the devil's workshop,"* her mother had often said. So Hen had kept busy from dawn to dusk, just as all the good folk of the church district did.

If any leisure time was left, it was spent walking in the meadow, visiting relatives, or going over to the little Quarryville library behind the police station to check out library books with Rose. Certainly there was no television or radio to lure them to sin.

*Or MTV!*

She lifted a strand of Mattie's pretty hair from her cheek,

slipping it behind her tiny ear. "I want you to learn the Old Ways," she whispered. "My already too-fancy girl."

The thought of asking God to forgive her for deserting His ways crossed Hen's mind. She lay there, keenly aware of her sins against the Almighty One.

She let her eyes roam about the room where she and Rose had made up fanciful stories and said their prayers before falling asleep in this very bed. The place where she'd ultimately revealed the secret of her forbidden beau. *"I really love Brandon,"* she remembered saying to her wide-eyed sister.

She and Rose Ann had been close from the day of Rose's birth, when her mother had asked Hen to help name the pretty little baby girl who'd arrived at the end of a whole string of brothers and one sister. At just five years old—*close to Mattie's age*—Hen had taken her baby sister in her arms and looked down at the tiny pink face. *"She's a rosebud"* was the first thing out of her mouth.

Delighted, Mamm had agreed the baby's name was to be Rose. Ann was added for her mother's sister Anna, although her mother had been concerned people might end up calling her Rosanna instead. Yet it was their mother who had begun referring to Rose as Rosie, dropping the middle name Ann altogether.

Hen shifted to face the windows, looking through the narrow space between the shade and the windowsill to the old oak tree, its branches nearly close enough to touch the house. Nature was on the very brink of turning to radiant autumn. *The glory of fall.* She brushed away a tear as she recalled her youthful love for that one beautiful and impulsive season.

It had been in early October that she'd attended her first Singing. Eli Mast had driven her home that night. The hardworking boy had raised a variety of animals—goats, sheep, peacocks, and all kinds of chickens—with his father and older brothers. Eli was pleasant enough, even a good conversationalist. But she hadn't felt a speck of emotion for him, daydreaming instead about the outside world and what it might have to offer. It wasn't any wonder that Eli had eventually lost interest in her.

Other Amish boys had followed, but no one had captivated Hen's imagination—or her heart—until Brandon Orringer had rescued her from the blizzard.

"And the rest, as they say, is history," she muttered into her pillow, assuming Brandon would be fuming about now. She'd told him she needed some time alone and would be heading to her father's before ushering confused little Mattie out of the house and into the car.

Reliving the scene now, Hen was surprised her husband hadn't tried to talk her out of leaving. Perhaps when she returned, he would not confront her about staying the night with her family. Not a single time since they'd married had he come with her to visit here, nor had he accompanied her and Mattie Sue to see her brothers and their families. Only once, when they were first engaged, had Brandon ever stepped foot into her father's house.

*My dear childhood home . . .* Her own radical change in perception was startling.

Mattie stirred in her sleep, and Hen stroked her long hair. Eventually they would return home, and Mattie Sue would once again be exposed to all the unwholesome forces Brandon thought of as simply entertainment. How was Hen going to protect her child's heart—her very soul—with Brandon working against her?

As for herself, tomorrow marked the start of Hen's job. Allowing her to work at Rachel's Fabrics was the least Brandon could do. And if he truly understood her motivation, he certainly would.

Looking again at her daughter's sweet face, Hen was torn. The job would fulfill *her* need, but it would do little for Mattie Sue. She couldn't take her away from Brandon like she had during last night's meltdown.

Getting up, she found her robe and slippers and crept down the hall to the large bedrooms that had been occupied by her brothers before they married. One of the rooms had been set up as a sewing and craft area, but the other room was entirely vacant, a shell waiting to be filled. She wondered why her parents hadn't furnished it for guests.

Moving toward the stairs, Hen assumed her sister had slept in Mom's daybed downstairs. Feeling a little guilty for taking over Rose's bed, Hen looked in on Rose, who was just waking up, burrowed beneath the quilts. "Good morning, sunshine," she said, going to sit on the edge of the bed. "I hope you don't mind giving up your room last night."

Rose yawned and stretched her arms. "Well, I won't if I get it back," she said. "But, seriously, you have me worried, sister."

Hen looked away, suddenly unsure of herself.

"You didn't run away from home, did ya?" Rose reached for her hand.

Hen grimaced. "I was much too hasty," she whispered, sorry for what she'd done.

"You're married now, Hen. You have to make lemonade . . . or however the saying goes, jah?"

Hen considered that. "I miss spending time with my family." She paused. "Something's changed in me. I really don't know when it happened."

Rose stared, her big blue eyes boring a hole in Hen's heart. "You *are* returning home today—going back to your husband?"

Hen nodded. "Sooner or later."

"Won't he be worried?"

"Well . . . Brandon knows where Mattie Sue and I are staying."

"He let you?"

She sighed. "We were very guarded about what was said in front of Mattie Sue."

"Poor little girl." Rose sat up in bed. "So, are you helpin' Mammi Sylvia make breakfast this fine mornin'?"

"This must be a no-Preaching Sunday, then?"

"Jah."

*Perfect*, thought Hen as she rose and went to the door. "I'll wake up Mattie Sue—she'll want to help make the pancake batter."

Rose pushed her waist-length hair back over her shoulders and offered a worried but faint smile as Hen left the room.

Emma was frowning at him as Solomon opened his eyes and awakened from a deep sleep. As his wife always wanted the shades up, the dawn was already inching into the room, about to spill forth with sunshine. She liked the shades that way even at night—*"so I can see the stars,"* she would say.

"You all right, dear?" He reached for her slight hand.

"Our prodigal's returned," she said, sniffling. "Hen seemed to be cryin' last night, when she first arrived. Did ya see?"

He'd noticed the swollen red eyes, all right. His heart had lurched, seeing Hen's car pull into the lane yet again. Right away, he knew it wasn't a good sign. *Especially her staying the night.*

"I'm betwixt and between, Sol," whispered Emma, her lower lip trembling.

He touched her ashen face.

"Never thought we'd see this day."

He hadn't expected it, either. Yet, here they were with Hen—and her little girl—in the house she'd run from more than five years ago. Oh, the years of sorrow that had ensued for the daughter they'd lost. *Lost to us . . . to God and the church.* "What's a father to do?" Sol's throat ached, but so as not to worry Emma, he pulled himself together.

Getting up from the bed, he went to the window and looked down at the barnyard. Soon the sky would brighten and another Lord's Day would begin.

"How long will she stay?" Emma said from the bed.

He turned around. "The question is: How long do we dare let her?"

" 'Tis a knotty problem." Emma coughed twice and he went to her, lifting her gently out of bed and carrying her in his strong arms to the upholstered chair he'd placed nearby for her comfort. He lowered her into the seat and reached for her favorite eggshell-colored afghan to lay over her lap.

"Might it be just a lover's quarrel?" he suggested, but the gnawing in his stomach told him differently.

"Hope so." Emma folded her hands and began to move her lips silently in prayer.

Befuddled, Solomon headed down the hall to the bathroom the bishop had allowed them to install following Emma's accident. "The Lord's sure got His hands full with our Hen," he whispered.

# CHAPTER 14

*H*en had planned to return home soon after the breakfast dishes were washed and dried and put away, but Arie Zook and her mother, Ruth, dropped by, of all people. Hen flinched as they walked toward the house, carrying a pie basket. The two hadn't spoken since Hen had run off to marry Brandon. Oh, but she should've known she would bump into Arie eventually.

*How will Arie react to seeing me?*

Surely the pending encounter wouldn't top the awkwardness of the breakfast she'd just endured, despite the delicious pancakes and eggs. She stiffened, recalling how Dawdi Jeremiah had studied her with a searing gaze, then looked sympathetically at Mattie Sue. No doubt he and everyone else were dying to ask what the world they were doing there without Hen's husband, staying the night like that.

She could just imagine the words buzzing around in his head. But it was her dad's inordinate emphasis on the weather during the meal that had been really annoying. Her sister had seemed to pick up on the strange dynamic happening at the table—at one point,

Rose had even rolled her eyes at her. No, today's meal had been nothing like the other evening at supper, when the atmosphere had been so relaxed and joyful, full of pleasant small talk.

*They must think I'm ferhoodled, leaving my English life for even a single night.*

Freckle-faced Arie stepped inside the house behind her mother, her reddish brown hair neatly swept up in a bun beneath her Kapp. Petite Arie hadn't changed much at all since Hen had last seen her.

Quickly, Hen put on a smile. She wondered what her former friend might be thinking of her, but there was no addressing that, of course. She'd always hoped there might come a day when Arie would forgive her—accept her as an Englisher. But when Arie caught her eye, she looked away.

Ruth gave a curt nod to Hen, then promptly lost herself in conversation with Hen's mother there in the middle of the kitchen. Holding her breath, Hen felt nearly as if she weren't present. Yet she couldn't blame Arie for rejecting her. After all, Hen had abandoned their friendship, even breaking their girlhood pact.

Sighing, she remembered the sun-dappled August morning she and Arie had gone together to BB's Grocery Outlet, not far from Quarryville, to pick up several cases of dented canned goods for Hen's ailing aunt. It was during the buggy ride there they'd promised to be each other's wedding attendants when they were brides. Hen had even suggested they have a double wedding, if it happened they got engaged around the same time.

"How about I serve up some of this pie, Emma?" Ruth's voice interrupted Hen's reverie. And just that minute, Mattie Sue came flying into the kitchen, her grin revealing that she'd heard about the unexpected treat.

"Aren't we still full from breakfast?" Mamm said, a twinkle in her eye.

"One small sliver won't add too many pounds," Ruth said and went to the utensil drawer to get the knife.

Hen wished she'd taken Mattie home immediately after breakfast. *What now?*

Rose was already setting dessert plates out and placing them around the table. Glancing at her, Rose pointed to a spot. *She's telling me to stay,* thought Hen, scooting onto the wooden bench with Mattie Sue next to her. *As a barrier . . .*

Everyone else gathered at the table, as well. Hen thought of saying something to Arie, but she decided not to force conversation. *If Arie only knew how much I miss Amish life . . .* Hen sighed, eager for this encounter to be over.

As soon as she'd finished the apple pie, Mattie Sue asked to go and see the barn kitties. "Please, Mommy?"

"We're heading home soon," she said quietly, getting up from her place on the bench.

Mattie pouted. "Aw, Mommy, why?"

*Here we go again,* she thought, hoping Mattie wouldn't cause a scene. *Especially not now.*

"You've seen the kitties this morning already," she said gently, taking her daughter by the hand and moving toward the stairs. When she got to Rose's room, she closed the door behind them. "Listen to me, Mattie Sue . . . you will not argue when I ask you to do something. Do you understand?"

Mattie backed away and went to sit on the floor—her typical response. At least she did not thrash her arms and throw a fit, but she was already starting to cry. "I want to go home!"

"We're leaving right now." Hen began to pack their belongings. She put Mattie's two dolls in her daughter's arms and asked her to carry them. Thankfully she obeyed without complaint. Hen was glad to have the chore of loading up the car to occupy them, in spite of the embarrassment of having to haul their suitcases past Arie and her mother. The pair was still sitting at the kitchen table as Hen and Mattie went through the kitchen and out the back door.

Rose came running after them. "I don't know how they knew yous were here visitin'," she said breathlessly.

"Well, maybe they didn't. Maybe it was just a coincidence."

Rose shrugged. "The grapevine's a fast communicator, though. Someone might've spotted your car."

"That's all right." Hen got Mattie Sue settled in the backseat, then closed the door. "It really doesn't matter."

Rose hugged her. "Did ya say good-bye to Dat yet?"

"No . . . should I?"

"Might be a *gut* idea." Rose hung her head. "I mean, the way he seemed all out of sorts at breakfast."

"I figured you noticed." Hen glanced at the back porch. "Stay here with Mattie for a sec, all right?" And Hen trudged off to talk to her father, sidestepping the chucking rooster.

Solomon had walked up and down the backyard in his bathrobe and oldest slippers for more than an hour in the middle of the night. Now here was Hen coming toward the porch, looking like she might burst into tears. "Weeping, comin' and goin'," he muttered to himself, rising and putting down his paper, *Die Botschaft*.

She gave a slight wave as she neared. "I wanted to say good-bye. Mattie Sue and I are leaving now." Her voice cracked.

"You take *gut* care," he said, his heart in his throat.

She lowered her eyes, nodding slowly. "I never meant to upset you and Mom . . . by coming."

Something welled up in him, and he moved quickly to her side. "You visit us anytime, ya hear? You're always welcome, daughter. Brandon and Mattie Sue, too."

Hen's eyes glistened in the corners as she blinked away tears. "Oh, Dad . . ." She reached for him and embraced him. "For the longest time, I've wanted to say how sorry I am for pushing you and Mom aside . . . out of my life." She paused, clearly struggling to speak. "I wish now I'd invited you to my wedding."

He could not speak but squeezed her hand. He nodded his head thoughtfully.

"Will you keep me in your prayers, Dad?" Her voice was as delicate as a child's.

"I never quit," Sol managed to say.

"Thank you," Hen said before she turned and left the porch.

By the time Ruth and Arie said farewell, Rose was nearly too full of pie to even think of going over to Mammi Sylvia's for some cold cuts and Jell-O, as they sometimes did on no-Preaching Sundays. Still, it was the appointed time to eat, so Dat wheeled Mamm across the back porch to the Dawdi Haus's separate entrance. Rose pondered Ruth Miller's thoughtful comment about how nice it was to see Hen again—the woman had genuinely seemed to mean it—and if Rose wasn't mistaken, Arie had given a slight bob of her head in agreement.

But no one said a word about Hen and Mattie Sue's visit during the meal at Mammi and Dawdi's. The closest anyone came to it was Dawdi Jeremiah. "Might be you gave the furniture in that one empty bedroom upstairs to Mose and his wife a bit too soon."

Rose caught her breath, wondering if Dawdi thought Hen might be fixing to come back home to live. Oh, she could not imagine such a thing. Much as her sister's marriage had broken her heart, the last thing she'd ever want was to think Hen and Brandon's love story might come to an abrupt end.

She watched her mother reach for another slice of Swiss cheese, Mamm's hand trembling as she did so. *If she knew what I was thinking, Mamm would say I've been reading too many romance novels.*

Later, before Mammi served up some delicious whoopie pies, Dawdi leaned back in his chair at the head of the table and told a story about their lippy ancestor, Yost Kauffman. Not only had

Yost courted a girl who'd chopped her hair in front, making fancy bangs, but he'd run around with some fellows who had worked some sort of "get rich quick" scheme in Big Valley. "It appears that ol' mustache we've all heard about wasn't the only thing that got Yost in trouble with the brethren," Dawdi said, smacking his lips and reaching for another whoopie pie.

Mamm's lips spread wide, and Rose's father chuckled. "There's some real fire in our genes, jah?" said Dat. Then, just as quickly, his face turned solemn, as if he'd suddenly thought of Hen. He changed the subject. "Where would yous like to go visitin' this afternoon?"

Mamm looked at Dat, as did Mammi Sylvia. Soon they were all looking to him for his opinion. "Since when's it up to me?" He glanced at Rose. "Why don't you pick this time, daughter?"

"Well, how about the bishop's family?" she said, thinking that perhaps some of the grandchildren might be there.

Dat's face paled. He shook his head. "Ought to be kin, ain't?"

Mammi Sylvia spoke up right quick. "They're our neighbors; we can go 'n' see them most anytime."

Dawdi quickly suggested Rose's brother Josh and his wife. "It's been some weeks since we dropped in over there."

They all agreed it would be nice to see the girls again—four-year-old Linda, three-year-old Katie, and the baby, Annie Mae. Rose washed Mammi's plates and silverware while her grandmother cleaned off the table, then came and wiped the dishes. Meanwhile, Dat wheeled Mamm over to the front room window, and they sat there for a time together, looking in the direction of the road and the fields across the way.

When Rose glanced over at her again, Mamm's head had drooped, and she was fast asleep. She couldn't help but think her parents both looked tired enough to simply go back to the main house and rest. Hen's surprise overnight visit had surely caused them a loss of sleep.

Rose finished up in her grandmother's kitchen, hoping they still might go and see Josh and Kate. But thinking about her father's decided disinterest today in visiting with the Petersheims made her ever so curious.

# CHAPTER 15

Early Monday, Hen thanked her sister-in-law Kate repeatedly, then kissed Mattie Sue good-bye. While driving her car to Rachel's Fabrics, she felt as carefree as a schoolgirl. Brandon's silence about her job—and her defiant attitude—at breakfast this morning had her stumped. Yet her nagging guilt disappeared when she pulled into the parking lot in front of the homey-looking store with window boxes on either side of its painted door.

"Come in, come in!" Rachel Glick called to her, all rosy-faced and bright-eyed. The friendly shopkeeper was probably only a little older than Hen.

Hen greeted her happily and followed her to the back room, where a quilting frame was set up, and hung up her coat and purse. She'd worn her long skirt with tiny blue and green print flowers and a ruffled cream-colored long-sleeved blouse. Her hair was pinned up in a French twist, but she thought she might roll it into the bun she'd worn before she was married. She could even pick up a Kapp at her father's house, if she had time to stop by later.

"Don't you look nice!" Rachel said.

"Next time you see me, I plan to look much more Amish," Hen told her, following her to the battery-run cash register on the counter.

"Oh?"

"I want to dress Plain again . . . from now on." She needed to say it into the air, to hear the words for herself.

Rachel squinted her eyes slightly, as if she wasn't exactly sure what Hen meant. But the People, and Brandon, too, would soon know just how serious Hen was about reclaiming parts of her former life.

The two of them moved about the shop, Rachel pointing out the shelves of quilting fabrics especially, before moving on to the shelves stacked with fabrics for dresses, aprons, and men's broadfall trousers and shirts.

"I'd like you to reorganize the quilting fabrics, beginning with the darkest hues of color on the top shelves, working down to the lighter shades below," Rachel said, her soft green eyes almost blue as she talked about her store.

"Sounds like fun." How Hen had missed this world!

The first few customers entered and appeared astonished to see her employed there at Rachel's. As they chattered together, Hen found herself enjoying the attention, though she wouldn't admit it to a soul.

Later, when there was a lull, Rachel showed her a picture of the Bars quilt she was working on at home. It was a replica of one her grandmother had made years ago and featured bright red, pastel blue, and black prints. "It's just beautiful, ain't?"

Hen wholeheartedly agreed, and she immediately imagined making a similar quilt of her own. She set to work arranging the bolts of fabric by color, picturing herself working on the quilt in her mother's front room. Somehow she couldn't see herself quilting in the modern living room in her home with Brandon.

During her short lunch break, Hen listened to a talkative

Rachel, who spoke glowingly of her English cousin, Donna Becker. "She lives neighbors to Gilbert Browning, ya know."

Rose Ann had told Hen about Mr. Browning, a relative newcomer to the area.

"Guess your sister has stopped by Donna's for tea a couple of times after her job."

"That's nice for Rose. I'm glad to hear she's able to take more time for herself again," Hen said.

"Donna says she seems to like workin' at the Browning house, even if Gilbert Browning is mighty strange."

"Strange . . . how do you mean?" Hen's antennae went up.

"Oh, I don't think Donna meant it's anything to worry about. The man's just peculiar in his ways, maybe because he's a widower." Rachel chuckled. "Seems a teenage Amish boy has been doing lawn work for Mr. Browning. He was even seen hangin' out the washing this past Monday mornin'. Isn't that an interesting howdy-do?"

Hen could not imagine a boy taking on so-called women's work. "Are you sure?" It sounded like someone hadn't gotten her story straight.

"Oh jah . . . ever so sure." Rachel glanced at a mail order for sewing notions in front of her, double-checking the numbers. "Once I was at Donna's to deliver some pinking shears and saw the young fella myself."

Hen had no idea where Mr. Browning had scrounged up such a boy—and one out of school, too!

Hen put away her lunch bag, then got back to work. The rest of the workday was fulfilling and fun, even inspiring, as Hen helped various Amishwomen who, once they got over their initial surprise at seeing her, were as welcoming and gracious as if she'd never left them for her English husband. As she and Rachel closed up shop that afternoon, Hen could hardly wait to work again on Thursday.

≈

Despite Hen's brazen move to accept the job at Rachel's Fabrics, Brandon was still noticeably quiet about it by Wednesday, not once confronting her about her outright defiance. And he hadn't said a word about her staying overnight at Dad's house, either. She and Mattie Sue had slipped back quietly last Sunday afternoon, only to find Brandon gone. *Just as well, considering everything.* Hen had put Mattie down for a nap while she unpacked, though she, too, was tired and emotionally drained. Eventually even Hen had taken advantage of the quiet house and slept for an hour, just as she had often done growing up.

Now that things had settled back into something of a routine between Brandon and her, albeit a somewhat uncomfortable one, Hen had returned to all the domestic things she loved—shopping for delicious sandwich fixings and other brown-bag food items for her husband to enjoy at work, keeping the house picked up and clean, and doing the laundry, including ironing Brandon's shirts lightly starched just the way he liked them. It was as if they'd swept their concerns under the proverbial rug.

Now, as Hen cut out a little Amish dress and black apron for Mattie Sue, she wondered if the reason Brandon had remained mum was due to being afraid he might say something he'd regret if he did confront her. Hen, for her part, was both glad and sad to be in such limbo, with Brandon not addressing her leaving or her working at Rachel's Fabrics. At this point, she didn't dare bring either up.

She'd already said all she could about her desire to re-embrace Amish culture to some degree. She just wished he might try to understand where she was coming from.

Yesterday she'd worked on the pretty wall hanging for Mattie's room, making brightly colored alphabet appliqués for several squares. Mattie had worn the little prayer cap Hen bought for her last week, and asked when she could learn to quilt, too. She'd also asked to help Auntie Rose make rag dolls sometime soon. Her daughter seemed to find her mother's new interests fun—she'd even parroted some of the Deitsch words she'd heard at her Amish grandparents' during their recent visits.

Hen's heart warmed at this, and she lost herself now in making Mattie's new Amish clothes, her own hair swept up in a smooth bun secured with one of her aunt Malinda's crochet hooks. Never once in the past couple of days did she consider how she looked to Brandon. Blissfully, she embraced the Plain world as she hummed at her sewing machine, stitching perfectly straight seams and well-concealed hems.

~

Rose simply could not understand how Mr. Browning failed to notice his rundown front porch. Each time she entered the door, she was all too aware of the repair and paint it needed.

*Maybe he just doesn't see it*, she thought, knocking now. *Things can become so familiar that you don't notice the problem any longer.* She made a mental note to talk to Nick about possibly sprucing up the place—squeezing it in between his other daily chores somehow.

Through the front window, she saw Gilbert Browning motioning her inside from his chair. "Is he too weak to answer the door?" Concerned now, she turned the doorknob and went inside.

"Morning," he said, folding his hands in his lap.

"*Gut* mornin'." She set her purse on the table, glad to see the African violets along the windowsill were thriving. "How are you today?"

"Oh, fine . . . fine." His usual response.

"How was the cake?" she asked.

"Uh, very tasty, thanks." He reached back and rubbed his neck, offering no further explanation about the treat's purpose.

Going to the sink, Rose noticed the cake pan was empty, except for a few dried crumbs still clinging to the sides. "Sure looks like it's all gone," she said.

Mr. Browning reached for the nearby newspaper, opening it wide. Apparently he was in no mood for conversation today.

Sighing, Rose turned on the faucet and began to wash the dishes. Suddenly, over the rush of the water, she heard what sounded like a thump on the ceiling. Another followed.

Shivers went down her spine. She turned off the water and looked up curiously and then at Mr. Browning, who remained with his head buried in the paper.

"I heard something upstairs."

He looked up. "Pardon?"

"Didn't ya hear that?"

He returned to his paper. "Must be the wind."

*Like fun it is,* she thought.

She thought of Lucy Petersheim's remarks and sighed. *Ridiculous.* But the shivers came once again. Feeling thoroughly spooked, she was anxious to finish her chores and get home.

As if to make up for not being permitted to dust or dry mop the dusty front room, Rose cleaned everything within her reach in the kitchen and the adjacent hall. Standing on a chair, she wiped down the tops of the cupboards, then continued with the counters and other kitchen surfaces, sometimes stepping near Mr. Browning, who remained planted in the doorway of the sitting room.

"Everything okay?" he asked later.

She swallowed hard. "I've heard stories about this house, is all."

He dropped his paper. "Stories, you say?"

"Silly stuff, like . . . ghost stories."

The man stared at her for a moment, then broke into a loud guffaw. "Well now, I can't say I've seen any ghosts."

"No, of course not," Rose whispered.

"But it *is* an old house," he continued, his steely eyes on her. "Every old place has . . . a personality, you know."

"Jah, maybe." She'd never heard this before.

"Thumps and bumps." He raised his bushy eyebrows. "Not to mention all the strange creaks and groans."

Rose sighed. "Maybe that's where the stories came from." *Must've started with Lucy. . . .*

Yet the man's expression did not convince her one bit.

When Rose was finished cooking and baking, she let the shoofly pie and apple rice betty cool, as well as a large tuna macaroni casserole and meatball chowder. Besides the hot dishes destined for the refrigerator, there were plenty of green beans, peas, and creamed corn in the pantry. Mr. Browning had assured her from the first day he didn't mind opening cans of vegetables—or heating soup from a can—to supplement the food she cooked ahead for him.

Making quick work of her morning duties, Rose soon bid him farewell and collected her pay in an envelope on the lamp table near his chair. "I'll return next week," she said, going to the door.

"Thank you, Rose."

She waved and reached to open the door, and closed it behind her. Welcoming the sunshine, she made her way down the steps and across the sidewalk to the waiting horse and buggy.

Suddenly she heard a knocking on a windowpane. Rose spun around to look at the house. Was Mr. Browning alerting her to something she'd left? Oddly enough, there was no one at the front room windows. Then, squinting into the sun, she glanced up at the attic and saw the flutter of *two* silhouettes move past the dormer window.

Shielding her eyes, Rose looked again, but no one was there.

*Is it my imagination?* She turned, dismissing her spooky thoughts, and hurried to untie Alfalfa. "Let's be gettin' home."

⌇

Following a delicious meal of veal, mashed potatoes, beef gravy, and buttered carrots and peas, Rose got Mamm settled for a rest, then rushed outside to her afternoon chores. She ran so fast, she nearly kicked the rooster. A few feathers went flying as he screeched and squawked and carried on. "*Acht gewwe*—watch out," she said, laughing at the friendless fowl.

She slid open the barn door and saw Nick, who smiled immediately. She hastened inside, relieved he was in a much better mood than the last few days.

They worked together, doing their daily routine. She enjoyed watching George consume his feed and waited until he was finished to stroke the gray and white markings on his forehead. He was so enormous as she stood there, looking up at him. Like a living, breathing wall, his breadth and stature made her feel small, as she did when dwarfed by the vastness of the night sky, sprinkled with more stars than she could count. At such times, Rose found herself pondering how grand and majestic the heavenly Father must be. *Are you small enough to hear my prayers, Lord?* she sometimes prayed.

She and Nick had talked about this once while out riding. He'd argued with her that God was much too busy—and far too great—to be bothered with people when He had the whole universe to look after.

"*That's just ridiculous,*" she'd said. She never felt it necessary to hold back with Nick. She had persisted, arguing what the psalmist David had said in so many words: *No matter where I go—whether I try to hide from God or not—He knows right where I am.*

The argument had ended in an impasse, and Nick assured her this was an issue they might never see eye to eye on.

Rose was rescued now from the glum thought by Dat, who came in from driving Upsy-Daisy. The gray horse headed directly to her stall, covered in sweat. Rose swatted dozens of flies off her back.

"She's parched," Dat said after Nick had taken the horse's lead. "I had her clear over to Mose's place and back mighty quick."

"We'll get her watered," Nick reassured him, and Dat gave

an appreciative nod before stepping back out into the blinding sunlight.

Rose tugged on Nick's shirt-sleeve. "Come . . . I must tell ya the strangest thing," she whispered. "Lucy said last week she thinks Mr. Browning's place is haunted."

Nick's eyes brightened. "No kiddin'? Haunted?"

"I didn't take her too seriously myself. Not until today." She shared a little of her own recent experiences. "And can you just imagine someone sitting in the doorway each day, blocking the way to the stairs?"

His face beamed with interest. "Sounds like a real mystery."

"That's what I thought!" Rose emptied the feed bucket and stood there holding it, a plan twirling in her head.

And, just that quick, Nick said aloud what she hoped he would. "We should go over there sometime."

"When?"

"Why wait?" He pushed his straw hat down hard. "It's been a while since we went riding, ya know." His dark eyes glimmered.

"Okay, then, let's go tonight."

"Meet at the clump of old oak trees, past the turn into the bishop's lane . . . out on the road." His gaze held hers.

*Same spot where I met Silas.* "Jah, I know where."

Nick was smiling to beat the band; so was she. Rose scarcely knew which was more exciting—trying to solve the perplexing mystery . . . or going riding again with her best friend.

# CHAPTER 16

$\mathcal{S}$olomon paced the length of his workshop that Wednesday afternoon, contemplating Bishop Aaron's reaction to the finished bench wagon. The bishop was not a man to shrink back when showing his pleasure for a job done well. Yet Solomon struggled within himself, not willing to take credit for the work he'd accomplished, fearful of sowing the seed of pride. Even so, he'd never seen Aaron so outwardly pleased—perhaps because Sol had done his special bidding and used a few of the old "still *gut*" boards salvaged from the deacon's barn in the construction of the new wagon. Solomon, too, had thought it an excellent idea to connect the past with the present in this manner.

On the way home from delivering the bench wagon to the bishop's, he'd taken the shortcut behind Aaron's buggy shed and the chicken coop. There, he came upon Nick and Christian arguing, their faces red with anger.

Sol had hustled nearer. "*Boys . . . boys!*" He'd had to raise his voice to be noticed. "*Just walk away now.*"

Nick turned to go, leaving Christian looking mighty sheepish.

"*Sorry, Sol,*" Christian had said, wiping his hands on his work trousers.

"*Might be gut to say the same to Nick,*" Solomon had replied. "*Make things right, ya know?*"

Christian had merely scowled over his shoulder as Nick headed for the barn, still saying nothing.

*Always too quiet,* thought Solomon of Nick.

This sort of thing had happened frequently through the years. Nick would say something hateful to his brother—or the other way around. But it was typically Christian who got fed up first and retaliated by hollering the loudest. More recently the feud had heated up to where the bishop confided he rued the day he'd ever brought Nick home. "*The boy can stir up trouble with just a look,*" Aaron had stated.

Solomon recalled all the afternoons he'd observed Nick with his daughter, working around the animals. Shaking off his niggling fears, he hoped with everything in him that his recent talk with Reuben Good might just remedy all of that. *And mighty soon.* Both men agreed their children would make a fine match, and Solomon again found himself thankful pretty Rebekah Bontrager had moved away to Indiana before she and Silas were old enough to court. The two of them had seemed awful sweet on each other some years back.

Brushing off the memory of Nick and Christian's heated squabble, Solomon straightened things up in his workshop. Tomorrow was another day, and he had two orders for pony carts to complete right quick—one from the deacon's son and the other from Emma's second cousin up near Strasburg. He reached for his broom and began to sweep up the last of the debris from the newly finished bench wagon.

～

From the moment Hen had seen Brandon that day in the swirling snow and wind, he had determined the direction of her life. She'd viewed him as a welcome escape, and his modern tastes and interests had shaped their years together.

Yet here she was, finishing up Mattie Sue's little dress and apron and humming "Must I Go and Empty-Handed," a tune Dawdi Jeremiah had often played on his harmonica. She rose and hung up the outfit in her daughter's closet just so.

Going next to Brandon's and her bedroom, Hen dusted and vacuumed thoroughly. When she was finished, she went into the walk-in closet to organize the shelving unit. Inside, her eyes fell on a plastic container of letters and cards from Amish relatives and friends—a written memory bank of sorts.

She sat down on the floor and began to sort through the stack for the ones written by Arie before she was courted by her husband, Elam Zook—before Hen had married Brandon.

She lost track of time, savoring the memories of her child-hood—of playing dolls with both Rose and Arie, making cookies to exchange at Christmastime, and sitting in the back of the Preaching service, helping new mothers with their babies. *Wonderful years,* she thought. She glanced up and was surprised to see Mattie Sue wearing the Amish dress and apron. On her head was the small white Kapp. The sight took her aback.

"I tried to make my hair like yours and Auntie Rose's," said Mattie with a frustrated smile. "Can you help me, Mommy?"

"Sure, honey." She left the letters on the floor and went with Mattie into the master bathroom to find a brush and comb. "We'll do the best we can to make a bob." Mattie's hair was long enough, but her bangs would have to be pulled back with bobby pins.

When Hen was satisfied with Mattie's hair, she set the prayer cap back on top of her daughter's head. "If you want to look like a real Amish girl, leave the Kapp strings untied," she told her.

"Well, I *am* a real one, aren't I?"

"Half of you is, yes." She leaned down to kiss her darling girl.

"Which half, Mommy?" Mattie Sue looked down at herself.

Hen couldn't squelch her laughter. "Aren't you something!" She held Mattie at arm's length, then picked her up and twirled her around, the dress billowing out.

Just as Hen set her down, the front door opened. And before she could stop her, Mattie Sue dashed out of the room. "Daddy, Daddy! Look at me!"

A long pause ensued. Then she heard Brandon say flatly, "That's nice, honey . . . now, where's your mother?"

In that moment, it dawned upon Hen that she might have underestimated the coming chaos her Plain cravings had the power to create.

~

There was not a sound in the air but the rustle of leaves as Rose crept out to the barn. High in the haymow, she found the hidden work trousers and pulled them on under her dress. Then she hurried to George's stall.

In a few minutes, she led the horse quietly down their lane, not wanting to cause attention by trotting past the kitchen windows. She'd seen Dat sitting near the lamp at the table with Mamm, reading aloud *The Budget*. Rose was not disobeying any creed by riding her father's driving horse—most church families she knew let their small children ride them occasionally for fun. But when a girl became a young lady, such frivolity was frowned upon— and she was certain her parents would disapprove of her doing so with a boy who was not her beau. *And one with both feet out of the church, too.*

The ridge of hills to the east was dreadfully dark as she made her way up Salem Road to meet Nick. The moon, if it were visible, would've helped greatly, but a heavy cloud cover blocked any hope of light. If George hadn't known the way so well, Rose might've been nervous about coming this far as she headed to the spot where Nick would surely be waiting with a flashlight.

She would have trotted right past him and his waiting horse if Pepper hadn't whinnied in the blackness. "Nick?" she said, wishing he wouldn't pull tricks on her like this. "Where's your flashlight?"

"It's more fun this way," he replied.

"Maybe for *you*." She could scarcely make out his outline as he sat atop the horse. She waited for him to take the lead up the right side of the road, with the flow of traffic, although there was rarely a car down here at this hour.

"Bishop wanted to know where I was headin'," said Nick as they rode side by side. "He caught me leading Pepper out of the barn."

She wondered if he ever referred to the bishop as his father to the man's face. But with Nick's irritable mood, it wasn't a good idea to bring that up now. *When isn't he tetchy?*

"Does he know you took Pepper riding last Friday morning, too?" She wanted to see what he'd say, having thought repeatedly it was Nick who'd brazenly ridden past Aunt Malinda's little Dawdi Haus.

He laughed. "Oh, so you *did* see me."

"You're crazy, Nick. You're goin' to get in trouble with the bishop, for sure and for certain."

"What he doesn't know, he won't have to worry about." He paused. Then he said, "Which way to the haunted house?"

"Not far. I always go up Bartville Road." She pointed toward the west.

"That's fine, but let's take the shortcut," he said, "through Bridle Path Lane."

She wasn't sure she wanted to ride down that narrow road on such a dark night. "Nick . . . why?" she protested. "You know how jittery I get. And there's no moon to light the way."

Nick chuckled. Feeling uneasy, Rose looked at the sky, hoping the heavy clouds might blow over. "We've never, ever gone that way," she continued.

"Then I think it's time. Look, if you don't make yourself go, you'll never conquer your fear."

"Maybe bein' fearful's a *gut* thing," she said.

"Well, I won't let the goblins get ya," he teased in a low tone. "You'll just have to depend on me." His laugh was a nervous one, and he seemed somehow different tonight, even for him.

"I'm turnin' back if you don't quit scarin' me." Rose meant it, although she might not find her way home without his help.

"Aw, Rosie . . . are you really so afraid?"

As they turned left on Bartville Road, all she could think of was Mamm's accident. Too soon, they were making a jog right onto the dreaded Bridle Path Lane.

When they were only a few yards onto the dirt road, the three-quarter moon appeared, creating eerie shadows on the trees and thick underbrush that lined the right side of the road. The ravine created a forbidding world even in the daylight, and Rose remembered the bishop's grandchildren's stories about this stretch of road. "Sure hope the hobgoblin's not out tonight," she said, trying to humor herself as they moved along.

"Haven't run into him yet, and I've been here many times . . . even when the moon's in its darkest phase," Nick said, sounding confident, like he felt at home here.

"*Him* . . . so, the hobgoblin's a fella?" Rose laughed a little. "Is there such a thing as a girl goblin? I s'pose you'd be knowing that, as well. Was it your Mamm who taught ya such things?"

Suddenly Nick coughed, attempting to clear his throat.

"You all right, Nick?"

"Why wouldn't I be?"

"You don't *sound* it."

He huffed loudly. "Just stop asking me, will ya?"

"I know you, Nick Franco, and there's something bothering ya."

He was quiet for a moment. Then he said, "I don't want to talk about it."

"About what?"

He sighed loudly. "I found out my mom died this week."

"Oh, Nick. I'm so sorry." Rose felt the air go out of her. "I shouldn't have said—"

"It's not like I even remember her."

"Still, she was your mother."

He hurried the horse, motioning with his head for her to keep up with him.

"You must feel very sad."

He shrugged. "Just more alone in the world, but so what?"

"Well, you're not alone," Rose said. "You have a *gut* life with the bishop and Barbara . . . and their family."

"I'm an add-on."

She shook her head and slowed her horse. "I'm sure they feel like you're their son, same as Christian."

"Well, you don't live under the bishop's roof."

"No, but I know how they've cared for you . . . raised you like Christian and the girls."

"Don't mention his name to me anymore."

"Ach, Nick . . ."

"I mean it. He's never been anything but spiteful to me."

Rose rode silently. The atmosphere was oppressively dank and dismal from more than just the overcast night. Several times Hen had shown her where Mamm's buggy had flipped over, but Rose was thankful she couldn't see well enough to recognize the spot now. She felt keenly aware of even the smallest movement in the shadows.

"I really wish you'd brought your flashlight," she said, her voice trembling.

"Your eyes should be used to the dark by now."

She wanted him to slow his horse to a walk instead of trot-ting on this precarious section. The road was a mere tunnel now beneath the trees overhead. "How'd your mother die?" Her voice sounded thin.

"Bishop didn't say."

"But she was sick for all these years, jah?"

Nick made no answer, and Rose knew she'd best be still.


After what seemed like nearly an hour, they made a right turn onto Pumping Station Road, then went northeast to Fairview Road. Rose's heart slowed its pounding when they were once again on a paved open road. Yet Nick remained quiet as they went, till even-tually they arrived at Hollow Road and turned right, not far from Jackson's Sawmill Covered Bridge. Mr. Browning's house was just a stone's throw away.

"Let's not go too far into the lane," she said, leading the way now. She stared at the gleaming second-story windows, a contrast to the attic dormer windows, which were as dark as the night sky.

"What're we lookin' for?" Nick sat tall on his horse.

"Anything peculiar."

"Like ghosts?"

Again she shivered at his tone. "Can't you be serious?"

He chuckled. "For you . . . anything."

"Don't be a tease."

"Then don't be so easy to fool."

She ignored his comment. "What about the sounds I've heard upstairs while I work?"

"Could it be a cat? Or a dog?"

She'd never considered that. "Wouldn't Mr. Browning admit it, though?"

"Or maybe evil spirits—ever think of that?"

Her skin crawled. "Will ya stop scaring me?"

"I don't see any hex signs anywhere," Nick went on, ignoring her. He clicked his tongue, signaling the horse to move forward.

"Not too close to the house," she warned. "I'd rather Mr. Browning doesn't know we're spyin' on him."

"On *them*."

"What?"

"Maybe there's someone livin' upstairs."

"Or . . . it could be only my imagination."

"You do have a big imagination," he replied darkly.

"It's all the library books I read."

He laughed softly. "Why read books when you can actually *live* nights like this?"

She wondered what he'd say if she revealed something to him that she sometimes pondered. Would he poke fun . . . or understand? "It's just that I've been noticing something in nearly all the stories I've read. The main character—usually a young woman—thinks she can have everything she wants. But almost always she finds out the hard way that she can't."

"Well, sure . . . that's because there are different rules in real life than in books."

"But even so, there's always a choice a girl has to make in every story . . . *and* in real life."

Nick didn't ridicule her like Rose thought he might. He actually listened, like a good friend. Not like a pesky older brother—*like Mose or Josh when they still lived at home*.

Quieter now, Rose wondered if Nick would grieve hard the loss of his mother. Was this the reason he'd been so glum last weekend?

All sorts of unrelated thoughts flitted through her head as she kept her eyes glued to the second-story windows. *Maybe Nick didn't like being my errand boy to Silas Good*, she thought. *Or maybe he dislikes Silas. Then again, who does Nick like?*

At that moment she realized there were four windows all lit

up across the second story. "Ach, there are two windows for each bedroom, ain't?"

"Well, I've got two windows in my room," he volunteered.

Her brother Josh's house seemed to be laid out similar to Mr. Browning's, and each of his upstairs bedrooms had two windows, too. "So, the windows on the right, over the kitchen, could be where another person sleeps."

"You're not makin' sense, Rose."

"Mr. Browning's bedroom could be on the left, over the front room. See?" She pointed as she tried to make heads or tails of the upstairs interior.

"And you think someone's stayin' over the kitchen."

"Maybe so. I know I heard noises there, overhead."

Then she saw it—the silhouette of a slender boy with hair cropped all around like her own brothers', standing in the window to pull down the shade. "Goodness, that's not Gilbert Browning!"

"*Nee*—no," Nick admitted.

Rose was stunned. "Ain't seein' things, neither." But now that her suspicions were confirmed, she was more perplexed than ever. Who on earth was living upstairs in Gilbert Browning's house? She thought of the Amish boy Donna had mentioned.

They turned the horses around and headed out to the road.

"Can we go home another way?" she asked, too jittery to return to the spooky dirt lane from whence they'd come.

"We'll cut through Mt. Pleasant Road, then down toward home."

She had to rely on Nick to see the way back—even George seemed unsure now as they rode through the night. When they arrived on the east side of Salem Road, she realized Nick's "shortcut" down eerie Bridle Path Lane hadn't been a shortcut at all. She trembled as she bade him Gut Nacht.

"You goin' to Singing next Sunday?" he asked her.

*Singing?* Nick never cared about the weekly gatherings. He was certainly full of surprises tonight.

She thought of Silas Good. "I just might for a change. How 'bout you?"

Nick snorted. "What for?"

"To meet a nice girl, fall in love, and get married, silly." The former mysterious mood around them had dissipated. She slid down off George and slipped a sugar cube into the horse's mouth.

"So, we're s'*posed* to pair up at Singings?" he said comically.

Now Rose was laughing. She glanced at the house, hoping no one was still up. "You've grown up Amish—you should know all this."

"Why are *you* goin'?" Nick pulled a small flashlight out of his pocket and shined it on her face.

"Ach, you had a light all along!" She turned to lead the horse into the lane. "How dare you fib like that!"

"Think back, Rosie . . . I didn't lie." He stepped in front of her, and the flashlight tumbled from his hand.

She felt both angry with him and strangely sad. "Why'd we have to go down that miserable old road?"

"It's like when I tumbled off the ladder, checking on the silage. I had to get back up on it eventually." He was gripping her arms now. "Sometimes ya have to travel down a road where someone you love got hurt. Sometimes you just have to."

"Nick . . ."

He released her and turned his back. "I'd better get goin'," he said, his voice suddenly devoid of feeling.

"You're awful upset . . . about your mother, ain't?"

"Why should I be? She was always too drunk to care about me."

"Maybe she was just too sick, jah?"

He stood there, unmoving . . . and silent.

Rose had often wondered why he hadn't returned to his mother on his own when he was of age. "Did ya stay round here because she was too sick to have you live with her . . . when you were old enough to decide?"

"I wanted her to search for *me* . . . not the other way around."

*Was he just that stubborn?* she wondered.

He breathed slowly and shifted his weight from one foot to the other. "I never stopped believing she'd get sober."

Her heart broke for him. "If she'd gotten well, I'm sure she would've looked for you." She paused. "Someone from the agency could've told her where you were, I'd guess."

"But . . . God let her die."

"Now, Nick, you know it wasn't like that," Rose said gently.

He reached to touch her elbow, his tone suddenly tender. "Did I hurt you before? When I squeezed your arms? I didn't mean to. I mean, I'd never . . ."

She stroked George's thick mane. "I'm fine."

He leaned forward to retrieve the flashlight at their feet. "Well, I'll be seein' ya."

"Nick—try not to be too sad."

"Tomorrow, Rose."

"Jah . . . tomorrow." With that, she led George up the lane and back to the barn.

# CHAPTER 17

*S*olomon had been unable to locate his horse George either in the stable or in the pasture earlier that evening. After searching much of his own property, he went on foot to hunt in the bishop's barn, too. Seeing that Pepper was also missing, and aware that Rose and Nick were nowhere around, he presumed the two were out riding together.

*Again*. He groaned—he had hoped they were spending less time together aside from chores. As reliable a worker as Nick had always been, the boy was not fit for his Rose. Sol could only pray that Silas might turn things around by the next Singing. The young man had been fond of Rose for quite a while, but according to Reuben Good, his son hadn't pursued her because she'd dropped out of Singings these past months. Thank goodness Sylvia was able to stay with Emma more often again, freeing up Rose Ann. There was a real possibility that romance might be winging its way to his daughter's heart.

Now Solomon stood beside the second-story window, peering

down at the front yard and Nick and Rose, who stood at the end of the lane. Nick's flashlight lay at Rose's feet.

Sol winced when Nick reached for Rose Ann's arms.

"Dear Lord in heaven." He shuddered at the possibility that his second daughter might also be lost to God due to an outsider. "Let it not be so. . . ."

~

Hen felt terribly tense. Brandon had decided to wait until after Mattie Sue was asleep to discuss the little Amish dress. He closed their bedroom door quite deliberately, the latch clicking in the stillness. It was apparent by the way he sat on the chair across from the bed where she waited that he was ready to speak his mind.

"Why would you do this, Hen?" He leaned forward, folding his hands in front of him.

She stiffened. "You saw her—Mattie Sue loves wearing it."

"Are you trying to interest her in being Amish?" His words were cutting.

"Well, she *is* Amish . . . partly."

He fixed his eyes on her. "But *you're* not, Hen. You never joined the church, remember?"

"Well, you know what I mean," she replied. "Besides, Mattie's just playing around. She's crazy about her dress and Kapp. Can't you let her enjoy the fun?"

"Fun?" He shook his head. "Why do you want to look back now, Hen . . . why?"

She pushed several more pillows behind her back and leaned on the headboard. "I just want my child to know her roots." Her voice trembled.

"*Your* child?"

"C'mon, Brandon . . . don't do this."

He rose in a silent sulk and headed for the shower. He grabbed his bathrobe off the hook in the closet, muttering something she couldn't make out.

"Can't we talk this through?" she asked as he pushed open the bathroom door. But he said no more.

She remembered driving by her father's house after Mattie's birth. Three-week-old Mattie Sue had been sound asleep in her infant carrier as Hen parked across the road from the old farmhouse and sat there with her window open, listening to all the sounds of twilight. It had been the first time she'd missed home.

"You're playing with the fires of hell if you marry that fellow," the bishop had warned. "A friend of the world is an enemy of God!"

She'd opened the car door and gotten out, just staring at the darkened house . . . waiting for Dat to bring in the gas lamps from the barn. She'd bit her lip, not wanting to spoil her glimpse of her childhood home with salty tears. No, Hen refused to cry when she had only herself to blame. She had disregarded the wisdom of her parents, as well as the ministerial brethren.

She had chosen her own way.

And now here she was all these years later, missing home more than ever. The memories and yearning had welled up and overtaken her until Hen could scarcely think of anything else.

*Why can't Brandon understand?*

It was impossible to brush their disagreement aside. But for tonight it appeared that Brandon had done just that. Hen rose and went into their spacious closet to find the letters she'd left out earlier. While she sorted through them, Brandon finished his shower and slipped out to the family room. She heard the TV on now and decided to steer clear of him. Let him think about what she'd said—what *they'd* said to each other. . . .

The tension between them could be felt across the house, and for the first time since they'd married, Hen hoped her husband might just sleep on the sofa again.

Settling down on the floor at the foot of the bed, she sat in her long cotton nightgown and read several of Arie's letters. It was hard not to compare her past friendship with Arie—who was happily married, according to Rose Ann, with three little ones already—to Hen's present relationship with Diane, who was altogether disgruntled with marriage and vowed openly that, now that she had one child, she was done having babies. *"I never want the hassles of another newborn."*

There were other differences between the two women, especially the way each viewed relationships. Diane, for instance, was just as quick to discard as to collect. Hen had noticed this with some degree of trepidation a few short months into their friendship. If Diane disliked your politics or thought you were closed-minded, she immediately brushed you off. No second chances with her. Hen had seen her do that with several work friends right before Karen was born.

Arie, for her part, had never been one to collect friends. She didn't seem to need more than one or two close relationships in her life. And for all the years she and Hen were best friends, Arie said she needed only Hen to confide in—until Hen had betrayed her, as she called it.

Hen sighed and opened another letter. Truth was, she'd pushed Arie into an impossible corner, where the only thing she *could* do was avoid Hen.

She heard Brandon changing TV channels, making more noise than was necessary. A frightening thought crossed her mind—what if her own husband rejected her?

Unable to consider such a thing for more than a fleeting second, Hen returned to reading Arie's encouraging letters—some written the year Hen was sick with a long-lasting flu. Others were penned the winter Arie and her family went by train to visit her mother's cousins near Sarasota, Florida, in a tiny village called Pinecraft.

Hen leaned down to lie on the floor, propping herself up on one elbow to continue reading. She missed her Amish friend terribly.

She wished she could talk to Arie tonight. She felt lost and quite alone, even here in the bedroom she and Brandon had created as a haven against the world. Why couldn't Brandon comprehend what had happened to her when Mattie Sue came into their lives . . . and into her arms? Hen merely longed to impart the wisdom of the ages to her darling little girl. Why was that unacceptable?

*Will I always regret my decision to marry outside the church?* The awareness that she felt regret startled Hen. Yet wouldn't all this fussing and fretting come to an end if Brandon simply allowed her what she wished for—a chance to work at Rachel's Fabrics, and more contact between Mattie and her Plain relatives? If he'd just be more flexible and open to the idea that good, simple living had something to offer her and Mattie—to all *three* of them—they could resume their previously happy relationship.

She glanced at the lamp table and saw her Bible tucked beneath the second shelf. How long had it been since she'd read it? She remembered years of reading aloud to her mother, confined in her wheelchair. . . . Oh, the joy the Scriptures brought to Mom, easing her pain in a way that Hen could not fathom. Whenever her mother couldn't sleep, she prayed. No doubt her mother was praying even now.

Hen took comfort in the thought and returned Arie's letters to the box.

Suddenly she got the idea to write to Arie. The desire had crossed her mind numerous times in the past five years, but never had she been as anxious to act on it as tonight.

She rose and found her stationery and best pen, then went to the small oak desk in the corner and began to write.

*Dear Arie,*

*Please don't dismiss me before you read this letter. After seeing you last Sunday at my parents' house, I've been thinking about our friendship. I know I hurt you with my choices. I hurt myself, too.*

*You were such a big part of my life, Arie. I realize this more each day. And I'm so sorry. I hope you can forgive me someday.*

*There are parts of my former life I still miss. I long to be around Plain folk again, and I've taken a job at Rachel's Fabrics. I'm really hoping you might stop by the shop sometime to see me. I'd love that!*

*I miss you, dearest friend.*

*With love,*

*Hen*

Rereading her letter, Hen realized anew how impulsive she'd been to marry. How ironic that *impulsive* was just what Brandon had called her. And now she must do her best to keep her yearnings for the Old Ways at bay, or she'd spoil their marriage. There was disgust in Brandon's eyes whenever she argued for a renewed connection to her Plain life. Amish culture—and faith—had never held any appeal for him.

The fact that he still hadn't mentioned her new job surprised her. Was he a pressure cooker, ready to explode in frustration? Until recently, he'd never said a harsh word to her, but then, she hadn't provoked such a disruption in their lives till now, either. *Though none of this is on purpose.* Hen was torn right down the middle of her soul.

She folded the note to Arie and addressed the envelope. Then, going to the kitchen, she located a stamp in a small drawer, as well as a return address sticker. She stared at it as she pressed the words onto the envelope: *Mr. & Mrs. Brandon Orringer.*

Hen belonged with her husband. No longer was she Sol Kauffman's little Amish girl. It was essential that Hen make a greater attempt to please Brandon—to try to make her unfulfilling English life a happier one for them both.

*Somehow, I must.*

≈

Rose was startled to hear the *click* of a stone against her bedroom window Sunday evening. Fully dressed for the Singing, she had been walking back and forth in her room, thinking of Silas. Would he ask her to ride afterward?

Going to the window, she raised it and looked down to see Nick standing there with his flashlight shining on his face. "What're you doin'?" she asked.

"Christian's takin' his buggy over to the deacon's," he said. "You can ride with him, if ya want. Unless you have another way."

Typically, brothers took their sisters to Singings so the girls were free to ride home with a beau. Always before, Rose had ridden with one of her married brothers, if they were going that way. Never once had she ridden with Christian Petersheim. "Are *you* goin'?"

"No."

She wished he would, but she wasn't surprised at the answer. "You never know who you might meet there," she urged. "It could be fun."

"Well, I'm sure not ridin' with Christian."

"Borrow the bishop's buggy, then—I'll ride along with ya."

Nick shook his head.

"Have it your way, then. Tell Christian I'll be right down." Rose felt bad for Nick as she closed the window. Heaven knew that if she couldn't persuade him to go, no one could. In all truth, he was as unpredictable and stormy as their autumn weather.

# CHAPTER 18

By the time Rose ran outdoors to catch up with Christian, she was surprised to see Nick still walking slowly up the road. "You should be getting your own courting buggy sometime soon, right?" she said.

"Puh! What for?"

"Well, so you can spend time with a girl you like. You'll never find one till you look."

He gave her a scrutinizing stare. "What are you so happy about?"

"Oh, I just haven't been to Singings in a while, is all." She folded her hands, glad she'd worn her mittens on this chilly night. Since Nick didn't have a sweetheart-girl, Rose didn't want to mention Silas Good. Didn't want to be rude . . . or sound all puffed up because she had a date and he had no one.

He walked with her to the turnoff to the bishop's lane. "Well, so long," he said and kept going.

"Good-bye." She glanced back—his shoulders were slumped and his head hung down. She chided herself for not being more gentle. Surely he was still brooding over his mother's passing. Oh, if only he could find it in himself to go along tonight! He shouldn't be alone when he felt so low.

Nevertheless, Rose hurried to hop into Christian's open buggy. "Denki for the lift," she said as she climbed in to sit at his left.

"Nick thought you needed a ride."

"Jah, my brothers have pretty much given up on me goin' to Singings anymore."

"You can always get a lift with me," Christian said.

She looked over her shoulder. "Why do ya think Nick doesn't care to go?"

"Have you ever known him to care about anything?" Christian held the reins and clicked his tongue to get the horse moving.

"Jah, he cares 'bout a lot of things. Don't you realize that?"

This brought a guffaw from Christian. "Aren't you spunky!"

"Ain't something I try to be."

"You mean it just comes natural?" Christian chuckled. "Prob'ly it's the reason you and Nick get along," he said. "Two of a kind?" He eyed her. "Except Roses are s'posed to be sweet, ain't?"

She shrugged off his comment and turned her thoughts to Silas, recalling his thoughtful letter and their date last Saturday. She was fairly sure he was serious about courting her, since they'd gone to spend the evening at his married brother's. Most fellows didn't want family to know who they were courting till closer to being published in church, two weeks before the wedding.

Christian interrupted her thoughts. "Nick seems more out of sorts than usual."

"Well, his mother just died."

Christian snorted. "No, it's more than that."

"Maybe he's missing his family . . . his kin."

"He's a burr in the flesh," Christian muttered. "That's what."

*What a thing for a brother to say!* Rose stared at him. "It can't be easy, losin' someone you loved." She refused to reveal more about what Nick had said concerning his mother.

"Seems he'll use any excuse to fall into a slump." Christian shook his head. "Nick's mighty stubborn, too. All these years, he's never tried to fit into the family." He huffed loudly.

Rose bristled. "Nick might be happier in the English world. Ever think that?" She didn't add, *"away from you,"* but she thought it.

Christian leaned back, the reins loose in his hands. "Believe me, I think on it plenty. And I wouldn't be surprised if my father suspects the same."

Rose suddenly felt disloyal, discussing Nick this way. Still, he'd taken no steps to build a life of his own among the People. "Maybe it's time he had his own buggy."

"Daed's offered a few times to purchase one, and a nice, fast trotter, too. But Nick keeps turnin' him down."

Falling into silence, Rose listened to the steady *clip-clop*ping of the horse. She considered several of the girls at church, wondering which ones Nick might find appealing enough to court and marry, keeping him in the community. Any number of pretty girls could make him a good wife. She could think of at least two who were her own first cousins, which would be right nice, making Nick her relative, too, if he married one of them. She was still kicking herself for not convincing him to go to Singing tonight.

Just then, she heard the sound of galloping behind them. She turned to look just as the horse and rider sped by.

Christian's young driving horse started and jumped, pulling jerkily to the left.

"Oh goodness!" Without thinking, Rose grabbed Christian's arm. *Are we going to tip over?*

She clung to Christian, not realizing for a moment that she might have caused even more chaos. Every nightmare Rose had ever had since her mother's accident careened across her mind, and by the time Christian managed to restrain the horse, she could scarcely breathe.

She gave a sigh of relief and wondered, as she moved back to her side of the seat, if Christian would chide her.

Instead, he touched her arm. "You all right?"

She nodded, keeping her emotions in check. "I thought . . . I wondered if what happened to Mamm might happen to us."

"Nick's foolish—he should've known better than to pass so close."

"That was Nick?" In her fright, she hadn't recognized him.

"Who else is so reckless?" Christian reined the horse over onto the side of the road and brought the buggy to a halt. He drew in a long, deliberate breath. "Jah, that was Nick for certain." He rubbed his hands on his face, covering his features, clearly upset.

"Christian, what is it?"

He adjusted his straw hat, then picked up the reins once again. "You ought to stay away from my brother," he stated.

She felt terribly weak all of a sudden. "I don't understand."

"He's a troublemaker."

She went silent, thoroughly frustrated and not at all surprised that Nick couldn't get along with as trying a brother as Christian surely was. Still, Mamm's comments years ago echoed in her mind. *"Nick ain't our kind. . . ."*

Up ahead, the rider leaned forward on his horse, holding on to the mane . . . riding bareback. Instinctively, she knew Christian was right—it *was* Nick up there.

Why had he changed his mind about going? It was downright flabbergasting, but even more surprising was his mode of travel. No girl would want to ride bareback with him after the Singing. *Why is he bothering to go at all?*

Unexpectedly, she felt like she had after Mamm's accident. Going up to the highest crest of the hill, behind Dat's pastureland, Rose had stood there a long time by herself, dreadfully upset about her mother. She'd gazed out at the sky, the velvety clouds floating behind the trees to the west. Everything—the buttonwood trees, the willows, every aspect of nature that she saw around her—seemed painfully significant in that moment. *Mamm got hurt because of me.* She'd told herself this so many times she believed it.

Now, feeling nearly as sad and helpless as that day, Rose imagined riding alongside Nick up ahead, on the hard pavement. All the while, Christian's spiteful remarks about his brother whirled round and round like the windmill behind their barnyard.

~

Once they arrived at Deacon Samuel's, Rose sat alone in the buggy, outside the large barn. The bishop had once told the deacon and his elderly father that it was mighty good to run a dairy farm, because the never-ending work with cattle kept the minister's sons busy—and out of trouble—from dawn to dusk.

Rose needed a few minutes to sort out her thoughts before going inside. Clearly Christian and Nick had some sort of feud going on between them, and anything more she might say to defend Nick would just add fuel to the fire. As far as she knew, there had never been a time when Christian had treated Nick with any kind of respect. *Like you'd treat a brother.*

After a time, she stepped down from the buggy and made her way around the side of the barn to the sloping pathway that led to the upper level. Almost immediately she saw Silas in the glow of the gaslight. He stood in a huddle with more than a dozen young men, all wearing their Sunday best—black trousers and coats over white shirts. Some even wore small bow ties, indicating they were a bit more fancy and from a more progressive church than her own district.

Nick was there, as well, standing back against the far wall of hay bales, his arms folded over his chest. It was his usual way at the few gatherings he'd attended.

Quickly, Rose looked to see if her cousins Mary and Sarah were there yet—the two she'd had in mind as possibilities for Nick. But neither girl was present.

She glanced again at Nick, who looked utterly disinterested and bored. Why had he come? Was it her pleading?

She momentarily caught his eye, and he gave her an *aw, shucks* sort of smile and a subtle shrug, as if to say, *I changed my mind.*

When they gathered at the tables to sing, Nick stood in the corner away from the rest of them, glaring at his brother. Later, too, his dark eyes followed Christian as he went over to talk to Leah Miller, one of Arie's younger sisters.

Rose kept an eye out for Mary and Sarah and wondered if they were already outside with other fellows. She happened to spot Nick, only to be surprised that the two girls had found *him.* As cheerful as they seemed, Nick appeared much less mirthful, and totally unimpressed by their playful flirting.

She watched for a moment, suppressing a smile. Her cousins seemed genuinely interested in Nick, and the longer they clustered around him, talking, the more she was aware of her own strange unsettled reaction. *Of course they like him*, she told herself, annoyed by the flicker of gnawing in her stomach. *What's wrong with that?*

Turning away, she searched the crowd for Silas. He caught her eye, and she smiled as he came ambling across the barn to her. The sparkle of fondness in his blue eyes made her feel shy all of a sudden. "Rose Ann . . . I'm glad you're here," he said, coming to stand next to her.

"Nice to see you again, Silas."

He gave her a warm smile and leaned near. "Would you like to go ridin' with me?"

"That'd be just fine."

As she turned to leave with Silas, Rose noticed Nick still standing in the corner. His hands were stuffed into his pockets now as Mary and Sarah continued their ceaseless giggling and gabbing.

Silas assisted Rose into his open buggy, making sure she was settled in the seat before he unfolded the woolen lap robe and placed it carefully over her, then over himself. "Might be too nippy for a long ride tonight." He reached for the reins.

The bone-chilling cold was already seeping into her feet. "A *gut* thing it's not raining," she remarked.

"I have an umbershoot, just in case." He grinned pleasantly. "Are we ready?"

She nodded and smiled. They rode along without talking much for the first half mile or so, and she looked up at the stars, spotting the Milky Way right away.

Then Silas asked, "How is your Mamm doin' this week?"

"About the same." She thanked him for asking.

"I hope it's not a hardship when you're away from the house for an evening."

"Oh no. Between Mammi Sylvia and my father, Mamm's looked after right fine."

"Do they depend on you mostly, Rose, during the daytime hours?"

"For the past months, jah . . . Mammi Sylvia had to look after my grandfather."

She found it interesting that he seemed to be asking, in a roundabout way, if she would be sorely missed for caretaking if she were out on dates, or even married and out of the house. Being careful not to let him know she guessed at the intent behind his questions, she inquired after his mother and siblings in turn.

He spoke warmly of them, and she found herself wishing she might become better acquainted with his family. Every last one of them just seemed so pleasant. It was no wonder Rebekah Bontrager had talked so highly of the Goods—and Silas especially—back years ago. Momentarily Rose wondered what might have come of Rebekah and Silas's friendship, but thoughts of her former friend quickly faded when Silas turned his handsome face to her.

Soon he was talking about the amount of honey they'd gathered in, as well as the wood that was already chopped, stacked, and covered for the winter. She, too, enjoyed talking about the things of autumn, saying she'd taken a short walk the other day to pick up the little balls the buttonwood trees had already shed. "I took several back to show Mamm. She's always said Hen and I liked playing with them when we were young."

Silas was quick to ask about Hen. Rose wondered if perhaps she'd made a slip by talking about her Englischer sister. "Hen's got herself a job over at Rachel's Fabrics," she said. "Do you know where it is?"

He said he did. "My, my . . . isn't that interesting?"

"She came by the house on Monday afternoon—her first day of work there—and picked up two of her old Kapps."

"You don't mean it!"

"She's just started wearing them again, at least to work."

"So, there's hope she might . . . ?" His voice trailed off.

"Seems she wants to spend a little of her time amongst the People." She really had no idea of Hen's future plans. Only what her sister had shared in confidence about missing her Plain heritage.

Soon they were back to talking again of her favorite season— the coming brilliance of leaves and the hickory nuts that would scatter on the ground, crackling beneath their feet.

"Have ya ever noticed the way the maple leaves crisscross so heavily on the bishop's lane, like an orange sunshade?" she asked. When Silas said he had, Rose also remarked about the thick new growth of hair on the horses and mules.

"It'll end up in the birds' nests, come spring," he said, reaching for her hand.

Her heart did a little skip. She breathed in deeply, slowly . . . and enjoyed the fresh, crisp air as the stars created a sparkling canopy.

"I want to ask you something, Rose Ann."

"Oh?" she said, filling the precious gap between his comment and the next lovely question.

"Will you be my steady girl?"

She didn't have to think twice. "I'd be honored."

Silas raised her mittened hand to his lips and kissed it. What was it about her hand in his that made her heart sing?

They continued on their way—Silas asking if he might meet her at their usual spot, up from her father's house, next Saturday evening. She happily agreed and replayed the curious events of the evening over in her mind: Christian's cruel words, Nick's unexpected appearance at the Singing, and the way Mary and Sarah had flirted with him—as if he were the most eligible fellow there. *And now this.*

Rose looked fondly at Silas as they rode beneath the dazzling sky. *Despite everything, this is the happiest night of my life,* she decided then and there.

# CHAPTER 19

With some good help from Mammi Sylvia, Rose took great care, as she always did, with the weekly washing, though she found herself hurrying a bit on this nippy Monday morning. She and Mammi talked cheerfully about baking pumpkin pies and cookies, and of needing to make a big batch of applesauce soon. But while Rose agreed there was plenty of baking ahead, she was eager to get out the door. She had a plan up her sleeve, one she would not tell a soul. She intended to go and visit her sister-in-law Kate, who lived not far from the Browning house.

So when the damp clothes were securely pinned to the line, Rose found her father, who'd said at breakfast he had errands to run near Josh and Kate. Since Mammi Sylvia was spending the morning with Mamm, Rose was absolutely free to go.

"I'll gladly walk home," she offered. That way, once she headed to Gilbert Browning's, she wouldn't have to scurry back to Kate's again just to get a ride home later.

Ever so pleased with her little scheme, Rose climbed into the gray family buggy. She could hardly wait to tell Nick about it, though that would have to wait till later this afternoon. Maybe then he'd tell *her* about Mary's and Sarah's silliness at Singing last night, too.

Dat rode quietly for a time, as was his usual way. Eventually he brought up the fact that both his horse and the bishop's Pepper had gone missing last week. "I suspect you and Nick were out riding."

She caught a note of dismay in his voice and didn't know how to respond.

"If you're thinkin' of letting him court you, well . . . I hope you'll think twice about such a thing."

"Dat . . ."

He looked at her. "Nick's not for you, Rosie."

She felt too shocked and upset now to enjoy the landscape rolling by or the familiar sway of the carriage. Why on earth did her father think she might have an interest in Nick . . . and he in her? Surely it would ease Dat's mind if he knew of Silas's renewed interest. But she wasn't about to break with tradition to say so.

After a time, Rose was able to shake off her discomfort and wondered instead what she might find at the Browning house on a day when she was not expected to arrive.

As they rode along, she noticed a plump red-tailed hawk basking in the morning sun. She pointed it out to her father, who nodded his head, straw hat perched atop his graying light brown hair. There was a shy ruffed grouse preening behind a fence post, and a red fox skulked in the grassy ditch along the road. Rose tried to soak up the quiet, allowing the peace of the ride to soothe her.

"Sure has been nice to have Mammi stay with Mamm after breakfast," she said, making small talk, wanting to discuss something completely different.

Dat's lips broke into an approving smile. "Anytime you want to slip away with a nice Amish boy, she's willin' to take your place." He paused, then added, "Things can always be worked out for your mother's care." Was he telling her it was all right to think ahead to her own future? *Just not one with Nick.*

When they arrived at Kate's, Rose thanked her father and got out of the carriage. She stopped to wave, then walked around to the back door.

Inside, she gladly accepted Kate's hot chamomile tea and a delicious sticky bun. She played with their youngest, fifteen-month-old Annie Mae, named for Kate's older sister. The baby jabbered as Rose carried her around while Kate showed her several small quilting projects she had in the works—potholders and table runners.

"It's time to start cookin' up lots of pumpkin, too," Kate said.

Rose said she and Mammi had been talking about just that this morning. "I like to make pies and cookies well enough, but I also like savin' some pumpkins for outdoor decorations, ya know."

"Well now, next thing you'll be talkin' of carving a face on them." Kate frowned.

"No need worryin' about that." *I'm not worldly like Hen,* she thought, kissing Annie Mae's soft, chubby cheek.

Later, when Kate said she needed to put Annie down for a morning nap, Rose excused herself to visit a neighbor "up the way." And Kate, being a busy mother, wasn't any the wiser.

～

Hen wound her hair into a low bun at the back of her neck in preparation for work later that afternoon. She didn't take the time to twist the sides, as she'd always done growing up. She did scrub her face, however, deciding not to apply any makeup this morning, hoping Brandon wouldn't notice. Or, if he did, that he wouldn't mind. *Rachel will be pleased,* she thought of her cheerful employer.

Hurrying to the kitchen, she saw that Brandon was taking his time getting off to work and was glad for the chance to cook his favorite hot breakfast—scrambled eggs with cheese and bacon, and jelly toast. She caught herself; it reminded her of the scrambled egg sandwiches her father had always enjoyed back home.

Brandon looked up and did a double take when he saw her. " 'Morning, Hen." He stared at her.

His frown made her feel strange. "Uh, hope you don't mind."

"What . . . that you're trying to match Mattie's hairstyle?"

She hadn't thought of that. But here came sleepy-eyed Mattie, her hair still in its little knot from yesterday. Part of it was falling out, and for a moment Hen thought of Rose's sometimes-mussed-up hair.

Mattie walked over to her daddy and crawled into his lap. Without looking at Hen, he began to pull the bobby pins out of Mattie's hair, one after the other, as he whispered to her. Hen couldn't make out what he was saying.

She really wanted to share what was in her heart this morning—something she had been pondering since sending her apology letter to Arie. But the likelihood of Brandon's agreeing was slim to nothing. Regardless, she forged ahead. "I'm hoping to visit my former bishop, Aaron Petersheim, sometime. There are certain things I want to say to him," she said, going over to sit at the table in the breakfast nook. "I'd like you to come with me."

"Hen . . ." Brandon looked down at Mattie and kissed the top of her head, her hair completely loose and hanging down her back now. "Why would I want to do that?"

"Well, can't I hope, at least?" She sighed and glanced at the table.

"Have you thought about this?"

"Yes, I have. And you're welcome to come, if you're willing."

He shook his head and set Mattie down, sending her back to her room to get dressed. "I guess you'd like me to say, 'Hey, thanks, Hen.' Am I right?"

"I understand why you're not interested," she said quietly. "I assumed as much."

"I have nothing to say to any Amish bishop—or to your father, for that matter." Brandon rose and went to start the coffee maker. He placed his hands flat on the counter. Then, turning his head, he looked at her from across the kitchen. "Every day there's something new with you, Hen. Where will this end?"

"Not 'end,' Brandon. It's actually a new beginning."

"Well, not for me." He raked his hand through his thick hair. "And it certainly isn't for Mattie, either."

She stiffened, apprehensive about his serious tone. Mattie Sue was her whole life, her everything. Well, so was Brandon. . . .

"I'd like to make an Amish dress and cape apron . . . for myself," she said. "Will that annoy you, too?"

He moaned and covered his face with his hands, then left the kitchen.

Feeling duly rejected, Hen wished she knew how to make this work for her and Mattie Sue while keeping Brandon happy, too. But how? It seemed absolutely impossible.

Actually, if she were honest with herself, dressing Plain—even working at Rachel's Fabrics—was only a fraction of what Hen wanted. She longed for everything she'd grown up with—time spent with family, openly living out her faith, and adherence to a lifestyle that promoted discipline and thoughtful child rearing.

She walked back to the bedroom, wanting to let Brandon know she did not intend to annoy him further. If the Amish attire bothered him, she would simply wear it to work. But she would not make the mistake of asking his permission anymore. She'd already blown it with that—taking the new job against his wishes.

He was brushing his teeth when she found him. Standing by the door to the bathroom, she figured he must view her as completely selfish, yet she didn't know how to go about changing that. She wanted him to take her into his arms and say he loved her even if she wanted to incorporate a few of the simple, peaceful ways of her childhood into her present life. That it was all right with him if she couldn't pull off being a modern woman, after all. She was still his devoted wife.

Straightening, Brandon wiped his face with a towel and started when he saw her there. "Good grief, Hen."

"Sorry." She touched his arm. "This is just so complicated."

He stared blankly at her. "Not for Mattie and me. We're fine."

"What do you mean?"

"Why don't you go back to your Amish foolishness . . . if you must. I'll keep Mattie here with me."

"Brandon . . . what on earth?" Her heart was throbbing.

"Isn't that what you're working toward?" He frowned hard. "A separation?"

"That's what you think?"

"Well, isn't it?"

"Honestly . . . no, Brandon."

"So, how's this supposed to work, then? Can you explain, because I'm clueless."

"That's just it . . . I don't know. I wish I could snap my fingers and be totally on board with your English life. But the older Mattie gets, the more I feel it's not possible."

Brandon walked to the window across the room, near the oak chest her father had made for her. Her hope chest. "Then I don't see any other way but for us to split up." He turned, his face pale. "Do you?"

"I love you." She swallowed, trying not to cry. "But I'm torn apart . . . and I don't know what to do about it."

He went to her, and she met him partway. "I didn't force you away from your Plain life, did I?" His arms were around her now. "You made that choice, Hen . . . as I recall."

"Yes," she managed to say. She'd wanted *him* more than her strict background. *Back then.*

He held her near, kissing her face. "I don't believe in that whole locked-in-time business—you know that. I'm fine with the real world. The world you chose when you married me."

"I really thought what I'm feeling might pass. . . ."

Hen heard Mattie Sue giggle while playing school with her dolls out in the hallway.

"But after our daughter was born," Hen whispered, her lips trembling, "everything started to change for me."

Brandon studied her, his eyes agonized. "What will you say to the bishop?" There was a catch in his voice.

"Offer to make amends . . . somehow."

"For your sin—for marrying me?" His eyes searched hers.

"We're unequally yoked," she murmured. "Bishop Petersheim told me that very thing once . . . with fire in his eyes."

"*You'll lose your innocence forever,*" the bishop had warned her. "*You'll never be able to come back . . . not as you are now.*"

Hotheaded and rebellious, Hen knew she'd lost everything important to the People. But with those losses had come the love of a man like Brandon . . . and their beautiful daughter, Mattie Sue.

Brandon pulled her into his embrace now. Then, after a moment, he clasped her wrist and inched back toward the bed, guiding her gently along. "Hard as this is to say, I think you should go back to your people for a while."

"What?" She struggled against her tears.

"Just listen." He ran his hands up and down her arms. "I see how miserable you are." He kissed her right hand and held it against his lips. "Why don't you go back to your father's home, Hen, and find out what you really want."

"Brandon . . . no." She blinked her eyes, fighting back tears.

"I'll take care of Mattie, and you can come visit her as often as you like."

Something rose up in her and she stepped back. "I could never

173

leave her," she declared. Then she suddenly realized what she'd just said. And what it implied.

His face looked as if she'd struck him. "And I will never let you take Mattie away from me."

"But it's for the best, Brandon. She knows nothing of the Lord and His ways." She sighed. "You know it's true."

His eyes grew dark and stern. "You'd rip Mattie away from me for something I don't believe in?" He got up and went into the closet, yanking a tie off the rack. "I'm serious, Hen . . . I was trying to meet you halfway, but you're making it hard." He finished looping his tie, then tightened it beneath his dress-shirt collar.

"Surely we can compromise."

*"You're compromising everything you've been taught,"* the bishop had said. *"Throwing away your very soul . . ."*

Brandon squinted his eyes. "Well, you tell me how to find some middle ground."

She thought of her new job. "What about my working at Rachel's Fabrics?" She paused for a moment. "It *would* help to have your blessing on that."

He stared at her. "You want me to sign off on your working for an Amish establishment?"

"It's just a fabric shop," she said. "And we could take Mattie Sue to visit my parents and my brothers' families more than just once in a blue moon."

He grimaced. "How often?" He ran his hand over his chin.

"Every other weekend, maybe."

"No, Hen." He paused to shake his head. "I see no reason to forge a closer connection with your family. There's no place for someone like me in their world. You know that."

"Well, then, I'll take Mattie Sue to visit them. Why couldn't that work?" She was pleading now.

He brushed past her. "Look, Hen, this just isn't working out for you, is it?"

Tears stung her eyes. Brandon knew the truth, could see into her soul.

"Go back to where your heart is, hon."

"You *are* my heart," she whispered. "You, Brandon."

He went back into the closet to get his dress belt, not responding.

She looked out into the hall and saw Mattie Sue's little stuffed dog, with its brown patch over its eye, sitting there on the carpet, along with several other toys. "What about Mattie Sue? I can't leave my baby girl." She was sobbing now, unable to stop the flow of tears.

He stood stock-still, then moved quickly to close their bedroom door. He leaned against it, his jaw twitching. "How long, Hen? How long do you need to deal with this craziness?"

She didn't know, and that was the worst of it. The bishop had said she had no hope of salvation marrying an English man, embracing the modern life. Brushing back her tears, Hen knew she could no longer function as a secular woman and mother. Or be the sophisticated wife Brandon really wanted. *Worldly-wise in the bedroom, too . . .*

No longer could she speak. She was walking on fragile ground—this was their marriage she was tampering with. *To love and to cherish . . .*

"Look, I'm going to be late for work." Brandon went to her again. "Listen, I get it. You're unhappy."

"But not with you." She had to reassure him, even though what she said wasn't making a bit of sense. "I just wish you'd understand that part."

His eyes gazed deep into hers as he pulled her to him, crushing her to his chest. "I *do* understand, Hen. I believe I do," he mumbled into her hair.

Hearing this somehow lessened her pain. "We'll come and see you," she said. "And you can visit us, too."

He shook his head, saying in no uncertain terms that he would not chase after her. "You'll have to come here, Hen. *Here*."

He went to the door, placed his hand on the knob, and turned to look at her. He studied her face, as if memorizing it. "If you end up choosing your old life permanently, then I'm warning you, it will be a whole new ball game. I'm talking an attorney and a custody suit—the whole nine yards. Not to hurt you, but it's important you understand my position, too." He opened the door to leave.

"Are you threatening me?"

"I don't want you making choices that isolate Mattie from me. She's *my* daughter, too."

Brandon's words lingered in her mind. She was certain he would not hesitate to fight for Mattie Sue, if it came to that.

Hen hurried to the kitchen to pour some coffee for her husband, her hands trembling as it dawned on her that this might very well be the last time.

~

As Rose finally arrived at the old Browning house, she looked around the driveway. There was no sign of Mr. Browning's car. *Interesting*, she thought, wondering how long he might be gone.

Quickly, she walked to the front door and knocked. She thought she heard movement inside, in the kitchen, but when no one came, she knocked harder. She waited, then went to one of the windows and peered in, cupping her hands on the glass. But she did not see Mr. Browning or his chair positioned in the usual spot.

*Wonderful-gut*, she thought, realizing she'd come on the ideal day. "Yoo-hoo, anybody home?" she called, tapping now on the windowpane.

To her great surprise, she saw a young woman with blond hair cut like an Amish boy's. The girl, who was surely in her late teens, pushed her chair back from the table and got up, swaying slowly back and forth. Her azure blue eyes were wide, like she wasn't sure what to do.

"Hullo?" Rose called again, knocking more gently this time. "Can ya come to the door? I'm Mr. Browning's housekeeper."

But the girl shook her head repeatedly and rubbed her fists on her eyes, like a little child might.

"No need to cry," she said through the glass.

The tomboyish young woman stared back, shaking her head in odd, jerky motions.

"I won't hurt you," Rose told her.

The girl just stood there, motionless now, her big eyes blinking. And now Rose noticed a slight resemblance between the girl and Mr. Browning. Was this his daughter?

"It's all right, honest," Rose said softly, leaning her face closer to the glass.

The girl made a frightened sound, then scampered off. Rose was mystified at the way she stumbled so awkwardly from the kitchen to the stairs, reaching out to balance herself along the wall before grabbing for the banister. *Is she sick—dizzy, maybe?*

Rose went to the door again and tried the knob, but it was locked. Still baffled, she walked around the side of the house to the back door, thinking it might be open instead. It, too, was locked.

*So someone is living upstairs.* She inched away and headed out to the lane now, toward the road. When Rose was halfway down the short stretch between the house and the road, she turned back and saw the same girl at a dormer window on the third floor.

*Why the attic?*

She waved to the anxious girl and felt a wave of sadness, then great hesitation. "I'm goin' to help you, little bird . . . whatever's wrong," she whispered. "I promise."

To Rose's amazement, the girl raised her hand in a half wave and held it against the windowpane for a moment, then slid it slowly down, as if she yearned to be made free.

# CHAPTER 20

Following her impromptu visit to the Browning house, Rose walked along the road, unable to erase from her mind the frightened face of the girl in the kitchen. It was hard to think of anything else.

There were a few dried clusters of wild flowers in the roadside ditch, and she recalled the way the little bees nestled down in the rose petals last summer, hiding in all the curls and layers. Might the girl at Gilbert Browning's be hiding away of her own accord, as well?

The days were moving quickly away from the lengthy, busy days of summer. Wedding season was just a month off. She wondered if either of her two engaged first cousins—Lydiann and Esther—might ask her to be one of their attendants. She hoped both girls didn't pick the same Tuesday or Thursday to wed. She simply could not choose between them.

Feeling the sun on her face, Rose knew there were nearly three miles yet to go, if she followed the roads and didn't cut through cornfields. She was glad she'd worn shoes instead of going barefoot as she often did at home, till the first frost.

Walking briskly along the grassy slope near the road, she heard a crow *caw-caw*ing overhead. She looked up and promptly lost her balance, stumbling forward, and just that quickly, her leg buckled and she tried to catch herself, instead falling hard onto a rock with her right knee. A jagged pain shot through it as she cried out in pain.

She lay there in the ditch, not moving, gasping for air. Then, managing to collect herself enough to sit up, Rose slowly raised her skirt to inspect her leg. Her knee was all banged up, and an ugly bruise threatened. Her entire leg was throbbing now as she tried but failed to stand up.

Falling again, Rose wondered how she was ever going to get home. She began to crawl, dragging her leg, determined to get back onto the shoulder of the road. Maybe an Amish neighbor would see her and give her a ride. *Mammi Sylvia would know what to do,* she thought, wishing her loving grandmother were here right now. The stinging pain in her knee was relentless, and tears pricked her eyes.

Oh, but she wasn't a crybaby! She must be as brave as dear Mamm had been in the ravine, lying there conscious but unable even to pull herself out of the rugged area to get help. *Thank goodness for whoever found her,* she thought now, praying that someone might also happen along for her soon.

Overhead, large clouds were building in the distance, and lightning flickered. She could only hope, selfishly, for a heavy downpour. Then the men filling silo might halt their work and head home for a while, perhaps seeing her there on the road.

As the minutes slipped by and Rose inched forward, she was more determined than ever to keep moving, lest she still be creeping along by nightfall. Yet the searing pain in her knee took her breath away, and she had to sit to rest. She stretched out her legs and rubbed her swollen knee and the muscle below it. If she weren't in such pain, she would consider cutting through the fields to home. The distance was much shorter, only a little over a mile. But there was no way she could make her way through uneven cornfields like this.

Then, as if in answer to prayer, she saw a market wagon rumbling down the road toward her. The horse, of all things, looked like Pepper! Could it be Bishop Aaron or Christian?

She moved farther into the road, so the driver might see her and stop. She was a bit surprised to see Nick perched atop the wagon, holding the reins.

Immediately steering the horse off to the side of the road, he stopped and jumped down. He ran quickly to her and knelt beside her on the ground. "Rosie . . . what happened?"

"I fell," she said, starting to cry. "Ach, silly me."

He didn't ask what she was doing so far from home on foot. He simply scooped her up into his strong arms and carried her to the wagon. She wrapped her arms around his neck, feeling terribly self-conscious this close to her friend.

Nick set her down gently on the wooden seat. "You want to stretch out in the back instead?" he asked, standing over her anxiously.

"No, I'll make a spectacle of myself." She could just picture people staring and wondering if she was half dead.

He dashed around to the driver's seat. "I'm headin' to Quarryville to pick up some tools for the bishop. I could drop you by the Amish doctor's." He glanced at her before reaching for the reins. "Or do ya want to go right home?"

"Might be best to take me to Old Eli's, jah," Rose managed to say, feeling dizzy. The Amish doctor would know if she needed more help than he could give.

Nick signaled Pepper to move forward. After they were on the road for a short time, he looked at her every so often as though he wasn't sure she was going to be all right ever again.

Nick was fairly quiet on the ride to Quarryville, but at one point he asked what Rose had been doing clear down there, near Jackson's Sawmill Covered Bridge. Clasping her knee, she explained that she'd gone to spy on Gilbert Browning's house. "I actually saw the girl—the one you and I saw in the second-story window Wednesday night."

"A girl, you say?"

"A teenager, I'd guess. She was down in the kitchen." Rose told him how she'd called through the window repeatedly. "I wanted so badly to talk to her."

Nick looked surprised. "Did ya?"

"Oh no. She was scared of me and ran right out of the room and up the stairs." She paused to catch her breath and felt a surge of renewed pain. " 'Tween you and me, I think she might be slow in her mind."

"Like Samuel's Abe?" he asked, referring to the deacon's special grandson.

"Come to think of it, very much like Abe." Rose remembered taking care of Abe recently while looking after Mamm, too. She'd seen Nick seek out young Abe, as well, after Preaching services during the common meals, or when the boys played cornerball and other outdoor games after corn-husking bees and whatnot. Abe always looked comfortable talking to Nick.

"There's just somethin' about Abe," said Nick. "He loves horses, 'specially Pepper."

"Jah, and he likes standin' right up close to your horse to pet him."

"Well, it ain't *my* horse."

"Might as well be."

Nick chuckled and raised his left hand like he was about to reach over and touch hers. Instead, he reached again for the reins.

"Bein' near the animals seems to help him." Nick began to talk about the Fresh Air Program, which allowed some disabled children to spend summers with a farm family. She'd heard about the program from folk involved with the seasonal foster care.

As they pulled into the driveway leading to the Amish doctor's place, the sky looked ready to open up in a deluge of rain. Rose felt the first few drops on her head as Eli Stoltzfus's house came into view. "Oh, just in time," she whispered, hoping to get some relief from the pain.

"You goin' to be all right?" Nick looked at her sympathetically.

She smiled faintly. She'd never seen him so caring, without a hint of his usual teasing.

He stopped the horse and jumped down to the hitching post, his ponytail jerking. Then he hurried around to lift her out of the wagon and carried her to the back door. There he stood with her in his arms, unable to ring the doorbell. He called through the screen door for someone to come and help.

"I feel so *dappich*—clumsy," she whispered, leaning her head on his shoulder.

"Just hold on to me. We'll get you better right quick."

A young woman came and opened the door. "Oh, dear girl, what happened to ya?"

Nick explained that she'd fallen along the roadside and followed the nurse inside. In the first available room, he lowered Rose onto the examining table, then awkwardly backed away, lingering only briefly to say he'd return for her within the hour.

"Denki, Nick . . . so much," Rose said. Then she leaned back into the fresh pillow the kindly woman tucked beneath her head.

~

Struggling to keep her emotions in check, Hen pulled the car out of the driveway. She knew better than to look too long at the pretty little house she'd always loved—*mine and Brandon's*. And she certainly hadn't known what to tell Mattie Sue as she loaded their suitcases and several large boxes filled with toiletries, mementos, and her Bible, too. Hen had already taken the liberty of packing all of Mattie's dolls, toys, books, and art supplies into the trunk. She'd also included the materials for the quilted wall hanging she was making, as well as Mattie's pillow and favorite comforter and matching sheet set. In short, she'd packed everything she thought her daughter would miss . . . as well as the things Hen most cared about, including Brandon's and her small wedding album. She did not take any family pictures off the wall, nor remove the large framed wedding picture from the dresser. Those would have been too obvious to Brandon.

Not wanting to confuse or upset Mattie Sue, she'd simply said they were going to see the barn kitties today. "We'll visit Grandpa and Grandma for a while."

Mattie seemed perfectly content in the backseat with her doll and perked up when Hen mentioned the kittens. Caught up in her own little make-believe world, perhaps Mattie Sue had been spared the earlier heartbreaking conversation between Brandon and herself.

Hen was also grateful Brandon had stayed around longer than she'd expected. He'd lingered over his second cup of coffee after breadfast. In fact, her husband had been downright pleasant at the table, interacting with Mattie Sue more than usual. For an instant, Hen had wished they might somehow frame the happy moment for always.

*How will he manage his meals?* she'd thought as she cleared the table while Mattie went to her room to play.

When he was done eating, Brandon hadn't rushed off to work as was typical but had taken time to kiss her and say he loved her. *"Don't be away too long, Hen,"* he'd said amiably, although his expression looked tense.

His words had echoed in her thoughts as she'd made quick work of organizing a week's worth of underwear and pajamas for both her and Mattie Sue. She'd left nearly all of their English clothing, planning to sew Amish attire for both of them as soon as she was settled at her parents' home again. Besides, she didn't know if she could bear spending more time than necessary in her and Brandon's lovely bedroom, reliving their happier days as she went from dresser drawer to closet to suitcase.

By the time she turned into her father's lane, Hen felt almost too limp and emotionally spent to walk. The future seemed at once joyful and heartrending. Glancing at the house, she saw the orderly lineup of wash hanging out to dry. She wondered if she should talk first to her dad about staying so as not to upset her mother. After all, he'd said last visit they were *"always welcome,"* but he surely didn't mean on a long-term basis.

Getting out of the car, Hen looked across the meadow toward the bishop's big spread of land and his beautiful farmhouse. What would the man of God say about Brandon's encouraging this trial separation? Hen cringed at the thought. She felt as ferhoodled as ever she'd been, wanting what she missed about the Amish community, yet already sorely missing her husband. How was Brandon doing right now? Could he pull off this workday, knowing he would return tonight to an empty house?

How long would it take for her to yearn again for the English life—or would she ever? From now on, every moment, every single day must count toward Mattie Sue's training in obedience and selflessness.

Hen dismissed the idea of going directly to speak with the bishop, although she desperately wanted his wisdom as soon as possible. Once she had her parents' consent, she would go and confess her sins, then ask for his wise counsel and prayer.

A superstition she'd heard from Aunt Malinda came to mind as she walked with Mattie Sue across the backyard. *"To keep a child from being homesick, offer a drink of cold water immediately upon arriving at a new location."*

She guided Mattie to the well pump and gave her a drink from the dipper. Then they headed to the barn to see the promised kitties. She collected her thoughts in the midst of the musty-smelling barn as her daughter made over the little mouse-catchers. Hen had asked her father to remember her in his prayers the last time they had visited. But never had she guessed she'd be right back here on his doorstep, asking if she and Mattie Sue could stay.

*A lot can change in five years,* she thought, looking affectionately at Mattie Sue, the precious result of her and Brandon's love. *I'm doing this so you can know the God of your forefathers, my dearest girl. . . .*

"Mommy?" Mattie Sue looked up at her. She held a tiny gray kitten in her hands.

"Yes, honey."

"Why doesn't Grandma Emma let kitties in her house?"

"Well, because they're happier out here with their brothers and sisters." *All twenty of them.*

"Do you think Grandma would let me take *this* one inside—just once?"

Hen knew all too well that her parents were sticklers about keeping cats outdoors. "Your grandmother isn't well, sweetie . . . so let's not worry her with your favorite kitty."

"But, Mommy—"

She shook her head. "Remember, it's important to obey," she told her. "It's not pleasing to God to whine and carry on, hoping you'll get your way."

Mattie's big eyes blinked slowly.

"When I was a little girl your age, my father or mother told me something once and that was the end of it."

"Did you ever get spankings?" Mattie Sue asked.

"Not after the first few, no." Hen sighed, remembering. "Aunt Rosie and I were expected to mind right away. We didn't argue with our parents."

"Why'd you get spankings, then?"

186

She smiled. "I needed to know what it felt like to be punished . . . for what I did wrong."

"Oh." Mattie's eyes were sad.

"My dad—your grandpa Solomon—believes that our heavenly Father wants us to obey Him. It is always best."

"Why?"

"Because it makes God glad."

Mattie Sue thought about that. "Daddy never spanks me."

"No . . ." She wished Mattie Sue were younger. Already, Hen had her work cut out for her. "When we love God, we want to obey Him . . . always." The words sounded right, but her life with Brandon was the poorest example of this. Hen was a terrible role model for her daughter. Yes, she had much to make up for, and not only her daughter's shoddy rearing.

Sighing, Hen bent down for the gray kitten's older brother, a larger black cat, and picked him up, stroking his neck. "Let's leave the kitties out here to play while we go in and see Grandma Emma."

"Okay, Mommy." Mattie Sue set the kitten down, took Hen's hand, and walked toward the sliding barn door without a single fuss.

*I'll talk to Dad in a little while,* she thought, feeling terribly chagrined.

# CHAPTER 21

The *Brauchdokder* massaged Rose's leg in downward strokes from the bruised area, gently at first, then stronger each time he repeated the movement. Rose cried out with pain as Eli's massage became deeper . . . nearly unbearable. Afterward, he placed first a cold pack on the elevated knee, and then a hot compress, alternating back and forth for nearly an hour before wrapping her knee in a soft bandage.

By the time Nick returned, Rose was able to gingerly hold her weight on the injured leg without severe pain. She'd almost forgotten how useful therapeutic massage could be to a strained and bruised muscle. *Mammi Sylvia would've remembered,* she thought as Nick offered to pay the old-timer for his services.

The gray-haired Amish doctor looked at Rose with watery blue-gray eyes. "This is Sol Kauffman's daughter, ain't?"

Nick said she was as Rose nodded.

"Well, then, you owe me not a dime," the doctor said with a toothless smile.

"Denki, so kind of you," Rose said softly.

"Can she use her bad leg?" Nick asked, coming over to offer his arm.

"Prob'ly not just yet." The doctor had urged her to keep her leg elevated and stay off it for twenty-four hours, using cold and hot compresses. "Why don't ya just pick her up and carry her. . . . like ya did before?" The old man grinned.

Rose felt embarrassed when Nick didn't hesitate and leaned down and lifted her right up into his arms. She smiled all the way out to the market wagon, where she could see that the rain had already come and gone. She didn't mind that the wagon seat would be wet—at least she wouldn't have to walk home.

"Better not get used to this," Nick teased, laughing.

"Don't ya worry!"

When they got to the wagon, he set her down carefully.

"Denki for rescuing me . . . comin' along when ya did."

"I go that way a lot. Besides, I had a feelin' you were in trouble."

Rose didn't ask what he meant. Today Nick was oddly different— so unlike himself. She guessed he was merely worried. What else could it be?

~

At the stoplight in downtown Quarryville, Rose noticed a handful of tourists strolling across the walkway in front of the wagon. Suddenly one of the young men focused his attention on her, his camera pointing. "Ach, no!" She turned her face as she'd always been taught to do.

Nick called to him. "You there—keep on walkin'!"

But the fellow ignored him and came closer to Rose. In fact, he walked right up to the wagon, repeatedly snapping pictures. "Never been this close to real Amish before," he said. "My friends back home won't believe it!"

Nick stood and leaned over the side of the wagon. "I said to keep walkin', ya hear?"

The light turned green, and except for the one with the camera, the tourists scampered across the street. As Nick signaled for the horse to move forward, the man ran around to the back of the wagon. With a gleeful look in his eyes, he grabbed hold of the side and leaped in.

"Better hang on," Nick hollered. "There's a steep hill comin' up."

"Take me to your leader," the tourist said, laughing. "The bishop, right?"

"Nick . . . let him out," Rose pleaded.

"I'll show him!"

"No, Nick. Please!" She glanced back to see the young man sitting in the wagon box, hanging on to the sides. "Turn the other cheek, Nick . . . like we've been taught."

But Nick urged the horse to a gallop.

"Whoa . . . okay, okay!" the tourist called.

Rose could stand it no longer. She called for the horse to halt, but with Nick's hands at the reins, Pepper just kept charging forward.

"Let the man get out, Nick. I beg you!"

Finally, when Rose was certain Nick was too stubborn to budge, he halted the horse a good half mile away from the intersection. Without saying a word, he hopped down from the wagon and ran around to confront the tourist. "Hand over the camera," he demanded as the man climbed out of the wagon. " 'Make not a graven image,' the Good Book says."

The man stared at him, openmouthed, not comprehending whatsoever.

Rose turned away, unable to watch. But she heard the camera hit the pavement, followed by what was probably Nick's boot smashing it. "There, that'll teach ya," he said harshly.

"Hey! You stupid—" A string of curses followed.

Rose spun around, embarrassed, as she watched the tourist flail his arms and shout at Nick.

"You little creep—you owe me a new one!"

Nick stepped closer, as if daring the man. But the tourist stumbled back up the road. "I thought you Amish were pacifists," he yelled over his shoulder.

"C'mon, Nick—let's get goin'!" she called, hoping he might get back into the wagon and they'd be on their way. The altercation had made her head throb even more than her wounded knee.

Then, lo and behold, she saw Silas Good's father, Reuben, getting out of his parked buggy behind them. He spoke sternly to Nick. "I want a word with ya, young man!"

Nick quickly pushed his ponytail under his straw hat.

Reuben Good stood near his horse, waiting for Nick to walk to him. "The bishop won't be taking too kindly to any of this."

"Well, he ain't here, now, is he?" Nick said.

Rose held her breath, stunned he'd talk up so to Reuben.

"I'll remind ya to respect your elders," Reuben said. "And to remember to do unto others as you'd have them do to you."

Even though he'd just demonstrated his rebellious side for all the world to see, Rose felt horrible for Nick. In a way, he'd only done what he had to protect her, however misguided his actions.

Just then Reuben raised his eyes and spotted her sitting there in the wagon.

*Ach, no!* Now Rose wished for sure she'd chosen to lie down in the back of the wagon instead of perch high in the seat. *Would've been far better to look half dead this minute!*

~

It was all Hen could do to carry on a merely casual conversation with her grandmother and mother while Mattie Sue played with blocks in the corner of the kitchen.

Mammi Sylvia didn't come right out and ask what had brought Hen here today, but her puzzled expression indicated she sensed something was up. She talked of the approaching work frolic this Saturday, when even a few of the men were planning to help make many quarts of applesauce. "Aunt Malinda's coming," Mammi said. "She'll be so happy to see ya . . . if you happen to stop by."

Mom didn't say much, and Hen heard her groan several times. She wished something could be done for the pain. But even the specialists her mother had seen following the accident had been at a loss for ideas when medications turned out to have too many unwanted side effects. *Poor, dear Mom . . .*

Mammi Sylvia showed Hen the pretty red and navy blue quilted potholder and a cross-stitch sampler her mother was working on, "just since you were here last."

Mattie Sue looked up from stacking blocks and came running over to see, as well. Hen tested the waters. "Look, honey, you can learn to do this, too," she said, glancing at her daughter's little hair bun and Kapp. So far, neither Mammi Sylvia nor Mom had remarked about Mattie Sue's Amish attire, nor Hen's own upswept hair.

*It must pain them to see me like this, knowing I'm not really Plain,* she thought. *Might be confusing, too.*

Hen told Mattie Sue about the starter patch she had begun when she was only six. "How would you like to learn to quilt like Grandma Emma someday?"

Mattie Sue grinned and nodded her head. "Maybe I could put a kitty on it."

Hen looked at her mother. "Can you tell she has kittens on the brain?"

"Well, there are worse things," Mammi Sylvia said, smiling.

Mattie's eyes brightened, and Hen could tell she was on the verge of asking if she might bring one of the barn kittens into the house.

Hen made eye contact and shook her head quickly. Surprisingly, Mattie Sue dropped the idea and returned to her building blocks. Meanwhile, Mom mentioned offhand that she'd kept some of Hen's dresses. "And your old aprons, too . . . if ever you'd like to have them."

Would she ever! She might have to pin the waist a bit looser, but if all went well, she could simply wear those, as well as use them to make a pattern for sewing more. "That's good to know," she said, trying not to let her excitement show.

Mom glanced her way, tears springing up in her eyes. "I saved them, as well as your woolen shawl and your best black leather shoes. Still have many of your hope chest items, too."

"How thoughtful of you." Hen went to her and kissed her cheek. "I'm really grateful."

Mammi Sylvia looked like she might drop her false teeth. And right about that time, Dawdi Jeremiah wandered over from next door, asking when the noon meal would be served. "Same time as always," Mammi Sylvia informed him comically. She glanced at Mom, and the two women exchanged knowing smiles.

Her grandfather pulled up a chair and sat next to Hen. "Fancy seein' you here again . . . and lookin' mighty nice, too."

*Mighty Plain, he means.*

Dawdi clapped his hands for Mattie Sue to come and sit on his lap. "*Both* of yous look real *gut*, I'll say," he added.

Hen hoped Mattie wouldn't blurt out that they'd piled their belongings in the car. Not before Hen could talk to her father. Mattie crawled onto Dawdi's lap, content to play with her great-grandfather's suspenders and to tickle his long beard. Hen was embarrassed when Mattie Sue asked if she could wear his hat.

"Why, sure . . . if I can find it," he said.

"Now, Jeremiah, she oughtn't be wearin' your hat," Mammi Sylvia piped up.

"Ah, don't be so superstitious!" he snapped.

"Why, Great-Grandpa?" asked Mattie Sue.

"Downright silly, 'tis," Mom said. "That's what."

Hen smiled as a great sense of belonging filled her. She remembered where she was the very first time she'd heard the saying that putting on a man's hat meant you wanted a kiss from its owner. She had been very careful which young man's hat she'd picked at one particular barn party, years ago.

"I'll show ya what it means, little girlie," said Dawdi, who planted a kiss on Mattie Sue's cheek.

Mattie's eyes widened. Then she asked, "Can I have a butterfly kiss, too?" She giggled in Dawdi's arms.

"Well, hold still now." Dawdi leaned his face close to Mattie's and fluttered his eyelash against her cheek.

"Do it again!" came the childish plea.

Mom offered a sweet smile through pained eyes, and Hen leaned back in her chair, absorbing the serenity of the house. *Ah, peace at last*, she thought, wishing there was a way to share with her husband how truly wonderful she felt here.

# CHAPTER 22

*R*ose sat beside Nick in the market wagon, relieved the morning's events were past. As they rode, she pondered what Nick had meant earlier by saying he'd had a feeling she was in trouble. There had been one other such time he had shown up and helped her out when she didn't see how he could've known. *Like certain twins*, she thought.

Shrugging off the peculiar notion, she asked if he might be able to go over to fix the railing and paint the front porch at the Browning house soon. "It's an eyesore."

"Once we're done fillin' silo, I can," he said.

"*Gut*, I'd appreciate it."

He smiled. "If you think it needs doin', then I'll see to it."

"Aren't you cooperative today?" she teased.

"Aren't I always?"

She had to laugh. "Not with that poor tourist you weren't."

"But didn't you see what he was doin'?" Nick was suddenly red-faced. "He wouldn't stop taking your picture. He deserved to lose his camera."

It was impossible not to think of Reuben Good just then. "Well, I don't think the tourist thought it was necessary."

"What do I care?" Nick shot back.

"And Reuben . . . wasn't he a bit startled?" She looked at Nick, whose countenance changed before her eyes.

"Let Silas's father think what he wants." He hissed Silas's name.

She stared at him, completely astonished.

"What're you lookin' at?" he muttered.

"Just forget it." And all the way home, Rose wondered how soon before she would hear, through the grapevine, about Nick's misdeed in Quarryville today.

*Even though he did it on account of me . . .*

Rose could kick herself for not watching where she was walking earlier—and falling like that! And she fumed at Nick's reaction to the scolding from Silas's father. Any other God-fearing Amishman would have said the same.

When they made the turn into Dat's driveway, she saw Hen's car parked near the back sidewalk, and something sank in her. She must've groaned inadvertently, because Nick asked if she was all right.

"Hen's here again." *This can't be good!*

"She must miss you."

Rose held her peace, not wanting to reveal her concern.

Nick was just as careful helping her out of the wagon as before, but this time she didn't wrap her arms around his neck, fearing she might give someone the wrong idea. *Especially if Hen's watching . . .*

As Nick carried her past the car, she could see inside the front seat to her sister's overnight bag. It was the same one Hen had packed with forbidden cosmetics before she'd run off and married Brandon. Was Hen coming home to stay?

She stiffened as Nick made his way to the back porch.

"What's wrong?" he asked.

Rose shook her head, not saying. Besides, Nick didn't need to know what she thought of Hen's being unequally yoked to an outsider. After all, Nick might actually find it comical, considering *they* were such good friends . . . and Nick wasn't a church member, either.

Hen heard the market wagon come rattling into the driveway, and Mattie Sue ran to the window. "Oh look, it's Auntie Rose!"

Mammi Sylvia stretched her neck to peer out. "That's odd. We thought she was comin' home on foot."

"Nick's there, too," said Mattie Sue, dashing to the back door to greet them.

"Ach, that boy." Mom shook her head. "You would think he wished *we'd* taken him in back when, 'stead of the bishop."

Mammi clucked and returned to her hand sewing. "Now, Emma."

"Well, isn't he round here more than my own sons?"

Hen stretched; she'd been feeling so mellow she might've fallen asleep right there. But she got up and went out to see Rose Ann, stopping at the screened-in porch. Mattie held the back door open for Nick, who was carrying Rose up the sidewalk, of all things. "What happened to you?" Hen exclaimed.

Rose's face pinked with embarrassment. "I fell and hurt my leg."

"Oh, you poor thing!" She followed Nick inside, where he set Rose Ann down slowly on the wooden bench next to the kitchen table.

Mattie Sue hovered near and reached to touch Rose's hand. "You gonna be all right, Auntie?" she asked worriedly.

"She took a bad tumble," Nick said, squatting down to Mattie Sue's eye level. "Hit her knee on a rock alongside the road."

He looked altogether concerned while Rose explained how she'd fallen into the ditch.

"*Simbel mir*—silly me," Rose said. "I was watchin' a bird, 'stead of looking where I was walking."

But it wasn't what her sister was saying that made Hen's inner antenna shoot straight up. Nick's expression was downright tender toward Rose as he lingered protectively, like he was her beau.

Hen shook off the inkling. Was she just imagining this?

Whatever the reason, something swelled within her, and she believed her return home was somehow meant to have a twofold purpose. Without delay, it was time to have a heart-to-heart talk with her sister.

The minute Rose saw Hen, she knew something was really wrong. Just the way her voice sounded all pinched up when she asked what had happened that Rose couldn't walk—her pretty face much too pale, too—Rose knew. *Has my sister pushed her husband to the brink?*

She didn't know why she mentally took Brandon's side on whatever had brought Hen here to visit again. Based on what Hen had shared with her last week, Rose had the terrible feeling that it was probably her sister's fault.

Now Hen was eyeing Nick, plainly displeased he was in the house, let alone helping Rose down onto the kitchen bench, then hovering near.

Hen quickly left the kitchen, taking Mattie Sue to the stable to see the twin foals. Her older brother Josh was there and promised to watch over Mattie while Hen went to talk to their father. When she opened the door of the woodshop, the air was thick with sawdust. She coughed upon entering, unable to stop.

Her father looked up. "Hen . . . for goodness' sake! I didn't expect to see you again this soon!" He stopped what he was doing and motioned her outside. "Can't have ya breathin' that dust into your lungs." He followed her, still wearing his protective mask.

"Do you have a minute?" she asked, walking with him toward the woodshed.

"For you? Plenty of time." His eyes were so bright and welcoming, it was hard not to recall the contrast in his countenance during the days before she had married Brandon. She'd seen great sadness there then, the reflection of her own betrayal.

They stepped inside the woodshed for a bit of shelter—he must've sensed her need for privacy.

"It's hard to know where to start," she said.

His eyes were serious. "What's goin' on, Hen?"

For Mattie's sake, she'd kept things all bottled up. And now as she opened her mouth to speak, she began to weep instead. "Oh, Dad . . ." She cried on his shoulder, wishing she'd never hurt him and Mom. Wishing she could help them understand, somehow, how bad she now felt about breaking their hearts. "I'm really sorry for everything. . . ."

Awkwardly he slipped his arm around her—he didn't seem to know what to say.

Hen wept so hard, she was glad she hadn't worn mascara as she had for the past few years. She cried for all the days and nights she'd been away from her family and her rightful heritage. But most of all, she shed tears for her struggling marriage, even though the mess was her own doing. Brandon was not to be blamed for seducing her willing heart away from the confines of her former life. She'd eagerly let him do so.

She tried to wipe away her tears, and her dad shook out his old blue kerchief and handed it to her. "Careful, lest ya smear sawdust in your eyes," he said.

When she had pulled herself together, she told of her discussion with Brandon that morning. "He knows how miserable I am . . . urged me to come home for a while."

"I 'spect he thinks you'll return to him soon, jah?"

She shook her head. "I doubt that." It was the hardest thing she'd ever admitted.

"Well, I certainly hope you will!"

She blew her nose. "I don't see how things can ever work between us now."

"What on earth is so different?"

"The world's pressing in on Mattie Sue . . . and on me."

"So you can no longer submit to your husband's English ways. Is that it?"

Her eyes met his. "It's my fault . . . jah."

"You're not thinking of movin' back home, are ya, Hen?"

"I know it must sound ridiculous." She dabbed at her swollen eyes.

Her father sighed. "It ain't right to leave your husband be, daughter."

Looking away, she said, "He wants us to visit him at home, but he refuses to come here."

"Will ya do things his way . . . at least what you can?"

She listened and nodded.

"You must work hard to salvage your marriage, Hen. It's imperative under God."

How could she expect him to say differently? There was no point in telling him Brandon's warning about their daughter's custody. *Too much at once.*

"Would you mind if Mattie Sue and I stayed with you and Mom for a while?"

He glanced at the house. "Well, the two rooms upstairs are all we've got in the main house. There's the second Dawdi Haus, though. Would ya want to stay there?"

She struggled to speak. "It would mean . . . so much. Thanks!"

He touched her elbow and led her back toward the big porch.

"I'll have to speak with your mother and the bishop about all this, of course."

"I don't want to upset Mom." Then Hen added, "Sometime after you talk to the bishop, I'd like to speak with him—make a confession."

"Well, since you didn't join church, you were never shunned, ya know."

"I shunned my family, though. And the Lord, too." Each time she thought of her loving heavenly Father, Hen could hardly keep her tears in check. "I really want to offer my heartfelt apology to the bishop and his wife. And get his advice, as well."

Her father gave a faint smile as they made their way inside. "I'll let him know."

Glancing at the gloomy sky, Hen realized the enormous challenge that lay ahead of her . . . a married *worldly* woman living here with a child from a union with a man the People had strongly opposed.

# CHAPTER 23

Hen had never anticipated that Rose Ann would burst into tears when she saw Dad and Nick moving Hen's and Mattie Sue's things into the cottagelike Dawdi Haus. It was hard to know if Rose's injured leg was partly to blame for her sorrowful outburst, or if her sister was truly heartbroken at what Hen's moving in signified.

Hen had been almost relieved to have to step away for a few hours to go to work at Rachel's Fabrics. She could not bear to stick around as Rose wept in the kitchen, her leg propped up on a chair. Why was her sister being overly dramatic? After all, *her* marriage wasn't at stake!

Now that Hen had returned and was unpacking in the small two-story house, around the corner from the main house, Mattie Sue sat on the floor in the middle of an oval rag rug, jabbering to her. She was talking about seeing the foals with Nick, who had let her follow him around the barn for part of that afternoon. Hen was surprised at how quickly she'd warmed up to him.

"I can sleep with my dollies here at Grandpa Sol's house, right, Mommy?" Mattie asked, suddenly looking more thoughtful.

"Of course." Hen went over and kissed her, pulling her close. "Give me a sweet hug," she said, cherishing the warmth of her little girl.

*How long before she asks to see her daddy?* Hen worried later as she set about arranging Mattie Sue's clothing into the empty drawers of the dresser in the smaller bedroom. *And . . . how long before I run back into Brandon's arms?*

Swiftly she redirected her attention to making the already furnished house into a temporary home for them, realizing that she would have to become reaccustomed to the lack of electricity. More than a few times she'd already reached for the light switch, even though it was still light outside. And cooking like Mammi and Rose Ann did on a woodstove might prove to be tricky, although Hen guessed it was like anything else—the ability would return soon enough. *With a certain amount of practice.*

Hen heard a rapping at the back door and went down to see who was there. Nick, dressed in his usual black, offered to help carry anything more for her. She took the opportunity to thank him for keeping Mattie Sue company earlier, as well as hauling in their things.

"That's fine," he said, ducking his head. "And Mattie's no problem."

Mattie Sue grinned at him from her spot on the carpet.

Hen wanted to ask how he had come to be the one to bring Rose Ann back from the Amish doctor's, but she didn't need to pry. In all the years she'd known Nick, she must've said five words to him.

"They're askin' if you'll come over for supper," he said, looking at her, then shifting his eyes away.

"Sure, thanks."

He frowned then. "Not to poke my nose in," Nick muttered,

"but why'd ya come back to . . . ?" He shrugged and glanced over at the barn. "To all this?"

Nick was the last person to whom Hen owed an explanation. "It's complicated" was all she said.

"It wonders me, is all." He turned to leave.

*You're not the only one*, Hen thought, going back to resume her unpacking.

$\sim$

After Hen had helped her grandmother with the supper dishes, she assisted Rose Ann up the stairs and into bed. "You've been through the wringer today," she said, carefully placing a pillow under her sister's leg.

Rose disliked being made over and grumbled when Hen covered her with the small afghan from the foot of her bed. "No need to baby me, Hen." She said it with a forced smile.

Hen ignored her. "Did the doctor say how long he thought it would be before your knee is strong again?"

Tucking the afghan beneath her chin, Rose shivered a little. "Not sure what's wrong with me. My leg has a fever in it and I'm chilled all over." She struggled deeper under the blankets. "Old Eli says I'm s'posed to stay off my leg for a full twenty-four hours."

"Then you should feel better tomorrow." Hen went to the window and pulled down the shade. She didn't think now was a good time to bring up her suspicions about Nick.

"I might seem ungrateful, but I'm just put out with myself," Rose said. "Denki for helpin' me get up here." She looked like she might start crying again. "I'm awful glad you're here, just when I need a big sister."

"Oh, Rosie." Hen knelt beside the bed and patted her hand. "I'll do all I can to make you comfortable."

"Will ya look out for Mamm, too?"

"Whatever I can do, sure." She kissed her cheek. "Our mother's not your sole responsibility."

"It seems so . . . some days." Rose closed her eyes. She took several breaths and folded her hands on her chest. "Were you upset earlier . . . when Nick carried me into the house?"

Hen touched Rose's cheek. "It *was* a little unsettling."

"He was just helpin' out." Rose's lower lip quivered. "I don't know what would've happened if he hadn't found me on the road, to tell ya the truth."

"Nick seems fond of you."

Her sister frowned and blinked repeatedly. "We've always been *gut* friends. You know that."

"But boys who are just friends don't look at girls the way he looked at you."

Rose gave a wave of her hand. " 'Tween you and me, I'm seein' someone else," she confided.

"Ah . . . so you think of Nick as merely a friend?"

"Why, sure. He doesn't care for me the way my beau does. I doubt Nick even notices I'm a girl."

Hen managed to squelch her laughter. "Rosie . . . goodness, what you *don't* understand." Hen rose to her feet. "But you rest, okay? Dad and I'll keep Mom company."

Rose was still stewing when Hen stepped out of the room and closed the door. Bewildered, Hen shook her head, trying to remember back when she was Rosie's age. She stopped to peer out the window near the landing, looking across the cornfields ready to be harvested for silage. Nick and Christian were heading toward their house, walking on either side of the road. *Still at odds after all these years . . .*

Treading softly on the stairs, Hen headed down to check on Mom, as promised. *Who, besides Rose, has Nick ever gotten along with?* she wondered, finding her mother alone in the small spare room. "You all right?" she asked, poking her head in.

Mom motioned to her. "Your father's just talked to the bishop, and Aaron wants to leave it up to us to decide how long you should stay."

Hen listened, anxious to hear what Mom thought.

"Marriage is a sacred trust, dear one—not to be tampered with."

She agreed. "I don't take it lightly, believe me."

"Your father and I want you to work things out with your husband."

"I've done what I can," she said, suddenly feeling tired.

"Well, keep tryin' . . . till something gives."

She nodded, though she felt little hope.

"That's all God asks of us," Mom said, her eyes fluttering shut.

Truthfully, Hen didn't know how anything would change as long as Brandon was dead set against her "backward" family, or the Amish community in general.

Rose felt dull and lifeless, like she was trapped in a cocoon. Her knee pained her, but so did her heart, knowing her sister and Mattie Sue were going to be living back home. The realization only served to make her feel worse. Her lofty dreams of a happily-ever-after marriage for her sister were dashed as she rested in the very bed where Hen had first told her of the "special love" she and Brandon Orringer had found in each other.

*Why can't it last forever—till death?* Rose stared at the ceiling. *And why does Hen pine for her childhood home more than the one she's made with Brandon?*

Tears trickled down Rose's face and into her hair. She turned and closed her eyes, letting her emotions go.

"Hen knows better," she mumbled into her pillow. "How could she do this?"

～

The little Dawdi Haus was too quiet now. Hen sat in bed, gazing out at the night sky, feeling isolated in the lonely room and too weary to bother getting up to pull down the shades. *Mom wants them up at all times*, she thought, understanding the quirk for the very first time.

When she was with Brandon, she'd never paid attention to the city sounds. Either that or the buzz had never registered. Rolling over in the empty bed, Hen thought back to her first night as his bride. She didn't recall hearing the traffic and other noises of the modern world. Was she so blinded by love, too willing to give up the tranquility of the country for a handsome husband?

She yawned deeply and slipped her hand beneath the cool pillowcase . . . one Mom had undoubtedly embroidered. When she thought of her mother, Hen felt sad, as if she had neglected her while living with Brandon. Now that she was here, Hen intended to make up for that.

Her thoughts turned to poor Rose. She'd really banged up her knee . . . and Hen hadn't meant to be so pointed about Nick. After all, no girl wanted a big sister meddling in her life. *Suzy did just that to me*. She thought back to the things her too-blunt sister-in-law, Enos's wife, had said about *"evil Brandon."*

But nothing Suzy or anyone else said back then had made a whit of difference. If anything it made Hen run to Brandon faster. She truly believed the difference between herself and Rose Ann was that her sister seemed innocent of Nick's attention. Actually, come to think of it, Hen had no idea what Nick's intentions were, considering his lifelong lack of interest in the church. Because of what Hen knew now, it was the thing that worried her most.

Frustrated and tired, she got up and went to the stark window to look out. Brandon must be sorely perplexed with her. Did he miss her? Had he fallen asleep on the sofa tonight while watching TV? Or had he stumbled into bed—*their* bed—tired as a dog, only to be reminded that Hen wasn't there to soothe away the stress of his day?

"O Lord, I need your help," she prayed quietly, tears falling onto her nightgown. "I chose the path of disobedience." She sighed. "But now I want to walk in the way that will please you most—whatever that may be. Amen."

She tiptoed over to the small room next to hers, where Mattie Sue lay sleeping peacefully, her arm around Foofie. The stuffed dog had been a birthday present from Diane Perlis and her daughter, Karen. She remembered how Mattie had protested that a year was a "long, long time" to wait for her next birthday. And Hen had agreed with her, saying a full year seemed like an endless amount of time when you were young. Now she knew all too well how the months skidded past, rolling along like a market wagon on a sharp decline. *Good enough reason to return to the Amish and make things right.*

"But how to do right by Brandon?" she whispered.

Tears blurred her eyes as Hen sat quietly on Mattie's bed. She leaned forward and touched her daughter's thick braids. "My darling girl, how will you ever cope without your daddy?" she whispered into the air. "How will *I* manage without my husband?"

# CHAPTER 24

*E*ven though her night had been a short one, Hen awoke feeling better rested than she sometimes did at home with Brandon, always being on edge due to their escalating disagreements.

She stretched, relaxing in the comfortable bed as she recalled that Dawdi Jeremiah believed wholeheartedly that if a person would simply lie in bed for twenty minutes before rising, the day would go more smoothly.

So she rested awhile and prayed a blessing on the day. She also asked God to make His presence known to her husband. "In spite of how things are between us now. Amen."

Later, once she'd showered in the makeshift bathroom just off the small kitchen—like an indoor outhouse, of sorts—Hen dressed in her most conservative print skirt and a cream-colored long-sleeved blouse with a tan sweater vest. The glint of her engagement ring caught her eye as she buttoned the sleeve of her blouse. Even if she were to set aside the showy diamond ring in favor of just her simple wedding band, Hen would never be mistaken for Old Order

Amish while wearing such a ring, no matter how Plain the rest of her attire. *Some things can't be helped. . . .*

She went upstairs to wake Mattie Sue but found an empty, unmade bed, with Foofie sitting atop the pillow. "Mattie? Where'd you go?"

Making her way downstairs again, she saw the back door was ajar. She headed first to the main house, and seeing her grandmother already stirring up the pancake batter, she asked if she'd seen Mattie Sue.

"I heard her squealing. She's out with Sol feeding the young goats," Mammi said.

Hen went to the summer porch and looked out. Nick and Christian were already working in the bishop's former potato field to the west, plowing and disking. "How's Rosie feeling today?"

"Oh, much better. She's up and hobblin' around."

"Bless her heart." Hen was glad to hear it as she continued scanning the area outside for Mattie. Then she noticed her father and Mattie Sue playing with two of the barn kittens over near the corncrib. Hen burst out laughing, her heart warmed by what she saw. "Looks like someone's getting spoiled," she said.

"Can't hurt none," Mammi agreed and poured some coffee, which she brought to Hen. "You'll be wantin' this soon, jah?"

"Thanks—I mean, *Denki*," she said, realizing she ought to start speaking her first language more. Especially around Mattie Sue.

"How long will ya stay?" her grandmother asked, eyes too serious.

"I'm supposed to get this out of my system, according to my husband."

Mammi's eyebrows rose. *"This?"*

"My Amish heritage." She doubted Mammi would understand.

"How can ya expect to ever do that?"

Hen nodded. "That's just it."

Mammi shook her head in disgust. "Brandon wanted an Amish girl back when—stole you right out from under our noses."

"Please don't dislike him, Mammi."

"Well, it ain't that, really."

Hen followed her into the kitchen. "What is it, then?"

"What he stands for."

*Sin, the flesh, and the devil.* Hen knew already . . . she'd heard it preached repeatedly when they were dating.

"And now here you are, back again." Mammi tested the griddle with several drops of water from her fingers. They spit and sputtered on the heat, so she reached for her favorite wooden cup and dipped it into the batter.

"It's good of Dad to let us stay." She watched Mammi at the cookstove.

"You prob'ly guessed, but your mother's awful worried."

"Not surprising." *So am I.*

"And your father was over talking to the bishop again early this mornin'."

A shiver ran up her back. If only she could come clean with everyone she'd wronged or caused pain. Hen wanted to have the right attitude when she talked with the man of God . . . wanted to make it known how very sorry she was, without abandoning the marriage vows she'd made to Brandon.

Not only was it a knotty problem, but as her husband had already said, it seemed quite impossible.

By the time Hen helped Rose Ann get situated at the table, with her leg propped on the wooden bench, their father had arrived in the kitchen for breakfast. Almost immediately, he motioned for Hen to join him on the summer porch. "Bishop wants to meet with you this mornin'," he said, his face drawn. "He's goin' to sit you down with him and Barbara—the three of yous."

*Sit me down . . .*

"I'm willing," Hen said meekly.

His face turned even more somber. "He has some important things to say."

She cringed, wondering what would transpire. Then, scanning the breadth of the backyard, she asked, "Where's Mattie Sue right now?"

"She saw Nick out with the mules, so she ran over there a bit ago. That's the last I saw of her."

"Well, *Dad*—"

"Just leave her be. She needs to run free, to explore the place."

"But—"

"Ach, she's just fine."

Hen had struggled from the first hours of Mattie Sue's life with being overly protective. And now she couldn't seem to keep track of her. More than ever she needed to look after her daughter, because when it came down to it, Mattie Sue might be all she had left.

~

Solomon watched his oldest daughter walk out to the road after breakfast, heading next door. *How will the bishop's remarks affect Hen?*

He turned to go to his shop and realized in that moment just how much he secretly enjoyed having Hen home again with Mattie Sue. It had been years since either Hen or Rose Ann were little girls. They'd loved holding all the barn kittens just as Mattie Sue did. He and Emma were blessed to be able to regularly see their many Amish grandchildren, but having Mattie Sue around was mighty special.

Stepping into the shop, Sol went to the wooden hook and took down his old carpenter's apron and tied it around his waist. He filled it with his favorite tools—a carpenter pencil and a fold-up wooden ruler, a tape measure, hammer, a bag of nails, tin shears, square level, pliers, screwdriver, and his safety glasses.

"Hen's marriage must not fail," he whispered, recalling the bishop's adamant stance earlier. Aaron had urged Sol not to encourage Hen to leave Brandon permanently. In fact, he had advised Sol and Emma to reach out to their son-in-law in whatever way they could. *Keep the lines of communication open at all costs. . . .*

So, under God—and the bishop—he had a duty to see that Hen did all she could to mend whatever rift she was experiencing with her husband. He'd noticed that both Hen and Mattie Sue were dressing rather Plain. Were their clothes the problem, or was there more to it?

Sol thought again of Brandon. How could he best extend himself to the son-in-law he hardly knew? These past several years he'd tried repeatedly through Hen to invite Brandon out for various work frolics and such, but he was always too tied up with his own work. Sol felt downright awful that there hadn't been any communication between himself and Hen's husband since before the wedding. And now here the bishop was, nearly demanding he get Brandon's attention somehow or other.

Moving to his workbench, Solomon wracked his brain, trying to think how he and Emma might successfully invite Brandon Orringer to have a glimpse into their cloistered world. How, indeed?

∼

Not knowing what to expect from the bishop, Hen hurried to the Petersheims'. Admiring their sprawl of land from the sloping road, she had to smile at the remembrance of the many picnics she and the bishop's three daughters—Verna and twins Anna and Susannah—had often enjoyed out on the front lawn. They'd especially liked to spread out an old blanket and have cheese and lettuce sandwiches out there with their doll babies.

She wished she'd kept in touch with the bishop's girls, all married now, just as she regretted her lost friendship with Arie. It was hard not to wonder if Arie had even read the recent letter Hen had sent. Hen sometimes found herself hoping Arie might drop by the fabric store, although since Hen didn't work there consistently, it would be difficult for Arie to know when to go.

The day had started out rather calm, with only a hint of feathery clouds out to the west. But now there were occasional bursts of wind, and she wondered if another rainstorm might be blowing in like yesterday.

Barbara Petersheim met her at the back door and waved Hen inside. "*Willkumm*, dear girl!"

"It's wonderful to see you," said Hen as she followed the very round woman into her warm kitchen.

"Made some brownies . . . if you'd like." Barbara presented a platter.

"Oh, they look delicious, but I'd better not."

"Aw, for goodness' sakes! Just look at ya, though. You could stand to put on some pounds." Barbara stood there frowning as if Hen had done something terrible by turning down the treats.

"Well, I'm trying to eat fewer sweets."

"Are ya sure?" The bishop's wife had often been a force to be reckoned with. Not to be outwitted, she stood there holding the brownies in front of Hen. "Just half a piece?"

Hen had to smile, knowing she'd never get out of the generous woman's kitchen without at least picking up one of her brownies. "All right—but only a half." When she helped herself to the smallest one, intending to halve it, Barbara whisked the platter out of her reach.

"Go on, now . . . you'll see how *gut* the whole thing tastes."

There was no arguing with Barbara. As Hen walked to the long trestle table, she wondered if this was a preview of things to come with the bishop. Still, she refused to get all worked up in advance over whatever the man of God believed was good and right in her situation. Hen would be much more receptive to his spiritual remarks than to Barbara's pleas to eat her rich, sugar-filled brownies. *Even though she means well*, Hen thought, taking a seat at the table to wait for the bishop.

~

Rose used her grandfather's cane as a crutch and managed to hop out to the barn after breakfast, eager to see George, Alfalfa, Upsy-Daisy, and the foals. And Nick. She hoped he realized how grateful she was for coming along when he had yesterday.

Soon she found him sitting in some fresh hay, holding a tiny gray kitten, with Mattie Sue sitting nearby. "Well, look at the two of ya."

"We're just wasting time," Mattie said, grinning up at her. "That's what Nick said."

He whispered something to Mattie that sounded like Deitsch, and Rose couldn't help but smile. "Go ahead and have your little secrets."

"How's your knee?" Nick asked.

"Some better."

"You need a ride to work tomorrow?"

"Where do you work, Aunt Rosie?" Mattie Sue piped up.

"Over yonder, near the covered bridge," Rose replied. "You know where that is?"

"I sure do." Mattie smiled. "It's where my daddy met my mommy—during a big snowstorm, too." She was all excited suddenly. "Mommy could've died if Daddy hadn't come along *right then!*"

Nick looked at Rose and nodded, his eyes piercing hers. "Just like I did yesterday, ain't so, Rosie?"

"Oh, you!" She picked up a handful of straw and tossed it at him. Several pieces stuck to his hat and lay on his dark shoulders. "And to think I was goin' to say again how nice it was you rescued me."

He sported a rare smile. "And don't ya forget!"

She didn't say it, but she thought he seemed just a bit too pleased about having been the one to find her after she'd fallen.

"So, when do ya think you'll be able to go ridin' again?" He picked the pieces of straw off his shirt and flicked them at her.

Rose frowned at Nick and glanced at Mattie Sue, shaking her head as a warning. But he shrugged like he didn't think it was a problem for her young niece to overhear their plans. "We'll talk tomorrow, on the way to Mr. Browning's," she said, eager to return there. "I really want to meet the girl I saw through the window yesterday."

Nick nodded and held her gaze. "Some mystery, ain't?"

"What is?" Mattie asked, looking first at Rose, then at Nick.

Nick leaped to his feet and snatched the gray kitten out of Mattie's lap. Just that quick, he flashed a mischievous look and ran off with Mattie's favorite cat.

"I like Nick," said Mattie Sue, jumping up. "He's silly."

Rose watched her chase after him, filling the stable with giggles.

She tested her leg and raised her cane to walk without it. Relieved her leg was already much more stable, she really hoped by tomorrow evening it would be strong enough to go riding again with Nick.

~

Hen could hardly keep her tears in check. "My husband is anything but interested in the Amish church—or *any* church," she said, her voice quavering. "So I don't see how what you're saying can happen . . . even in the future."

The bishop's graying bangs rimmed his bushy eyebrows as he folded his hands and leaned forward on the table. "This is how things must be, Hannah." He'd always called her by her given name, ignoring the popular nickname. "If you want to join church someday, then Brandon must also be baptized with you. I will not allow you to become a voting member as a single woman . . . because you are quite *married*." He paused, his hazel eyes boring into her. "There can be no exceptions."

She absorbed his words. "My husband won't even darken the door of my parents' house, let alone a Preaching service." She shook with sadness.

"God works in mysterious ways at times, so we will trust Him for the outcome. And always remember, His mercy holds us up when we reach the end of our own strength." He pushed his chair back from the table, signaling the end of the discussion.

*God's mercy*, thought Hen, wishing for a greater sense of it even now.

Barbara added, "Meanwhile, dear, you just keep showerin' *dei Mann* with love."

"Invite your husband to come visit ya in the Dawdi Haus," the bishop said before leaving to return to the barn. "Don't give up."

Barbara advised Hen to talk to her mother about this, too. "See what she might suggest. Emma says very little, but when she does, it's often wise counsel."

Hen stared at the brownie before her—she'd yet to take a single bite. "I don't know what to do."

"The Good Lord will show ya ways to reach out to him, Hannah. Your father mentioned possibly invitin' Brandon for a meal with your mother and you and Mattie Sue." Barbara glanced toward the eastern window that faced the Kauffman house. "Might you write a dinner invitation to him, just maybe?"

"I can try."

"After all, the way to a man's heart can sometimes be his belly," Barbara said, apparently trying to lighten things up. She reached for her plate of brownies and rose, carrying them to the counter. "If it helps to know, I'll be prayin' for ya, Hen, dear."

"That's kind of you. Denki." Then, holding her hand over her trembling lips, Hen stood, grateful for Barbara's loving arms as she came to embrace her.

"That's all right . . . you'll feel better soon. You just go ahead and cry, honey-girl."

Hen's pent-up tears flowed freely now—she felt overwhelmingly sad because she knew Brandon would never budge. There was not a smidgen of hope for that. In some ironic way, she'd trapped herself in no-man's land, by choosing a way of life and love she could no longer reconcile herself to.

*The worldly English life smothers my spirit . . . and I'll never be able to join this one,* Hen thought, stumbling miserably up Salem Road.

# CHAPTER 25

Rose was surprised how much better her leg felt Wednesday morning. She was glad she'd gone to get help from Old Eli, though he was not a medical doctor. His therapeutic massages and herbal concoctions had gone a long way in helping her family through the years, as well as many others in the community. And Mamm, too.

She was ready and waiting when Nick arrived with the bishop's family buggy. Still using Dawdi's cane to steady herself, she shuffled out the back door and down the walkway. Nick hopped out and came over to walk close to her.

"I don't need to be carried *today*," she said, laughing.

He followed her around the buggy and stood there watching her struggle to get in. "So, ya think you're doin' fine on your own, then?" Now he was chuckling.

"Just be still." She smiled. "And give me a little boost on my *gut* foot," she added, anxious to be back to normal again. Once she was settled inside, she realized how very sore she still was.

"Are ya up to ridin' tonight?" he asked when they were out on the road.

"Not sure I can manage a horse well enough," she admitted. George could sometimes be rambunctious, although she loved the horse all the more for being so.

"Well, if it would help, we could ride Pepper together," he suggested. "I'd be careful hoisting you up."

"Let's see how my leg's doin' later. Maybe I'll be able to take George on my own."

He fell silent suddenly and turned his head away to look at the other side of the road.

"What's wrong?"

"Nothin'."

"You looked awful disappointed."

Nick nodded slowly. "Just tryin' to please the bishop." He sounded glum and sarcastic. "He's eggin' me on to spend time with ya."

"Whatever for?"

Nick shrugged his shoulders.

"You're makin' this up, ain't so?"

He looked surprisingly serious. "No, Rosie. I'm *not* kidding."

She pondered this while they rode in the buggy, beset with the idea their bishop would *want* his unbaptized boy spending time with her. "You can't mean he wants us to be more than friends," she said quietly, still puzzling this over.

"He didn't say that, no."

"Well, what, then?"

He paused and glanced at her, then away. "Even if he did want us to court, you've already given your heart away, jah?"

She stared at him. "How on earth would ya know that?"

"So, I guess I'm right." A flicker of a frown crossed Nick's ruddy brow.

True to the People's age-old tradition, she was not going to reveal what she'd agreed to with Silas. "Just because I left with someone after Singing doesn't mean anything," she spouted back.

"No need to holler 'bout Silas Good."

She shot him a quick look but decided not to bother with a response.

"By the way, I'll come over and fix up that porch." He motioned toward the Browning house, his tone suddenly more conciliatory.

She nodded abruptly, unsure now why she'd felt so upset with him. "I'll tell Mr. Browning to expect ya."

"Tell him I'll be there first thing tomorrow."

Rose didn't wait for him to come around and help her down. Instead she inched carefully out of the buggy, making sure she was ready to land on her good leg. But she slipped and landed unsteadily all the same, and Nick was there just in time to catch her. "Denki," she said, stepping back quickly, not waiting for him to say more. "Can ya pick me up around eleven o'clock today?"

"Only if you go ridin' with me tonight."

"To please the bishop."

"It'll please him no end."

Rose limped up to the front porch, considering again what Nick had said about the bishop. *Supposedly*, she thought as Nick circled the lane and headed out with a mocking wave of his hand.

*Whoever heard of a man of God encouragin' such a thing!*

~

While Rose washed the week's worth of dishes, she listened for sounds overhead, thinking surely the young woman she'd seen on Monday was upstairs somewhere. Might she still be asleep? She'd heard from Hen that some English folk slept in late.

She looked over at Gilbert Browning, who was reading a magazine. Every so often he glanced at her, which she found curious. Peering down the hallway toward the back door, she wondered if there was another access to the second floor, and if so, where it might be. She'd cleaned the back hall and small bathroom nearby enough to know there wasn't a second stair there. As far as Rose knew, there was no other way upstairs. *The reason Mr. Browning plants himself in the doorway . . .*

The man's odd habit annoyed her greatly, and it was all she could do to keep from asking right out to see the girl he was hiding.

Going now to sort through the papers on the kitchen table, she came upon a few pieces of mail. She turned her back to Mr. Browning while furtively glancing through. Rose noticed a utility bill, a receipt from the nearby general store for two spiral notebooks, and a letter from Arthur, Illinois, addressed to *Miss Beth Browning*.

"Beth?" she whispered. "Is that the girl I saw?"

Rose finished redding up and quickly wiped down the counters, wondering again if Beth Browning was Gilbert Browning's daughter. She'd appeared young enough to be just that. Yet if that was the case, why hide her?

Rose measured out some rolled oats, cinnamon, baking powder, sugar, and salt and mixed them together. Her employer liked a hearty oatmeal, and it had been a couple of weeks since she'd made her favorite baked oatmeal recipe with pieces of apple, cinnamon, and walnuts.

Rose was breaking an egg into the mixture of cooking oil and milk when she heard a chair slide across the floor overhead, then the distinct sound of footsteps. The noise grew even louder as she set the oven to two hundred seventy-five degrees and the timer for thirty minutes.

Looking over at Mr. Browning, who'd dozed off, Rose could no longer contain herself. She limped over to his chair and stood in front of him, her arms poised on her hips. "Mr. Browning, please wake up!"

He mumbled in his sleep.

"Someone's moving about upstairs."

He rustled and his head came up . . . his eyes opened. "What?"

"Don't you hear it?" she blurted, anxious that he not do as before and deny the sounds. "It must be Beth!"

He startled, then scowled. "How do you know that?"

"I saw her name on an envelope."

He muttered, head down again.

"I want to meet her," she said firmly.

He scratched his jaw, his eyes blinking rapidly. "You don't know what you're talking about."

His confounding behavior made her feel both angry and helpless. Rose stepped back and folded her hands in front of her. "Beth must know I'm here—that's probably why she's making noise upstairs."

He straightened himself in the chair. "Have you completed your work for today?"

Ignoring the question, she said, "Beth waved to me when I dropped by Monday morning."

His eyes were fiery. "You had no right!"

"I only want to befriend her," Rose pleaded, hoping he might understand she meant no harm. "Why do you keep her up there?"

"You don't understand." He lumbered to his feet. "No one would." Gilbert Browning got up and moved the chair aside before heading into the sitting room, where he looked toward the stairs. But Beth had suddenly grown quiet. He shook his head, obviously worn down.

"You can trust me," Rose persisted. "Please?"

He leaned on the banister and gazed toward the window, a glint in his eye now. "Beth's all I have left," he said, as if resigned to telling Rose the truth. "I lost her dear mother, and I couldn't bear to lose her, too."

"So, Beth *is* your daughter?"

He nodded slowly, as if his heart were breaking.

Rose felt overwhelmed with his sadness and loss. "Is that why you keep her locked away?"

"It's best this way," he said. "But I only keep her upstairs when people are around—like you, on Wednesdays." He glanced at the stairs once again. "I need to protect my Beth . . . it's not safe for her to be known."

*Protect her from what?* Rose considered entreating him yet again, wanting more than ever to meet his daughter. "Makes no sense to me."

Mr. Browning moved away from the stairs, back toward Rose. "If you'll excuse me, I must look after her now."

Rose felt desperate—she didn't want to leave. "Might I finish cleaning the kitchen?"

"You've done enough for today." His expression was less harsh now. "I'll put a check in the mail."

She hesitated, hoping he might change his mind, yet not wanting to push the man further.

"All right, then. Good-bye," Rose said reluctantly and turned to gather up her things.

~

"You told him *that?*" Solomon said to the bishop as the two men stood around in Sol's workshop.

"Well, isn't it obvious Nick's fond of your daughter?" Aaron helped steady the board while Solomon continued sanding by hand. "It may be our last hope to keep the boy in the fold."

"You honestly think usin' my daughter as bait is a *gut* idea?"

Aaron's eyes were pleading. "Sol . . . it's all I know to do."

Solomon did not appreciate this idea whatsoever. Rose Ann was a special and beautiful girl—lily-white inside and out. Even Emma said they were blessed by God to have such a remarkable daughter. He could not understand why the bishop would put him—and

Rose—in such a predicament, particularly when he'd already lost one daughter to a worldly fellow.

"Ain't a *gut* idea, Aaron . . . puttin' it bluntly."

"Ah, Sol. It's up to Rose in the end, jah? The two of them have been friends for years. Why not just wait and see how this all plays out?" the bishop added.

Solomon clenched his toes in his work boots, and he realized he was shaking his head. The thought of Rosie sacrificed to bring Nick to his knees before God and the church irked him no end!

# CHAPTER 26

By midmorning the sun was hidden by heavy clouds, and the atmosphere had turned hazy. Hen asked to borrow some of her mother's stationery. "I never thought of bringing along writing paper," Hen said as the two sat in the kitchen.

Mom, in her wheelchair, had been trying to darn some socks but kept stopping, obviously struggling to manage her pain today. She pointed to the corner cupboard, across the kitchen. "There's a tablet in the middle drawer," she said, her words clipped just now.

Hen, Mattie Sue, and Mammi Sylvia had just finished mixing together ingredients for chicken mushroom bake, one of Mom's favorite recipes for the noon meal. Before that, Hen had driven over to talk with Rachel Glick about changing her week's work schedule to this afternoon and tomorrow morning, which was just fine with Rachel. The woman seemed quite accommodating.

Nick had surprised her by dropping by to see if Mattie Sue wanted to go over with him to visit the bishop's wife, who was baking snickerdoodles with two of her granddaughters Mattie's age. Hen remembered what Dad had said about letting her roam about the farmland freely, so Hen agreed, but only if someone went along with Mattie Sue. Nick had seemed more pleasant than she'd ever remembered him being, but she wondered if it was just that Mattie Sue brought out the best in a person—even Nick Franco.

With Mattie Sue off at the neighbors', Hen was alone with her thoughts. She looked lovingly at Mom, who persevered in her attempt to darn socks, and wondered how many more years her mother could endure such suffering.

*Will she live to see Mattie Sue grow up?*

Hen closed her eyes and asked God to help her mother. And to help Hen know what to say in her invitation to Brandon—*my own husband!* She stared out the window, to the wind rippling the grass in the yard and beyond, in the pasture where the horses grazed leisurely. *Oh, to live such a trusting life . . .*

To think she had to ponder her words so carefully, even in the first line of her letter, somewhat alarmed Hen. Yet she wanted to respect the bishop's wishes and write before it was time to set the table here in the main house. She was still getting acclimated to the daily schedule of eating right at eleven thirty on the dot. The early hour gave Dad all afternoon to accomplish his farming work, as well as his woodworking projects. Dad had mentioned writing an invitation of his own to Brandon, but she'd asked him to hold off until she first sent hers. "*I'll see how he responds to mine,*" she had said, fairly certain the outcome would be negative.

Wishing for a resolution to their dilemma, Hen picked up the pen and began to write.

*Dear Brandon,*

*I think of you all the time . . . and miss you. I hope you're doing all right.*

*Mattie Sue is having an exciting day today, enjoying the farm and feeding the animals. It's so cute to see her chasing after all the kittens around here!*

*Both Mattie and I want to invite you to have dinner with us this coming Saturday night. We'll cook something very special for you— we're staying in the smaller "grandfather" house for the time being, so it will be just the three of us.*

*I'm mailing this note today hoping that you can get word back to me soon. Either that or I will follow up with a call from the phone shanty in the neighbor's field down from us.*

*We really hope you'll come, Brandon!*

*With love,*

*Hen (and Mattie Sue)*

Before she lost her nerve, Hen hurried back to the Dawdi Haus and found her purse, then rummaged through it to find a stamp. She gripped the letter and made her way out to the road. *Will a dinner invitation make a difference?*

Perhaps Hen should have started with something simpler and offered to make a meal for Brandon in their home together. But she felt unready to return to the English world so soon. Honestly, she felt torn, uncertain how to implement the things the bishop and Barbara had suggested.

What she truly longed for was to interest Brandon in joining the Amish church, and had started to ask God to soften his heart toward the Plain community. "Why does this seem so ridiculous, dear Lord?" Hen whispered as she walked back to the main house to check on her ailing mother.

$\sim$

Reaching for his carpenter's pencil, Solomon marked the surface where the next board would adjoin. Several hours had come and gone since Rose Ann left with Nick for her job over at the Browning house. All the while, he'd struggled to keep his mind on his work—finishing up the orders for the two pony carts—and pondering what he and Emma might do to reach out to Hen's husband. The bishop had been quite direct with him about opening wide the door to a relationship.

As soon as Sol could come up with something, he would talk with Emma, who really didn't have much of an opinion these days. Just marking time, he sometimes thought, till she passed on to the Hallelujah Shore. This made him downright cheerless when he thought of it. Yet wouldn't he wish for the same if he were forever laid up? Nothing more could be done for her, poor thing, and she was resigned to her immobile state.

"What can we do to include Brandon in our family?" he whispered. He placed the square level back in the pocket of his work apron.

A few minutes later, his father-in-law, Jeremiah, came wandering into the workshop and asked about the pony carts. "Are ya nearly done with 'em?"

"Oh, 'bout three more hours or so. Why?"

"Just wondered if you might run me over to BB's right quick. Sylvia wants some kidney beans for her three-bean salad."

"Well, either I can take you or Hen can drive ya later today after work."

"In her fancy car?"

Solomon smiled. "It's a mighty perty blue, ain't?"

His father-in-law grinned and looked at him. "How long before you ask her to park it somewhere . . . well, out of the way."

"Might be best to let that come up on its own, I daresay."

"No, no . . . ya need to say something," replied Jeremiah. "She best be hiding it under a tree somewheres . . . or out back behind the barn."

"All in *gut* time," Solomon said. "She's only been home a couple days."

"Fair enough." Jeremiah changed the subject. "I hear we're hosting the applesauce-making frolic this Saturday."

The notion that Brandon Orringer might be interested in seeing how this was done popped into Solomon's mind. "Do ya think Hen's husband might come, if we invite him?"

"I've never even met the Yankee, so I can't really say."

"Well, I'm tryin' my best to get Hen's husband over here, is all."

Jeremiah smacked his lips and pulled on his beard. "A mighty big hurdle the bishop's got you about to jump over."

Sol agreed. "Still, if the Lord's in it—which He must be, to put it in Aaron's mind—then things'll fall into place."

"Fall into the Englischer's lap, ya mean."

Sol had to chuckle at this. Fact was, God had either called Hen's husband to be one of the People or He hadn't. It would be interesting to watch and see how Brandon responded to a divine tug, if that's what you could call an invitation to make quarts of applesauce.

~

Thanks to Solomon's mother-in-law and Rose, by the time his prodigal daughter had arrived back from working at the fabric shop, the supper of roast beef, new potatoes, carrots, and onions was piping hot and ready to serve. Solomon had been over in the main house, savoring the aroma and hoping to catch Hen before she walked in the back door.

He stepped outside to wait and saw her coming down the steps of the addition. "Hen!" He went to meet her.

She smiled, looking more rested than when she'd arrived the day before yesterday. "How was your day, Dad?"

He told her the pony carts were finished and that he'd even had time to deliver them. "How 'bout you?"

"There were oodles of customers at the shop this afternoon, so that's good," she said. "What's on your mind?"

"I've been thinkin' about what the bishop asked your mother and me to do." He took off his straw hat and pushed a hand through his hair. "What chance is there that Brandon would spend time here with us this Saturday? We're goin' to make applesauce to divide amongst several families."

"Oh." Her smile faded instantly. "I really doubt he'd come."

"Well, we can invite him anyways, jah?"

"Can't hurt, I guess," Hen said. "But I already mailed him an invitation to join Mattie Sue and me for supper that night . . . over in our little Dawdi Haus."

"If he accepts, then all the better."

"It'll be a miracle." Hen glanced toward the big house.

"God ain't short on those." Sol offered a smile. "Just look at *you*, standin' here like this."

She hung her head. "And I said I'd never darken your door, didn't I?"

Sol remembered too well how those unbearable words had spewed forth. "You're followin' what's right." He sighed. "Now we'll hope and pray you can interest your husband in the same."

Hen sighed and they fell into step together, following the sidewalk to the main house. "I suppose Mattie Sue's been helping Rose and Mammi cook," Hen said.

"Last I saw her, she was over yonder with Nick, riding one of the bishop's ponies."

"Why's she so drawn to him, I wonder?"

"Maybe she's like Rosie," he said before thinking. Then he added quickly, "Nick does have a gentle side when it comes to children. I've seen it many a time." He opened the screen door.

Just then, they spied Mattie Sue running across the meadow. Nick stood a ways back, waving to them. "See? He's watchin' out for her," Solomon said.

"And Rosie . . . who's looking out for *her*?" asked Hen.

He rubbed his forehead. "You're worried 'bout that, too?"

"My sister's eyes sparkle when she talks of Nick," Hen said. "I doubt she even realizes how fond she is of him."

*Like a moth to a flame . . .*

Solomon felt a wave of nausea as he hung up his straw hat. He hoped to goodness Hen was wrong. Even so, he asked, "And Nick—how's *he* feel about her?"

"Oh, he's a goner."

"You're sure?"

"Totally smitten," said Hen.

"Can Rosie point him toward the church, do ya think?" Sol leaned down to remove his work boots on the porch.

"How determined is he to leave the People?"

"He's never said, but just look how he refuses to wear the traditional men's haircut. And I heard he picked a fight with a tourist in Quarryville on Monday, according to someone who witnessed it himself. Jah, I fear Nick's on his way out . . . and sooner than any of us realizes."

Hen grimaced. "Unless Rosie stops him . . ."

Stricken, Solomon said no more as they made their way into the kitchen for supper.

# CHAPTER 27

Rose never expected Nick to shine his flashlight on her bedroom window that night, like a beau coming to propose marriage. But there he was all the same, and when she opened the window, he asked her to go riding with him.

"I . . . don't know," she said, still holding her library book, Jane Austen's *Emma*.

"Is your knee better?"

"Well, jah . . . quite a lot."

"We could go through the meadow, instead of taking the road." His voice was insistent. "I'll be careful with ya, Rosie."

Against her better judgment, she reluctantly agreed and closed the window. When she'd donned her warmest sweater over her dress, she put on her woolen shawl for good measure. Outside, she asked Nick to go to the haymow to get her britches. "My hiding place," she told him.

He seemed surprised. "You keep 'em in the barn?"

"Always have." Rose waited on the back porch for him to return. When he did, she went inside to pull the trousers on under her dress in the small room where her mother napped during the day. Rose felt tired enough herself to simply lie down on the daybed and fall asleep. She assumed it was all the reading she'd done and hoped the night air might perk her up.

Back outside, she let Nick help hoist her onto Pepper. Then he went around and slung his right leg forward over the horse, careful not to bump Rose. "Grab hold of me when we ride, all right?"

Rose agreed, glad she'd worn the britches, even though now Nick knew where she hid them.

"Are ya ready?" he asked.

She held lightly onto Nick's shirt. "Go slow, all right?"

"Nice 'n' easy," he said, directing the horse to move toward the grassy lane leading out to the bishop's field.

"Aren't we goin' to the high meadow?"

"We'll end up there."

The night was still . . . the sky clear and dark. She wanted to enjoy this ride through the night. But Rose thought of her book and wondered if quick-witted and spoiled Emma Woodhouse was destined always to be a matchmaker and never a bride. Few young women Rose knew would've taken the same stance on marriage as that character. And yet, as she contemplated it, Rose realized she, too, had once nearly given up on ever having a husband, though for wholly different reasons.

*Thankfully, Silas didn't forget about me,* she thought as she watched the meadow rise to meet the sky over yonder.

"Your leg's doin' all right?" Nick asked over his shoulder.

"It's fine."

"Ready to try for a slow trot?"

"Thought ya said we were going to dawdle."

"Well, must we go *this* slow?" Clearly, he was itching to increase Pepper's pace.

"All right, but just a little."

Nick clicked his tongue and the horse moved into a trot. Taken off guard by Pepper's quick movements, Rose lost her grip on Nick's shirt and began to slide. "Oh!" she cried out.

Nick reached behind him and caught her left arm, then halted the horse. "I got ya . . . you're all right."

"You scared me half to death!" she said, catching her breath and getting situated again. Nervous now, she wondered if it wouldn't have been wiser to remain home, burrowed in with Miss Emma Woodhouse.

"Now," said Nick, "try wrapping your arms around me instead."

*How unladylike!*

Nick didn't wait even a moment for her to dispute it before they were off again. She had to grab hold of something, since she was lurching out of control with each jog of the horse. So Rose did as Nick suggested, holding tightly around his middle as he trotted the horse ever closer to a gallop.

All at once she began to feel much steadier—safer, too. She was keenly aware of Nick's strength. What freedom, riding this way! Never before had she felt so unfettered, yet also truly connected to someone. No, not just someone . . . her best friend.

*Does Nick feel it, too?*

Rose had to suppress the wild and enlivening sensation that rolled through her as they rode through the darkness together. It was akin to the first time she'd leaped off the long tree branch and let herself fall helplessly into the swimming hole below . . . disappearing into the muddy waters, over her head with happiness. Her whole body had seemed nearly weightless that day as she swam toward Nick—completely at one with the water, the hot sun, and her own body.

Just as she felt now.

But no. She couldn't let herself think this way. She was Silas's girl, not Nick's. In fact, she could never be anything more than Nick's friend.

Rose tensed up just then, her arms turning stiff.

Nick slowed the horse, quickly bringing Pepper to a halt. "What's wrong?"

"Nothin'."

"You don't fool me, Rosie." He got down and held out his arms to assist her. "You need to rest, maybe."

She let him help her down, easing carefully onto her feet. Quickly, he removed his black work coat and insisted she sit on it. "I'm not an invalid," she said as she stood there looking down at it. "Besides, it's starting to get cold."

"Just sit for a spell . . . won't ya?"

From his tone, she realized he had something on his mind. She knew him too well.

But suddenly he was walking away from her, shoving his hands into his pockets. He stared at the sky, his hat and head a shadowy silhouette.

Slowly, she lowered herself down onto his coat, her legs stretched out in front of her on the cold ground. Cushioned only by the coat and its flimsy lining, Rose felt sure he was going to tell her something dreadful. "I'm here, Nick . . . listening," she said.

He turned, pausing before coming back to meet her. Then, sitting on the bare ground next to her, he said, "I've been makin' trips into town."

"Quarryville?"

"Farther." He leaned back on one hand. "To the edge."

*The edge?*

"Never heard of that. Where is it?"

"I hoped you'd ask," he said quietly, his face alight. "Just this side of the city of Lancaster. It's what I call the line between the Amish and the English worlds—like the modern life I came from."

She took that in, feeling befuddled. "Sounds like something

you could fall from, like a precipice." Just saying the word reminded her of the dreaded ravine with its jagged outcroppings.

"It's only imaginary." He sighed, removed his hat, and placed it on his leg. "Have you ever been as far north as the bypass around Lancaster, Route 30?"

"No . . . too fast for a horse and buggy."

"Sure, it's fast—*and* dangerous." His robust chuckle lifted to the sky. "I want you to see it sometime."

"Why, Nick? *This* is our world . . . all the tranquil miles of farming land are what I love." She sighed. "I can't picture anything else."

"That's exactly it," he continued. "If you don't ever go beyond what ya know, how can you choose?"

"I don't have to. I joined church years ago."

Abruptly, he stopped talking.

"I'm *Amish*, Nick. And so are you . . . it just hasn't dawned on ya yet."

They sat there in the darkness without speaking for a moment. Then, when she was certain he was put out with her, he said, "I'm looking into borrowing a car."

"Oh, Nick," she groaned.

"Please listen." His voice was softer, almost tender. "You're my only friend. . . ."

She looked at him, wishing for some light to see his face better.

"I'll take you through the whole city. You can see how the fancy folk live—the way I used to . . . before the bishop plucked me away."

"You already know how to drive a car . . . is that what you're sayin'?"

He admitted he could.

Rose shivered at the thought. "Why don't ya tell me about the city instead . . . spare me going and lookin' clear over on the worldly side of things?"

He studied her. "Before I came here, I lived with my mother on the third floor of a brick row house for ten years."

"A row house?"

"It's connected to two other houses exactly like it—the whole block's a string of houses. Sometimes there are alleyways running between them, every two houses. But there's no place on the street to park a car."

"Must be awful crowded." *And horrible*, she thought. "I'd never be able to breathe."

"Well, the city's more than just that. Think of the most exciting place you've ever been and multiply it by one hundred. Movie theaters, restaurants, and bowling alleys, too. Lots of fun things to do." His eyes found hers. "You can see them for yourself if you go with me."

"But I'm happy here—Dat's farm's the most exciting place I know." She was shocked at his fascination with all of this, because he'd always seemed so at home in the country. *In the wild.*

"Aw, Rosie." He leaned his head close to her shoulder. "Promise me you will . . . sometime."

She was astonished and so cold she was shivering. "I won't promise anything of the kind!"

The ride back was not nearly as exhilarating as before, even though Rose clung to Nick and pressed her left cheek against the middle of his back. She felt like a sinner being so close to someone who craved the outside world, yet she wanted to be near him while she still could.

Soon they came to a stop near her father's woodshop. Rose didn't bother to thank Nick for suggesting the ride or for helping her down, neither one. Rather, she reminded him about scraping and painting Gilbert Browning's porch. "Tomorrow morning, remember?"

"I won't forget," he muttered.

Wanting to cry, she shuffled across the yard toward the house.

Then he was behind her, running after her. "Ach, Rosie . . . don't be mad." He turned her around and she lost her balance, falling right into his arms. "I wouldn't have told ya if I thought you'd be so upset."

She pushed away, yet he still held her hands. "How could I not be, Nick? *How?*"

He touched her face with the back of his hand. "I've always told ya things. You know that."

She nodded. "We've shared too much all these years, maybe," Rose whispered, a tear escaping.

"How can that be? That's what friends do, ain't?"

She felt his fervor in his grip and realized that now he was the one holding on to her for dear life. She'd been a part of nearly every boyish thing he'd ever wanted to do over the years—including riding double on Pepper. And she'd shared with him almost all of her thoughts, too.

*He asks so little of me. . . .*

"Just think about it, won't ya?"

"I s'pose *thinkin'* might not hurt anything," she said softly.

Slowly, he released her. "There's something more. . . ." He paused and looked up, staring at the sky. "I'd like to see my mother's grave."

Rose knew he hadn't received word of his mother's death in time to travel to Philadelphia for the funeral.

"And I want you to go with me."

*Past the edge*, she thought.

"Why didn't you say so?" Rose was the one reaching for him now, her hand on his arm. "Is this what you meant, then, earlier? Instead of all that talk 'bout the modern city life?"

He shrugged.

"Well, when?" she asked, her heart in her throat.

"Honest, you'd really go?"

"Just there and back," she said. *Only for you* . . .

And with that, Rose headed into the house. By now, it was too late to continue reading *Emma*. She would simply go to bed and pick up the book another time . . . and try to put the emotions of this strange night behind her. *Oh, if that is even possible.*

# CHAPTER 28

The damp, windy weather wasn't exactly the best for fixing Gilbert Browning's front porch, but Nick would still make quick work of the scraping. Rose guessed he would need to match the paint in Quarryville and come back to do the priming and painting another day.

She'd looked for Nick from the kitchen window earlier that Thursday morning and saw him out near the barn, talking with Dat and Christian. It was strange to think now of being held in his strong arms last night—out there in the backyard, of all places! What *was* he thinking? And, worse, why had she been so taken by his sudden affection?

*No, it wasn't like that,* Rose assured herself. Although, now that she considered it, she had no idea just what she'd felt at all.

Around eight o'clock, she noticed Nick with his tools slung in a bag on his shoulder, riding out toward the road on Pepper. *Our horse,* she thought, surprising herself with the thought.

She wondered why he hadn't bothered to hitch up to a carriage.

Nick was taking this sort of shortcut a lot lately. *Surely the bishop frowns on that.*

Seeing him fly down the road reminded Rose again of Nick's odd behavior last night. For the life of her, she could not understand his keen interest in going to a big city. And if it was truly a visit to his mother's grave in Philadelphia that drew him, why had he waited so long to say so? *Or is he using it as an excuse?*

She also wondered if his interest in his modern beginnings was the reason he'd never joined the church. This made her tremble—not for her sake, or for the possible loss of their friendship—but for Nick's very soul.

~

It was all coming back to Hen—making meals from scratch and cooking on a woodstove, relying on gas lamps and lanterns at night while lingering at the table after supper with her family . . . and reading the Bible afterward. Even bowing her head with the family for silent prayer.

*Living in one accord*, she thought as she opened the door to Rachel's Fabrics. She could hear Rachel and several ladies already at work in the smaller back room, chattering softly in Pennsylvania Dutch while working on a quilt. For a moment it made her feel homesick to hear them, and then she remembered she was right back where she'd longed to be. While half of her felt so alone without Brandon, her heart was at home.

She had been grateful for her sister-in-law Kate's eagerness to look after Mattie Sue once more this morning. Mattie's little face had brightened like a Christmas bulb when Hen brushed her hair back into a bun and told her she would be spending the day with her Amish cousins.

Mattie had asked if she was going to work again, and Hen assured her it was not going to be more than twice a week. It pleased her to see how rapidly her daughter was taking to this way of life, soaking it up like a thirsty sponge.

*Hopefully she's beginning to appreciate people more than things.*

In fact, when Hen had arrived with Mattie at Josh and Kate's farmhouse, Mattie ran straight into the kitchen and hugged Linda and Katie, then leaned into the playpen and kissed Annie Mae right on the lips.

*She's finally getting the chance to know my side of the family.* Hen looked up from the cash register, apprehensive about calling Brandon this evening. How would he receive her? She felt terribly cut off from him without a phone. Aside from the letter, she hadn't contacted him since arriving Monday morning, three days ago.

*Too long to be silent.*

Looking out the shop window, Hen spotted a bank of dark thunderheads rising in the north. Lavina Zook, one of the regular customers, was getting ready to leave. "Thanks for coming in today," Hen said. The middle-aged Amishwoman was trying to push her wallet down into her overflowing pocketbook.

"It'll be makin' down real soon," Lavina said, frowning with a glance out the window. "I best be getting home."

"There was a stiff, cold breeze earlier. You take care now."

"Oh, I'll be just fine. Will prob'ly be back next week for who knows what."

"And we'll be here to help," Hen said casually, but her mind was still on her husband. How would she feel if he turned down her invitation? She had tried not to expect anything remarkable to come of her letter so that she wouldn't be hurt if he either snubbed or totally rejected it. Was he even missing her?

*Lord, will you work in Brandon's heart?* she thought, then assisted a pair of customers with color choices for their quilt patterns.

Later, Hen was straightening up the counter where fabric samples and thread were strewn about when she looked up to see her old friend Arie Zook coming through the door with her baby. "Arie, hi!" she said, holding herself back from rushing over to hug her.

Arie's freckled cheeks flushed red beneath her black outer bonnet, but she looked right at Hen. "I got your letter."

"Did you?" Hen felt nearly embarrassed now—such unpleasant awkwardness between former bosom buddies. The gulf between the counter and the few yards to the door seemed unsurpassable for a moment.

"Denki for writing to me."

"I've wanted to for the longest time," Hen replied.

"You're lookin' nice and Plain," Arie observed. "How do ya like workin' here?"

"Rachel's really wonderful." She glanced toward the quilting room. "I'm enjoying it."

"That's *gut.*"

"I haven't decided on a pattern yet," Hen forged ahead, "but I'm determined to make a quilt for Mattie Sue sometime this winter." She glanced about, glad no one was shopping on this side of the store. Oh, all the months and years she'd missed Arie!

"Such an ambitious project for one person."

"I'm hoping my grandmother will help, and maybe Mom, too." She said she was presently living back at her parents' home.

Arie's face fell. "Oh, so very sorry."

"My little girl and I are staying in the small Dawdi Haus. Lord willing, it will only be for a short time," Hen added.

"I hope things work out for ya," Arie said, eyes solemn.

Hen moved out from behind the counter and went to her. "I'm glad you came by."

Arie offered her a small smile. "I want to apologize for how I behaved that Sunday at your parents'." She sighed and set the baby carrier on the floor. "I haven't been able to stop thinkin' how it must've hurt you."

"But I hurt *you* years ago. . . ." Hen couldn't finish and was comforted by Arie's tender embrace.

"I don't know how things are going to be for Mattie Sue and me," she said softly when they'd walked over to the corner, out of earshot. "I'm going to need your prayers, I know that."

Arie nodded her head. "I'd be happy to help out with your daughter, too, if you ever need it. All right?"

Hen blinked back her tears. This longed-for reunion with Arie was as sweet as it was timely. She truly needed an understanding friend.

When Arie was finished shopping for a mere handful of sewing notions, she paid cash for the items and turned to leave. "I'll look for ya on Sunday at Preaching, Hen."

"Denki. I'll be there." It was in that moment, Hen realized with a smile, that Arie had come to Rachel's Fabrics primarily to see her.

∾

While Mamm sat in her wheelchair and did her needlepoint, Rose read aloud from *Emma* to fill up the silence. She fell easily into the appealing setting, which struck her as a very romantic time. Mamm stopped her occasionally to comment on all the many social events and gatherings—or the women's frivolous preparations for them. Such occasions seemed to occupy all of their waking hours, and at one point, Mamm mused that the young women were "downright obsessed" with wondering who would be their dance partner.

The rumble of thunder caused Rose to look up from the book, and her eyes met Mamm's. "Read from the Scriptures awhile, Rosie."

She went to retrieve the old family Bible. "Would ya like to hear a psalm?"

"Oh, Psalm Ninety-Eight would be ever so nice," Mamm said. "Practice reading it in German, jah?"

Rose faltered in places but managed to get through all of it.

" 'O sing unto the Lord a new song,' " Mamm whispered once Rose was finished. "His mercies are new each and every day. Never forget."

Rose wondered if her mother might need to rest, but when she suggested moving her onto the daybed, Mamm set down her sewing. "Let's just talk a bit."

Bless her heart, Mamm sounded downright lonely. "That's nice," Rose said.

Her mother folded her slender hands in her lap. "Your sister's car . . ." she said. "Can ya see it from the road?"

"Jah."

This clearly troubled Mamm. "Ach, I wonder if one of us shouldn't say something to her."

"Well, who's to know how long Hen will stay?"

Mamm shook her head. "Heaven knows she best be makin' up with her husband. And mighty soon, too."

Rose agreed. "Does it make ya feel better to know Hen was over to see the bishop and Barbara early this week?"

"Your father told me." Mamm reached out to clasp her hand. "Oh, Rosie, who ever thought our Hen would return like this?"

"Seldom happens, ain't?"

"Never, as far as I know. Once a person leaves, they tend not to look back."

Rose realized the same might prove true for Nick. Concerned, she said, "Besides baptism and an interest in community and the Old Ways, what would keep a young person in the church?"

"Well, a hunger for spiritual things, first and foremost." Mamm gave a rare smile. "But a perty girl can sometimes thwart a young man's worldly plans."

"So courting an Amish girl might actually keep a fella from goin' fancy?"

"It's kept many a boy in the church through the years."

Was the bishop trying to do that—encouraging Nick to spend time with *her*?

Just then Rose thought of pretty Sarah, the fairer of her two cousins who'd flirted with Nick. Oh, if she could only be the matchmaker Emma Woodhouse was in the wonderful-good book she was reading! But . . . how to go about it?

"Why do you ask?" Mamm said softly, eyes fixed on her.

"Just wondered, is all."

"Not thinkin' of anyone in particular?"

She wouldn't lie. "Let's just say I'm hoping to match up the perfect girl with someone . . . and mighty soon."

"Could be a daunting task."

Rose looked at her, wondering if Mamm suspected what she was thinking. "Well, I'll tread lightly." They were venturing into unfamiliar territory, having never discussed romantic relationships before. Quickly, she changed the subject to the applesauce-making frolic. "Who all's comin' Saturday?"

"My sister Malinda and Barbara, next door. And Verna and her husband, Levi, and Christian, too."

Rose supposed Nick might help haul away the apple skins and cores with his brother like other years. "Will Josh and Kate come, as well?" She hoped so for Hen and Mattie Sue's sake.

"Kate talked 'bout bringing supper for all of us, but I doubt they'll come early enough to put up applesauce." Mamm went on to say that Barbara and the bishop were going in with them on two kinds of apples—Staymen Winesap and Golden Delicious. "I daresay the work should go quick."

"Are we removin' the stems this year?"

"Barbara prefers the lighter sauce, so we'll pull them off."

"Might be a *gut* job for Mattie Sue and me, then."

Mamm was getting sleepy, nodding her head either in agreement or fatigue—Rose wasn't sure which. Reaching for her book, Rose began to read again, quickly reentering the early-nineteenth-century tale right where she'd left off. The humorously capricious Emma had struck a nerve in Rose, seeing as how the character was the exact same age as she was at the outset of the story, and had the same name as Mamm. But, goodness, if Emma Woodhouse wasn't careful, she was going to matchmake herself right into spinsterhood!

# CHAPTER 29

They were in the midst of a heavy rainstorm by the time Rose saw Hen—from the front room window—turning off Salem Road into the driveway. She was very close to finishing *Emma* and hoped Hen would take her to the library so she could replenish her supply of novels. They could get there and back before suppertime preparations should begin.

*The benefits of having a car in the family . . .*

Only Hen knew of the armloads of books Rose had borrowed from the Quarryville library from her childhood on. Twice each month when they were young, Hen and Rose had gone to the small library, taking along the same box to fill with books. During the warmest months, Rose had read in the barn amidst the horses and mules. The librarian had joked when she returned the box that they'd have to air out the books for days on end, and Rose knew she wasn't kidding.

"Do ya have time to run me up to the library in Quarryville?" Rose said, holding her umbrella as she tapped on Hen's car window.

Mattie Sue was sitting happily in the backseat, playing with the new rag doll Rose had made for her.

Hen looked at her wristwatch. "I don't see why not." She turned and asked Mattie Sue if she'd like to go and check out a few books, too.

Nodding, Mattie was all smiles, looking like any other little Amish girl in the community. "I want a storybook about a puppy dog, Mommy."

Hen turned back to Rose. "How soon do you want to leave?"

"Mamm's asleep, so let's hurry 'n' go now," she said, excited. "I'll let Mammi know right quick and get my stack of books." *Except for the last one*, she thought, having a delicious inkling that Emma just might end up with Mr. Knightley . . . and hoping so.

~

At the library, Hen silently rehearsed her upcoming phone conversation with Brandon. She planned to call after she made supper for the family, eager to help out as much as possible. Rose Ann and Mattie Sue were presently engrossed in finding "puppy" books to read later that night. Rose had promised Mattie Sue on the drive there that she would come over to the Dawdi Haus and spend some time with her.

Hen would've sat with Mattie, too, helping her choose which stories to check out, but one particular book had caught Hen's eye on the way to the children's section of the library—an adult self-help book that addressed common differences in most marriages. She'd picked it up to see if the author had Christian credentials but found it was written by a secular marriage therapist. Even so, the chapter lineup tackled so many of her and Brandon's issues that Hen was determined to read it.

*The sooner, the better . . .*

~

256

Once Hen returned from the library, she and Mammi Sylvia managed to whip up and serve a meal of roast chicken, mashed potatoes and gravy, buttered corn and green beans, and two pies—Dutch apple and cherry.

After eating with the family in the main house, Hen left Mattie Sue with Rose Ann to dry dishes for Mammi Sylvia. Feeling pleased with herself for having remembered all the tricks of woodstove cooking, she slipped outside to walk across the field to the east side of the house.

The air had turned nippy after the day's rain, and the sky was faint with light. The shanty phone booth stood in the middle of the wet pasture, near a few trees, still looking as if it threatened to topple over in the least bit of wind—something it had done in several windstorms. As Hen went inside, she recalled the times she'd come here to use the phone, sometimes for emergencies, sometimes to call Brandon just as she was now. She searched for the tiny initials she'd carved with Brandon's pocketknife: *H&B*. There they still were, less vivid with the years.

Hen felt the heat of tears rising in her eyes, but blinked them back. She felt almost as if this call tonight were an emergency of the heart. She dialed, and Brandon answered, sounding uneasy and distant.

"Hi, hon . . . it's Hen."

"I wondered when—or if—you'd call."

She guarded her words. "We needed some space . . . like you suggested."

"No, Hen, *you're* the one who needs space." She heard him breathe out in a huff.

"Mattie Sue and I are doing all right here. But we miss you, Brandon."

"It was outrageous what you did." He sounded like he'd been storing up his frustration until this minute. "You cleared out Mattie's room!"

She sputtered, trying to make an excuse. "I wanted her to feel . . . comfortable."

"Do you ever listen to yourself?" he said. "You aren't planning a short stay, are you?"

"Don't jump to conclusions."

"Am I?"

She sighed. This was deteriorating quickly. "Mattie Sue would love to see you."

"Well, bring her home."

She ignored his comment, trying to remember all the good times they'd shared. Right now, in the heat of their discussion, she hardly recalled any. "Did you get my letter?"

"I told you what you could do about visiting before you left."

"Mattie Sue and I really hope you'll come," Hen said, trying to do what the bishop's wife had said, but she was failing miserably. "I'd love to cook a nice hot dinner for you—your favorite."

"On an old cookstove, right?"

"Actually, yes." She said more softly, "I think you might like it."

He hedged, like he wasn't sure, despite his usual bravado. "I *would* like to see Mattie . . . and you, too, Hen." He paused for what seemed like minutes. Then he added, "But why not cook here?"

"It would mean a lot to us if you'd accept our invitation . . . here." She waited, hoping he might change his mind. "I'll make steak with the rich gravy you like."

Another long pause. Was there any chance he'd accept?

Then, with a sense of great deliberation, he said, "I'll come on one condition."

"Yes?" She held her breath.

"That dinner is only with you and Mattie."

"That's fine. I'll look forward to it, and Mattie Sue will be so happy."

"By the way, I was planning a little surprise for Mattie, so maybe I'll bring it along," he said almost cheerfully.

"Any hints?"

"Nope . . . you'll just have to wonder."

She almost smiled. So the real Brandon was definitely alive and well. "We'll eat around five o'clock, okay?"

He said he'd be there, and she hung up the phone. Overwhelmed with relief, Hen did a little jig right there inside the rickety phone shanty. *He's not as stubborn as I thought!*

~

Hen waited until after Mattie Sue was ready for bed to tell her the news. "Daddy's coming for supper this Saturday."

"Goody! I'll help set the table," Mattie Sue volunteered, surprising Hen as they sat at the small table in a circle of gaslight. "And, Mommy, do I have to wear my old clothes? The fancy ones?"

"No, darling. You can wear your favorite Amish dress."

"The blue one!" Mattie Sue hurried off to the front room and returned with her two library books. "Can I show these to Daddy, too?"

*You sure won't be watching TV together!*

"If you want to."

Mattie Sue looked up at her. "And, Mommy?"

"Yes, sweetie."

"Is Daddy coming to live with us?"

She hadn't expected this. "Well, he didn't grow up like I did, so he's not as interested in Amish ways, honey."

"I didn't grow up here, either, Mommy."

*She has a good point!*

There was a knock at the door, and they looked up to see Rose Ann waving at them through its window.

"Come in," Hen called as Mattie Sue ran to give her aunt a hug.

Rose greeted her niece and watched as she spun around in her little Amish dress till Mattie squealed, "I'm getting *daremlich!*"

Hen laughed. *She's not only dizzy; she's picking up Deitsch very quickly.* And in that moment, she startled herself, realizing how happy she was to use her first language more freely. *It would be easier if I felt that way about everything, like not driving a car.* She had a strong attachment to her sedan. Yet Hen understood Dad's concern in asking her to park it somewhere less obvious. *"Hide it under a tree somewhere,"* he'd advised just before supper. Despite the lack of power lines, anyone passing by who saw it might immediately gather the house was occupied by Englishers.

"Pick a storybook," Rose Ann said as she settled down onto the little settee with Mattie, near the window.

Mattie Sue was teasing her auntie, shuffling the books—both were stories about puppies. "I can't decide! Eenie, meenie, miney, moe . . ."

"Close your eyes, then." Rose Ann placed the books behind her back. "Okay, now point to one of my hands, either the right or the left, and that's the book we'll read first."

Mattie Sue giggled and waited, shilly-shallying, undecided as to which hand to choose. Hen was amused by her daughter's inability to make a decision—*how the bishop must think of me now.* The realization made her chagrined. She wanted to open her arms to her husband—embrace him fully without accepting the worldly things he stood for. There was the biggest catch, and the most difficult challenge. But to obey the man of God, she must figure out how to combine the two.

*Maybe Saturday's supper will prove helpful,* Hen thought, still shocked that Brandon had agreed to come.

Yet the confident ring in his voice when he had mentioned a surprise made her not only wonder, but also shelter her heart.

While Rose Ann read to Mattie Sue, Hen paged through the small wedding album she'd brought. She stared at her own happy face as a young bride and recalled how giddy she had been that day. Brandon had jokingly suggested they marry quickly to keep from sinning—certainly they'd hardly known each other long enough to make a rational decision about a lifelong commitment. But they *had* grown as friends since then, although now when Hen thought of it, she wasn't sure what commonalities they shared. They didn't see eye to eye on rearing a child, that was evident.

With her pointer finger, she traced her wedding veil in a picture. *What did I set out to give to this marriage? Am I still this Plain-turned-fancy woman inside?*

She glanced over at her sister, all curled up with Mattie Sue. The endearing sight brought tears to her eyes. *How can I not stay the course here with my darling girl?*

There had been more than a dozen opportunities since returning home to point out to Mattie Sue the importance of embracing honesty, generosity, patience, and kindness in one's life—all the lovely character traits she had been taught as a child. And Mattie was receiving the loving instruction more receptively than when they had lived at home with Brandon. Surely it was the worldly environment that had made the difference, she thought.

*How hard will Brandon laugh if I ask him to join the Amish church with me?*

Hen was feeling especially lonely, so she was delighted when Rose Ann stayed around until after Mattie was tucked into bed. Putting on a kettle of water for tea, she sat at the kitchen table, across from her sister.

"Mattie seems eager to learn our ways," Rose Ann pointed out. "It surprises me, really."

"She's young . . . and open to it." Hen set two cups and saucers on the table. "I was actually worried she might already be too ensnared in English life for any of this to take."

"What are ya hopin' for, Hen? I mean, for Mattie Sue?"

She placed several kinds of tea bags in a small bowl and put them on the table next to the sugar. "Between you and me, I haven't felt this free since I left home to marry. This life"—and here she gestured with her hand—"is what I believe in. It's true and has eternal value. I feel as if I have to break through to it somehow . . . because I want Mattie Sue to grow up Amish."

Rose Ann smiled. "Maybe it took leavin' your fancy life to grasp this."

"Jah . . . I had to find out the hard way."

"Are ya filled with joy now?"

It was a strange question coming from Rose Ann, who was usually not this reflective. "I once read a Shakespeare sonnet that reminds me of how I feel right now," Hen said. "When I'm walking on Amish soil, I feel my losses are restored and my sorrows have ended."

Rose looked unexpectedly sad. "Not when you're with Brandon?"

"I don't know how to explain it, other than to say that things have radically changed. Yes, I did experience all of those things when we were first married. But I was in a much different place then . . . and conceited as a crow."

Rose sat quietly, rearranging the tea bags. "I guess if you can figure out what's different now, then you can try 'n' remedy it somehow."

"I must appear disloyal to Brandon," Hen admitted. "I'm not exactly sure what's going on myself." *Why am I so eager to raise Mattie Sue in the Anabaptist tradition?*

"Brandon's coming for supper this Saturday," she told Rose.

"Seriously?"

"It's surprising, but yes."

Rose clapped her hands. "Oh, sister, this is wonderful-*gut*!"

"Well, I hope so."

Rose leaned forward. "You should be jumpin' for joy."

"I actually was." She described her little dance in the phone shanty. "But I have a feeling something's up." The teakettle whistled, and she went to get it off the stove. "He's bringing a surprise."

"Look on the bright side—might be something nice."

Hen shrugged. "Brandon can negotiate like nobody I've ever known. You don't know my husband."

"No . . . and I wish I did. He's family, after all." Rose chose peach passion herbal tea and held her cup and saucer while Hen poured boiling water over the bag.

*Poor Rosie.* Hen didn't have the heart to tell her that Brandon had made a point of wanting to see only her and Mattie Sue. *He doesn't care about my sister or brothers and their wives and children . . . or my parents, either. And never has.*

As she sat down and dripped some honey into her tea, Hen began to understand precisely why she felt so lonely—and why it was so critical that Mattie Sue become familiar with her Amish heritage. This life brought peace with it . . . and was far better than anything else the world had to offer.

# CHAPTER 30

$\mathcal{A}$s surprises go, Gilbert Browning's arrival at the Kauffmans' on Friday morning was most unforeseen. Rose was enjoying the final chapters of *Emma* with her mother when she heard a car coming up the driveway. Looking out the window, she recognized the old rattletrap with Gilbert Browning sitting in the driver's seat.

"Well, lookee there!" She quickly explained to Mamm that the widower she worked for had just arrived.

Before her mother could say much of anything, Rose kissed her cheek and said she'd go and call Hen to come sit with her, since Mammi was doing some shopping for tomorrow's work frolic. She did that as quickly as she could, then hurried back through the yard to meet Mr. Browning, who'd already stepped out of the car. "What a nice surprise," she told him as he gave the countryside a once-over.

"You've got quite a spread of land here," he said. "I had the hardest time finding your place, until I asked the fellow over on Bridle Path Lane."

"You came *that* way?" Rose winced. "You must've talked to Jeb Ulrich."

"He seemed to know about your family . . . said your mother had an accident not but a few yards from his little hut."

She wished he hadn't brought that up. "At least he steered ya in the right direction."

Mr. Browning mentioned the stacked rock sculptures found at random up and down Bridle Path Lane. "Have you ever seen them? Flat rocks piled up in graduated sizes from large at the base to very small at the top. They're quite the works of art."

"I know what you're talking about," she said, though she didn't know who'd created the curious piles.

"There are even garden turtles and other decorative things set under the large bushes there in the hollow," he said. "Beth might like to see them sometime."

"I've seen 'em, too," Rose said, then offered to take him around the farm. "How long can ya stay?"

"Thanks, Rose, but I'm here for Beth." He paused and turned to look at her. "She hasn't stopped asking to meet you since you were at our place Wednesday. It's been a while since she's had her heart so set on something."

Rose smiled her delight. "I'd love to meet her, too."

"She asked if I would bring you back with me today." He wore a slight smile of his own. "I don't know if it will suit or not."

"Right now?"

"If you have time."

Rose didn't skip a beat. "Sure, I'll go with ya." She explained that she must let her Mamm and sister know. "Just let me run inside right quick." Oh, she could hardly wait to meet Gilbert Browning's secret daughter!

~

Rose took along some freshly baked sticky buns she and Hen had made earlier that morning. Carrying the plate into the Browning house, she was met by Beth, who sat stiffly in the very chair her father always sat in, although it had been moved off to the side, near the lamp table.

Beth's hair was flax gold and as cropped as any Amish boy's. Her eyes looked as blue as the sky when the wind had swept it clean, framed by thick lashes. The young woman Gilbert Browning had been hiding from her was beautiful. "Are you Rose?" Beth asked hesitantly.

"Jah, I'm your father's housekeeper and cook. It's nice to meet you." *Finally,* she mentally added.

"I'm glad you came with Daddy," Beth said, staring at her.

Rose realized she must look peculiar to the young woman. She held her breath, hoping Beth wouldn't be upset.

Beth eyed her Kapp and long dress and apron. "I thought you might be Anne of Green Gables on the porch the other day."

"My hair does look reddish in the sunlight."

Beth smiled faintly. "I sometimes wear Amish clothes, too—except britches and a straw hat."

*So that's who Donna Becker saw!*

"Do ya like wearin' boys' clothes?" asked Rose with a glance at Beth's father, who appeared chagrined.

"They scratch me," Beth said.

Rose didn't say that she, too, sometimes wore trousers beneath her dress and knew exactly what she meant.

Mr. Browning looked at his daughter. "Beth, honey, would you like to show Rose your room?"

"Oh yes!" Beth jumped up and then waved for Rose to follow her. "But wait until I say to come up," she told Rose before scampering up the stairs, leaving Rose alone with Mr. Browning.

"Beth is very different," he said, lowering his voice. "She's not like other girls her age."

Rose nodded. "Is she . . . troubled?" She didn't dare ask if Beth was slow in her mind, although Rose suspected as much.

"No more than anyone who's lost her mother, I suppose."

He paused before continuing. "Beth nearly died at birth. The doctor initially couldn't get her to breathe, and it affected her development."

"I'm so sorry."

He nodded, his face less dour. "After her mother died, Beth sank into herself even more." He explained that Beth had attended special classes at the high school in Arthur, Illinois. "Before we moved here last year." Mr. Browning shook his head and sighed. "I don't know why I'm telling you this."

Rose felt sorry for him . . . and for his daughter. "I'd like to try to help Beth, with your permission. Surely she could use a friend."

"Well, she's always been very shy. I'm quite surprised at her interest in you."

"I would never frighten her. I can promise you that."

"Beth doesn't comprehend the outside world too well," he stated. "Most likely she'll never hold down a job or drive a car . . . or even marry." He looked at the ceiling momentarily. "I pulled up stakes in Illinois to come here . . . to protect her. A girl like Beth is extremely impressionable and naïve—susceptible to those who might wish to take advantage of a pretty girl."

Rose noted the nervous expression on Mr. Browning's face. Despite the explanations, he seemed reticent, as if holding back more. She saw his struggle as he reached into his pocket and took out his kerchief, hands shaking.

Slowly, wearily, he wiped his wrinkled eyes. "I hope I won't end up kicking myself," he said, motioning for Rose to take the stairs. "I'll go along with you. Beth's waiting."

Rose followed Mr. Browning, making her way up the forbidden staircase, gripping the railing as she favored her weaker leg. At the top of the stairs, she saw there was only one room with a closed door, and Rose paused, waiting for Mr. Browning.

He stopped to catch his breath. "Keep in mind everything I

just told you." He turned the knob and the door opened. "Follow me."

Rose stepped into a fairly large room. It was a lovely space with several pieces she was almost certain were Amish made. The solid oak dresser might have been built by her own father, or her next-to-oldest brother, Enos, who made furniture when he wasn't raising tobacco and puppies to sell.

She looked around and saw a comfortable upholstered dark blue chair near the window, with a lamp table that matched the oak dresser. The single bed looked quite rumpled, as if it had been laid on after it had been made. One of the small throw pillows was lying on the floor, and there were many dozens of stuffed animals—mostly teddy bears and cats. In the corner stood a wooden cupboard containing numerous books and what looked to be rows of blue spiral notebooks.

Rose moved farther into the room. There, in the corner, sat Beth, clutching a stuffed cat, her eyes blinking rapidly. The idea of being dropped smack-dab into a story came to Rose's mind as she looked into the haunting blue eyes of Gilbert Browning's daughter.

"Beth, honey . . . Rose can't stay long," he said.

Rose was careful not to move closer to the girl. "Call me Rosie, all right?"

"I thought I was dreaming when I first saw you," Beth said, standing up suddenly, just as she had downstairs.

Rose held up her hands and wiggled her fingers. "Oh, I'm real. See?" *Just as real as you are.* She saw that Mr. Browning had slipped out of the room.

"Where'd Daddy go?" asked Beth, looking agitated. She shifted her weight from one foot to another, back and forth.

Rose pointed to the doorway. "He's just outside."

Frowning, Beth shook her head.

"I've been wantin' to meet ya, Beth."

The girl scurried uneasily to a window and sighed softly, her breath clouding the glass. She leaned her head down oddly and stared at the center of the window. It wasn't clear what she was looking at, but she positioned her hand on the glass just so. Then, slowly . . . inch by inch, she began to slide it down the windowpane.

"I saw your hand on the window the other day," Rose said quietly. "It's so *gut* to finally talk to you."

Beth turned. "You say you cook for Daddy and me?"

"And clean a little, too." Rose had a sudden idea. "I made the most delicious cinnamon sticky buns. Would ya like some?"

Beth's eyes brightened.

"They're downstairs on the table." Her heart was overjoyed that the treat seemed to appeal to the girl. "Melt in your mouth."

Beth removed her hand from the window and crept closer, though still staying at least a good three yards away. "Will Daddy eat some, too?"

"I wouldn't be surprised." Rose moved toward the doorway. "Come down in a few minutes, if you'd like."

Beth sniffled just then, like she might cry.

"You don't have to be sad, Beth. You can come right away if you like. And if you want to, every Wednesday you can watch me bake, all right?"

The girl nodded slowly. Her expressions appeared much more childlike than her body. "I'd like that."

Rose's heart warmed. "Me too," she whispered.

Beth scurried past Rose and went to sit on her bed, her arms wrapped around her knees. She leaned back against the pillows and the many colorful teddy bears there. "Stay upstairs longer, Rosie."

"All right."

"I want to know more about you."

"Ask whatever you like."

Beth asked all sorts of questions—why Rose didn't ride in a car to come to work and why she dressed like a girl from the 1800s. "I like to read books from the time before there were any cars."

Rose answered as best she could, then said, "I really like your room, Beth. Thanks for showing me."

"But it's lonely up here." Beth pointed to the ceiling. "Especially in the attic, where I stay sometimes, too." She got up from the bed and went to her bookshelf to pull out one of the notebooks. "I write in this when my father says I must stay here or in the attic room he made for me."

"So you've been in the attic when I come to work?"

"Mostly." Beth nodded slowly. "And if a neighbor or the milkman or the mailman comes, too." Now she was looking at Rose curiously. "Why do they call you Rosie?"

"It's just a nickname." Rose thought of her sister's name. "Have you ever heard of *Hen* for a girl?"

"That's a chicken." Beth smiled.

"Well, it's a nickname, too—for my sister, whose name is Hannah. 'Cept she doesn't go by that anymore."

"Rosie sounds like a horse's name," Beth said, still smiling. She glanced at the window. "Where was your pretty horse on Wednesday?"

"In the meadow back home. But you'll prob'ly see Alfalfa next week when I come again."

"He's your horse?"

"Well, my father's."

"Alfalfa. I like that name." Beth leaned her head back and closed her eyes. "Why didn't you come with Alfalfa and your carriage on Wednesday?"

"Because my friend brought me."

Beth was quiet for a moment. "The boy with the long black hair?"

Now it was Rose's turn to smile. "Jah, Nick."

"Is that a *nick*name, too?"

They both started laughing, and Rose said, "You're a very bright girl."

Beth's eyes saddened. "No, not really . . ."

"Well, you love books, right?"

Beth glanced fondly at the cupboard. "I write, too." She opened the notebook in her hand. "Things that I think about, letters, some prayers, and poems that never rhyme."

"Your dad says you went to school."

"Yes, in Illinois . . . but not with the smart students."

*A long way from home*, thought Rose. "Do you miss your friends?"

Beth shrugged. "Never had many. Besides, Daddy doesn't want me to talk about that."

Rose was confused. "But . . . why not?"

"I finished school more than a year ago. I'm eighteen. My birthday was a couple weeks ago."

*So that's who the chocolate cake was for!* "Well, happy belated birthday, Beth!"

"Thank you, Rosie." Grinning, Beth pulled one of her teddy bears close and kissed the top of its head. "I don't feel like I'm eighteen, though."

Rose thought again of the breakfast sweet rolls. "Will you come down and have something to eat?"

Beth nodded her head up and down, quite eager now.

When Rose left the room, she felt pleased with herself—thankful, too. She went to the top of the steps and sat down gingerly, scooting from one step to another to avoid putting undue pressure on her improving knee.

At the bottom of the stairs, she saw Mr. Browning pacing in the sitting room.

"How's she doing?" he said as Rose hobbled toward the doorway between that room and the kitchen.

"She wants one of my sticky buns."

His eyes brightened. "She's never taken to anyone so quickly," he said. "She was so close to her mother . . . God bless her." Mr. Browning's mood had markedly improved. He sported a smile as he went with Rose into the kitchen, offering to set the table while Rose warmed the sticky buns in the oven. He opened the narrow drawer and set out three of each utensil as if this was to be a true celebration.

The African violets Rose had placed on the windowsill were beginning to flourish, and Rose welcomed how they brightened the space. Beth wandered downstairs and took a seat next to her father at the table as Rose placed the sticky buns before them. Rose poured some milk for Beth and coffee for Mr. Browning.

Beth asked if she might say grace, and Rose smiled as the young woman said a familiar one. "Come, Lord Jesus, be our guest, let this food to us be blessed. Amen."

"Thank you, Beth," Rose said, reaching for the sugar for her hot tea. "My Dawdi Jeremiah taught me that same prayer when I was little."

"Dawdi?" said Beth, looking puzzled.

" 'Grandfather' in Deitsch," she explained.

"What's grandmother, then?" Beth reached for a bun.

"Mammi."

Mr. Browning stirred sugar into his coffee. "You're very talkative today, Beth, honey," he said.

"I like Rosie." Beth looked right at her and smiled. "Me and Rosie are friends," she chanted happily.

"I wish you could come over and see our new foals sometime," Rose ventured, glancing at Mr. Browning to see how he'd react. Too late she realized she should've talked to him first before bringing it up to Beth out of the blue.

"Foal . . . that's a baby horse, isn't it?" Beth turned to her father. "Would you let me, Daddy—please?"

Her father glanced from Beth to Rose and back again. "I . . . don't think it's wise."

"Rose would look after me, wouldn't you, Rosie?" It appeared that Beth had latched on to the idea.

"I'm sure she would." Mr. Browning spooned sugar into his coffee. "But let's not rush this."

*This, meaning Beth's social life*, thought Rose. She had planted a seed and watered it, and poor, thirsty Beth had more than responded. Now it was up to Gilbert Browning to decide whether or not to shine sunlight on his daughter and allow Beth to blossom.

# CHAPTER 31

The assembly line for the applesauce-making frolic was in place by eight-thirty Saturday morning. Rose and Mattie Sue worked together to remove the stems, while Dat and Dawdi Jeremiah rinsed the bushels of apples, and Barbara Petersheim and her daughter Verna cut them in quarters. Aunt Malinda and Mamm removed the seeds, preparing them for the Victoria strainer.

Throughout the long process, Nick and Christian alternated turning the handle of the strainer as the other carried away the apple skins. Rarely were they in the same proximity at the same time. *Will their feuding ever cease?* Rose wondered. Christian's mouth had been in a sharp line all morning.

"I'm having so much fun!" announced Mattie Sue, looking up at Rose with her bright eyes and long lashes.

She realized then that her young niece would have missed out on this family tradition if Hen hadn't returned home when she did. With all of her heart, Rose hoped the delicious meal Hen had planned for tonight might set the right mood for Brandon's visit.

Rose had her own reason to look forward to this evening, since she and Silas would be riding under the stars. Still, she wouldn't fail to send up silent prayers for Hen and Brandon, trusting that their love might be saved. *Somehow!*

After a time, Dat and Dawdi got the canners going on the woodstove as the womenfolk chattered like magpies about the upcoming canning bee. It did Rose Ann's heart good to see her sister fitting in so well. Goodness, but Hen could already make hearty breakfasts that rivaled Mammi Sylvia's, and she'd only been back home less than a week.

"I'm gonna eat applesauce at dinner . . . and for breakfast tomorrow, too!" said Mattie Sue, who was getting quick at twisting off apple stems.

"You can do like your mother always did when she was growing up," said Rose.

"Put whipped cream on top?" asked Mattie.

"Well now, how'd you know that?"

"Mommy always does."

"With cinnamon sprinkled on first?" asked Rose.

Mattie Sue nodded her cute little head. "Mommy taught Daddy to eat it that way, too." Her lower lip trembled just then.

Rose thought it best to change the subject. Leaving home was surely the most harrowing thing poor, dear Mattie had ever experienced—drastically changing her way of life.

By the time they were finished, Mamm reported that they had canned over a hundred quarts of the applesauce. Barbara's face fairly glowed; she'd gotten her wish to make a light-colored sauce.

When the many jars were out cooling on the summer porch, Rose Ann followed Hen back to her Dawdi Haus and sat with Mattie Sue to reread the picture books aloud to her for at least the fourth time.

≈

Remembering Brandon's stipulation that dinner be just the three of them, Hen sent Mattie Sue out to the back porch to watch for him at a quarter to five o'clock. Mattie carried Foofie with her, talking to her stuffed animal while she waited.

Mattie looked like an Amish girl, her hair parted evenly down the middle and swept back into the bob. She hadn't wanted to wear the little white Kapp so she could show her daddy how "big Amish girls" twist their hair on the sides.

Hen had never felt so nervous about serving a meal to her husband and daughter. It was as if the years at their house in town had faded into oblivion. This night had to count toward getting Brandon interested in the Plain community. *My people.* Their life together depended on it.

So with the bishop's words of admonition still echoing in her mind, Hen stood at the door as Brandon's car pulled into the lane and Mattie ran out to greet him.

When he opened the car door, Hen saw that he was dressed in one of her favorite casual sweaters and dress slacks. Her heart did a flip as she opened the screen door to welcome him. "Hi, Brandon." Her voice sounded tense even to her.

"Hello, Hen." He leaned down to kiss her cheek before stepping inside the house, still holding Mattie's hand.

"I helped Mommy set the table," Mattie Sue announced, showing him where to sit.

Brandon cocked his head slightly and smiled down at her. "Thanks."

"Can you say 'Denki'? That's Amish for 'thank you,' " Mattie Sue told him in a singsongy voice.

Hen flinched. "Mattie Sue . . . please wash your hands."

Without blinking an eye or whining whatsoever, Mattie hurried to the rustic washroom around the corner.

"Impressive," Brandon remarked. "She's been in obedience training, what . . . less than six days now?"

Hen felt the color rush to her face. Her expectation of immediate obedience had been one of the many disagreements they'd had over rearing their daughter. Brandon was much more lenient, and his brusque comment wasn't a good sign. There was no sense in taking the bait.

Trying to remain unflustered, Hen lifted the thick steak out of the large black skillet and spooned the gravy on top. Mattie Sue appeared again just as Hen dished up Brandon's favorite scalloped potatoes, then another one of his favorites—baked beans with bacon, onions, dark brown sugar, ketchup, mustard, and molasses.

"Looks like you outdid yourself." All of a sudden his smile seemed genuine.

She and Mattie Sue sat down, and as Brandon picked up his fork to dig in, Hen bowed her head and Mattie Sue folded her hands in prayer. Together, they offered the silent prayer, just as her own father was doing undoubtedly at this moment in the main house. Josh and Kate and their family, along with the bishop and Barbara, were gathering there for a small celebration following the applesauce frolic. Mattie Sue's eyes were still closed when Hen raised her head and said amen.

"Hungry?" Brandon asked Mattie when her eyes flew open. A big smile followed.

"We say *two* blessings at the meal now, Daddy. One right before we eat and one afterward."

Hen noticed Brandon's controlled smirk. They ate for a time without anyone speaking, and Hen breathed another silent prayer for God's blessing on their time together.

"After we finish eating," Brandon told Mattie Sue, "I have something to show you."

Her eyes literally sparkled at him across the table. "What is it?"

"You'll have to wait and see."

"*Where* is it?" Mattie Sue pressed.

"Outside . . . in the car."

"Why didn't you bring it in?"

Hen intervened. "Mattie Sue . . ."

Brandon shook his head. "It's okay. Let her play along."

Backing down, Hen let him have the upper hand.

"Give me a little hint, okay, Daddy?"

Brandon shook his head. "After you're done with your meal, I'll take you out to see it."

Hen cut into her steak, pleased with its tenderness. She'd marinated the meat since early morning.

"What did you do today, Mattie?"

"I twisted the stems off lots of apples," answered Mattie Sue, her mouth still full.

"Wait to talk until you're finished chewing, honey," Hen prompted her.

Brandon ignored the comment. "You weren't making candy apples, were you?"

"Applesauce, Daddy!"

He was laughing now, and the sound of it made Hen ache for the happier times. *Can we ever get those days back, dear Lord?*

When Hen offered seconds to her husband, he took a smaller portion of meat this time but passed on the side dishes, saying he was watching his weight. "I know—this is new, right?" He smiled fleetingly.

"Amish don't exactly count calories," she replied.

"What's a calorie?" Mattie Sue pushed back her plate.

"You'll know soon enough." Brandon reached for his glass of root beer. "This is delicious." He stared at the glass.

Mattie Sue piped up. "Mommy made it . . . just like at home."

"Honey . . ." said Hen.

"It's all right," Brandon said. "Guess I never really noticed it before. Overworking can do that."

The meal was topped off with Mattie Sue's choice: applesauce with cinnamon and a dollop of whipped cream. "See? We made more applesauce than I've ever seen in my whole life." Mattie Sue giggled.

When they'd eaten their fill, Brandon pushed back from the table and thanked Hen for the terrific meal. Then he turned to Mattie Sue. "Are you ready for the big surprise?"

Hen had no idea what her husband was up to. She stood at the window and watched as Brandon took Mattie to the car and opened the door on the passenger's side. He reached into the front seat and brought out a small pet carrier. "Goodness, he must've bought a puppy," she whispered, moving to the back door. *Unbelievable!*

Mattie Sue put her hands inside the carrier and lifted out an adorable cinnamon-colored cocker spaniel puppy. Hen heard her squeal, then rush back to the door, excited to show off her new dog.

Brandon followed closely behind, his face beaming with the pleasure his gift had brought their daughter. "What would you like to name her?" He squatted down to Mattie's eye level.

Mattie's eyes glowed with delight. "I can name her? I really can?" She slipped one arm around Brandon's neck, still holding the beautiful purebred puppy.

For the next full hour, Mattie and newly named Wiggles were inseparable. She showed Brandon her picture books and asked him to read one, all the while cuddling the irresistible dog, who slept in her lap.

Hen sat across from them, glad she'd brought in this particular gas lamp before Brandon's arrival because it looked similar to an electric lamp. She didn't want the lack of electricity to be a point of discussion for his first visit. She eyed the book on marriage, lying on the table near where Brandon and Mattie sat.

A knock sounded at the door, and Hen rose to open it.

"Hullo there," her dad said, coming in. "Saw a car parked over here and wondered if it was Brandon, just maybe."

"Dawdi, lookee here," Mattie Sue said, jumping up and showing off Wiggles.

Hen stood quietly, her hands folded, hoping her husband would be courteous about this impromptu visit. She held her breath when Brandon got up, still holding the picture book, and went to shake hands with her father.

"Nice to see ya," her dad said. "Come anytime."

"Thanks," Brandon said and looked down at Mattie Sue with Wiggles. "Guess you've got yourself a grandpup." Brandon chuckled at his own joke.

"You wanna hold her, Grandpa?" asked Mattie Sue, holding up the puppy.

"Sure do!" Dad squatted down and took the puppy from Mattie, putting her up on his shoulder like a newborn babe.

Brandon cast a sideways glance at Hen, as though he assumed she'd put her father up to this visit. Hen was helpless to say or do anything—in spite of Brandon's request, she refused to rudely send her dad on his way. She tried to walk the fence for both men, knowing her husband was offended that she appeared not to have kept her word.

Later, when Mattie Sue went outside with her father, still carrying Wiggles, Hen told Brandon she hadn't known her dad was going to drop by.

He shrugged. "Well, what can you do? You live all clumped up together here . . . like a commune or something."

She wanted to defend that but caught herself and said nothing. Changing the subject, she said, "Mattie Sue's responsible for her own chores—indoor and outdoor," she said, making small talk.

"Sounds like child labor."

"Brandon, please." She reached to touch his arm. Why was he so belligerent tonight?

"Do you *really* think this is the best place for our daughter?"

Hen sighed. "We've already talked about this."

"Right." He headed for the back door. "Well, thanks again for the good meal."

Her heart sank. She'd wanted to share so much more. "I spoke to the bishop," she said, hoping he might stay while Mattie Sue was over next door.

He nodded. "Hope you got everything about your sinful past squared away."

Disheartened, Hen stood at the door, watching him pause there on the little porch. Everything the bishop and Barbara had said came rushing back to her—about being kind and accommodating to him. *Shower Brandon "with love.". . .*

"I hope you'll come again," she said quietly. "For supper . . . or just to visit."

He didn't respond, nor did he ask what she'd discussed with the bishop. But he did turn slightly and said with a straight face, "Mattie's puppy will stay with me."

"Aw . . . Brandon."

He shook his head. "She can have it when she comes home."

Her heart flew into her throat.

"Listen, Mattie doesn't have to live your very weird life, Hen. Let her decide where she wants to live—and how." He turned and headed for the car just as Mattie Sue came across the lawn, caressing the puppy.

*Mattie Sue's too young to know where she should live!* Hen watched helplessly as Brandon leaned down and talked to their daughter, touching the back of her head.

*He's telling her the puppy's going with him!*

It was all Hen could do not to rush out the door and cause a scene. Mattie Sue glanced back at the house, not seeing her. Then she looked up at Brandon, so trusting . . . so naïve about what was ahead.

Mattie reached to take her daddy's hand and nodded her little head as she followed Brandon to the car.

*No, dear Lord . . . please don't let this happen!*

# CHAPTER 32

$\mathcal{S}$ ilas was waiting for Rose beneath the grove of trees right after the bend on Salem Road. He stood beside his horse, wearing a crisp white long-sleeved shirt and black vest and trousers. Rose was incapable of keeping her smile in check. Oh, how handsome he looked in his black felt hat. She recalled him saying his straw hat was "wearin' thin" last Sunday evening after Singing.

"Rose Ann." He nodded his head.

"Hullo, Silas." It had been nearly a full week since she'd last seen him. *Almost that long since Hen has seen Brandon, too,* she thought as she got herself settled in the open buggy.

As they pulled away from the shoulder of the road, her thoughts and prayers were with Hen, who might still be spending time with her husband. Rose had seen the sweet gift from Brandon, Mattie Sue's new puppy, before she'd managed to slip away to meet Silas.

*Surely a hopeful sign,* she thought of the cute cocker spaniel. Mattie Sue had been so giddy, she could hardly speak. Mamm, too, had been delighted to pet the dog and said she must bring him over so they could play with Wiggles together. For a woman who did not care one scrap about having animals in the house, Mamm was certainly taken with Mattie Sue's new puppy.

Rose shared the story of the little dog with Silas, and about meeting Beth Browning for the first time. She also told him that Hen and Mattie had moved home for a while. "All of this in the space of a single week!" she said.

But Silas was quieter than any other time they'd been together. It wasn't until they'd ridden in near silence for quite some time that Silas said his father had seen her in Quarryville. Rose had hoped Reuben Good might not bring it up to Silas, since her being with Nick had no bearing whatsoever on her and Silas's courtship.

"Daed noticed you were riding with another fella," said Silas, not looking at her.

"Well, it was strange how it all came about," she replied. "I'd fallen and hurt my leg—could scarcely walk. Nick happened by and took me to Old Eli's."

"My father wondered why one of your brothers didn't take you instead."

"Jah, it must've looked a bit odd, 'specially if he knows you and I are courting."

"Daed was troubled by it, I'll say." Silas paused and glanced at her. "Mainly because it was Nick you were with."

Rose felt put out suddenly. *No one knows him like I do*, she thought, but she was smart enough not to refute Silas.

"That no-*gut* Nick . . . he's caused so much grief for Bishop Aaron. Christian too."

Rose knew Silas and Christian were longtime close friends. "Some brothers tend to argue too much at times," she said in Nick's defense, not knowing what else to say.

"Oh, but not many carry a grudge for years."

"A grudge? On whose part—Christian's?"

"No . . . Nick's." Silas sounded so adamant she was taken aback at his loyalty to Christian.

"Well, what about?" she asked.

"He's carried a chip on his shoulder since the bishop brought him here, is what Christian says. Nick despises anything to do with the Plain life."

"Then, why's he still here?"

"Mighty *gut* question." Silas turned to look at her again. "But Christian has a theory 'bout that."

"Oh?"

He nodded his head emphatically. "He's certain it's because of you, Rose Ann."

"Me?" She remembered Nick's pleading with her to go to visit his mother's grave, to visit the English world. "That's mighty farfetched."

"Christian says the two of you—you and Nick—are much closer friends than anyone knows."

She stiffened. What anyone had to say about that, well, she really didn't care. Truth was, she and Nick *were* close, but they'd guarded their friendship to keep tongues from wagging—and to keep folks from jumping to the wrong conclusion. "We work together in Dat's barn most afternoons," she offered. "I'm sure Christian told ya."

"He did indeed."

She held her breath, hoping there wasn't more to defend. Yet why should she have to? She and Nick had done nothing wrong.

"Christian suspects the two of you go ridin' alone sometimes."

Rose sighed. This was not turning out to be a very good night!

"I hope he's mistaken about that," Silas said, "since you're *my* girl now."

For a brief moment, just to demonstrate her innocence, Rose thought of describing a few of the adventures she'd had with Nick.

But something powerful stirred within, and she recalled having a similar ominous feeling that terrible day so long ago when her mother left for market. This time she heeded her intuition. "I *am* your girl, Silas . . . and happy to be," she said and left it at that.

In saying what she did, Rose had also protected her friendship with Nick, which was as important to her just now as sitting there beside Silas Good, who smiled and reached for her hand.

∽

In that moment of sheer blackness, Hen watched her world tip and plunge upside down. She pressed her hand to her heart.

*Mattie Sue, my precious child!*

Her heart cried out for her daughter, yet she was mute. Her legs were as useless as her mother's, who was surely over next door in the main house talking with the bishop's wife and Kate . . . her little granddaughters at her knee.

Hen's anger filled her beyond reason as she watched Brandon take the puppy from Mattie Sue and place the pet into the carrier in back, behind the driver's seat. Then, like a robot, he marched around the car and opened the door on the opposite side, waiting for Mattie to get in.

Just when Hen's heart was in the process of shattering, Mattie Sue looked back at the house—and saw Hen there at the door. She raised her little hand to wave. Brandon urged her to get inside, but Mattie Sue dug in her heels and shook her head. Then, like a dart, she moved quickly away from the car and dashed toward Hen, her long skirt and apron flying. "Mommy . . . Mommy!"

Hen thought she must be returning to say good-bye, but her little girl's face was wet with tears. "Oh, M-Mommy . . ." Mattie Sue stuttered, unable to do more than sob in her mother's arms. "Daddy's t-taking . . . Wiggles away from . . . me."

"But you're here, baby . . . you're still here."

"I thought Wiggles was mine."

Hen continued to hold Mattie Sue, then carried her into the house and closed the door behind her. She leaned against it, her daughter clinging to her neck and crying for both the puppy and for Mommy, all in one sorrowful blend of betrayal and confusion.

≈

The next morning Rose Ann awakened with Hen and Brandon heavily on her mind. She hadn't gone over to talk to Hen after arriving home last night because Hen's gas lamps had already been extinguished. But she'd discovered her distraught father in the kitchen, unable to sleep, all bent over his Bible as he prayed for Hen and her little family. It was at that late hour she'd learned of Brandon's trickery. Poor, poor Mattie Sue!

Now, as she stretched out her feet in bed and slipped her hand beneath her cheek, she wondered if Hen might not be wishing this Lord's Day were a Preaching Sunday. Rose couldn't help but think such a gathering might do her sister some good. *Next Sunday*, she thought, anxious herself for worship with the People.

She heard Hen downstairs—at least, she assumed it was her sister—starting breakfast. Soon she also heard Mattie Sue's birdlike chatter. *Mamm must be down there, too*, she guessed. Who better to comfort Mattie over the loss of her puppy than dear Mamm? It pained Rose when she thought about Brandon's cruel deed.

*How could a father do such a thing?*

≈

Later, after the noon dishes were redd up and put away, two of Rose's cousins, Sarah and Sadie Kauffman—and their parents—stopped by on their way home from having also visited the bishop. After a time, Rose and Sarah slipped out of the house and went walking together. They'd invited Sadie to join them, but she'd wanted to stay and visit with Mattie Sue instead.

"Are ya planning to come to the next Singing, Sarah?" Rose asked as they strolled through the meadow behind the barn.

Sarah's pretty eyes twinkled in the sunlight. "I hope to."

Rose leaned near to whisper, "Is there a chance you might flirt with Nick again . . . like last time?" She felt strangely blunt, yet she wasn't at all adept at this sort of thing.

"Honestly, do you really think I'd waste my time with the likes of him?"

Her response surprised Rose. "I was just wondering. You and Mary seemed bent on getting his attention . . . well, last gathering."

Sarah moistened her lips and smiled. Now it was her turn to whisper in Rose's ear. "He's a cold fish, seems to me."

"Why would ya say that?"

" 'Cause he's not interested in me or in Mary—neither one." Sarah looked away, frowning, then back at her. "You tryin' to look out for him, Rosie?"

She was, but Rose wouldn't say why. "Sure is hard to understand why he never had a girlfriend, ain't so?" said Rose.

"Might be he's not thinking of stayin' round long enough to settle down and marry. 'Least that's how the grapevine has it."

She was afraid of this kind of talk. "Guess we'll have to keep prayin'."

Sarah looked around, her golden hair catching the sun's rays. "Jah . . . 'specially since he's disappeared somewhere—and on the Lord's Day, yet."

"So, Nick wasn't at home when ya visited over yonder?"

Sarah's eyes were gentle now as she nodded. "Bishop looked awfully worried for Nick. I s'pose we all should be. Still," Sarah added, "he's never seemed Amish to me. And that disgraceful ponytail!"

"Why'd ya flirt with him, then?" Rose had to ask.

Sarah's eyes registered instant disdain. "Ach . . . you must think

I'm like your sister, Hen. Well, I ain't!" With that she picked up her skirt and marched away, heading back to the house.

"What a terrible matchmaker I am," Rose muttered to herself. Oh, but she wished to goodness Nick wasn't raising eyebrows by vanishing like he had.

Why had Nick picked the Lord's Day to go off to the English world? Had he gone to his mother's grave without her? *And did he take a car there?* If so, why choose the most sacred day of the week? So many questions tumbled through her mind.

She glanced at the bishop's house and wondered why on earth Sarah and Sadie's parents had gone visiting there today, too. Unless . . . was Sarah actually hiding something about her—or her sister's—feelings for Nick? After all, her cousin had not denied being interested in Nick just now, had she?

As Rose slowly turned to walk back toward the house, here came Christian, making a beeline for her. "Hullo," she said, wondering why he looked so glum.

"Rosie . . . any idea where Nick's gone off to?" Christian's eyes probed hers.

"No." She shook her head. "How long's he been away?"

"Far as Dat knows, he never came home last night."

"Did ya run him off? You two are always quarreling."

He smiled severely. "He needs a *gut* whippin', that's what."

"Christian—bite your lip!"

He laughed scornfully. "That boy's never had a hand laid on him by Dat or anyone." He lowered his voice, stepping closer. "Between you and me, I 'spect my father was afraid of the caseworkers checkin' up. But I say a hard thrashing might go a long ways with Nick Franco."

"Ain't a *gut* idea to think that way," Rose said. "Don't ya listen at Preaching?"

"Well, you just try 'n' love a brother like *him!*" Christian shot back as he rushed off.

*For pity's sake*. Rose wondered if Nick hadn't run off for the day just to be free of Christian. But deep inside, she feared Nick had been so enticed by what he called the edge that he'd crossed over and was never coming back.

# CHAPTER 33

$\mathcal{S}$eeing Silas two days in a row—their Saturday evening date and again late Sunday afternoon for an impromptu volleyball game at his oldest brother's house—was unusual but also very nice. Because of the sudden drop in temperature Sunday evening, they'd shortened their time together after the game. The sizzling-hot brick he'd put on the floor of the buggy had cooled much too quickly.

Truthfully, Rose Ann had been kept so busy she'd scarcely had time to ponder Nick's peculiar absence over the weekend, at least not until Monday afternoon. By then he had returned from who knows where, having slipped into the bishop's house late Sunday night—or so Nick told her himself while they hauled feed for the mules. Rose listened, trying not to make much of it—trying not to reveal her concern, either. She presumed that if he wanted her to know anything about his disappearance, he would say. But he didn't breathe a word.

Rose busied herself with a canning bee on Monday morning while Mammi Sylvia looked after Mamm. Rose and Hen and several of their close cousins, including Sarah, Sadie, and Mary, worked together to put up dozens of quarts of chowchow for the deacon's family. Arie Zook had come to assist, as well, which seemed to make Hen very happy. Then on Tuesday, after breakfast, Rose and Mamm helped Hen cut out two new dresses and aprons, using paper bags for homemade patterns.

By Wednesday morning, the week was beginning to feel completely out of kilter without her usual banter with Nick. Yet all the while, Rose attempted to avoid her friend . . . for Silas's sake.

∼

When Rose arrived at work Wednesday, she was delighted to see Beth sitting in the kitchen, waiting for her. Gilbert Browning was nearby in his usual spot in the corner of the front room, reading the newspaper. Rose said hello and set about brewing coffee and making oatmeal and apple fritters. Sighing, she glanced at the sink filled with dirty dishes.

Beth broke the stillness. "Daddy, can I *please* go to see Rosie's baby horses?"

Rose kept her attention on mixing the oatmeal, but Mr. Browning did not reply.

"I really, really want to." Beth reached for the glass of orange juice Rose had poured.

"Beth . . . listen."

"Daddy, please!"

Rose couldn't help herself. "What if you brought Beth to my house this Friday, after the noon meal?" she suggested to Mr. Browning. "I could bring her home in, say, two hours?"

Beth's eyes were alight as she turned to see what her father might say. She looked to be holding her breath.

Once again, Mr. Browning appeared quite unwilling, and Rose was fairly sure he was going to nix the whole idea.

"I'll keep a close watch over her," Rose added.

He shook his head. "It's too risky."

"Aw, Daddy . . ." Beth slumped back. "Rosie *said* she'd take care of me."

"But I'm your only parent, Beth, honey. Someone has to make good decisions . . . for you."

Beth looked devastated, like this was her last hope of getting away from the house—and from her overly protective father.

"Maybe another time, then." Rose realized it was best to drop the idea, lest Gilbert Browning take issue with *her*. She was merely an employee, after all.

Rose poured more coffee for herself and thought Mr. Browning might want his warmed up, too. Going over to the lamp table, she poured some into his cup. Then she returned to the kitchen, thinking about all that had already transpired in a few days' time in this not-so-haunted house. She'd gone from suspecting someone was being hidden upstairs to discovering it was, in fact, Mr. Browning's own daughter. And, goodness, but Beth had quite an interesting personality—she loved life as much as Rose did. *She's just not permitted to live it fully!*

When the hot oatmeal and fritters were ready to serve, Rose set the table, then went to the sink and drew water to wash the dishes while Beth ate. Mr. Browning put his paper away and stated that he wasn't hungry before heading outside through the back door, mumbling to himself. Rose assumed he was either disturbed at what she'd suggested, or still pondering it.

"Daddy won't let me go. I just know it," Beth whined.

"He might need time to think it over."

Beth had tears in her eyes. "No, he never will."

Rose glanced over her shoulder. "How patient can ya be?"

Beth blinked her eyes, wiping back tears. "It's no fun being stuck here. The only time I get outside is when I dress like an Amish boy and help in the yard for a while."

Rose felt sorry for her yet again as she scrubbed the dishes. It occurred to her that Beth was surely bright enough to do some easy kitchen chores. "Would you like to dry the dishes and utensils?"

"Daddy says I might break something, so we just leave them be."

*You aren't kidding—you leave them for me!* "Well, if I showed you how to carefully dry, would you like to try?"

Beth scratched her head and moved her weight from one foot to the other. "Um . . . I don't know."

"Isn't it time you learned how to take care of a kitchen?"

Halfheartedly, Beth finished eating her oatmeal and a whole fritter before coming to the sink. She brought her dirty dishes and silverware and handed them to Rose. Then she picked up the dish towel Rose had placed there.

"Are you right-handed?"

"Yes."

"All right, then. Pick up the plate in your left hand and dry with the towel in your right." Rose showed her what she meant with the first bowl. "Always make slow movements when stacking plates and other breakable items. That way you won't chip or crack them."

They worked side by side until all the dishes were washed and dried. Then Beth went down the side hallway to the rear door and peered out. "Daddy looks real sad out there."

*Everything's changing for him,* thought Rose.

Beth came back down the hall and opened the kitchen pantry door. She disappeared in there for the longest time, talking to herself all the while. Then, just when Rose was about to check on her, Beth brought out the broom and dustpan. "I hoped and hoped I'd get to see your baby horses," said Beth, sniffling. "Hoped so hard it hurts." She began to push the crumbs about in un-predictable patterns, attempting to sweep under the table without Rose prompting her.

She smiled empathetically at Beth, who was clearly eager for more independence.

When the floor was swept, Beth went to sit in her father's usual chair, across the room. Hoping to join her, Rose walked to the petite armless rocker and was about to sit.

"Oh, not there!" Beth said, eyes wide.

Rose stepped back.

"That chair was Mommy's." Beth's lower lip quivered. "She made the pretty needlepoint there on the seat cushion."

Rose leaned down to look. "Your mother was very *gut*. Mine does needlepoint, too."

"We stopped sitting in her chair when she . . ." Beth's voice faded off.

Sighing, Rose said she knew her mother had passed away. "I'm awful sorry."

"Daddy said Mommy was too young to die."

Rose thought on that. "Well, it's not our place to question God's timing. Did you know He plans when we enter this world at birth—and He knows the day we will draw our last breath, too?"

Beth blinked. "Never heard that before."

"It's written in the Bible," she told her. "Our heavenly Father is sovereign. That means His plans for us are far better than what we could ever begin to plan ourselves."

Beth looked at her. "Is it easy for you to trust God, Rosie?"

"Believe me, I'm far from perfect, but I try not to let myself question the Lord."

Shrugging nonchalantly, Beth got up from the chair and wandered back through the sitting room, nearly stumbling as she headed toward the stairs without saying more.

*Did I say something to upset her?* Rose wondered.

∼

Even after returning home, Rose continued to think about her discussion with Beth. How much of it had Mr. Browning's daughter understood? And what of his reluctance to allow Beth to visit the farm?

Rose tried to keep her attention on her latest novel as she snuggled into her bed that night, about to drift off to sleep. Suddenly she saw a flash of light on one of her windows. *Ach, is it Silas?* She scurried to find her bathrobe and slipped it on. Not having time to put her hair into a respectable bun, she wound her waist-length hair up into a knot before opening the window.

There below stood Nick, his flashlight shining on the ground. "Will ya come for a ride, Rosie?"

"Aw, Nick . . . I was nearly asleep already."

He nodded solemnly. "It's maybe too late . . . jah." He sounded glum.

"You all right?"

"Sure."

The cold night air pressed into the room. "Well, I'll see ya tomorrow, then."

He turned, his shoulders slumped as he crept away . . . alone, back toward the bishop's farmhouse.

*Something's not right.* Rose closed the window and tried to dismiss her fears.

~

On Thursday afternoon, there was a pretty white quilt to complete for the upcoming wedding season. Rose accompanied Hen in the family carriage to Aunt Malinda's, where she was glad to see her sister and her aunt getting further reacquainted. In fact, Aunt Malinda made a special point of drawing out Hen. Mattie Sue was spending the day with Kate and her little ones, so Hen was free to soak up their loving aunt's kind attention.

On the ride home, Hen surprised her by taking up the driving lines for the horse—she'd left her car parked behind the barn at Dat's for the day. Rose realized Hen had not been using her car much this week, not even to go to her job yesterday—Dat had taken her over in the family buggy, of all things.

Most noticeable, though, was Hen's countenance, which had begun to change from concerned to carefree. Her smile lit up the entire area, no matter where Hen happened to be, including the stable. "I want to become familiar again with Dat's driving horses," she explained. *An interesting, yet worrisome sign . . .*

&

Hen was happy to see Rose that evening after supper, when Rose invited her and Mattie Sue to family worship at the main house. Pulling up a chair next to her mother, Hen listened as her father read from what he called the "love chapter" in the New Testament book of Corinthians. She couldn't help wondering if the passage had been chosen just for her—*love beareth all things, believeth all things, hopeth all things . . .*—but she didn't mind. Eager for God's wisdom, especially in the form of Scripture, she welcomed whatever spiritual guidance she might glean from her father.

After an evening prayer from the old German prayer book, *Die Ernsthafte Christenpflict*, Rose took Mattie Sue over to play at the bishop's with three of his visiting granddaughters. Dad left the house to head out to the stable to see the foals, and Hen was glad to sit quietly with her mother, who seemed more interested in talking than at other times.

"Are you free of pain tonight?" Hen asked, touching her mother's hand.

"A little more bearable than sometimes." Mom smiled thoughtfully. Then, after some time, she said, "My dear girl . . . I hope you'll keep the door wide open where Brandon's concerned—invitin' him for meals, finding ways to be with him."

"I'm doing what I can."

"That's wonderful-*gut*, Hen." She went on to encourage her.

"Couples need to make things right with each other, submitting to one another in love, as God instructs us in Scripture."

Hen honestly wondered if her mother knew what that might involve in her case. "I'm going to write him a letter . . . every few days."

Mom smiled faintly. "The Lord woos *us*, that's for sure."

"Jah," whispered Hen, falling silent for a moment. Then she said, "Brandon's never been one to attend any church, let alone care at all about the Lord."

"Nothing's impossible with God, dear one."

Hen sighed. "My husband says he's an agnostic."

"I have no idea what that is."

"No, and neither did I, either . . . back when we were dating." She didn't think her mom would care to hear that Brandon was lukewarm toward God. His aversion to things of the Spirit made her tremble. "Brandon's not interested in the Bible, prayer, or the Christian faith."

"All the more reason to trust the Lord to work in his heart," said Mom.

"It'll take God's doin'," Hen agreed, glad to have the kind of support she'd so longed for and missed. "Thanks, Mom. And please keep Brandon in your prayers."

"Oh jah . . . no question about that." Her mother reached over and squeezed her hand.

"Denki," Hen caught herself saying.

≈

That night Nick shone his flashlight on Rose's window at an earlier hour to ask again if she'd ride with him. This time, she didn't have the legitimate excuse of being ready to retire to bed, so she wavered and held back, not wanting to hurt him. But she knew full well Silas would never approve. Her beau hadn't come right out and said she couldn't spend time with Nick, but it was strongly implied.

"I'm sorry . . . but I can't." She paused. "I shouldn't, really." Her heart went out to her best friend, who turned away looking even more dejected than last night . . . downright hopeless.

"Nick," she whispered but did not raise her voice. What could she do? She was Silas's steady girl, and it wouldn't be long, she was rather sure, and *his* flashlight would be the one twinkling off her window. The fact that Nick was using this method to get her attention was not suitable at all.

When Rose really stopped to consider it, nothing much made sense about their friendship, and hadn't for years. What could possibly come of it? Nick had secretly cherished the modern world since his childhood, and this now colored everything between them.

The logical thing was for Rose to back off from seeing him and simply honor Silas Good's implied request. Yet why was it so hard?

# CHAPTER 34

All week the leaves had been falling and cluttering the front lawn, so Rose, Hen, and Mattie Sue went out to rake Friday morning. Rose had positioned Mamm's wheelchair near the front window so she could enjoy the sunshine, content to watch "her three girls" work together, making neat piles as Hen and Rose had done as youngsters. Several times, Hen let Mattie run and jump into the piles, which brought a round of giggles from not only Mattie but Hen, too. Rose had never seen her sister this peaceful, and she took heart in her sister's hope to win Brandon to the Plain life . . . for God.

*Brandon should see her now!* Rose found herself thinking more and more this way, wishing her brother-in-law might come to understand how through the years he'd deprived Hen of this joyful life she was born to . . . and still loved. No matter how hard things seemed each time she pondered Brandon and Hen's situation, Rose prayed for divine wisdom. And Mattie Sue's near-constant pleading to go and see her daddy and Wiggles "back home" wasn't making the situation any easier for Hen.

Rose knew something had to change, and soon. Would her parents insist on Hen's return to her husband?

◇

Rose was surprised and delighted when Gilbert Browning arrived with Beth that afternoon. She'd wondered when he might realize that most anyone would be safe on an Amish farm.

She offered her hand to help Beth out of the car, remembering she was sometimes wobbly on her feet. "I'll take very *gut* care of your daughter," she promised Mr. Browning.

The man pursed his lips and inhaled slowly. "I'm counting on that."

Rose placed Beth's arm through hers and led her to the back walkway. There they stood, giving her father a wave when he got into the car and backed out to the road. "We'll have a nice time," she told Beth as they turned and slowly made their way to the barn.

Seeing the baby horses through Beth's eyes made the experience all the more moving for Rose Ann. Beth was not at all fearful of the young foals, and neither were they of her. She whispered to them like a child. "Aren't you the prettiest little thing?" Beth said over and over while she let them smell the back of her hand, like one might approach a strange dog. The foals blinked their eyes at her.

Soon Beth was down in the straw, just sitting there, and they came right to her. At one point she was eye to eye with the gentle creatures, and Rose caught her breath and blinked tears away.

"You're just so precious," Beth whispered as the smaller horse moved his face right up next to hers, licking her chin, her face, her neck, till Beth couldn't keep her giggles inside.

When Mattie Sue came wandering into the stable, Rose introduced her to Beth. "My niece loves the foals, too," Rose said, but

Beth was not very interested in either Rose or Mattie Sue just now. All her attention was focused on the young horses.

Mattie went and squatted down next to Beth, and Rose was pleased that it didn't take long before Beth became comfortable with Mattie Sue. Now and then, Beth turned to look at Mattie, smiling tentatively, both of them just inches away from the foals. And to think Beth had been too frightened to come to the door a little less than two weeks ago!

"Looks like you're makin' some new friends today," Rose said, overcome with joy as she watched. Without a doubt, her efforts to seek out Mr. Browning's daughter were truly worthwhile.

Beth made no reply as she stroked the foals and shared the same space with Mattie Sue, lost in her own world.

Later, when it was time to take Beth back home, Nick waved to Rose from over in the pasture. Beth stared at him for the longest time, even as they were pulling out of the lane.

"Rosie, I didn't want to leave today," Beth told her on the ride home in the buggy.

"Well, I understand that feelin'," Rose replied.

"Like when Daddy and I lived in Illinois—I felt just like that all over again," Beth said.

"And what was that?"

Beth grew quiet; then she began to sniffle.

"You all right?"

Looking away, Beth wiped her eyes. "My daddy won't let me tell."

*Tell what?* Rose wondered, beginning to worry.

"That boy—the one who waved at you—is he your boyfriend?"

"No."

"He looks like—" Beth stopped.

"Who, Beth? Someone you knew in Illinois?"

"I'm not supposed to say."

"Well, I believe you're wrong about that. You can tell me

anything," Rose said, gripping the reins and feeling terribly uneasy.

Beth was silent for a time. At last she said softly, "He reminds me of Tommy Walker."

"Is Tommy your friend?"

Nodding, Beth continued. "Daddy didn't want my boy to take me away from him. That's why we moved here. Daddy says it was for my own good."

"Was Tommy your boyfriend, ya mean?"

"We loved each other a whole bunch."

Rose did not know what to think. "Was Tommy nice to you?"

Beth said yes and wiped her face with the back of her arm.

"Your father brought you here to get away from a *nice* boy?"

"Daddy likes the Amish community—says it's a safe place for girls like me. That's why we lived in Arthur, too."

"Was the boy you liked Amish?"

"No, Tommy was from my school. He loved me, he said. And he wanted me to go away with him. Daddy caught us kissing one night and started making plans to leave."

"You must miss Tommy."

Beth sighed. "I'll never, ever forget my sweet Tommy."

"A girl never forgets her first love."

"Who's yours?" Beth asked, looking at her.

"Well"—Rose gave her a conspiratorial grin—"his name is Silas Good. But you can't tell anyone, all right?"

Beth's eyes widened. "A secret—like Tommy?"

"Not exactly the same way, no. But we Amish don't tell it around who we're seein' till it's closer to the time we get married."

Beth nodded, her eyes fixed on Rose. "Is that so no other boy can push his nose in and spoil things?"

Laughing softly, Rose said, "I guess you could say that."

"Well, if you love each other, then no other boy can come between you, right?" Beth said.

Rose considered that and found it to be quite profound. "Jah, I s'pose so." She felt that Beth had not only been separated from the physical world on some level, but also separated from life's sweetest moments. Lonely as she was, no doubt Beth was hungry for affection.

"Would you like to come to my house again?"

"If Daddy lets me."

"Well, maybe on Wednesdays, after I'm done with my work, I could bring you home with me sometimes."

"Goody!" Beth smiled so wide she showed her gums. "I hope so."

"Why don't you let me talk to your father about it, all right?"

Sitting straighter now, Beth agreed, then turned to watch the road. "Do you think I could ever learn to drive a horse and buggy?" she asked softly.

"Maybe, with plenty of practice."

"There's lots of things I hope to do . . . one day."

"Hope is a wondrous thing."

"My aunt in Illinois—her name's Judith—she says I have to put wings on my hope, but I don't know how to do that."

Rose listened. "Your aunt sounds like an encouraging person."

"She has lots of time to write me letters every week."

"Why's that?"

Beth pressed her lips together tightly and looked away. "She never got married."

"Lots of women don't," Rose said. "One of my mother's sisters has stayed single her whole life."

"She's happy?"

"Sure."

Observing Beth's forlorn expression, Rose wished she'd never said a word about her beloved Maidel aunt. "I'm so glad your father brought you to visit me," she said as they pulled into the driveway.

Mr. Browning hurried out the door, coming to meet Beth, a relieved smile on his face. Beth stepped down out of the carriage and into her father's arms. "Oh, Daddy . . . this was one of the best days of my whole life!"

Rose struggled to keep her emotions in check as she waved to the two of them. "Good-bye, Beth . . . and thank you so much, Mr. Browning."

~

Rose awakened in the middle of the night with a sudden fright and stumbled across the room. Going to the nearest window, she raised the shade and looked out, anxious to see the bishop's farmhouse in the near distance. She had the strangest urgent need to talk to Nick. All week she'd suppressed it. Had she done the right thing by putting him off? The only difference in their relationship now was her courtship with Silas. Surely, if she revealed the reason to Nick, he would understand.

Standing at the window, she wished she might see a speck of light coming from Nick's upstairs bedroom. Was he awake, too, and looking back this way, wondering something similar?

Rose pressed her hand to her chest—she did not know what to do with this peculiar tugging on her heart. The days of obligatory separation from Nick felt nearly like a deception on her part. She hugged herself in the darkness, feeling as if part of her had been severed somehow. But wasn't that silly? Maybe these thoughts were merely part of the odd web of irrational notions the mind spun in the wee hours. Things could seem terribly skewed in the bleak hours before sunrise.

The thought of going without seeing Nick indefinitely—*really* seeing him, not just working alongside each other, but riding together and talking freely—rendered her almost unable to breathe. It was all she could do to keep from crying.

"But why . . . why should I miss him so?" she whispered into the shadows.

# CHAPTER 35

uring Rose's ride home from her Saturday afternoon visit to Aunt Malinda's, she happened upon Christian, who was kicking stones along the road as he walked away from his house. She slowed up the horse and waved, wondering why he looked nearly as down in the dumps as Nick had all week.

She was surprised to see him begin to run alongside the carriage as she passed. "I need to talk to ya, Rose!" he called.

"I'm late getting home," she answered, not interested in more of his nonsense about Nick. "I need to help with supper."

"Well, soon, then . . . very soon," he shouted back. "Jah?"

Rose headed up Salem Road, hoping Christian might just forget and leave her be.

~

While tossing feed to the goats after supper, Rose kept telling herself there wasn't anything she could do for Nick. She must live her life and he must live his, even if it meant he went to the English side of things. What he chose to do was none of her concern. *He has a free will . . . and he has not chosen the right way.* It was not her place to pressure him to follow the Lord in holy baptism—if anything, it was the bishop and Barbara's. Yet they had failed to win him over.

Rose turned from the barn to go to the house, and there was Nick, standing under a tree, hatless, his back against the trunk and arms folded. He was staring at her, his long black hair pulled into its customary ponytail. "Nick . . . what're ya doin'?"

He motioned to her. "Rosie . . . I think we should go ridin'."

She disliked rejecting him again. Still, she needed to honor her commitment to Silas. "My beau could get wind of it," she said softly.

"What right does *he* have to pick your friends?" Nick said defiantly.

"Well, Nick"—and here she offered a smile—"it's not like you're one of my girlfriends, ya know."

He smirked good-naturedly. "Might as well be." He glanced at the sky. "Come on, Rosie . . . while it's still daylight."

"I . . . really shouldn't."

He ignored her remark. "Your knee's much better, ain't?"

It was, and had been for a while now. "Well . . ." She hesitated, though she still didn't feel it was right, not when Silas had been so clear about where he stood on the matter.

"There's something I want to show you in the ravine."

"You'd say just about anything now, jah?"

"Come and see—you won't be sorry." He left her standing there as he strode across the yard. "I'll meet ya up the way. Bring George; he's surest on his feet."

What was she supposed to do—leave Nick waiting out on the road?

"Hurry, Rosie," he called over his shoulder. "The ravine gets dark quick."

*Why's he so taken with that place?* She glanced over at the Dawdi

Haus where Hen and Mattie Sue were staying. Hen easily could've seen her with Nick if she was anywhere in her kitchen. Rose could only hope her sister was resting upstairs.

Groaning, she made her way to the barn, up to the haymow, and found her old trousers. Quickly she pulled them on under her dress. Since she intended to be gone just a short while, she decided to take only the old lightweight shawl from the row of hooks in the stable.

She then removed her Kapp and left it on one of those same hooks.

George was ready and raring to go, and Rose wondered how on earth she could walk him past the house without being seen. So she took the long way around, through the meadow behind the barn, out of sight.

Carefully, Rose hoisted herself up. *Forgive me this one last time, Silas.* She also wondered if she shouldn't ask the Lord to forgive her, too.

# CHAPTER 36

*L*et's go to the bottom of the hollow," Nick suggested as he and Rose rode side by side on the narrow strip of Bridle Path Lane. "Down by the crick."

"I despise this place," she said. "It's creepy."

"It's an adventure, Rosie."

"Well, I'm not comfortable here, are you?"

"Puh!" He blew air out of his mouth. "Don't ya know I'm the hobgoblin who lives deep in the ravine? The one the bishop's grandchildren talk about."

She shivered. "Don't make jokes 'bout that. Please . . ."

"I'm *kidding*," he said. A shadow seemed to cross his face.

She'd noticed this happen before. "You look different sometimes, Nick."

"I'm the same fella you've always known." He stopped talking till they'd gone past Jeb Ulrich's ramshackle place. "Promise me you'll never, ever turn your back on me again."

His words stung her. "What do you mean?"

"All this week, you refused me."

"Nick, I told ya why."

"And you know what I said to that."

She sighed as she followed him down the craggy cliff, leaning forward on her horse, steadying herself with her knees. His black ponytail marked the way ahead.

"No one has any business interfering with *gut* friends," he said, directing his horse into the narrow gorge. "You know it, Rose Ann, and so do I."

What had gotten into him, using her two names? He never referred to her like that. He was starting to sound like one of her father's uncles—sharp-tongued and without regard for her feelings. Even so, she refused to argue. Nick was smarter than he was letting on about her and Silas. Goodness, they were on the threshold of engagement. *Surely he suspects . . .*

The descent grew steeper, and the horses had to pick their way around large boulders, then slow even more as they moved near treacherous outcroppings. "Did ya come here last weekend, when you were gone overnight?" she asked.

He laughed. "You're just dyin' to know, ain't?"

"Well, I hope you didn't sleep in the brambles and thorns."

"We're almost there," he coaxed her and the horse. "Keep on comin' now."

Once they'd made the difficult passage through the thick underbrush and heavily treed areas where the rock face was more dangerous, Nick stopped and got off his horse. He gave Pepper a cube of sugar and led him to the creek to drink. "Go over there, Rosie, and look behind that boulder." He pointed behind her.

She dismounted and went to see what Nick was talking about. Leaning behind the enormous stone, she reached down and felt something hard sticking out of the mound of earth. It felt like a tree root petrified over time.

Then, peering down, she cried, "Can it be?" She saw the grimy silver top and pulled the object up out of the mesh of leaves and twigs. Caked with debris, it was her mother's long-lost money tin. "I can't believe this!"

Nick stood between Pepper and George as both horses drank from the creek. "I found it Wednesday night, when I was down here, ridin' *alone*."

"Well, how on earth?" Lovingly, she removed the leaves and pieces of mud as best she could.

"I was sitting right where you are, and my flashlight rolled back into the crevice behind me. I started fishing around for it and bumped into the hard tin and realized something was lodged in there."

"What do ya know . . . after all this time!" Holding the tin box, Rose sat on the stony ledge and pried open its rusty top. Her heart was pounding as she looked inside and saw the dollar bills and coins her mother had placed there so long ago. "Won't Mamm be surprised?" she said, looking up at him. "Oh, Nick! Denki, ever so much." She set it down and went to him. "You knew how much it would mean to me to find this. Thank you!"

He chuckled, looking at her hair. "You look like me, all schtruwwlich without your Kapp."

She raised her hands and felt the loose strands of hair. "Ach, goodness."

"That's all right. Ya look *gut*, Rosie."

She smiled up at him. "Denki again for findin' Mamm's tin box."

"I said you wouldn't be sorry."

"It's a family heirloom. She'll be so happy to have it back."

"But how can ya take it home?"

"Well, why not?"

"Think about it—you can't say you've been down here, now, can ya?"

She moaned. "You're right. They'd never expect me to come here by myself."

"They'd suspect you were here with *me*," he said. "And the bishop or Barbara might've seen us ridin' up the road together earlier."

Rose was torn now, because she couldn't show her mother or take the tin and the money safely home again. She could not even tell Mamm she'd found it. And if word got out to Silas's father, or to Silas himself, who knew what might happen? "Guess I have no choice but to leave it here." She felt like crying.

"It's just like everything else, Rosie."

She raised her apron hem to dab at her eyes, listening. "What is?"

He looked at the boulder, his gaze rising up the steep ravine. "We can't be honest and show anyone what we know. Or how we feel."

*What do you mean?* she almost said, but she knew. She knew all too well. Tears welled up in her eyes.

"We have to hide our feelings behind a boulder, like that tin box. Keep them hidden away like Mr. Browning kept his daughter a secret out of fear." Nick looked into her eyes, pleading. "Come with me to the modern world, won't ya, Rosie? For *gut*."

"Leave the People?"

"We'll disappear before dawn." He reached for her hand.

She hesitated, shocked by his request. "What are ya sayin', Nick?" She stared at him, aware of the ache in her throat.

"We've known each other nearly all our lives. I know how you are with me. I saw you lookin' my way when your cousins were talkin' and flirting with me at Singing. Aw, Rosie, I know you care for me."

"Sure, I care, but . . ."

"What?" His eyes urged her to continue.

"I belong to . . ." She stopped.

Nick took both her hands in his and drew her near. Her cheeks felt too warm, and a strange feeling nearly took her over . . . like the night they rode Pepper together. "It's always been you, Rosie. Always."

She felt so horribly confused in his arms. "But . . . we're just friends!"

He nodded. "The best kind of friends, jah. I'm the one who's listened to you talk a blue streak since we were kids. I *know* you better than anyone. Come away with me. We can live in Philly."

"But that's where *you* long to be." She shook her head. "My life is here."

"Shh. Just listen." He cupped her chin, his eyes searing hers. "Think ahead twenty years from now," he whispered. "Who do you see yourself with?"

*How dare he ask me this!*

"Think, Rosie . . . whose wife are you—and are ya happy?"

"Nick, don't." She pulled away.

"Please, just let me have this moment—the two of us together." He caressed her cheek, then pressed her face gently to him. She felt the rise and fall of his chest. "Not a single day goes by that I don't think of you—*us*—this way. I can hardly wait to see you every afternoon. And I remember each place we've ever explored together."

Oh, she could rest in his arms for always, embrace this strange, exuberant feeling. Yet Rose felt wicked for even thinking she should allow herself this pleasure.

But he'd said it himself: They truly were best friends! "I do care for you, Nick."

"Then come with me," he said again. "It's that simple."

Rose searched his eyes, this familiar face she'd grown so accustomed to. A long moment passed between them, and in that span of time, she felt it, too—she *wanted* to be with him, to be where he was. How many years had she cherished their friendship? Nick was the one she'd run to first when she had something to share.

Her heart was beating much too fast. Was this how Hen had

felt with Brandon? Her dear, dear sister, who'd thrown her life away for the world? She thought also of Beth's father, who'd rescued his daughter from a boy who would surely have taken advantage of her innocence. Was Nick any different from either of them? Could she trust her heart to him?

*No,* she thought. *This is just like the books I read—it's not real!*

"It wouldn't be right," she said at last. "I can't go with you."

Nick drew a slow breath. Her heart was breaking for him, for the rejection he must feel. "Then I'll stay here and join church."

"No, you'll never be happy unless you take the kneeling vow for the right reason. I see you livin' your life for the bishop, miserable day in and day out. I can't let you do that for me . . . for the rest of your life. I won't." She stopped to brush back tears. "Besides, I'm sure you must know—I belong to Silas Good. I'm his steady girl."

Nick never even flinched—he simply refused to acknowledge what she'd said. "I know you love me, Rosie."

*If that's true, what kind of woman falls for two men?* She shook her head.

Nick leaned down to kiss her forehead, her cheek. "Have you saved your lips for your beau?" His voice was raspy, his breath near.

She kept her head bowed. " 'Tis best, jah."

He sighed audibly. "I loved ya first. . . ."

Rose knew in her core this was the last time she could ever show him any depth of affection. Raising her hands to his shoulders, she stood on tiptoe and gently kissed his face. It was wet with tears.

He reached for her so quickly, it took her breath away. She yielded to his strong embrace, thinking of poor Beth Browning, who'd loved and lost when her father had intervened. *"Daddy says it was for my own good,"* Beth had told her in a quivering voice.

*What would my father say if he saw me now?* Rose wondered.

"I'm leavin' the Amish." Nick's dark eyes shone with resolve. "If I can't have you, I don't want to stay." He sighed again, his head resting on hers. "I couldn't bear it."

"How soon?" Rose asked.

He shuddered and released her. "When the time is right."

Their eyes locked; Rose stepped back slightly. "Then God be with ya, Nick Franco."

"And with you, my sweet Rosie."

# CHAPTER 37

*S*unday morning, Hen held Mattie Sue's hand in the long line of women and girls who waited to enter the deacon's house for Preaching. She was filled with a great sense of joy to be attending church for the first time in years. It seemed like longer than five years since she'd heard the old *Ausbund* hymns or listened to the sermons.

Looking now at Mattie Sue—beautiful in her blue dress and white apron, her Kapp atop her head—Hen wondered how her little girl would manage the nearly three-and-a-half-hour service. Hen had already decided to sit close to the back, if she could, not being a member anyway. *A good choice for Mattie's first time.*

Once the line moved and she was indoors, she saw a space on the wooden bench beside Arie Zook, who was holding her infant son and had her three-year-old daughter, Becky, with her, as well. The women sat in one section of the long room, facing the men and boys, the age-old way. Hen fought back tears during the familiar *Loblied*. She had not forgotten either the words or the tune and joined her voice in joyful praise to her heavenly Father, trying to forget the many Sundays she had not kept the Lord's Day holy, or acknowledged it with reverence in even the smallest way.

As she looked around, she was reminded that being in attendance was significant for even the elderly folk, three of whom sat in rocking chairs, too feeble to sit on the hard, backless benches. Seeing Mamm perched in her wheelchair next to Mammi Sylvia touched Hen deeply, and as the ordained men offered testimonies, she committed anew to following the code of conduct of this, the church of her birthright. Bowing her head, she prayed silently that God would guide her and Mattie's future. Was it His will for them to remain indefinitely within the protective confines of the People?

She thought of Brandon and wondered if being a father to Mattie Sue might not eventually turn his hardened heart toward the Lord. Oh, for his sake—and theirs—she prayed it would be so.

She embraced not only the hymns but also the time of prayer, when the People turned to kneel at their seats. Quietly, she thanked God for this wonderful opportunity to worship with others of like faith.

Later in the service, when both Mattie Sue and Becky became restless, Arie took out a clean white hankie and made twin "babies" in a handkerchief cradle to entertain them. Then she undid the cloth to start over again, silently showing the girls how to roll the "babies" while five-month-old Levi slept peacefully in the crook of her arm. By the time the second sermon was finished, Mattie Sue was able to do it on her own.

Hen, meanwhile, attempted to focus on the orderly worship service, which struck her as exceptionally meaningful. How long would she have waited to return if Mattie Sue hadn't been born? Was it purely because she'd become a mother that her heartstrings were tugged toward home?

After the final prayer, Hen and Arie had an opportunity to sit and chat. After being shushed repeatedly during the actual service, now Mattie Sue and Becky were permitted to talk, as well. Hen expected Mattie to tell Becky about Wiggles, but she was more interested in baby Levi. "Can I have a baby brother, too, Mommy?" she asked, startling Hen.

Hen's eyes met Arie's and the two women were at a loss for words. Soon, though, the two little girls were busy playing again with the white hankie.

Hen sighed with relief.

"We'll have you and Mattie Sue over for dinner real soon," Arie said, adjusting a cover-up as Levi began to nurse.

"Can we go to their house, Mommy?" asked Mattie Sue.

*If we stay around long enough,* Hen thought.

"We'll have fun," little Becky babbled in Deitsch, and Hen had to translate for Mattie Sue.

"Jah," giggled Mattie Sue. Hen's daughter wriggled on the bench, sneaking glances at Arie's cover-up.

*She's never been around a nursing baby,* Hen realized, thinking yet again how different Mattie Sue's childhood had been from her own.

∽

Hen awakened early on washday to tend to her laundry before helping Rose Ann and Mammi Sylvia, too. Once the week's washing was out on the line, she checked on Mattie Sue, who was sitting and playing with her dollies close to Mom's wheelchair in the kitchen, near the cookstove. "I'll be back in a bit," she told them, hurrying to the little house next door.

Taking out some writing paper, she began to write her thoughts to her husband.

*Dear Brandon,*
*Would you like to meet for coffee whenever it's convenient?*
*There's a little café not far from the fabric shop where I work, near*
*Quarryville. I'd be happy to meet you there.*

*Also, Mattie Sue talks constantly of you and Wiggles. She would like to visit you and see the puppy, too, if that's all right. We can talk more about that when we get together for coffee.*

*I'll look forward to hearing from you.*

*With love,*

*Hen*

As she signed her name, she suddenly felt more hopeful. And when she ambled to the mailbox, she relished the soothing sounds of the country around her.

Raising the flag on the wooden mailbox, Hen happened to see the bishop's wife up the road, also mailing a letter. She waved to her, knowing it was too far away for her to hear Hen call a morning greeting. But Barbara did not see her, and head down, she walked slowly back toward their house. *She looks awfully sad*, thought Hen, praying all was well.

~

Nick was distant and brooding that afternoon, keeping to himself in the corner of the stable. *Away from me*, thought Rose, second-guessing her resolve in the ravine. Had she made the right choice, dismissing her best friend?

He would not even allow her to catch his eye. He was either furious with her or had sunk back into a state of despair. In many ways Nick's sullen expression reminded her of his first troubled months here, after the bishop brought him here to live. *No wonder*, she thought sympathetically. *All this time, he missed his fancy life. Like a maverick wandering in the woods . . .*

When Rose could take it no longer, she slipped over to him. Checking first to see if anyone was watching, she touched his arm. "Nick . . . can we talk?"

He frowned. "What's left to say?"

"I don't want you to go."

His face softened. "Have you changed your mind about—"

"No, but . . . I don't want you to leave like this. The way things are . . . between us, I mean." She choked back tears. "I don't know how to make you understand."

"Understand what, Rosie?" He leaned toward her, then glanced about furtively. "We can't talk here."

She nodded. "I know. But somewhere . . . before you do anything rash."

"Leavin' here's rash?"

"Yes."

Dat came into the barn just then, and Rose ducked down to hide. Nick walked away, taking his shovel with him, and she held her breath, hoping her father had not seen them standing so close, her face wet with tears.

~

Later that afternoon, as Solomon approached the bishop's horse barn, he spotted Christian and Nick scuffling near the corncrib, their faces almost purple with anger.

Suddenly Christian shoved Nick hard against the wall and demanded he get on his horse. "Now!" Christian shouted. "Let's go!"

The two were clearly unaware of Sol. Stunned at the fury in Christian's voice, he realized their flared tempers had gotten completely out of hand. "Fellas . . . stop!" he called to them, but they paid Sol no mind. It surprised him, and he was further amazed when Nick obediently mounted Pepper and followed Christian, who was already on his own horse, galloping off toward the road.

Riveted to the spot, Solomon wondered, *Where are they going at this hour?* Surely their chores weren't finished for the day. He watched them head clear out to the road and turn west toward the main thoroughfare, shaking his head.

Making his way into the barn, Solomon wasn't sure whether

to say anything to his good friend, the bishop. But, as it turned out, Aaron was equally flustered. "I'm mighty fed up . . . the way those two are treating each other." Sol let Aaron blow off steam. "With all the horseback ridin' they do, they might as well be drivin' cars!" Then Aaron added quietly, "I fear Nick's goin' to get himself one."

Sol had seen Nick and Rose Ann head off together on driving horses through the back meadow just yesterday. The sight had made him heartsick, yet he'd told no one. Especially not Emma . . . the dear woman had enough on her mind lately, what with Hen living apart from her husband.

"Nick wants a car?" Sol asked.

Bishop shook his head. "He's certainly savin' up for something big. I can't get him to contribute to the house anymore."

"Nothin' at all?" Solomon was shocked, because he'd been so generous with his pay to Nick through the years.

"The boy's out of control."

"And Christian . . . what about him?" asked Sol.

"He's mighty upset, to tell ya frankly." Aaron drew a long sigh. "And between you and me, the ministers have been here yet again, urging me to set things right with my own household . . . so I can serve the Lord and His People more effectively."

Sol suspected what that signified. The two preachers and Deacon Samuel had to uphold the traditional qualifications for bishop, which meant all of Aaron's adult children were required to be church members for him to continue in the office.

"Christian insists Nick be baptized."

"Well, how can that help?"

Bishop brushed his brow with the back of his hand, then wiped the perspiration on his work trousers. "Christian's adamant that Nick owes me, so he's twistin' his arm, so to speak."

"To join church against his will?"

The bishop nodded.

"That's a terrible idea."

Bishop exhaled loudly. "Must sound thataway to Nick, too."

Solomon clasped Aaron's shoulder. "I'll keep this quiet . . . and in my prayers."

"Denki, Sol."

Hearing this so soon after having seen Rose Ann and Nick ride off together left Solomon painfully aware there was much to beseech the Lord God for, indeed.

~

A few of the bishop's grandchildren were sitting out on the front porch telling stories when Rose Ann headed over there after supper. Nick was nowhere to be seen, which was just as well, since she had been stewing all day about what to say to help soften the blow of her rebuff.

As was often the case, the older boys were taking turns outdoing each other with their various tales, and several of the younger girls shivered with fright as the setting once again became the ravine.

For Rose, that location would now always be taboo. Nothing good could happen deep in a chasm like that. *A dangerous path away from the real world.*

She trembled as she recalled Nick's caresses, so inappropriate considering she was nearly engaged to someone else. Even though she'd found Mamm's money tin, she deeply regretted having gone to such a secluded place with Nick.

Thinking back on his impulsive declarations, she worried she might have led him on simply by being there. To think he'd said right out that he'd loved her *first*!

The twilight was very still, without a hint of a breeze. The smaller girls edged closer, till she had her arms around two of them on each side of her. "Just remember, it's all make-believe," she whispered to them, no longer convinced she herself believed that.

Rose looked at the sky and took in the changing shades and

colors. Within minutes, the first star of the evening appeared as the sky grew darker.

The children were clad in coats or woolen shawls, but she knew it wouldn't be long before they went inside to Mammi Barbara to get warmed up with hot cocoa and to sit near the woodstove. Soon, too, the outdoor storytelling would become a faint memory as another year slipped away.

Glancing across the field to her house, Rose was glad Mattie Sue had stayed put with Hen and Mamm. Even though her niece would've enjoyed seeing the children gathered here, Mattie Sue was much too young for the foreboding tone the older ones seemed to enjoy giving their "tellings."

Then, looking back at the sky, Rose saw a falling star.

"*Ach, guck emol datt!*—just look at that!" several of the children said in unison as it streaked a white line down to the horizon and was gone.

"Someone's going to die tonight," one of the boys said.

"Well, sure they are," said another. "People die all the time."

"No, someone *nearby*," an older girl piped up. "My Mamma says so."

Rose suddenly felt cold. "Maybe we should go inside now," she said, and the girls scrunched up next to her nodded and quickly stood up.

"That's the silliest thing I've ever heard," said the boy who'd had his story interrupted, but even he followed the rest of the children inside.

Rose Ann decided to accept Barbara's kind invitation to stay and have hot chocolate and some fresh brownies, a favorite treat. In short order they were all talking and sitting around the table, along with the bishop and Verna, and the twins, Anna and Susannah, whose husbands had all gone together on an errand.

"Your Dawdi Aaron's got something for each of ya," Barbara was saying.

Bishop wiped his mouth with his handkerchief. "It's time I gave ya some of your inheritance," he said with a quick smile as he pulled out a handful of silver dollars. Amidst their *oohs* and *ahs*, he presented each of the eight children there with one bright and shiny coin.

Rose heard a horse whinny outside, and turned to glance through the window behind her. She gasped. Coming up the driveway were the bishop's sons, Christian draped head down over Pepper and being steadied by Nick, who led his brother's horse behind his own. Blood covered nearly all of Christian's head and face.

"Ach, no," she whispered, tears springing to her eyes. "Hurry, Bishop . . . go outside right quick!" she said, pointing to the window.

His eyes registered panic. "*Was is letz?*—what is wrong?"

Swiftly she rose to pull down the shades, instructing the children to stay in the kitchen as their grandfather rushed out the back door. She could see curiosity in their eyes, though they were obedient when Barbara suggested they all go quickly upstairs.

Nick trudged into the kitchen a few seconds later, struggling to carry his brother into the house. The bishop directed him to lay Christian on the table, where he stood over his unconscious son. Then, as if a light had gone on in his head, he pressed his fingers into Christian's neck, checking for a pulse. " 'Tis awful weak," he uttered, shaking with emotion. "Nick, what happened?"

Nick's face was as white as last winter's snows, his mouth turned down severely. He looked dreadfully guilty. "He fell," Nick muttered.

Barbara and Verna had gotten a bowl of cold water, the water rippling as their hands shook. With a cloth, Barbara dabbed at the gash still gushing blood from Christian's head. His face was deathly white and his chest did not rise and fall as before. Rose stood stock-still with horror . . . not knowing what to do.

She looked again at Nick, who'd slumped back against the wall, leaning as though he might collapse without its support.

Then, she saw it—his long hair had been cut roughly, as if someone had taken a knife to it. His short, dark locks fell forward, cropped off just below his ears. Nick's breath came in a short gasp, and his arms hung limp.

*Did he lose his temper?*

"I'll run for help." Rose dashed out the back door and lifted her skirt as she ran as hard as she'd ever run through the bishop's pasture, then into Dat's own immense field, her lungs burning. *Oh, dear Lord in heaven!*

Never once did she slow her pace till she reached the old phone shanty. "Someone's terribly hurt," Rose told the operator, then gave the location of the bishop's house. "Please send help right away!"

# CHAPTER 38

*A*fter calling for help, Rose ran all the way back to the bishop's house. She found Nick still standing in the kitchen, leaning hard against the far wall, his shoulders hunched forward, eyes glassy. He glimpsed at her, but she looked away. For the minutes that followed, they watched together in somber silence as the bishop made repeated efforts to keep Christian alive.

*O Lord, please let him live. . . .*

But despite the attempts, by the time the ambulance arrived, Christian had drawn his final breath. Rose wept quietly as men wearing white rushed into the house and began yet another fruitless attempt to revive Christian. She bowed her head, shielding her view.

Despite the activity in the room, she heard the bishop and Nick talking in the corner. Nick was describing Christian's fall, saying he'd cracked his head on a boulder deep in the ravine. She wondered, from the bishop's skeptical tone, if the minister thought Nick was lying. And the bishop continued to ask Nick pointed questions even as his son was being wheeled out on a covered gurney.

Suddenly Nick moved away from the man of God and plodded off toward the barn. In disbelief, Rose watched him go, struck by how exposed he looked without his thick black mane.

Shaken, she returned to the house to sit with Barbara and Verna, who were huddled near the woodstove in the kitchen. Anna and Susannah had gone upstairs to be with the children, and she could hear their soft footsteps just overhead. Oh, how she wished Mammi Sylvia would come to comfort the bishop's wife—the woman's constant weeping ripped at Rose's heart. She was relieved when her father and grandfather arrived to inquire about all the commotion, what with the siren swelling up and down Salem Road.

Not long after, Mammi Sylvia arrived in time to help Rose and Verna get Barbara upstairs to bed. Then, kneeling on either side of her, the women prayed for God's presence to be near, especially to the mourning mother. *Fill the room and our hearts with your sweet solace, O Lord,* Rose prayed silently. She did not know what else to pray at such a dreadful time.

Her grandmother reached for the Bible on the nightstand and began to read softly from the ninety-fifth psalm, still on her knees. " 'O come, let us worship and bow down: let us kneel before the Lord our maker. For he is our God; and we are the people of his pasture. . . . ' "

Rose waited till Barbara's heartbreaking cries had faded to soft whimpering, like an inconsolable child's, before slipping out of the room to the stairs. In a state of shock, Rose stepped out the back door, wondering, *How can it be—Christian is dead?*

She couldn't help but remember her brief conversation with him just yesterday. *"Soon, very soon,"* he'd said with such urgency. What had he wanted to tell her? And why, oh why, had she dismissed him so quickly?

Trudging back home, Rose was sick with worry for Nick. What would become of him now? The words of King David's psalm plagued her. Mammi had stopped reading just short of the plea for people not to harden their hearts—*as in the day of temptation in the wilderness. . . .* Many times Dat had read the entire psalm for evening worship: *It is a people that do err in their heart, and they have not known my ways.*

∾

Family worship that night was a somber scene—Mamm looked terribly forlorn as Dat read the Bible, his face serious and drawn. Rose's grandparents joined them, as well, and nary a one of them spoke once Dat offered the evening prayers. Afterward, Rose hurried to her room, tears falling uncontrollably as she wept for Christian . . . for Nick. For all of them.

Though she tried, it was impossible to erase the image of Christian's broken body upon Barbara's long table as he lay there, bleeding. Or Nick's strange demeanor—his unevenly chopped hair, his face wracked by shame. She suspected Christian of forcibly cutting off the ponytail, inciting Nick's long-simmering rage. With all of her heart, she hoped what followed had been an accident and nothing worse. Yet . . . the two had been enemies from the very first day of Nick's arrival.

When Rose lay down to sleep that night, her dreams were shrouded in darkness.

∾

The next day, Nick was gone. "Disappeared in the night," Dat told Rose, his face as grim as ever she'd seen it. "Left his Amish clothing behind . . ."

"Will the police find him and arrest him?" she asked.

Dat shook his head solemnly. "According to the bishop, they already talked with him last night—and several neighbors, too. But no one saw or heard anything unusual, so in the end, they believed Nick was tellin' the truth."

Rose felt her breath escape her. "Do you believe he's innocent?"

Her father hesitated. "We might never know for sure, Rosie. But it's not our place to judge. Nick's soul is in God's hands now."

She trembled at the thought.

The rest of the day, she felt as heavy as a bale of hay. Rose slogged through her chores, keenly aware of Nick's absence. The hours passed in a haze of grief. Surely Christian's untimely death had been an accident, just as Nick claimed.

Still, as much as she cared for him, the rumors were spreading. Soon there were more than a few fingers pointing at the boy who'd never embraced their culture—his hasty disappearance seen as the most damaging proof of all.

All the years of their friendship . . . had Rose ever *really* known him? To think she'd come that close to Nick's beloved "edge," and nearly fallen into the chasm, right along with him.

~

Following Christian's funeral Wednesday morning, Rose and Hen walked to the burial service in the fenced Amish cemetery. The bishop and his wife were surrounded by their married daughters and sons-in-law, all ashen with sorrow.

The hole that had been dug for the newly built coffin was filled halfway with dirt before the men removed their hats and the preacher read a hymn from the old hymnal. Afterward, the grave was filled with the remaining soil. Christian's mother nearly fainted when it was time to take leave of the mounded earth, and Verna's husband, Levi, quickly steadied her and helped her back to the gray carriage.

*So this is grief.* Rose could not imagine what Bishop Aaron and his family were experiencing. *My own anguish is nothing compared to theirs,* she thought as clusters of families slowly returned to their buggies. Several headed up the road, back toward their homes, while the bishop and his extended family walked silently to their own farmhouse for a private meal.

"The bishop lost two sons in the space of one day," Hen whispered to her as they walked toward home together. "His *only* sons . . ."

"One from this life, the other to the world," Rose managed to say, feeling awfully conflicted. In the short span since Christian's passing, she'd had plenty of time to think. And to reconsider, too. She missed the Nick she knew, but she was also relieved he was gone from their midst. Wasn't it best? After all, he'd rejected everything that was good and noble . . . each of the valuable life lessons he'd learned from the bishop. *He rejected God*, Rose realized anew. *And at what cost?*

Even so, despite Nick's stubbornness, part of her wanted to believe the Scripture he'd heard had *not* fallen on unfertile soil. Or deaf ears. She prayed that Nick might one day understand fully the reason he'd been handpicked to be brought up as an Amish Christian. Surely there was still hope for him.

As they walked, Rose glanced at Hen. The Lord seemed to be calling her sister to return to Him. Hen gave her a sad little smile and reached for her hand. Rose was glad for her sister's comforting touch at such an unspeakable time. Thankful, too, she hadn't had that final conversation with Nick, as she'd originally hoped. *Best to just push that out of my mind*, she thought, wondering how Nick could possibly find any happiness now . . . wherever he ended up living.

Rose sighed. Truth be told, there were moments she wished she'd never known him. And yet, how could she forget him? Indeed, she must continually remember him in her daily prayers.

She thought back to the afternoon in the ravine and shuddered. Nick had given her the freedom to choose—nearly impossible as that choice had been. Despite that, perhaps the time Nick had spent amongst them could be deemed providential, just as his leaving was, as well.

≈

Solomon could envision a hot meal and an invigorating shower. This final October day had seemed longer than most as he had finished up baling corn fodder. Still, there was another good hour or so before supper.

He wandered outside and across the long expanse of pastureland to look in on his bishop neighbor, mighty worried for him. Since Christian's death, the bishop's ruddy face had turned as withered as some of the shriveled grapes that still clung to the vine. The poor man was carrying the deepest kind of grief a soul could bear.

*A father shouldn't outlive his son*, thought Sol as he pushed open the bishop's barn door. He was surprised to hear Rose Ann's voice. Moseying over the cement floor, toward the stable area, he could see her tending to Nick's favorite horse, Pepper. She was currying him nice and slow, making long, steady strokes—talking to him all the while, though Sol could make out but a few words.

"Nick would want me to look after ya," she was saying.

He was struck by her remarkable tenderness. Why hadn't he comprehended it before? Had he been too distracted by Nick's fondness for Rose to pay close attention to Rose Ann herself?

With a great sigh, she stopped what she was doing and leaned over to caress the horse's mane, crying softly now. It startled him to witness such raw emotion, no doubt intended for a fellow who wasn't worth giving the time of day. *As we now know . . .*

Solomon's bearded chin quivered suddenly. The last thing he wanted was for Rose to notice him there, struggling to keep his own feelings in check. Turning silently, he headed back toward the barn door and shoved it open again. He stepped into a shower of the sun's dusty rays and made his way to the big farmhouse where ungrateful Nick had put his feet under the bishop's table . . . and heard the Good Book read each night. *Where he learned about almighty God at the knee of our bishop*, thought Sol, shaking his head in dismay. *But what he learned just never took.*

Thus Solomon consigned the worldly young man to the judgment he seemingly deserved.

~

Rose was perched on her bed that early November night, still wearing her brown choring dress as she tatted a doily—a birthday gift for a cousin. Suddenly she was startled by a light whirling over the window glass.

*Could it be . . . ?*

She hastened to open the window, almost expecting to see Nick there. Peering down, she saw Silas below. Her heart fluttered in unexpected wistfulness. It wasn't her old friend after all.

"Hullo, Silas," she said softly.

"Will ya meet me downstairs?" His voice was restrained.

She nodded, her heart beating ever so fast. "I'll be down in a jiffy." When she greeted him at the back door, Silas asked if everyone was asleep.

"All but me," she whispered, scarcely able to speak.

"*Gut*, then," he said, stepping inside. Together, they made their way to the woodstove, where the metal box stored a few chopped logs. He leaned down to add another couple pieces of wood, then waited for the fire to brighten.

They sat side by side on the long kitchen bench, making small talk for a while—about the weather and the youth activities centered around the numerous weddings to come.

After a time, Silas rose to stir up the fire again before returning to her side. "I've been waitin' a long time for this day," he said, his eyes reflecting the firelight. "*This* night . . ."

She listened intently, memorizing every word.

He reached for her hand, and the feel of it made Rose's pulse leap.

"Will ya have me, Rose Ann," he asked, "as your husband?"

She did not hesitate, not even for a moment. She said, "I'd be pleased to marry you, Silas."

He leaned forward, eyes searching hers as if to see whether she'd permit him to come so close. Then, with great tenderness, he kissed her cheek. "You've made me mighty happy, Rose."

She knew she must be simply beaming. "And me, too," she whispered.

"We'll wait till our wedding day to lip-kiss," he said, his gaze fixed on her mouth, then her eyes, and back to her lips.

"Probably should, ain't?" she said, now holding her breath, dying to know what it would feel like—his lips on hers.

Pulling back, he drew a long breath. "Jah," he said, though reluctantly, and raised her hand to his lips instead. "We best be waiting."

Rose smiled, enjoying this surge of pure delight.

"My father asked me to take over his dairy farm," Silas added. "He'll likely be ready for us to live in the main house, once we tie the knot, possibly next wedding season."

*Such wonderful-gut news! To think, in a year we might be wed.* Oh, how bright and happy her future looked now. Silas squeezed her hand again, and Rose smiled into his handsome face.

Later, after he bade her a sweet and lingering farewell, Rose tiptoed back upstairs. When she'd put on her nightgown and let her hair down, she slipped beneath her mother's beautiful quilts. There, in the moonlit room, she whispered, "Sleep well, Silas . . . and when you dream, dream of me, my dear beau."

# EPILOGUE

The flame of suspicion about Nick's role in Christian's death—whatever it may have been—has slowly burned out in me, turning to ashes at my feet. And I am left with a deep *Zeitlang*—longing—to go on foot down Bridle Path Lane on this unseasonably warm November day.

*Indian summer, Dat calls it. . . .*

And it's the official start of the wedding season. Esther Kauffman, my first cousin, just stopped by to whisper her appeal to me: *"Please, perty please, be one of my wedding attendants."* Since she asked me before Cousin Lydiann, I happily agreed.

Just maybe it was observing the alluring blush on Esther's cheeks that got me thinking about Nick again. He's been gone now for almost a month and no one's heard a word from him. The police questioned the bishop and his family shortly after Christian's death, but as is our way, no charges were pressed. There was simply not enough evidence anyway.

Even so, when Mamm and I sit and read together afternoons, sometimes she'll look deep into my eyes and say, "If you're ever tempted to feel sorry for that boy, Rosie . . . don't. And remember he was never really Amish."

*He knew it, too.* I guess it does all boil down to faith. But for Nick's and my friendship, it was truly something else. Something ever so precious and free. I can't begin to describe it.

Hen continues to cling to her renewed walk with the Lord now more than ever. And here lately, Brandon's been writing her letters. He's apologized for showing Mattie Sue the puppy dog, then taking him away. Hen's actually thinking of taking Mattie Sue to see him—and Wiggles, of course. Far as I know, Brandon hasn't darkened the door of Hen's house since that supper she made for him, but she expects to meet him again for coffee sometime soon. So my sister's not giving up on their love . . . or on swaying her husband toward God. And I am filled with a gnawing angst over the seeming loss of their storybook romance. Still, my parents say Hen belongs at home with Brandon, regardless of his spiritual leanings. Honestly, I look for Dat to impose a time limit on her stay here, and very soon.

Hen says Rachel Glick, her employer, has read between the lines, encouraging Hen to trust God to quicken a desire in Brandon for a peaceable Christian life. I think, as with Nick, Hen must realize it's up to her to relinquish her will—and Brandon—to the sovereignty of God. Because where God's presence is, all good things abound. I must remind myself of this daily . . . especially where Nick's concerned.

~

Turning onto Bridle Path Lane, I walked along the dirt road, then picked my way cautiously down the side of the ravine, once I passed Jeb's shanty. Carefully I inched over the steepest outcroppings, trying to avoid the brambles and thorns at every step. It would never do to slip and fall when no one knows where I've come this sunshiny day—so similar to the sun-dappled afternoon Nick brought me here.

Dozens of birds sang and flitted in the canopy of trees as I made my way to the bottom of the gulch. I was after one particular boulder, and I walked right to it, eager to find Mamm's tin money box once again. Reaching into the crevice, I pulled it out and opened the corroded lid. I was surprised to see a note tucked inside atop the money.

> *Dear Rosie,*
>
> *I hoped you'd come here one day and find this note.*
>
> *It's only right that you should hear this from me. I was stupid to go riding with Christian that day. And now, because of me, he's dead. I say let your God be the judge.*
>
> *We never got the chance to talk one last time. It haunts me. But no matter what you must think of me now, dear Rosie, I will always miss you.*
>
> > *Your friend,*
> > *Nick*

> *P.S. Will you look after Pepper for me?*

Tears threatened to spill down my cheeks as I folded the note and placed it in my dress pocket. I rejected the visions of Nick shoving Christian off his horse—striking back as he sometimes did. Knowing Nick as I had all these years, I wondered how such a thing could've happened . . . if it did. How will I ever know for sure? How will any of us?

I pressed the lid down on the tin box, a strange longing making me wish I could write a note back to him to tuck inside. But such a note would be seen only by God, down here in this deserted ravine.

Returning the tin to its muddy crypt, I covered it with the leaves of eleven autumns, a way to say good-bye to the past. "Help

Nick find forgiveness, O Lord," I prayed, "but most of all, help him to find you. . . ."

I struggled back up the small canyon, fighting back tears for what might have been . . . if Nick had joined church. And for all the lost years of Nick's life with the People, for his rejection of the Lord, too.

I marched straight home and burned Nick's shocking letter in the woodstove. There was nothing I could do now to help save Nick. That was up to God alone.

Forcing my thoughts away from the past, I looked toward the future—the wedding attendant's dress I will sew and the many dried-corn casseroles I plan to bake for Silas. This is to be the very last winter of my singleness, and there is much to do to prepare for setting up my own household. So, quite happily, I look forward to becoming Mrs. Silas Good one year from tomorrow, on Thursday, November twentieth. The dear Lord willing.

# Author's Note

$\mathcal{I}$ was delighted to discover Salem Road and the overall setting for this series just southeast of Quarryville, Pennsylvania, in the autumn of 2009, while visiting my mother's family—and thanks to the kindly suggestion of one of my dear Strasburg friends. My husband, Dave, and I enjoyed exploring the oldest graveyard in all of Lancaster County during that visit, as well, and I stumbled upon the strikingly beautiful name of Rose Ann, as well as the Amish nickname of Hen, while doing my research.

But it was the picturesque and rugged ravine below Bridle Path Lane that enthralled me most, and I remember getting out of the car and creeping over several boulders to peer down the heavily treed slope to the narrow creek below.

Dave snapped many pictures while I had my little adventure. My imagination soared as the setting for Emma Kauffman's mysterious horse and buggy accident sprang to life. The secluded area would also become the spot where Nick reveals his true intentions toward dear Rose Ann.

The lovely sun-dappled setting seemed to demand the birth

of a story—a trilogy, no less. My heart and mind were also gripped by idyllic Farmdale Road, as well as scenic Cherry Hill Road, and Hollow Road, which runs through the historic Jackson's Sawmill Covered Bridge. The whole of this rural farming area in one of the oldest Old Order Amish communities in Lancaster County truly sparked my creativity, and I am thankful God led us to this most captivating place.

Special thanks to Erik Wesner, Judith Lovold, and Hank and Ruth Hershberger.

As always, I am grateful for the support of my wonderful husband and our family, and for the remarkable people at Bethany House, who create strong links in the chain from story idea to bookstores, actual or online.

To God be the glory! *Soli Deo Gloria.*

## The Judgment

*Book Two in* THE ROSE TRILOGY

—AVAILABLE APRIL 2011—

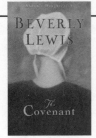